The Rhino Keeper

A Novel

Jillian Forsberg

ISBNs: 978-1-963452-03-7 (pb);
978-1-963452-04-4 (hc);
978-1-963452-05-1 (eBook)

Book Cover Design: The Book Cover Whisperer, OpenBookDesign.biz
Interior Book Design: Inanna Arthen, inannaarthen.com
Maps designed by Annika Wooton
Library of Congress Control Number: 2024932350
First Printing: 2024
Printed in the United States of America

Names: Forsberg, Jillian, author.

Title: The rhino keeper : a novel / Jillian Forsberg.

Description: [Roseville, Minnesota] : [History Through Fiction], [2024]

Identifiers: ISBN: 978-1963452-03-7 (paperback) | 978-1963452-04-4 (hardcover) | 978-1963452-05-1 (ebook) | LCCN: 2024932350

Subjects: LCSH: Indian rhinoceros~Europe~History~18th century~Fiction. | Ship captains~ Netherlands~History~18th century~Fiction. | Women college students~Netherlands~ Fiction. | Archives~Netherlands~Fiction. | Priests~ Europe~History~18th century~Fiction. | Love~Fiction. | LCGFT: Historical fiction. | BISAC: FICTION / Historical / General.

Classification: LCC: PS3606.O748661 R45 2024 | DDC: 813/.6~dc23

To Cody

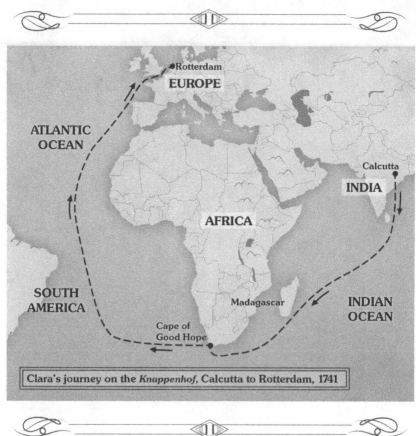

Clara's journey on the *Knappenhof*, Calcutta to Rotterdam, 1741

Douwe's Travels with Clara, 1740s

Prologue
Andrea
North Carolina
2022

Andrea shut the car door as hunting dogs brayed, their chorus of howls a discord. Her soft brown boots hit gravel in front of a white-columned manor. She tugged at her second-hand yellow sweater and stretched her legs from the hours-long drive. Jake lifted her overnight bag from her hatchback and carried their luggage toward the house. Waving pampas grass and trees dripping with southern moss lined the long drive.

The house's wraparound porch was golden-lit by black sconces. It was Thanksgiving Day, time for dinner. The last rays of the North Carolina sun sank below the house, and a rippling chill brushed Andrea's cheeks. The place looked like the cover of a luxurious Southern charm magazine. Her palms tingled. She didn't realize just how wealthy Jake's family was until now.

Jake's house was an eight-hour drive from campus. A copper touch of autumn had waved through the trees on the postcard-like road trip. She was glad to be out of the car, excited to meet Jake's family, incredibly excited to see the heirloom engagement ring his mother had retrieved from the family's safety deposit box. She grinned at the thought, tucked her dark hair behind an ear. The hunting dogs continued howling behind the willow trees lining the long, winding driveway. Jake whistled with two fingers in his mouth, and they quieted, whimpering.

"Sorry," he said. "Wild beasts."

Andrea slowly followed him up the steep steps, taking in the three-story manor.

"1775," he said, tossing his honey-brown curls off his forehead.

"What?"

"1775. The house was built in 1775."

Andrea's mind flickered. Many things happened in that year. Ready to spout facts and historical figures' names like a card catalog, her brain opened up. So did the wide navy-blue door. Behind her, a flagpole clinked in the wind. She glanced at it, recognizing the markings of a twisted Confederate flag. The dogs cried.

Jake waited by the door, beckoning Andrea in. She quickly stepped inside. A chill finger rippled up her spine. A *Confederate flag?*

A thin blonde woman wearing a magenta floor-length gown and dangling earrings rushed forward to embrace her, squishing a tiny fox-colored dog held in her arms. She smelled of bourbon and Chanel perfume. Andrea felt a wave of nausea.

"So nice to finally meet you," the woman said. The dog squirmed, and she set it down. It wagged its curled-up tail as Andrea knelt to pet it, angling her face to the door to see Jake hauling the luggage. The twisted flag around its pole pulsed in the dusk.

"Don't worry about Primrose. She's a mess, just like me," said the woman. "Jake's told me so little about your past, Andrea, only that you're also a history major. Tell me everything about where you come from."

The dreaded question of the past, so quickly? Andrea opened her mouth to answer, to reveal that she was fatherless and poor, the daughter of an artist, college paid by government grants and student loans, but Jake grabbed her hand.

"Let's get her settled, Mom, before the interrogation begins, alright?"

"Don't patronize me, young man," she said, voice slurred by liquor. She bent to pick up the little dog. Primrose growled, showing the whites of her eyes. Jake's mother frowned and let her be. "Andrea, you must be so tired. How about you head into the parlor while we get your bags upstairs? I'll get my dear husband and join you with cocktails."

Andrea was ushered to a darkened room nearby, passing a grand staircase. Her boots clicked on shining hardwood floors, and behind her, delicate paw taps from Primrose revealed the dog followed. Jake turned the light on, Andrea's small suitcase in his hands.

"See you in a second," he said. He kissed her briefly on the cheek, leaving a lingering scent of cool cologne, and rushed up the white-banistered stairs. Primrose sat at her feet, pink tongue lolling.

Andrea realized she hadn't been allowed a single word and pursed her lips. She exhaled and bent to the little dog, expecting a growl. There wasn't one. Andrea picked her up and the bell on her collar jingled.

"I wonder if the dogs outside have pink collars with silver bells, eh, Primrose?" she asked. Primrose's tongue darted toward Andrea. "My mom has a service dog that looks like you, girl."

Andrea then turned to the room and gasped, startled. Taxidermy animals loomed from the walls. Primrose wheezed. Animals only seen in zoos stared back at Andrea with glass eyes—a lioness's mouth was open, teeth bared. Primitive-looking wooden nails held a crocodile skin to the wall, essentially crucified. Andrea's heart beat rapidly, body tingling with sweat. She put the dog down. A half-dozen deer mounts lined the wall below the coffered ceiling.

Brown leather furniture, animal-skin rugs. The smell of hides and dust and sour fear filled her nose and mouth. A ringing sounded in her ears. Primrose pawed at her.

There was a framed picture on the wall. Jake. A massive rifle by his side. He and his dad leaned into each other, kneeling. In front of them was a male lion, eyes closed, tongue out. Blood pooled on the dirt below. Bile rose to Andrea's throat. The male lion's taxidermy mount stood in the corner of the room, illuminated by a single dramatic spotlight from the ceiling.

Jake's feet sounded on the staircase. She rushed to the couch.

"Y'all right?" he said.

"Not...not really."

"Yeah, I thought this might bug you some, but they're dead already, see?" Jake tapped the horns of a black water buffalo.

"Bug me some?" Andrea trembled. "Jake, this is a nightmare to me."

"People've hunted for thousands of years, girl," he said, sitting beside her. She scooted away. Primrose leaped up between them and placed a paw on her lap.

"This isn't thousands of years ago, Jake; this is this century. I... I can't be here."

"This is my family's stuff, Andrea. My grandfather brought some of these home decades ago. They're antiques now, you love antiques."

"Jake, they're endangered animals, and you've got them hanging on your living room walls."

"This isn't the living room."

Andrea scoffed. "What the hell...?"

"This is the parlor. The living room is across the foyer."

She blinked at him, eyebrows knit together.

"You really don't understand, do you?"

"Relax," he said, smirking. "I've got a surprise for you."

From his pocket, he pulled a baby-blue ring box. If her heart raced before, now it was a jackhammer. There was a silver "A" embroidered on the velvet box top. He opened it. It was the ring he'd told her about: his fourth great-grandmother's, sparkling and white, made before the Civil War.

Just then, his mother walked in, tray full of cocktails, followed by the handsome, tan-faced man from the hunting photo. They both grinned from ear to ear.

Jake stood from the couch and dropped down to one knee. Primrose growled. Jake was proposing to Andrea in a room full of nightmares.

Her mouth went dry when she tried to speak. The room began to spin. Jake spoke but Andrea's muffled heartbeat filled her ears. Primrose began barking at Jake, still down on his knee, beautiful toothy smile flashing brightly. In one hand he held the ring, and with the other he swept the little dog onto the floor. She landed with a thud and a whimper, silver bell tinkling.

Andrea rose from the couch and set her fists. She could not quell her trembling. She pulled her car keys from her thrifted purse and inhaled through her nose. She looked at Jake, and at his eager-eyed parents.

"No," she said, her voice strong. She longed to scream but ran from the room. Eyes bored into her back, though she could not tell if the feeling of being watched came from Jake and his parents, or the ghosts of the animals hanging on the walls.

Chapter 1
Andrea
Leiden, The Netherlands

Andrea sat on a sheetless twin bed, feeling the now normal stomach-churning ache of missing Jake. Her analytical brain knew she didn't actually miss *him*. She missed who she thought he was. Her brain understood why she left him, though her heart still ached. A dizzy wave of jet lag consumed her, and she squinted, head pounding as she took in her dorm room. Her new place was a campus apartment at Leiden University, with cold tiled floors and a cracked, silvery-paned cathedral-type window. A relic of a writing desk took up a quarter of the space, bolted to the floor with stripped screws.

What kind of college was this, to leave a once-valuable eighteenth-century antique in a dorm room?

Andrea embraced the weird. Traveling across the world alone felt necessary to rid herself of everything from her past. Her mother told her to apply for the semester abroad project in a series of relentless but loving phone calls and texts. Out of a thousand applicants, she was chosen. The impressive history work on her resume got her here, helping her escape the rumors on Charleston's small campus. *Did you hear how Jake and Andrea broke up over Thanksgiving break? She ran out of the house before they carved the turkey!*

The rumors hadn't caught up to the proposal. Andrea wondered if the other girls on campus, given the opportunity, would have said yes to the ring despite it all. She couldn't move forward with the relationship, knowing what awaited her future and shrouded his past.

Andrea tried to remember what people told her about recovering from jet lag. Stay up? Sleep? Coffee? Her phone dinged, battery dying. She found her charger and a plug-in, then cursed under her breath. The prongs wouldn't fit. She had buried her European converter plug in her checked bag.

She hauled her suitcase to the edge of the bed and unzipped it. The bag toppled off, contents tumbling out. The same yellow sweater she wore to Thanksgiving dinner was on top. A tuft of Primrose's fur was stuck to the sleeve. *The only nice family member,* Andrea thought. She picked up the sweater and threw it in the corner.

She rifled through her clothes and toiletries, sending the converter plug clattering under the writing desk. It was partly visible between the shallow arch of the floor and the claw foot leg. Andrea dropped down and cautiously slid her hand into the narrow gap, a dry film of dust coating her fingers.

Pulling on the charger did no good. It was wrapped around something. Using her dying phone's flashlight, Andrea saw it was caught on a small metal lever, flashing bronze. She wiggled the charger cord out of its grasp. Curious, Andrea pushed the metal piece upward into a slot. A gentle click sounded.

She slid out from under the desk and splayed her hands out, feeling the warm-wood surface. The thing was once beautiful with hinges, a locked front piece, and drawers, now scratched from years of student use. It was helpful even if it took up too much space. There was no way it would fit through the door. Who had bolted it down, and why?

Did the click mean something moved? This was the kind of desk seen on Antiques Roadshow—full of hidden compartments and secret drawers. Silver coins from the Dutch East India Company in a velvet pouch, pulled from a secret compartment, flickered in her mind. But the only thing out of place was a slender wooden column.

She slid out the column carefully. It was a narrow box, far too small for a pouch of coins, but it wasn't empty. Inside was a yellowed document covered in scrolling brown script—an artifact—a gorgeously archaic one. Andrea's heart pounded.

Andrea carefully unrolled the ancient crumbling parchment with trembling hands, desperate to read it.

Chapter 2
Douwemout van der Meer
Calcutta, India
1740

Douwemout van der Meer's palms sweated. It was his first time at his commander's house—a gleaming white palace inside and out, the porticos and open-air rooms surrounded by a palm-heavy garden. It was a stark contrast to his small, temporary apartment.

The mansion was furnished in a European fashion: imported French furniture with delicate legs and velvet cushions, walls decorated with fine Indian chintz tapestries. The drawing room was stifling despite the open archways. Jan Sichterman rose from a spindly-legged chair, bowing in greeting.

"Captain van der Meer. Come, it's cooler in the garden." He ushered Douwe outside.

A Dutchman in a white wig was a strange creature to behold in the exotics of Calcutta. Sichterman dripped with sweat in a waistcoat, linen shirt, and deep blue velvet doublet. Even in late November the sun drenched the jungle city, the opposite of the late fall climate of their native Netherlands. Douwe observed his commander, mimicking his gestures to fit in. It was the first time he'd seen him without his Dutch East India Trading Company medal, usually strung about his neck during formal speeches, indicating his position of power.

Sichterman was in charge of all of the Dutchmen and their trade in Bengal. The VOC was the largest company in the world. Douwe captained one ship, the *Knappenhof*, a colorful East Indiaman that hauled 650 tons of trade goods back and forth from India to Europe, South Africa to Batavia, and onward to Japan.

Jewels, spices, shoes, fabric, and silver jewelry created a kaleidoscope of vibrant colors in the hull of Douwe's ship. Stacks of fabrics and silks, specially selected for his European customers, softened the ship's dark stores. The weavers made magic in India, and the fabric was sent to the finest tailors in Europe, who fawned over the florals and scrolling patterns.

The coins Douwe earned were stamped on one side with the Vereenigde Oostindische Compagnie's initials: VOC. On the other side was a lion roaring over a striped flag. The lion was a warning—the VOC was the apex predator of the seas. No other beast dare challenge it and survive.

Fabric was a common trade good for the company, but Douwe thrived in his specialty: delivering exotic creatures from around the world to European masters. While the hulls of the *Knappenhof* were stacked with fine goods and fragrant spices, above decks was the smell of livestock and the rattling cages of beasts. He was responsible for the trade and care of these creatures, great and small.

"Thank you for the invitation today, Captain. Your home is impressive." The sun made them squint, the garden path bright.

"Tell me, Van der Meer, why are you in Calcutta?"

"Sir, surely you don't mean I brought the *Knappenhof* here by mistake?"

"You are not present at social activities. You stay for months, I see you twice for your papers, and you are gone again with a full ship and a deck crawling with animals."

"Yes, sir," Douwe said. He hesitated.

"Do you not find yourself longing for more, Captain?" Sichterman said.

"I find fulfillment in my work," said Douwe. "Especially the deck of animals."

Sichterman humphed.

"Do you know why I am in Calcutta, Captain?"

"Commander?" Their boots sank into newly laid gravel.

"Thirty years ago, I won a duel," Sichterman said. "I was born to nobility but fled when I killed another man. My father managed to get me on with the VOC before the body hit the ground. I did not ever desire to live here."

Douwe's mouth was dry. He slicked back his chestnut hair, hustling to keep pace with Sichterman, who was significantly taller.

"The duel ended in my favor, and yet I was punished. Not unlike our work—even if we succeed and make our shipments and the coin, we are punished by the sea, Africa's cape, or India herself."

Native palms spilled over the walkways despite a gardener's obvious attempts to tame the place to formality. A fountain gurgled in the middle, its brightly colored tile shimmering with water. A banyan tree shaded a distant corner of the garden, innumerable arches mimicking the chalk-white mansion's curves. Bright floral smells filled the garden, and Douwe closed his eyes in the glaring sun. The gravel dusted his brown leather boots, stained with sea salt.

"I do not long to live in India, either, sir," Douwe said. "I want to see more of Europe. Rome, Paris, Vienna. I have lived longer in India and Africa than in my own bloodlands."

"Were you a boy when you joined?" Sichterman asked.

"Fifteen, dropped off in Amsterdam by my father. I begged to go. Now I've spent more of my life at sea than on land. I suppose I thought my career would be short. That I'd meet a woman and settle. Yet here I am twenty years later, and my only woman is a ship called the *Knappenhof*."

"Well, she's a true beauty. And you, a true careerman," Sichterman said. "Though you can make a home here, if you like, or one in the Netherlands."

Douwe pursed his lips. He did not stay long enough in any port to allow the rocking of the ocean to leave his body, let alone call a place home. He opened his mouth and shut it abruptly. Sichterman led him onward through the garden and a flickering thought entered Douwe's head: how would it feel to own a place like this and stay?

"I have invited you here today because I have a cargo that I can no longer support, Van der Meer, and a proposition for you."

Douwe's heart quickened. He straightened, hazel eyes scanning Sichterman's sea-tanned face.

"Your experience with animals is well-known," Sichterman said.

Douwe felt more comfortable around animals than people. Plus, money was abundant when taking on animal cargo, even if it was easy to get attached. On his last voyage, a flock of parrots and a small white-faced monkey became hard to part with. Pigs and chickens were kept for food, goats and cows for milk, and, if needed, slaughtered. But the creatures delivered to noble families to fill their menageries made him feel important. Horses, camels, peacocks, and monkeys departed the decks and entered royal households, filling Douwe with a sense of wonder upon delivery. He was responsible for the rarest creatures in Europe, even if he was the middleman.

"I enjoy the transport of livestock and have a cat around my apartment," Douwe said, smiling cautiously.

"I've heard cats on the *Knappenhof* were not keen to leave your lap. And the monkey meant for Louis XV grew rather attached to you."

The monkey was fun to be around, and the ratter cat was useful against the plague of vermin. She gave birth to five kittens in the cargo hold and the crew grew fond of them in the six-month journey. Douwe loved them, especially the black mother cat he named Betsy.

"Helpful along the way, cats," said Sichterman.

Douwe did not respond. They neared the edge of the gardens. Palms and heavily burdened fruit trees filled the beds. Outside the stone garden wall was a stable and a small paddock for grazing.

"I have come across a creature that is not as helpful as a cat. I know you'll want to see it."

Sichterman kept Arabians transported across the Himalayas the year prior. They were specimens befitting a king—their shining coats caught the eye of every passerby in Calcutta during the nightly airings on the concourse where Dutchmen socialized. Surprisingly, the horses were inside in the heat. The paddock was occupied.

A gray mottled monster grazed there. Douwe's heartbeat echoed in his head. He had patted an African elephant and held a white-faced monkey. Swaying camels draped in golden tassels carried his goods in the streets of Calcutta. Across the world, he saw wild beasts and things living in the sea unknown to land-bound men. He did not recognize the beast in front of him. The book of Job echoed, recited in the lofted church of his home in Leiden, Holland:

Look at Behemoth, which I made along with you and which feeds on grass like an ox. What strength it has in its loins, what power in the muscles of its belly! Its tail sways like a cedar; the sinews of its thighs are close-knit. Its bones are tubes of bronze, its limbs like rods of iron.

Sichterman whistled. The Behemoth raised its head, black tufted ears perked. Its skin was like plated armor, gray and mottled like the Black Sea in winter.

"Douwe," said Sichterman, "this is Clara." The beast stood within arm's reach. Sichterman put a hand between the fence posts and waited for the snuffling mouth.

Douwe's throat caught—what was it? He was draped in excitement and apprehension a few feet from the creature.

Sichterman chuckled. "Clara is an Indian rhinoceros. She's a little thing now but will get much larger. I have heard she could live one hundred years."

Douwe swallowed. A rhinoceros. His schoolteacher taught him from the writings of Pliny the Elder that rhinoceros were enemies of elephants: vicious animals that killed men and devoured them without hesitation. This creature did not seem dangerous—it was absolutely devoted to the sun-scorched grass and paid little mind to the two men.

"Clara. What a pleasant name for a Behemoth. Where is her horn?"

"Seems they are not born with horns," Sichterman said. "Behemoth indeed!" He rolled on the balls of his feet in a bouncing laugh. "She's harmless despite her stink and her weight. Hunters downed her mother last month. My wife could not resist her."

Douwe inched closer. Clara's ear fur skimmed the earth as she grazed. Her skin had pink folds between each joint. Was she smooth, like a dolphin? Rough like the elephants in Louis XV's menagerie? Was her mouth soft and warm, like the muzzle of a horse? The cobbles of her skin were tempting, as was the thought of touching her feathery ears. Her lip worked quickly over the grass, her padded pink feet rounded as she slowly paced.

"She eats grass already? I would assume she needs her mother's milk."

"She drinks goat's and mare's milk. I have asked the locals, and they say she is better off with a mother rhino, but they cannot find one. Even if they did, we do not know if it would take her as its own or trample her to death. Soon, she will be too large for my stables."

Clara raised her curved, finger-like lip to the sky and sniffed, snorting as she did. She was, despite her oddities, a fine addition to Sichterman's collection. Europeans would pay a handsome sum to own such a rare animal. Men took pride in the trend of curios: taxidermy birds and creatures, beautiful shells and bones displayed in the fine homes of Europe and the European homes of Calcutta. Menageries held the same appeal with living creatures.

"Douwe, you must come for dinner. Clara will be the evening's entertainment. I will part with this animal for the right sum."

"Of course, sir," Douwe said. "Who would you like to sell her to?"

"To you."

Thirty minutes later, Douwe was on the winding street back to his apartment, sweat dripping down his parchment-thin shirt. The breeze only touched the tops of the palms. Calcutta was a delightful puzzle to a European who grew up in the formality of Amsterdam. There, the straight-gabled homes and shops created order.

In Calcutta, the juxtaposition of rambling shacks neighboring fine houses looked like the buildings were picked up, shaken, and tossed down with no care where they landed. But paces away, the Ganges Delta connected the cream-tea-colored Hooghly River to the sea, beckoning sailors onward to the shores of the world. In a roundabout way, the Netherlands' harbors beat with the same waters.

Douwe preferred the sea. As a boy in Leiden, he shaded his hazel eyes against the sun to spot whales in the harbor. Their waterspouts blurred the horizon. He tugged at his mother's dresses when he found them, squealing with delight. Shells filled his pockets, sand lined his shoes, and the smell of the North Sea rarely left him. Douwe became the farthest traveled in his family of sailors when he made it around the treacherous horn of Africa, where the Indian and Atlantic Oceans collided.

On the balcony of his modest apartment, the black mother cat twitched her tail. A green pigeon teased her from the adjacent palm. The pigeon cooed, and Betsy chattered, baring her fangs. Douwe felt more like the pigeon than the cat.

It was an honor to be invited to dinner, but Douwe never enjoyed formal society parties. He preferred to spend his evenings watching the sunsets from his apartment and listening to the sounds of the city, black cat on his lap, poring over trade routes, marking sandbars, and dreaming of what creatures or people waited at his next stop. He had few longings to make lasting connections. Each place felt temporary, like his feet weren't quite on the ground, like the next best thing waited for him.

He had little time to get ready and batted dust off his pea-green formal coat, praying it still fit. The clock chimed the quarter hour. He slicked his curly brown hair with a tortoiseshell comb, petted Betsy from her ears to the tip of her tail and clicked shut the door despite her protesting mews.

The formal meals were held early in the day, lasting hours. The party was not as exciting as the prospect of owning the baby rhino. He wondered why Sichterman had chosen him to buy the Behemoth. Clara. He should call her Clara.

The white manor was bathed in palm shadow. The elegantly dressed khansamah greeted partygoers at the door and led Douwe to the parlor, where VOC officers mingled, clinking their silver wine goblets. The air was thick with the earthy-sweet smell of rice, swirling incense, and men in hot wool.

An elephant tusk was mounted above the fireplace, a tiger skin rug tucked into a corner. An Indian fruit bat dangled in a cloche on a bookshelf, and a curio cabinet was filled with treasures. Inside were swirling seashells, small mammal skulls in a row, a glistening ammonite, and a fragile, translucent porcelain locket featuring the portrait of a fair European lady—her eyes were sad and brown. The locket hung on a simple gold stand.

The curio held leather-bound books, rare in this part of the world. Douwe slid a big book off the shelf with a sea-calloused hand. Could it be? Yes—a Gutenberg Bible. Douwe felt a pang in his gut. The Bible had opened to the book of Job.

"Douwe," Sichterman said. He clapped him on the back. Douwe's knees collapsed, and the Gutenberg nearly dropped. He steadied himself and slid the book back to its home. "I see you found the Gutenberg. I was about to board the *Rooswijk* with it. Some sort of god looks out for me, though I cannot confirm it is the one in this book."

The *Rooswijk*. Douwe had friends aboard that vessel when it sank. None survived.

"May they rest in peace," Douwe said. "Death at sea means their souls wander the fathoms, not bound to earth."

"That is comforting," Sichterman said, smiling broadly and handing Douwe a silver goblet. "Though one a bit morbid for a man about to embark."

"I leave in two weeks. I do not expect the gods of the sea to support my sails on every voyage. I work alongside them, and they guide me." Douwe drank. The tang of alcohol burned his throat, a wave of heat following.

"The gods of the sea are cruel, Douwe. May we be ready when we meet them face to face," Sichterman said. He raised his glass. Douwe met his goblet.

"I am sure you know most of these men," Sichterman said. He turned his back to the curio cabinet, gesturing to the room. A dozen men were sweating, laughing, talking. No one seemed interested in Sichterman's collection, though they were surrounded by it. They were more interested in the future: deals and silver to be earned. Douwe could practically smell the metal coins in their hands.

Douwe nodded at them, raising a glass in their direction. They returned the gesture and promptly returned to their conversations. Their mouths formed his name—he was being reintroduced.

The kanasmah escorted the party to the white dining room. The women were led in simultaneously, trailing their gowns across the floor from the opposite parlor. Servants plated food: rice and roasted fowl cooked with herbs. Fruit dripped with honey, piled high in gilded porcelain bowls.

Sichterman examined his long table with a satisfied smirk.

"You may all be wondering why I have brought you here on such a fine and heavy-hot day in Calcutta." A small bird wove in and out of the dining room through an open archway, gulping an insect mid-flight. "I have received notice from the VOC that I have been promoted. My new title, effective immediately, is Councillor Extraordinaire of India, and we have received the funds for thirteen new trading ships."

The room burst into applause, and the men shifted eagerly in their seats. This meant a payload. Their eyes shone like VOC silver. Douwe quickly counted: thirteen men plus Sichterman sat at this table. It meant a ship for all except Douwe.

"We are celebrating tonight, and we will have news for you all over the next months. Proost!"

Sichterman thrust his glass into the air, and the others followed, drinking heavily after a raucous cheer. Their waistcoats bulged as they tucked into dinner, excitedly talking about the future of trade in Calcutta. Dinner jackets were tossed onto chairs, trailing their velvet tails on the white tile. Wine glasses were refilled in earnest.

Douwe listened and did not say much. He thought about Sichterman's offer to buy the rhinoceros in the paddock. Was the animal such a burden that Sichterman wanted it gone before he could show her off to his underlings?

The servers and kanasmah were acutely aware of the diners. Douwe did not want for anything. Sybilla Sichterman, however, was particularly vocal about her needs. She snapped her fingers at the wine bearer when her goblet needed refilling. A woman in a shimmering green dress was seated to her right. Douwe, a fabric expert, knew the quality of her gown— it glowed olive and clover depending on the light. A servant spilled a single drop of red on the chintz tablecloth. Sybilla seethed but stopped at her friend's gentle touch on the wrist.

Sybilla's skin was dull—powdered and pasted. She had deep lines under her eyes, the corners of which were in a permanent position of mourning, drenched with elegant sadness. She was a much older version of the woman in the porcelain portrait that swung in Sichterman's curio.

Douwe stared at the woman to Sybilla's right. She had an aquiline nose, auburn hair, eyes that danced with laughter. She was an emerald gem at the table. Drops of pearls dangled from her ears. He liked her even more after she touched Sybilla's wrist. She demurely put a fan in front of her mouth as she reprimanded her friend, and Sybilla calmed immediately—a snake charmer.

Sybilla was unpleasant a few more times. Each time, the white fan popped up in her companion's gloved hand, fluttering like a moth, and when it withdrew, Sybilla was calm. Douwe glanced their way, smiled, and raised his glass to her.

"A lovely hostess, indeed," he said. "Thank you, Mrs. Sichterman, for inviting me to your home today."

Sybilla smiled, the lines of her powdered makeup creasing around her eyes and mouth. Her teeth were crooked and purple from the red wine.

"Who are you?" Sybilla said. She did not raise her glass or remove her smile.

"Douwemout van der Meer," said Douwe, lowering his goblet. "Captain of the *Knappenhof*."

Sybilla closed her lips over her teeth.

"What a pleasure to meet you, Captain van de Meer," said the woman in green. "I am Johanna van der Weijden. It must be your first time at the estate of the Sichtermans."

"It is, Mistress van der Weijden. A magnificent home that fits the leader of the VOC and his lovely wife."

Sybilla stared at Johanna. Johanna smiled politely and turned to her friend. "Sybilla said she knew all of her husband's captains. It is a surprise to be meeting you now."

"I understand, madams," Douwe said. "I do not regularly socialize here in Calcutta. I am here and gone again before anyone notices me." He gave a small laugh.

"We have certainly noticed you, Captain van der Meer," said Sybilla. "No wife, yet no interest in the single women at the table. You keep staring at the married ones."

Douwe blushed. "I apologize, ladies. The two brightest gems in Bengal shine at this table. I shall turn my attention elsewhere."

Johanna fanned herself. Flattery went far with Sybilla, and she raised her goblet to him. Johanna breathed deeply—a sigh of relief, perhaps? The fan waved wildly. The ladies turned their conversation inward, and a drop of sweat ran down Douwe's back.

Dancers and musicians filtered in and out. Douwe anxiously fidgeted. Sichterman signaled to the hookah burdars to bring forth pipes and tobacco. Servants carried in hookah pipes and desserts. Plates covered the table, full of round, colorful sweets.

Hookah bottles rested on the crimson and camel-colored carpets. The air thickened with dense smoke, the heat of bodies, and Calcutta's humidity. Douwe had no desire to linger in the cloud. The rhino had not been mentioned and he wanted to see her.

Douwe grabbed several desserts from a silver platter. He excused himself politely, though no one noticed. An arched open-air doorway led to a chorus of crickets in the garden. The sun had set. The breeze picked up and the temperature melted; it was finally, blessedly, cool. A blue-white moon, nearly full, rained light on the palms.

The stable glowed white beyond the fountain in the distance. Douwe took a bite of the crumbling, sticky sweet meat that tasted of cardamom and honey. He heard the diners behind him laughing and glanced back. Coils of blue smoke curled under the archways.

He took the winding path to the stable. The voices in the house grew in volume as the partygoers smoked and drank and dripped honey into their mouths. Ahead, the paddock was empty.

A boy sat on the threshold step of the stable, playing a ball-and-cup hand game Douwe recognized from childhood.

"Fine night," Douwe said. The boy startled. His focus had been on getting the ball in the cup.

"Sir," said the boy dismissively. He was thin, with coal-black hair that framed his long face. He had warm, tawny skin and overly large front teeth.

"Is Clara in there?" Douwe said. "The rhino?"

"She is," said the boy. He furrowed his brow and flicked the ball toward the cup. A miss. "Why?"

"I'd like to see her," Douwe said.

"Why?" He played with his toy. "She's coming to dinner. Just wait." The ball did not land in the cup.

"Coming to dinner? Dinner is over, my boy. The hookah is on the floor as we speak."

The stableboy leaped to his feet.

"I'm done for! I was supposed to lead her in for dessert! Sichterman will have my neck!" The ball-and-cup clattered to the ground. Douwe picked it up.

"Let me help you," Douwe said. The boy hesitated, panicking. The ball landed in the cup. The boy smiled.

Chapter 3
Andrea
Leiden, The Netherlands

The document was delicate with crunched, crumbling corners and smelled of a once-wet place made of stone, dry and musty. Andrea carefully unrolled it and laid it flat on the writing desk, putting her cell phone on a corner to hold it flat.

"Holy shit," she said to no one. The page was illustrated, some kind of advertisement. There was a man wearing breeches and a long overcoat, a staff in his hand, and a feathered cap on his head. He was looking at an armored rhinoceros. Andrea's memory returned to the nightmare room at Jake's house with its taxidermy looming, and her breathing increased.

She stilled herself and turned on the academic part of her brain, focusing. The script was German, which she could barely read, but the date and place were clear enough. Vienna, 30 October 1746. A rhinoceros? In Vienna? The animal looked fabricated, with metal plates stacked on each other.

Her phone buzzed, sliding. The document curled closed. It was her mother.

"Hi, Mom." She held the document down with one hand.

"Hi, Andrea!" She was usually happy, but lately, there was caution in her voice. "You made it. How's Holland? How are you doing?"

Andrea paused, unsure of how to answer her. Truthfully, she was still shaken up.

"I'm fine. I've slept pretty much all day, but the flights were good. Lonely, but good."

"I think you're making the right decision. What's on your schedule?"

"I meet with my adviser and see my work site tomorrow." She wanted to get off the phone and flip the document over. She didn't want any questions about Jake.

"The graveyard, right?"

"Yeah. Not every day an amateur historian gets to work in a historical graveyard."

"You're not an amateur, honey. You're good at this stuff. You wouldn't have gotten picked for this project if you weren't."

"Thanks, Mom. It's hard for me to take a compliment right now."

"Separate the things in your life. What happened between you and Jake has nothing to do with where you are now. Remember to let go of what you can't control. But if you meet a nice Dutch boy..."

"It's only been a month since we broke up, Mom."

"If you wanna have some fun, do it. You deserve it. Someone who sees your worth will come along, and they'll fit with you better than Jake did."

Andrea sighed. Her mother was the only person who knew the truth besides Jake himself.

"Thanks, Mom, I'm sorting through my trauma. No safari rooms with illegally poached animals here."

"Don't discount what happened to you. You had every reason to leave that boy. Your values didn't line up."

On the surface, Jake's family legacy seemed admirable: generations of wealth, a house held for centuries, abundance. But the secrets gave her nightmares. Andrea felt blinded by the attention of someone popular, influential, well-spoken. It was all an illusion.

"I know, Mom. It's hard to know that someone else will be fine with the things I'm disgusted by."

"You're not someone else, Andrea. You're you. I would have done the same."

"Thanks, Mom. I'm gonna go back to bed. I'll call you after my meetings tomorrow."

Her mother said goodbye and Andrea immediately flipped the document over. On the backside was a hand-written list in French, barely legible, faded to brown. What was this?

She typed the words into Google Translate:

Seventy pounds of hay

Twenty loaves of brown bread

3 gallons of water

Apples, oranges, and ale

Beside it was a list of dates from the 1740s and places: Berlin, Vienna, Dresden, Leipzig, Versailles.

In her vast, whispering history brain, nothing clicked. Unusual. Delicate flicks of penmark were photographically saved to her memory. But the rhino stopped her short. She couldn't see it, with its broad shoulders and proud, intelligent face, and not think of the taxidermy room at Jake's parents' house.

Someone else would have wandered in there with admiration. But Andrea grew up in a house with her mom's service dog and stray cats, where the most expensive gift each Christmas was a zoo membership. Seeing a taxidermy clouded leopard, lioness head, Cape buffalo horns, and the draping eyelashes of the elephant looming from the walls was panic inducing. Even if the soft blue ring box was in that room, too.

There wasn't a rhino there, but on this historic document, there was, completing the big five, the dream of every trophy hunter: a lion, an elephant, a leopard, a Cape buffalo, and a rhino. The rhino in this illustration was portrayed alive, and the list on the back looked like it might have been its diet. Andrea tried to focus on what was real, in her control, in front of her. This was real history right here. Jake's parlor was far away.

Andrea snapped a picture of the document before rolling it back up to preserve the crumbling corners. She put it back in the hidden drawer, taking a few deep breaths to calm her mind. She slid into bed, thinking about animals in the 1740s. Even as a historian with a brilliant, immediate memory of everything she read, she knew nothing.

The next morning, Andrea rummaged through her suitcase for her robe and towel and put her dark hair up in a clip. A scalding hot shower helped to shed her jet lag. She couldn't stop thinking about the document, a far cry from thinking about Jake's heirloom ring.

She dressed quickly, desperate for coffee, and found a campus map on her phone. A winding staircase led to the commons a few buildings over. The university was beautiful, the air crisp. Brown brick buildings with archways and tiled roofs and straight clear canals surrounded her.

Minutes later, she was in line for blessed coffee and pulled up the picture of the document, zooming in close on the details. The rhino illustration was beautiful, if primitive, and she began to make out more of the words. She typed a paragraph into Google before ordering.

"Vanilla latte with oat milk, please," she told the barista. He laughed and slid a cup of thick, black Dutch coffee over. She laughed back, embarrassed.

Her phone read: October 30, 1746. Drawn by wagons, the rhinoceros with skin like shields comes to Vienna, the only one of its kind.

Skin like shields...fascinating. How did a rhino come to be in Vienna, alive? Better alive in a foreign place than dead and hanging on someone's wall. Andrea stared at her phone, coffee in hand, when she rounded a corner on the cobblestones of campus and slammed shoulders with someone, hard. Hot coffee slid down her arm.

"Pas op!" the man said.

"Ah, I'm sorry." She shook coffee off, mortified. The man had dark hair and copper skin.

He wiped coffee from his black pea coat.

He shrugged it off, though clearly irritated, and walked on. Andrea trembled. Any conflict left her reeling lately.

She pulled up the campus map again. Her meeting in ten minutes was in another ancient building, the Gravensteen. Unlike her dorm room, which felt like a prison, the Gravensteen actually used to be a prison. The professor's office was in one of the old cells. Repurposing places with disturbing pasts was revolutionary to the history of a community. Andrea scanned the building with pride.

She took the stairs slowly, admiring the brickwork. A placard said part of the masonry dated to the twelfth century. Her brain went to the 1740s document, crisply detailed in her mind...this building was 600 years old when the document was new.

She knocked on the professor's door. It was covered in inclusivity and safe space posters and a giant sticker of a pirate ship. There was no answer. Andrea slid to the floor, tried to stop her anxious habit of rubbing her fingertips together, and sipped what was left of her coffee. She pulled up the picture of the document again, zooming in on the rhino.

Footsteps sounded near the stairs, and Andrea hopped up, eager to make a good first impression. A pair of black Chuck Taylors rounded the corner. She smiled, thinking, check this guy out. He wore loose-fitting jeans, the hem damp from puddles, a puffy red jacket, brown knitted mittens, a rainbow scarf, shoulder-length blonde hair, thick glasses, and a gray newsboy cap. He automatically made Andrea happy.

"Hi!" she said, smiling.

"Andrea?" he said gently, extending a mittened hand.

"It's pronounced awn-dre-uh, no emphasis," she said. "Blame my mother."

He smiled genuinely and unlocked his office door.

"I'm Professor Hahn. Call me Paul."

His office was lined with books, but where it wasn't, the brick was painted with beautiful, faded murals.

"Original?" she said, drawing near to the painted wall.

"Likely eighteenth century, so kind of," he said. His gray eyes twinkled.

"You're American?"

"Yeah," he said. "Hopped a flight and never went back. I remember your application well. Photographic memory, right? Welcome to the Netherlands, Andrea."

He made a point to say her name correctly: awn-dre-uh. She felt comfortable around him, like he was a kindergarten teacher, and it was her first day.

"Here's everything we know about the campus graveyard." He pulled out a folder.

Inside was a map with details of each grave printed in full color. Some headstones were so faded they had no visible markings at all.

"We'll be documenting these so we can relocate them."

"I'm excited," she said. "Preserving history."

"Yes. The river has changed course, and we have to preserve these remains. Common folk and known historical figures are buried there," said Paul. "The museum has a mausoleum ready and plans for the gravestones."

"What's our plan of action? Schedule?"

"All inside your folder," Paul said. "We're scheduled to be on-site in fifteen minutes."

"Should we go?" Andrea asked.

Paul lazily looked at his watch and smiled again. "Probably."

Chapter 4
Douwemout van der Meer
Calcutta

The stable was dark save for the blue-cream moon streaming through the windows. Sichterman's Arabians perked their ears but made no noise.

"What's your name?" Douwe said. The boy hustled to a back stall, the one nearest the paddock.

"Zubin. You've met Clara?"

Clara was asleep. She was the size of a large hound, curled onto her bumpy legs in an awkward position. Her breathing was deep; the sides of her armored body rose and fell like an ebbing wave. She was adorable.

Her ears twitched and she blinked her small brown eyes open. Zubin, now with rope in hand, was in her stall. Clara was delighted. She perked her fuzzy black ears and stood. Clara stuck out her tongue several times and yawned as Zubin wrapped the leash around her neck. He made ticking noises and urged her forward with a piece of banana.

She followed, her padded feet rolling under her as she walked. Douwe smiled.

"Does she like this?" Douwe said. He gestured to the rope. Zubin walked backward, lightly pulling her. She followed with little hesitation.

"With me, she does, sir. She doesn't do this with everyone."

"How is it you know what she likes, Zubin?" Douwe said. He pressed his back to the stable door to allow Clara to pass. He resisted the temptation to touch her gray skin. It felt forbidden—like she was still Job's Behemoth.

"She's a baby animal," Zubin said. He ticked at Clara repeatedly. "Most baby animals want the same things."

"Those are?" Douwe said. He picked up a banana from a barrel nearby and tucked it into his pea-green evening coat pocket. Zubin and Clara moved at a steady clip through the stable and crossed the threshold.

"Treats, warm things, milk, and play," Zubin said. "I've seen plenty of baby animals in my day. More than you, where you're from."

"Is that so, Zubin?" Douwe laughed again. This child was leading a baby Indian Rhinoceros through a dark moonlit garden. He spoke the truth.

"Yes, sir. Elephants, tigers, rhinos like Clara, even a cheetah," Zubin said. He put a piece of banana flat in his hand and extended it to Clara, who used her tongue and lip to eagerly eat. Her eyes brightened.

"A cheetah? Have you been to Africa, boy?"

"No. A cheetah, a baby, here. Like Clara, its mother was shot by the Mughal's men in a hunting game and bought at the market by one of you firangis."

Douwe frowned. He did not consider himself a firangi, an invader-foreigner. His time in Calcutta was short and purposeful, but Zubin used the word with malice on his tongue.

"Zubin, where did Clara come from?"

"The market," Zubin said. He paused by the tiled fountain to allow Clara to drink deeply. The white manor glowed. "Lady Sichterman's son turned seven, so she's lonely."

"Why would Sybilla's son turning seven make her lonely?"

"Each of her children has turned seven here in Calcutta. After their birthday, they are put on the next VOC boat and are sent back to Amsterdam," Zubin said. He tugged gently on Clara's lead. "Lady Sichterman has not been back to Europe in fifteen years. Her oldest child left before I was born, but Lady Sichterman has not seen him. Or any of the others."

Douwe's heart sank. "So, you thought—"

"That Clara could be her last baby." Zubin lingered in the doorway. Clara stood in the candlelight, her mottled armor skin lavender in the smoke.

A group of musicians joined the party, and the hookah pipes were refilled. The hookah burdars filled the bowls with water and opened tobacco pouches for the guests. Remnants of dessert lingered on the table, and empty wine bottles were carted away. The cream and carmine floral chintz tablecloth was dotted with red wine and food stains.

"Sir," Zubin said. He tapped Sichterman on the shoulder, holding Clara's lead. Sichterman rose, smiling.

"My dear guests!" Sichterman said. "May I introduce to you the wonder of the Indian jungle, my latest addition to the stables, and my wife's lovely pet, Clara the Rhinoceros!"

None of the guests had been warned of Clara's arrival. The women shrieked excitedly, and the younger men leaped to their feet as if to defend them from Clara. Zubin led her in, and she trotted eagerly after him.

Zubin raised a banana in the air, which caused Clara to look up suddenly. Her behind whumped to the floor like a sitting dog. The women collectively "awww'ed," and the men chuckled. Her feather-tufted ears wagged. Zubin lowered the banana, and she grasped it with her lip.

The reaction from the crowd was varied:

"Fascinating!"

"Look at the ears!"

"Her feet are like tree stumps!"

"Her armor—like it was made for the Habsburgs!"

"That's a little monster!"

"Sichterman, she's your crown jewel!"

"Look at her rat tail!"

"The Behemoth of Job!"

Zubin led Clara farther into the dinner party to eat leftovers off dessert plates. Clara was spellbinding. Her movements were foreign and unnatural but smooth. Her focus was mainly on food—she found each crumb on the floor, each scrap on the table and the seemingly never-ending supply of bananas in Zubin's pouch.

Douwe weaved his way to Clara's side as she rolled a sticky honey ball off Johanna's plate. Johanna removed her gloves. Her hands were small and dotted with chestnut freckles but milk-pale. Her green dress shimmered.

Douwe knelt beside the rhino and held his hand out to Zubin, who gave him the lead. Douwe felt his heartbeat in his ears. Would this be what it was like to own her? Johanna held her plate with both hands, rising from her seat. Douwe and Johanna's garments touched—his pea-green velvet and her taffeta. The colors blended. The roses in her perfume floated.

"Captain van der Meer," Johanna said. She took a small step away, holding the plate still for Clara. "This animal frightens and delights me. I hear they can devour a man!"

"Not sweet Clara," Douwe said. He touched her. She was smooth, dry. A chill ran down his spine. She felt like a rock on the beach, a pebbled surface warm from the sun.

"The name of my first daughter is Clara," said Johanna. "My husband is at sea. Captain Abraham van der Weijden."

"I recognize you from the docks last spring," Douwe said. He pried Clara away from the plate, now thoroughly cleaned.

Johanna blushed and turned her attention to Clara. When he came to check on the *Knappenhof*'s cargo, she was at the docks, belly full of child, weeping at white sails on the horizon, the only woman there.

Zubin slipped Douwe two banana pieces. Clara's attention turned. Her pink top lip slid over his palm: slimy, strong. He rubbed where her horn would be. Clara leaned into him, chewing. Douwe nearly toppled over. He gave the second banana to Johanna.

Clara's total weight was on him now. It seemed he had little reason to feel brave. The so-called Behemoth was a gentle creature. Clara teased the banana from Johanna's hand, not as trusting of her as she was of Zubin or Douwe. This revelation also came to the partygoers, who watched with closed-mouth smiles and twinkling eyes. Sybilla Sichterman left her chair.

"Isn't she a joy?" Sybilla said. Her pink silk gown swept the floor with fabric gleaming. It was accented with silk roses, French lace, and blue ribbons tied into bows. Her petticoats swayed as she walked. Johanna's fan was far away.

"Lady Sichterman," Douwe said. He rose, and Clara slid to the floor. He held out Clara's lead to Sybilla.

Sybilla shook her head and smiled wryly. She pushed his hand away.

"Zubin handles Clara. We paid for him to do so. She is a wild creature."

The party stood still. Zubin rushed forward, grabbing the lead. He stared at the floor. Johanna straightened in her chair and placed the plate on the table. She reached for her fan.

"I shall take Clara back to the stables, madam," Zubin said. He bowed low and began to back away.

"Stay," Sybilla said, offering Zubin a poisonous smile. "I am not done with her. I am sure each person surely wants to feel the exotic hide of a magic rhino."

"Our special animal," Sichterman said. He drew near Sybilla and Clara, trying to take control of the situation. "A most rare and misunderstood beast. Gentle as a lamb, we have seen, though the universities will tell you they are wild and dangerous."

"She's not the same as their writings," Sichterman said. He smiled at Sybilla, but she was on edge. "But how would they know? There has not been a living rhinoceros in Europe for 200 years."

"Perhaps, sir, she's unusual because she's domesticated?" Douwe said. "How long have you had her?"

"Three weeks," Sichterman said. "If we are being sensible, it's not long enough to tame a creature that could kill an elephant."

"An elephant?" A man in a powdered wig laughed, gingerly touching her bumpy skin. "This creature seems more interested in food than fighting."

The partygoers laughed in agreement. Clara's only downfalls were her size and clumsiness.

"We must guess then, my friends, that the universities and men of science don't know everything," Sichterman said. "She is not unique in her species, either. A bull rhino may charge, but this docile creature has eaten food from your hands."

Sichterman raised his glass to Clara. "She is more than what meets the eye; we are the privileged few who get to see her."

The crowd toasted Clara, who was licking a porcelain plate. A man nearby in a marigold-colored overcoat dropped to one knee. Clara sniffed the beer in his tankard, then drank deeply and messily to great amusement.

Beer slopped down her chin and onto her bumpy neck. Her ears flicked upward as the tankard was taken. She eagerly followed. The guests laughed. She was curious, innocent, and truly adorable, moving elegantly on her rolling, pink-soled feet.

A servant offered a large pewter bottle. Zubin took it with a shallow bow and presented the metal tube of a nipple to Clara, who nursed.

"Mare's milk," Zubin said to the crowd. "She cannot get enough!"

"She'll need more than that to outweigh the ale in her belly, now, lad!"

Sybilla wore a sly smile as if she were responsible for the joy Clara brought. She weaved with too much wine.

"Must I remind you of the tragedy here?" Sybilla said. "Her mother shot in the wild, horn ground for the apothecary. I saved her from the market before she was slaughtered as well. You should all be thanking me for her presence."

The women looked away. The men took puffs of hookah, entertained by the drama. Sichterman took a long draw of his pipe, blowing blue smoke in clouds toward Sybilla.

"Leave your pipes and your glasses. Tell Clara goodnight," Sybilla gestured, both arms up, dramatic and drunk, to Clara. She ripped the bottle out of Zubin's hand and Clara's mouth. A large billowing cloud of blue smoke hit Sybilla from behind, and the sleeves of her dress moved like a bird taking flight. Clara bolted.

Sybilla screamed and stumbled backward. Clara panicked. Zubin had hold of the lead, and though Clara was a baby, she weighed twice as much as him, and the lead slipped from his hand. Clara reared again, coming down on the hookah burdar's rug. A glass bowl smashed under her feet, shattering. Shards scattered to the floor. The snake-like pipe tangled itself around Clara's legs, and she tumbled.

Clara hit the table, rearing and rolling. The table's legs snapped like saplings in a storm. Plates and wine goblets flew into the air. Clara smashed into the seated Johanna, the chair underneath her crashed to the tile leaving Johanna pinned to the floor.

Clara's legs were tangled in the hookah pipe, and when Johanna tried to stand, the heavy young animal slammed her leg to the tile viciously. The VOC men did not move to help.

Zubin leaped into the scene. He ripped the hookah pipe from about Clara's legs and snatched her flailing lead. The pipe wove through the air like a snake in the sea. Clara's high-pitched call filled the room and the women screamed with her. She was out of control, tangled in the glass and table linens.

Douwe rushed to Clara's side, shoving the other guests out of the way. Douwe ripped the tablecloth from under her and tossed the chintz over her, capturing her like a wild bird. He swaddled her and pulled her to the ground. Zubin went with her, crunching his shoulder bluntly. Clara moaned, blood was smeared on her swaddle. Douwe bundled up the fabric and dragged the screaming animal into the moonlit garden.

Douwe looked back. Johanna was pulled from the chaos by a servant. Green silk ripped. She did not move.

Clara did her best to remove the heavy tablecloth. Douwe pulled her behind the banyan tree and unfurled the chintz. It was unclear which red spots were blood and which were wine.

Clara lay on her side, soft armor heaving with panic. The whites of her eyes showed. Her feet were spattered with red. Douwe ran his hands over them and pulled back, seething. Glass shards cut his palm. He grimaced and pulled a sharp piece out. Clara kicked. A panting Zubin was suddenly sitting on her. Douwe and Zubin looked at each other briefly, then dug out large glass shards while Zubin's weight held the squealing animal.

Douwe's white shirt and cream pants were smeared in blood. He'd seen worse at sea with the deaths of his crewmates, to be sure. He found himself envious of Clara's thick hide. She would have no lasting marks.

"I shall lose my head," said Zubin.

"Nonsense. I shall lose mine before yours. They need you to care for her."

"They won't keep her now." Zubin sat; his hands balled up on either side of his face. "Any animal hurts a firangi and they turn the muskets on it. Remember the cheetah?" Zubin cried loudly. Clara rolled to her belly and kept her feet curled underneath her. She whistled low.

Zubin wrapped his arms around Clara's neck. The whites of her eyes showed again. Douwe pulled Zubin gently off, surprised when Zubin turned and embraced him. He had not been hugged in a decade or more. Douwe sighed and petted his black hair, feeling ribs through Zubin's white servant's tunic.

The boy was right. Clara had injured or perhaps even killed Johanna van der Weijden. And she had embarrassed Sybilla. This was a disaster. Douwe swallowed hard. He had to make a deal with Sichterman and get Clara away from here.

"Take Clara to the stable," Douwe said, wiping Zubin's damp face with his thumbs. The boy's eyes were bloodshot, his thin face pale. Zubin's lower lip trembled. "Listen, Zubin, I have some pull here, I think. I shall not let her die this night."

Zubin nodded. He pulled a banana from the pouch. Clara perked up and slowly stood to great relief. Her wounds were superficial, though some of the cuts bled.

"Her armor saved her. But is she truly safe, sir?"

"If I don't return by dawn..." Douwe hesitated, looking at the cream-blue moon. The banyan tree cut its light like a knife shadow on his face. "Take her to the grasslands beyond the river and let her go."

"I could never." Zubin knelt by her side. Clara ate, her eyes fixed on Zubin. "I would go into the grasslands with her and live my life in the jungle."

Douwe wiped blood from his hands onto the chintz tablecloth, gathering it.

"By dawn," Douwe said. "I will meet you outside the city by the bend in the river across from Fort William at first light. You won't be alone."

A slow, limping Clara and a weeping Zubin made a meandering path back to the dark stable. Douwe was frustrated. His life was smooth, unremarkable. A sea with no wind. And now he risked his life for a Behemoth and a boy.

This feeling startled him. Clara captured him the moment Sichterman called her to the paddock fence. He shook his head, the knot in his stomach twisting. He must save her.

Douwe last felt something similar to this when he was fifteen, boarding a frigate bound for the southernmost point of Africa. Adventure awaited him. Now, as the chintz tablecloth dotted with rhino blood dragged the garden path behind him, he felt more purposeful than ever. He prayed Johanna was alive. And to save Clara, he had to make a deal with Jan Sichterman.

The dining room was void of people. Fragments of dinner remained reminiscent of a battlefield: shattered china, smeared food, overturned chairs, and dried blood on the tile.

Douwe tossed the chintz near the table, which leaned on three legs, and left the room. Voices sounded from an upstairs bedroom. Sybilla, Captain Sichterman, and an Indian doctor in a mid-length dressing robe looked over an ornate bed. In the bed was Johanna. Her green dress was tossed to the side. It had been roughly cut off of her. Only her cream-colored chemise remained. She was breathing.

Douwe stalled—should he leave? The woman was clearly alive. This was his opportunity to flee with Clara and Zubin. But if he made the purchase right, he'd be free and clear.

He stepped into the room and cleared his throat, conscious of the blood on his white pants. Sybilla rose. She was still in her pink dinner gown, her hair swept back in an elaborate design that had not moved. Her mouth was tight and no longer painted. The kohl around her eyes tumbled down her cheeks in a gray rivulet.

"Where is the beast!?" She stomped a tiny satin-clad shoe.

"Outside the gates, on its way to the wild," Douwe said, showing his palms. "She is far away, Mistress Sichterman."

Jan Sichterman turned to Douwe. "You did not kill it?"

"I did not, sir. It did not occur to me to do so."

Sybilla Sichterman hissed, her chin rising. Douwe took a step back.

"The beast is uncontrollable. It should be killed."

Douwe tilted his glance. Clara showed fear, not aggression, and though he had not seen the incident from Sybilla's eyes, he did not feel that his life was in danger. Why would Sybilla, who wanted this creature to be her last baby, show such malice?

"The Behemoth," said Sybilla, fire reflecting in her eyes, "cannot be controlled by the unrighteous."

"If you mean Zubin, madam," said Douwe, "then you are far from the truth. The boy is perfectly capable of caring for her."

Sybilla grasped the pink silk of her gown so tightly it began to rip at the seams. Sichterman placed his hands on her trembling shoulders. She did not blink. He gently grasped her powdered chin, and their eyes met. She collapsed into his arms in wracking sobs.

Douwe and Sichterman exchanged glances. Sichterman swept her up, white petticoats and satin shoes both dotted with blood...from woman or beast, Douwe did not know.

Chapter 5
Andrea
Leiden, The Netherlands

Snow piled in corners on campus. Professor Paul and Andrea walked to the graveyard near the river adjacent to a massive church. Huge black slate tiles made up the floor, shining with the remnants of melted snow and student footprints.

The graveyard was small, maybe a half-acre, and someone had shoveled the snow away, revealing verdant green. Fifty or so gravestones, some bent and broken with age, leaned toward the glassy river, some faded to nothing but rock.

"Who clears off the snow?" Andrea said. Her breath fogged the air.

"The groundskeeper," Paul answered, as he opened the black wrought iron gate. "He's been watching these graves for decades now, knows them better than anyone.

Paul gestured to a man in coveralls holding a red shovel in the corner. He was bundled up tight with huge boots and a real fur trapper hat. Andrea cringed. Real fur was triggering. It seemed everywhere she turned there were reminders of hunting. At least his hat was functional, not a trophy on a wall. He offered a low wave, and Andrea returned it sheepishly.

Paul explained they were working in the winter because the river swelled in the spring, and according to the campus environmental team, the river would overflow its banks this year, taking the graveyard with it. Working alongside museum staff, the students involved had to photograph, clean, take life-size rubbings front and back of the graves, and document the size and material of the headstones. Then, the museum's archaeologists were slated to dig.

Andrea's section was in the back right corner, nearest the river. The gravestones leaned precariously toward it. It was past time for the remains to be moved. Andrea paused, thinking of the lives these people had lived.

She felt a particular passion for final resting places. Regardless of their status or rank, people from history deserved to have peace wherever they were entombed.

Her first gravestone was easy: a nineteenth-century duke whose stone was nearly perfect, minus its dramatic leaning. She documented it in her logbook: 4' tall, 2.5' wide, granite, and added his name. Paul had given her a box of supplies, and she pulled out the rubbing crayons and taped a piece of butcher paper to the top.

Her first rubbing was done in about twenty minutes. She thought about the line between the dates—what history had he seen? What was his daily life like? Who did he love? She did not think of Jake or the safari animals once. She moved to the second grave, enveloped in her work.

The second grave was impossible to read. Small, rounded at the top, black and green with age. The words were faint, like it had been etched too lightly at its creation. Andrea put a hand on it. There was an emblem deeply set at the top inside a carved circle. Andrea expected a flower or an angel or a cross, but it wasn't any of those things.

"Hey, Paul?" She rubbed her hands together. His Chuck Taylors squelched in the muddy grass.

"Whatcha got, Andrea? Ooh, this one's old."

"What do you think this is?" she said, pointing to the emblem.

"Probably a religious symbol," he said, removing his glasses to look closer. "It's too faded. Let's use our tools, yes?"

He grabbed a bucket from the maintenance golf cart parked nearby. The maintenance guy hovered closely, watching all of the students work with raised brows and eager eyes. Paul motioned him over to see their grave, handing Andrea a horse grooming brush.

"Remove the debris, and then we'll use our chemical cleaner," he said. "Remember, our goal here is preservation above all else. We do our best to keep the original stone intact. Sergei, know anything about this one?"

The groundskeeper knelt by the grave and rubbed a gloved hand over it.

"It's an old one, something unusual about the carving here," Sergei said. "Take care, it's badly eroded. We don't want to damage it further. You can do it."

Sergei's fur trim fluttered in the breeze and distracted Andrea as he walked away. She put the brush to the stone, feeling the vibration through her gloved hands. Layers of dirt and mud lifted from the bottom, but the lichen, hunter-green and black, didn't want to budge. Paul helped wet the headstone before applying the chemical cleaner.

"Can you see anything?" Andrea asked, squinting at the carved emblem.

"It's easier to see while it's wet from an angle," Paul said. He snapped a photo on his phone.

She removed a glove, fingers sore, and zoomed in. Her heart pounded. It looked like a rhino.

Paul taught Andrea how to use the chemical cleaner and she scrubbed again with the horse brush. An hour later it was cleaner, but the words were still soft, unreadable. An animal emblem could mean a million things. Was it a coat of arms? A last name represented by a creature? The more she scrubbed, the clearer it became. Paul came to check on her.

"You'll have to wait a few hours for it to dry before you do your rubbing," Paul said. "This is a large mammal of some kind, but not a horse."

"No, not a horse," she said, kneeling by the wet stone. They took a second photo with Paul's phone, but the writing still didn't reveal itself. "Can I show you something?"

This animal on the stone reminded her of the document in the desk. Andrea showed Paul the picture she'd taken the night before.

"Where did you find this? I know this animal."

"I...well, I found it in an old desk bolted to my dorm room floor," she said. She wondered what he would ask her to do with the document. She wasn't ready to give it up. The image was filed in her mind with precision.

"Ah, you're in the 'newly renovated' women's dorm." He chuckled. "They made some curious choices. Do you know what this is?"

Andrea shook her head.

"Obscure University history, that's for sure. There was a rhino on campus sometime in the 1700s," said Paul. "The museum had an exhibit on it. We should ask if they recognize this document."

"Do you think this gravestone—"

"Hard to say what that is," said Paul. "Could be a horse or a dog. It could be a rhino but that would be awfully coincidental. We won't know until your rubbing is done and we see these pictures on a bigger screen. I'll ask Sergei about it, too, he might know."

"No, let's not bother him."

Paul raised an eyebrow at Andrea.

"It's just he has so much to do with the moving of the stones, surely we can rely on the museum exhibit."

"We'll exhaust every resource we have. We'll check with Sergei and the museum both. After lunch?"

A museum exhibit on the rhino in the document sounded promising.

She'd rather seek help from documents than people, she had to admit. Andrea let out a shaky breath of relief. If Paul knew the animal on her found document was alive in the 1700s, Andrea likely wasn't dealing with another set of trophy hunters. She reluctantly left the damp stone behind. As she walked away, Sergei stepped around her and knelt by the grave.

Chapter 6
Douwemout van der Meer
Calcutta, India

Sichterman swept Sybilla away, and Johanna did not stir. The doctor felt her forehead, watching her breathe, then rummaged in a satchel and produced a thumb-sized bottle.

"Will she be alright?" Douwe asked.

"She has a few cuts, a bump on her head, a deeply bruised leg and tender ribs. The genda scared her into sleep."

"She fainted?"

"Yes, and she will wake as soon as she smells this." The doctor uncorked the tiny bottle.

"If you knew she would wake, why not do it with the Sichtermans still in the room? Wouldn't it improve Sybilla's disposition?"

"My good sir, nothing could improve Lady Sybilla's disposition without upsetting Lady Johanna. Sybilla's worry would be too much for the lady at this moment," he said. With a wave of his wrist, an ammonia smell woke Johanna.

She fluttered her eyes gently, then, blinking largely, stared at the men with confusion.

"Lady Johanna," the doctor said. "There has been an accident. Do you feel pain?"

Johanna tried to sit up. Douwe and the doctor grabbed her under an armpit.

"Pain?" She was dazed. "Yes, my leg." She reached to raise the blankets with a wince and gasped. "And my ribs."

"Johanna," Douwe said. "You gave us a fright."

"You came for me," she said, blinking widely. "What happened?"

Douwe explained to Johanna about the smoke and Sybilla's billowing sleeves. He told her his plan to buy Clara and leave with her. The doctor explained Johanna's injuries—Clara crushed her leg, but it was not broken. The blow to the ribs was from the overturned table, the cuts were from shattered glassware.

"Sichterman already had this plan in place, Johanna," Douwe said. "He invited me here tonight to see if I wanted to purchase Clara."

"Why would he deny his wife her last shred of happiness?"

"I do not think he realized the trouble Clara could bring. I have experience with exotic animals, and I promise you I can do this." But he doubted himself.

Johanna's eyelids fluttered. In a whisper, the doctor asked Douwe to stay so he could check on Sybilla. Johanna's porcelain skin and disheveled hair glowed red in the firelight. He memorized her profile, the turn of her curls.

The doctor returned, Sichterman by his side. Douwe wiped his hands on his blood-stained breeches.

"Sybilla is resting. Both of them will be fine."

Sichterman motioned to Douwe to follow. "We will check on Johanna within the hour." The two men left the room together.

"Is your wife alright, sir?"

"She will be once Johanna speaks with her, and the memory of the night fades," Sichterman said, turning a corner to a wood-paneled study.

"Fades?" It felt impossible to forget what had happened.

"My wife has trouble with her memory, Douwe. She relies on Johanna. She is aware of it. It started shortly after our third child was sent back to Groningen."

Sichterman sat behind a dark-wood desk, fingers on his temples. A large window looked out over the garden. The stable in the distance was bathed in lantern light. Where were Zubin and Clara now?

"She...she will not remember what happened?"

"She may remember some things, but they're distorted. Sometimes things are made worse, sometimes more pleasant," Sichterman said. "Her mind is unpredictable, not unlike the sea. I try to keep her calm and contained. I should have known better than to bring the animal in."

"It's not your fault, sir. You were trying to bring her happiness, another baby."

Sichterman closed his eyes. "Yes, I suppose I was. The ways of India are too much for even me, let alone my fragile wife. Sending our children back to a home they have never seen to live with people they have never met...? They are our children, for god's sake." He popped the heel of his hand on his desk and rose, moving to the window.

"Would it be better or worse for Clara to stay?"

"If Sybilla wants Clara gone, she will be killed, chopped, and sold at the market for a pretty penny, Douwe," Sichterman said. He did not turn. "If Sybilla wants Clara to stay, she would get so large that she would have to leave, and Sybilla is dealt another heartbreak."

Douwe swallowed, his throat dry. There was no correct answer.

"I am not a man driven by emotion, but my wife has been through too much."

Sichterman put a fist gently on the glass. "Clara should go, Douwe."

"I will take her, Captain."

"Go as far away as you can."

"Sir, may I ask, why me?"

Sichterman turned, eyebrows up.

"I see something in you, Douwemout van der Meer. You are a man of dedication. I asked you here tonight to solve a problem, knowing you would do it, though I did not expect it now."

"You always wanted me to take her?"

Sichterman nodded. "You were my best option, Captain. No family, no ties. Let's negotiate this. Clara was expensive."

Minutes later, Douwe had a bill of sale in hand and prayed that the coin in his chest would cover the sum. Two hundred ducats and a gentleman's agreement to take Clara and leave, never returning to Calcutta. His pace quickened as he passed Sybilla's closed door. The stairs and wide white door below were in view when Johanna stopped him.

"Johanna! You should be resting. Aren't you in pain?"

"I am stronger than I look, Douwe," Johanna said. She struggled to stand, leaning heavily into the stair railing. "Will you stay, Captain?"

Douwe took a long exhale. "I never planned to," Douwe said. He unrolled the bill. "I'm taking Clara and Zubin and leaving, all cleared with Jan."

Johanna took the parchment and skimmed it. Sadness crossed her countenance. She handed it back to him and sighed deeply.

"Seems settled then." She blocked the stairs.

"May I take my leave, madam?" Douwe said. The clock in the foyer struck an hour precariously close to dawn. Zubin and Clara would soon leave.

Without warning, Johanna kissed him. Douwe kept his eyes open, shocked. When she pulled away, she was red in the face. Passion stirred in him, but Johanna was as out of reach as a star in the sky.

"Go," Johanna said. She limped toward the bedroom door. "Every man who leaves Calcutta leaves me in tears, and I stay here longing."

"Your husband will return," Douwe said, shaking his head. "He is an honorable man."

But Johanna's husband would be gone for many more months. A kiss was one thing, but more than that, and the woman risked everything. Adultery was punishable by death.

"You have not met my husband," she said. She paused at the doorway. "His last European visit was long enough for me to get a letter from his mistress, demanding recompense for the child left in her belly."

Douwe could not count the number of times anger had filled him in the last twelve hours. He stepped forward, sweeping Johanna into his arms and carrying her to the four-poster bed. The fire had died. He lay her down gently. Tears hit his shoulder. She clung to him, longing to stay in his grasp.

"It's been so long since a man cared for me, Douwe."

Douwe gently removed her arms from his shoulders and pulled the blanket over her. He wiped the tears from her skin with his rough thumb. She grasped his hand, brought it to her mouth, and stared at him. He did not desire to lay in this bed with her, though his body warmed at the thought of it.

He smiled gently and kissed her forehead. She trembled at his touch. Douwe stepped out of the room, lingering in the doorway. Johanna did not look at him. Her profile was backlit by a single candle on the nightstand. He thought of Clara and Zubin.

"Goodbye, Johanna," Douwe whispered. "I am sorry."

Johanna closed her eyes, perhaps to wish him back into the room, but Douwe was out the wide white door.

Calcutta under moonlight made things clear, especially passing the concourse where high society spent evenings in fancy coaches and on Arabian steeds. It was empty save dust and wind, wheel marks, horseshoe prints. Had he ever belonged here? Douwe turned the corner to his apartment and took the steps two at a time.

The heavy black door swung open, skeleton keys jangling in the lock. Douwe filled his trunk for sea travel: clothing, a few books, parchment, quills, and VOC charter. He groped under his bed, face and shoulder pressed into the floor, and wiggled his black box of coins close.

The money chest was a German corsair, wrought iron with a fine black polish. As tall as Douwe's hand and as wide as his forearm, it was intricate and locked tight. A false keyhole decorated the front. It could be turned, but no action took place, no matter how good the lock-pick. The keyhole was hidden under a rivulet, part of the design. The key was fastened to a silver chain around his neck.

Bright silver and copper coins from all over Europe shone, though the valuable ones were VOC silver: lion and crest, year plainly stamped.

The entire chest contained 360 ducats. More than enough to own Clara. He removed the coin for Clara's purchase and locked it tight. Soon, all that remained in the apartment was a stub of a candlestick, quickly swept into his pocket.

In the quiet, Douwe heard a mewl. His heart sank. Betsy was climbing the trellis. She leaped in through the balcony window, black tail swishing at him, saying: Where have you been?

"Hello, Betsy." Douwe picked her up. She purred, rubbing his stubbly cheek. "I will come back for you midday if everything goes according to plan, little miss."

He put her down. She wove through his legs like a seabird. Douwe stroked her from head to the tip of her tail, black fur dancing in the moonlit air. He grabbed the trunk by its rope handles.

Across from Fort William, the southwestern edge of Calcutta was marked by a big bend in the Hooghly River where a banyan tree grew in curves like a jumbled cathedral. Hopefully, Clara and Zubin waited there, safe under the roots. Douwe hauled a cart through the winding streets, wondering how long past dawn Zubin would wait. He stumbled in the dark, legs heavy.

Douwe stopped at the tree, breathing heavily. He wiped sweat from his brow and stepped around a root. Under the lifted root, Zubin's face and shoulders rested on Clara's bumpy shoulder, settled under a knitted blanket. Clara's skin was draped over her like a thick cloth. They were both fast asleep. Douwe lay down nearby, relieved.

Day broke an hour after Douwe fell asleep under the towering roots of the banyan. The Hooghly rushed past to the Bay of Bengal, and the shipyard bustled. The shouts of men on water woke Douwe with a start. Zubin and Clara stirred.

"Zubin," Douwe said. Zubin grabbed Douwe's shoulders as if making sure he was real. "You're alright?"

"I was worried you wouldn't come."

Clara slowly stood. Zubin had a canvas bag of supplies taken from the stable. He produced his never-ending pouch of bananas and two full pewter milk bottles. Clara was held by a soft brown leather collar.

"We ran through the streets," Zubin said, staring at Clara with a furrowed brow as she suckled. "I went to the stables first and took all her things and extras, too. Douwe, they will know it was me who took it and I shall be punished."

"No, no." Douwe grabbed the pouch and waited to feed Clara a banana. She was more eager to take her bottle from Zubin. "I have arranged it with Sichterman. He will meet us this morning to receive payment."

"Where will we go?" Zubin's hand dropped. Clara unlatched and raised her ears. Zubin eyed Douwe cautiously.

"Away from Sybilla," Douwe said. He showed Clara the banana. She flicked her ears before licking his palm, nudging him with her lip. She took the banana and looked back at Zubin for more milk.

"The wild?" Zubin asked.

"I don't think we will make it out there." Douwe shook his head. "Clara's not used to it, and we couldn't live there long. I think we should take Clara out of India."

"Out of India, sir?" He stepped closer to Clara and clung to her lead. "You mean to sell her."

"She has already been sold. I have saved her."

"That is not true!" Zubin took a fist to his chest, fire in his words. "I am the one who saved her. They would have paraded her at dinners forever until she was too big, then chopped her into bits and sold her horn to be ground to magic dust."

"Zubin, I..." He needed Zubin. "I have purchased Clara and all that goes with her for a fine sum."

Douwe put a hand on the boy's shoulder. Zubin's eyebrows lowered, nostrils flaring.

"I purchased your services, too, Zubin." Douwe knelt beside the boy. "I did it so you could have a choice. If your family waits for you, then go to them. If you want to come with me and Clara, so be it, but Sichterman does not expect you back."

"I have no family," Zubin said. "I began my life with the baytar, the horse keeper, and that is all I have known. He took me to Sichterman's stables when I was old enough to lead a horse alone."

"Come with me and Clara."

"And how shall we live? You will trade and command a ship with a rhino and a stable boy in your apartment?"

"No," Douwe said. "Part of the agreement is that this is my last voyage with the VOC."

Clara had wandered and was grazing nearby. She violently ripped out the tall grass near the riverbank with her lips, head to the ground. Her feet were pink on the bottom and showed when she scraped at the tender roots. Her lead trailed behind her.

"Then who do you work for now?" Zubin walked toward Clara.

"I work for Clara." Douwe gave a half smile. "Zubin, have you ever heard of a wunderkammer?"

"What is this, wunderkammer?"

"A way to see the world you do not live in, a wonder cabinet. The people last night were amazed by Clara, yes?"

Zubin nodded. "She is amazing."

"Imagine how the rest of the world would respond to her, Zubin. She is different from what I thought a rhino would be. No one has seen a rhino in Europe in two hundred years. Those who see her will be changed."

"And how do you know Clara won't die?"

"Because of you," Douwe said.

Zubin led Clara out of last night's chaos and lulled her to sleep away from her stable. He knew her needs like his own. They were bonded. Clara loved him. Douwe had to keep them together if he wanted what was best for Clara. If Zubin had not helped him, he might learn how to keep Clara alive, but his life and Clara's would be better with Zubin.

"What is your plan?" Zubin sat, legs extended, scratching Clara's shoulder.

Clara flicked her ears and looked at Douwe, expecting a banana. The man and the Behemoth locked eyes, and for that moment, there was something beyond the texts of the Bible or what he had read from Pliny. Here was a creature most people were wrong about. Here was a beast of wonder.

"We board the *Knappenhof* in two weeks," Douwe said. He touched the black fur of Clara's fringed ears. She glanced across the wide river to the port. "And we shall go to Leiden with Clara."

"If she goes," Zubin said. "Then I go."

"I cannot tell you how happy that makes me, my boy."

Chapter 7
Andrea
Leiden, The Netherlands

Andrea sat next to Paul at a high-top table in the student union and locked eyes with black pea coat guy. Same guy she'd dumped coffee on that morning. Of course, the first cohort she met was someone she had already angered.

"Hi," Andrea said.

"Coffee girl," he said. He raised a dark eyebrow at her.

"Yeah, sorry about that," she said. He was handsome, naturally. Her mother's voice was in her head: Andreaaaa!!

She blushed and turned away, stomach leaping, hoping he wouldn't scold her. She was jittery. She tried to force herself to relax, but her hands trembled.

"You've met our American student for the semester already, Lucas?" said Paul. He had such a calming voice. Her trembling eased.

"We bumped into each other this morning," he said. He shrugged off his pea coat to reveal a coffee-stained t-shirt. Andrea turned crimson, ears burning.

"Andrea is from the University of Charleston," said Paul. "She's here to help with the cemetery project. Want to show Lucas the stone you were working on earlier?"

Andrea was glad for the refocus. She pulled her phone from her coat pocket and brought up the picture. Lucas had a gorgeous, hooked nose, his warm brown eyes were serious but lively. He took the phone and zoomed in, bringing it to his face.

"An animal of some kind?" He furrowed his brow. "Does Sergei know?

"We haven't asked him yet," Andrea said. "I'm not exactly sure what it is. We hope to get a closer look when it dries this afternoon."

"Animals are uncommon," said Lucas. "Unless they are doves. But most of the time, we see crosses and wreaths. Can you read the dates yet?"

"I can make out the seventeen," she said. "So definitely eighteenth century. But the other two numbers I can't make out yet."

"It looks like a zero? Or an eight? Maybe a six?" said Lucas. His fingers pinched the screen of her phone to look.

"Right," she said. "Too hard to see."

"Well, you've got a good one," he said. He swiped to the previous picture, looking for another shot of the grave. "Oh!"

It was the document picture, rhino blazing in red-brown ink. Lucas's eyes widened, showing lust, joy, or something in between.

"I found that yesterday," Andrea said, leaning in. He smelled like coffee and light cologne.

"You found this? Linen?" he asked. "Lucky you."

She told him about the desk in her dorm room. "It's definitely old," she replied. "And printing ink. This is a mass manufactured item, but on the back was iron gall ink."

Paul chuckled. "You know your historical inks? What a cool student. I didn't know there was anything on the back."

"I didn't get a picture of it. It was a list in French, supplies, I think, and dates."

"This is German on the front," said Lucas. "An Indian rhinoceros? There are no rhinoceros in Europe. The climate won't support them."

"Right. I thought it might have been from the VOC, from their days in India, but the dates are wrong," she said. "In the late 1740s, the VOC lost control of India in a huge battle. I don't remember all the details, but by then, the Dutch wouldn't have been promoting a spectacle like this. Their world was turned upside down."

Lucas nodded. "That's my heritage. The British took over India in the 1750s, and the Dutch essentially abandoned their ports. My family can trace its roots to that chasm. The question is, how did this Indian rhino get to Europe?"

"I'm glad it was alive when it made it here," Andrea said, wondering how long the journey was. "Too many things could have gone wrong."

"It's lucky indeed," Lucas said. "Rhinos have always been valued for their horns and skin, people thinking it can be medicine. Large animals like this were pretty common in menageries, though I don't know about rhinos. Mostly elephants, probably treated poorly."

"Crazy for sure," she said. She brightened, put in a position where she could talk about animal rights with someone who seemed to think the same, but she felt cautious.

"But we don't know what happened to this animal in the end."

"We know it was alive for a while at least," said Lucas. "Better than seeing a similar broadside advertising an auction for its parts."

A lump grew in Andrea's throat, and she tried to swallow, but the elephant mounted to the wall in Jake's house popped into her mind's eye. She wanted that place to be cut from her photographic memory.

"Remember how I told you the museum had an exhibit on a rhino?" Paul said.

Lucas nodded. "It was up a few summers ago. I knew this looked familiar, but I don't remember much. I don't spend as much time there as I used to."

"How'd you get involved in the gravesite project?" Andrea said.

"I grew up here, watched the river shift. It's different now, even from my own childhood. The river touched the gravestones last summer. We feared the ground would open up and the caskets would float to the surface. I spent a lot of the time moving sandbags around."

A more welcome vision than the elephant came to mind: Lucas, shirtless in eighteenth-century breeches, moving sandbags around the cemetery in the summer sun. Andrea allowed herself a half-smile.

"I wondered what the University would do with the graves, and I met Paul and Sergei out there one day. They told me about the project. I was a music major before, but this was too appealing to me. I switched majors, and here we are."

She completely understood. It was impossible to ignore real history in front of you.

"How much involvement does the museum have?" Andrea said.

"A lot, considering they'll be the keepers of the records and remains," said Paul. "We have a great connection with them, valuable for all parties. Sergei's really connected this project to the institution. They're planning an exhibit once the graves are up. We'll move the remains to the mausoleum."

"Sergei's connected to the museum?" Andrea said.

Paul and Lucas nodded at her.

"He's dedicated to this," Lucas said.

"Can we go to the museum and figure out more about the rhino exhibit?" Andrea said. She tried to shrug off her apprehensions about Sergei. "Should I go get the document?"

"Not without instruction," said Paul. "It's too damp outside, and with something so old, we definitely need help moving it. Heaven forbid we drop it in the snow."

"Or spill coffee on it," said Lucas. He raised an eyebrow and smirked.

Chapter 8
Douwemout van der Meer
Calcutta, India

Douwe and Zubin headed to Apollo's Tavern, near Fort William, to meet Sichterman. It had everything a sailor needed: upstairs rooms for rent, quick and easy food, golden pints of beer. The tavern's cobbled street was strung with colorful buntings. It reminded Douwe of Holland.

"Captain van der Meer!" said Hirzet. The Scottish barmaid recognized Douwe.

She wiped her hands on her brown apron. Hirzet smiled coyly, blue eyes bright. Douwe usually made straight for Apollo's after he docked for a few reasons. He was partial to the fish dishes and to Hirzet, all blonde curls and curves.

"What do we have here?" She gestured to Zubin and Clara.

Hirzet came around the bar and put her hands on her knees. Her bust mounded like ripe pale pumpkins. Zubin blushed. Hirzet put her hand out to Clara, rubbing her fingers together and clicking her tongue like she was calling a kitten. She wore an orange scarf in her hair that suited her beautifully.

Clara's feet padded on the wooden floor, and she gazed uneasily around, perhaps still nervous about last night's dinner. But Hirzet produced a carrot for her, and Clara ate it happily. Hirzet knelt on the floor and stroked Clara's side. She smiled widely, a small gap between her front teeth showing.

"Two fish today, then?" Hirzet said, softly eyeing Zubin, who took the place in.

Clara leaned into Hirzet with enough force to knock her over if she wasn't braced for it.

"Please. We're early, expecting Commander Sichterman in an hour," Douwe said. He motioned for a bottle of milk from Zubin's satchel.

"Would you like to feed her, Hirzet?"

Hirzet nodded and took the pewter bottle. "What's in it?" She sniffed it, fighting Clara away. Hirzet rose to her feet and Clara latched on, guzzling happily.

"Mare's milk," Zubin said. "From Sichterman's Arabians. I've only got one bottle left."

"Ach, when does she go back to the stables?" Hirzet held the bottle firmly, but Clara was a glutton.

"Never. Captain van der Meer bought her."

"Didja now? And what on earth will you do with a rhinoceros, Douwe?"

Douwe blushed at Hirzet's use of his shortened name. "Well, Hirzet, I plan to show her to the world. She's not what people think."

"Certainly not. A gentle creature, eh?"

Clara guzzled her milk. Hirzet was entranced.

"Her name is Clara," said Zubin. "She should probably go outside for a while now." Zubin shrugged sheepishly as Clara began to squat.

"This way, out back, where you can be safe from passersby until Douwe is finished with Sichterman."

Zubin led Clara out the kitchen door to a courtyard scattered with chickens. The yard was small but had two gates, one leading to the street and one to the alley behind the tavern. A fabric overhang shielded the yard and chicken coop. Clara chased the chickens through the yard, snuffling at them. Douwe checked both gates and made sure they were latched. Once he was confident the boy and the rhino were secure, he returned to Hirzet.

"Thank you, Hirzet. I owe you a debt."

"Not yet you don't," Hirzet said from the kitchen. "I have a donkey that's given birth and milk to spare. I'll give you that, then you'll owe me." Hirzet shook the skillet, the fish sizzled.

Douwe made a sound through his teeth—phew. He was grateful for others who offered to care for Clara.

"Thank you. I plan to take her to Europe in a fortnight. Let the University at Leiden study her. The only thing they've seen of a rhino is Albrecht Dürer's woodcut, but that's two hundred years old. It's wrong, too. Clara doesn't look like Dürer's rhino."

"University? Sure, let them get a good look at her. Then make your money."

"Money?" Douwe said. The kitchen was warm. Hirzet wiped her brow with a cotton rag.

"D'yknow how many royal families would pay to have her be part of their menagerie?" Hirzet asked, flipping the fish in the skillet. "In Versailles, King Louis has a bunch of animals, but no rhino."

"And how do you know what animals Louis has?"

Hirzet motioned to dishes on a wooden slab behind him, and Douwe handed her two tin plates. He was well aware of the menagerie in Versailles. The white-faced monkey he transported was bound for the cages there.

"Worked in the kitchens before comin' this way," Hirzet said, heading to the door with Zubin's plate. Zubin hollered a quick thanks and scalded his fingers on the fish, rushing back to play with Clara. "Servants come in and out of that place quicker than a tide rises. I was gone in a week. But learnt plenty. He bought an elephant for twenty-five thousand francs. I had to prepare that feast once. I was not fit for chopping vegetables for a beast bigger than a house."

"Twenty-five thousand? I could never sell Clara, not with Zubin about. They're... well, we're all attached."

"Then make yer money and show her off," Hirzet said. "People'd pay a pfennig to see her, I'm sure of it. Make 'em pay five to pet her, seven to bottle feed her like I got to."

"Sounds like you owe me eight pfennigs, Hirzet."

"Do I now? That'll be fifteen pfennigs for fish and beer, Captain van der Meer." Hirzet slid a mug across the table. She cocked her head to the side and laughed.

Douwe envisioned taking Clara from university to university and royal households. The academic community would pay. But would a commoner? It was simple to find joy with Clara. Hirzet and Zubin were not royalty or natural philosophers, but they were taken with her.

Clara could correct the falsehood about rhinos being ferocious man-eating beasts and expand the perspective of people who never left Europe. But without money, Douwe would be stagnant. He was saddled with providing Clara's food, space, care, and transport. Would people actually pay to see her, pet her, feed her? He had two weeks in Calcutta to find out.

From the Dutch door, Douwe watched Clara charge at Zubin, who dodged her and spun, laughing. Clara trotted, flaring her nostrils, backed away, and charged again. Two children. Clara chased the chickens to the delight of Zubin, who smiled. His mouth was missing teeth from childhood.

A bell on the door told him Sichterman had arrived. Douwe exited the kitchen and opened his trunk. The coins were pre-counted and heavy in their leather sack. Douwe replaced his skeleton key under his tunic and joined Sichterman at a worn table.

"Captain." Douwe placed the coin down.

"What are your plans, Douwe?" Sichterman weighed the bag in his hand and swiftly pocketed it.

"I have been considering. But first, please tell me how Johanna and Sybilla are faring?"

"I told Sybilla Clara was gone. She's made her own assumptions," Sichterman said. He motioned to Hirzet, approaching with two pewter mugs of ale. "Johanna will be alright. She was still asleep when I left."

"She went through a lot last night. I hope she will still help Sybilla after everything."

"Johanna would not abandon us. Tell me, how do you plan to keep Clara?"

"I'll be leaving India. I'm on my way to Leiden with her in a fort-night. She may as well be studied. She's not wicked or violent. She's scarcely different from a dog."

"She's a wild animal. Have you forgotten last night?" Sichterman said. "She nearly killed Johanna."

"Perhaps the best place for an animal is not a dining room, sir," Douwe said. He straightened in his chair. Sichterman bristled.

"Whatever your choice is, Van der Meer, I do hope the animal brings you a fortune." Sichterman stood. "Your voyage with the VOC is over after this. I expect you may want to re-up when your animal meets its demise. I may make an exception for you."

"Sir." Douwe rose. "No thank you."

"Tot ziens, Douwe," Sichterman said. "I wish you the best."

Douwe went back to the Dutch door. Clara and Zubin were taking vegetables from Hirzet. Clara's presence felt like freedom and a chain simultaneously—an adventure with a few unexpected passengers.

"Hirzet, may I ask a favor?" Douwe examined the outdoor courtyard. "Could I try your method out here?"

"My method, love?" Hirzet wiped a rhino-slimed hand on her apron.

"A pfenning a view." He motioned to Clara.

"Ach, Douwe. That means I get to keep her for two weeks, yes?"

"And Zubin and I, if it's not too much to ask. And my cat, Betsy," Douwe said sheepishly. "I must fetch her."

"A cat, a child, a captain, and a rhino?" Hirzet laughed. "Sounds like a full house. Pay me half of what you make, and I'll feed you all."

Soon, Douwe heard the patrons asking after Clara. Her ears perked at the sound of voices and shuffling feet. She was curious—intelligent-ly so. She was excited to see people and showed little fear of them, but quick movements spooked her. She liked other animals and chased the chickens.

Part of him was nervous about keeping her. He had cared for horses in his youth as they were his family's primary mode of transportation. But this animal—she was risky. He had an unanswerable question—how much would she actually eat? Zubin told him what he knew, but she was a baby. Soon, she would be double or triple the size. How could he properly stock his ship?

"Zubin," said Douwe. Zubin had been resting in a hay-filled corner. He perked up, took his cap off his eyes.

"Yes, Douwe?" said Zubin, black hair shining in the sun.

"Do you know anyone around here who has raised a rhino?"

"People in the market might know someone. Then there are the hunters, but I do not think you want to speak with them."

He did not. Poachers hunted tigers, rhinos, elephants, bears—all of the large animals in India were subject to the shikar. They even imported British hounds to flush out jackals in the wilderness. Nausea crawled up Douwe's throat when he considered the death of Clara's mother. How did Clara survive? Perhaps because she did not yet have a horn.

"No, no hunters. Who did you learn from? Would he know?"

"The baytar. Near Fort William, not far. He knows a lot."

"Let's go see him now."

Zubin sighed and lazily crawled to his feet.

"Are we taking her?" he said, extending a hand to Clara, who was sleeping in the shade near the chicken coop. The hens pecked at the dirt, sending her ears twitching.

Douwe hesitated. The gates did not lock. Hirzet was busy with her customers.

"We'd better," Douwe said.

Zubin led Clara through the fence to the crowded alley beyond. The people parted with amusement as Clara tromped through. She was clumsy, with a bouncing walk like a puppy. She loved the attention.

A few oxen pulling a cart, as did the raucous laughter and broad swinging of a tavern door, startled her. Douwe placed his hand on her shoulder when something that might frighten her passed by. Clara made it through the street with him on one side and Zubin on the other.

Despite the palm trees and excessive heat, Fort William's neat walls and orderly paths were so reminiscent of Rotterdam that Douwe forgot he was half a world away. Zubin led him catty-corner to a stable full of horses. The boy and the rhino paused with Douwe, waiting for his guidance. Douwe wanted to avoid taking Clara into a stable with prized horses—she was not a common sight, and the horses might startle.

"Alright, you stay here with Clara," Douwe said. "I will find out where the baytar is. Zubin?"

Zubin looked up at Douwe, squinting in the mid-morning sun. He shielded his eyes with a dirty hand.

"Do not leave this spot." Douwe pointed to a white post.

The boy nodded, tying a sheepshank. He pulled out another banana chunk, and Clara grabbed it from his hand. Douwe left them apprehensively.

Fort William was built by the VOC. It had European-style buildings with towers and battlements, a garden, stables, offices, a chapel, and plans for a larger church. It was surrounded by a star-shaped wall, except where it dumped into the river with an enormous ramp, beyond which ships waited for loading, bobbing in the Hooghly.

Inside the walls was called the factory: a huge market where ship captains and dock workers unloaded and loaded their treasures. Trinkets, spices, cloth—Fort William's factory was the central hub for goods leaving via the Hooghly River bound for Europe, including animals. Outside the wall were Bengali buildings. They were beautiful and otherworldly. The archways, stonework, charm, detail—it did not exist in the clean, straight lines of the Fort.

The baytar was called upon to assist with sailors and captains' livestock. The stable was framed in archways, old construction. The stone building harbored damp and cool air. The familiar, welcome smell of horse and hay surrounded him. Douwe breathed it in. He closed his eyes for a moment and was transported back to his childhood home in Leiden.

The stables there were warm in the winter with glowing wood and hay rustling with dormice. His old bay mare nudged his hands until he took his gloves off. Lost in the memory, Douwe startled when an Arabian nickered nearby. The horse curiously peered over its headstall.

"May I help you, sir?" a stableboy carrying water buckets asked.

"I am looking for the baytar. Tell him Captain Douwemout van der Meer is here to see him."

"And why?" the boy asked, latching the gate after he emptied a bucket in the Arabian's stall.

"I need to see if he can help me care for...ah..."

"For what?"

"A rhino, a genda," said Douwe. "A rhino calf."

The stable boy laughed and grabbed another bucket. The horses chuffed.

"He's at the end of the stables, in the tack room," the boy said through his laughter. "I can't believe you want him to help you."

"What do you mean?" said Douwe.

"He sold a rhino calf at the market. It must be the same one."

Douwe flushed. Either the man knew nothing of rhinos, so he sold Clara or got rid of her because she was too much work.

The horses nickered at him, some eating loudly, some thrusting their soft noses at him and sniffing. The tack room door was ajar. Silver bits and leather bridles hung on the walls. The baytar shuffled inside.

"Excuse me," Douwe said, rapping lightly on the door frame.

The man inside was dressed in white robes, with a beard extending to his chest. He had a hooked nose and kind eyes framed by animated eyebrows.

"And who are you in my stables? I do not recognize you."

"I am Captain Douwemout van der Meer, and I believe I bought your rhino."

"Rhino? From the market? About three weeks ago? Not possible. I sold her to Jan Sichterman."

The baytar stepped over piles of fringed horse saddles and bridles. They were red and gold, fancier than any Douwe had ever seen.

"Sichterman sold her to me," Douwe said, stepping into the hall to give the baytar space. "I took her out of an unpleasant situation, and I am in need of assistance. I need to know how to care for Clara."

"Clara, is it?" the baytar chuckled. "What a silly thing to name a wild animal."

"I did not name her. But I am now her keeper, and if you know anything about her, please help."

"I know plenty. My knowledge of animals is generations long. My father's father cared for the same bloodline of horses that you see before you. But I learned about rhinos, gendas, from experience. When the calves arrived at the market, bleating unbearably, I helped."

Douwe thought. Though rough on the surface, the baytar softened at the mention of baby rhinos.

"Perhaps we go see her? She is outside."

"I would love to see Clara again," he said.

"Sir, you know my name. May I know yours?"

"I am Fateh Khan. This is my stable, and these are the horses of the VOC, Indian royalty, and my own. I train them until they are ready to ride or board them while captains are at sea."

"Why not keep Clara here?"

"She adds complication to the stables," Fateh said. "I am not inclined to keep wild animals."

"But she seems so tame," Douwe said. He and Fateh stepped into the sun.

"She is a baby, but she will grow large. Captain, she will not fit through this doorway when she is fully grown. Her size and appetite will only grow. Her care is complicated. I would not repurchase her from you."

Douwe's mouth dried.

"I'm not selling her," Douwe said, bracing himself. "I am attached to her and plan to take her onward. I will show the whole of Europe how wrong they are about her kind."

"Have you considered releasing her?" said Fateh. He stopped under an arched doorway, backlit by the sun. "Her kind roam the wilds in the forest beyond Calcutta."

Zubin could have accompanied her to the jungle, and they would have lived with her, but not for long. Danger was abundant there. Douwe was conflicted—was Clara able to return to the wild? Had he purchased her to let her go?

"I am considering it now, sir." Douwe was crestfallen.

"I am glad to hear it, but now that she has connected with people and her mother is dead, she cannot go back. Rhinos are solitary creatures. She will be killed if she trusts the wrong people or animals now. Her growing horn also presents trouble, temptation."

"Then why mention releasing her at all?"

"To see if your intentions for the sacred genda are pure or poison."

The men stepped into the courtyard, but it was crowded with people. Zubin's white post was surrounded. Douwe glanced at Fateh and darted away, heart beating wildly. How could he have left them alone?

"Zubin!" he called. "Zubin!" But Zubin did not answer him.

Zubin was at the post with Clara. She ate bread from a woman's hand. Zubin rubbed two coins together, his smile bigger than anyone else's. A flash of silver shone from the ground. The crowd tossed coins in Zubin's cap in the dirt.

In exchange, Zubin passed a chunk of banana. Clara ate readily from their hands. A few members of the crowd produced their own food for her. Clara indulged them with happy ear flaps. Douwe did not want to break the spell. He was about to approach the crowd when Fateh stopped him with a subtle hand on his arm.

"She is precious. A rare gem," Fateh said.

"She is worth protecting and worth showing the world that even though she is not the most beautiful of creatures, there is beauty in her," Douwe said.

"And joy," Fateh said.

An elderly man leaning on his cane dropped to his knee. Zubin offered him a banana. The man shook his head and withdrew a dull orange from his pocket. He peeled it a little and let Clara smell it.

To the crowd's surprise, Clara squealed. She grasped the orange with her lip and ate it, eagerly looking to the man for more. She was so desperate for another orange that she nearly knocked him over. The old man chortled with laughter. Douwe nodded to Fateh, and they joined the crowd.

Zubin was happy to see them. He motioned to the crowd to signal their leaving, gathered Clara's lead, and swept his heavy cap from the dirt. Douwe untied Clara from the post.

"Douwe," Zubin whispered excitedly. "Look at what Clara earned!"

Clara was not as excited to go. She looked behind her for the elderly man with the oranges. He tossed one toward them, and Douwe caught it. Clara followed him at the promise of citrus and Fateh laughed.

"I think you've found her favorite food," Fateh said. "But easy on the oranges. She should have more greens than citrus."

"Zubin, what did she eat?"

"Oh, the orange, bread, some sweets, banana, oats, an old cigar, and a few swigs of beer."

"Perhaps not the cigar in the future, Zubin?" Fateh said. "The rest is fine as long as she has mostly hay, grass, vegetables. And milk until she refuses it."

He spoke to Zubin like a grandson, with some pain in his eyes. Douwe thought of Fateh, losing both Clara and Zubin at the same time when Sichterman bought them, and his heart sank.

"That reminds me," said Zubin, reaching into his pouch. He wagged the metal bottles at Douwe. Empty.

"Lucky for you, I have a barn full of mares and a generous heart," said Fateh. "I'll give you milk to last a few days. May I lead her?"

"Of course, badeh." Zubin bowed as he handed the leather leash to Fateh.

Fateh motioned for the orange from Douwe and held it aloft. Clara followed it with her eyes and huffed at him. She trotted, then full-on ran.

"Good," said Fateh. "She's alert, strong. She'll need to keep her skin moist. Look how the sun has burned her. You'll need fish oil unless she's bathing herself in the mud like her wild family would do."

"What can you tell me about her wild family?" said Douwe.

Fateh led them into the paddock, where Clara was let off her lead and roamed. She kept her nose to the ground, searching for food.

"Rhinos in the wild tend to be alone or just a mother and calf," Fateh said. "You can find them wallowing in pools and rivers on hot days. They sleep in the shade of banyan trees. I have seen bulls taller than a man. They're a special creature, but targeted. Their horns are sacred."

"Why hunt them if they are not for eating and no threat to the livestock?" Douwe had difficulty imagining her tough hide pierced with a bow and arrow.

"They can threaten crops as they trample and strip the plants of their leaves," said Fateh. "But it is more of a power thing—the beasts are so strong, therefore only the strongest can take one. They think the horn is magic; drinking from it cures any ailment."

Douwe shook his head. His father had taught him how to hunt. They hunted for food—fowl, deer; never for sport or a magic token. Clara drank deeply from a wooden trough in the paddock.

"Come," said Fateh. "I'll show you how to check her feet for sores and clean between her skin folds. I'll get you the milk. Has she had goat's milk?"

Zubin nodded. "Not as much goat as mare, but yes."

"Find a goat for your voyage. I can help you find hay, but you'll have to pay a pretty penny for it," Fateh said.

"No problem," said Zubin, jingling his cap at them with a grin.

Douwe obtained a plan of care for Clara. As long as she had three main things she would survive: food, milk, and water. The food had to be hay, vegetables, and vegetation. In a few months, Clara would refuse the bottle. The *Knappenhof* was due to leave in twelve days, and Douwe now had to procure all of Clara's needs for the long journey.

Chapter 9

Andrea
Leiden, The Netherlands

The copper-roofed, red-brick Academic Historical Museum had a Rembrandt statue and windmill sculptures out front. Inside, the first thing on display was a seventeenth-century taxidermy swordfish. Despite her anxieties about taxidermy lately, Andrea swallowed big, read the placard, and attempted to change her mindset. This animal was historic and used for education, not a trophy. It was not illegally poached or endangered, and it was old.

Andrea relaxed a little. Museums did something to her—gave her that effervescent feeling of stepping back in time. She could place artifacts in her memory alongside dates and places, recalling them instantly, bringing history to life. Everyday items and unique artifacts from centuries ago opened the door to the past. She wanted to jump in and leave her problems behind.

The place had a medieval feeling, with large displays of documents and artifacts from the early years of Leiden and the University. It felt warm, like most museums. Charcoal-colored walls, gilded frames, glass cloches. Things used to make the past come alive to people without the context of what happened before their existence.

Exhibits were spotlighted in bright LED bulbs, and she was pulled to a golden goblet in a case. "Wow," Andrea whispered, forgetting that Paul and Lucas were behind her. They chuckled at her near sprint.

"This place is amazing," she said.

"I've visited here for years," said Paul. "The exhibits change somewhat regularly, but Lucas and I know most of the museum."

"Let's head to the offices and see what they say about your document," said Lucas. He led the way through the winding exhibits. Andrea longed to stay and look, but they walked too quickly. She kept up, coming to a wall of university presidents painted in epic sixteenth, seventeenth, and eighteenth-century glory.

"Amazing," she said. "Who do you know here? Curator? Director?"

"Yes," said Paul, opening a warm wood door to the offices. The sign said STAFF ONLY.

The back looked like typical offices, except in a two-hundred-year-old building. The windows were curved and lead-paned, but the ceiling was dropped, and fluorescent lights hummed.

A few cubicles were set up with computers on each desk. Most had black screens, but Andrea recognized a museum artifact software pulled up on a few. It was one she was familiar with, PastPerfect. Manila folders were stacked on desks, and she strained to read artifact documentation papers. Cataloging artifacts was a true delight; learning their provenance and how to preserve them felt like real history work.

Paul knocked on one of the closed doors, and a rustling sounded.

"Komen!" said a woman with a thick Dutch accent.

Paul opened the door and ushered Lucas and Andrea inside. The office was a perfect combination of past and present. Sunlight streamed in through the thick glass. A massive potted monstera strained at the window in a terracotta pot, and a poster of the unicorn tapestry from The Met was framed behind the desk.

The original stone walls remained, but an electric kettle, BlueTooth speaker, and glowing MacBook threw everything into the twenty-first century. The fluorescents were off, and a Tiffany-style floor lamp softly illuminated the space. There was a Squishmallow, a Kate Spade purse, and a glass case full of artifacts within two feet of each other. Perfect.

The desk looked like the one in Andrea's dorm room. Dark wood, rosy insets, ornate carving. Its legs were not bolted to the floor, however. The woman behind it was a graying redhead with thick green reading glasses perched on her nose. She had bright blue eyes and soft, fuzzy hair.

"Ah, Paul!" she said, rising from a red armchair. She came around to kiss him on both cheeks, and Paul blushed. Lucas waved, removing a hand from his pea coat's pocket. "And who have we here?"

She turned to Andrea, folding her glasses and smiling. There was extreme intelligence in her eyes, but she was also adorable. She was precisely who Andrea imagined herself to be in thirty years.

"I'm Andrea Clarkson, in for the semester from South Carolina."

"Ah! Paul told me he'd have an international student this semester. How nice to meet you. I'm Janice, the director of the Academic Historical Museum," she said. "Well, director, curator, toilet cleaner, ticket taker, gift shop clerk. I do it all, unfortunately."

"I'm so excited to meet you," Andrea said. "This place is a dream!"

Janice smiled politely. Andrea shrank a bit—European people didn't get as outwardly exuberant. She tried to tone down but was genuinely pumped to be in the museum's offices. She hadn't felt this good in months.

"My graveyard project was attractive to you?"

"Yes." Andrea pulled out her phone. "Can I show you what we found today?"

"By all means," she said. "Within the next week, Sergei and I will remove the caskets and remains. I meant to be out there today, but you've interrupted this game I play with my printer. I send it a document, and it prints two hours later. Technology for you. I'd love to see what you've been working with."

She showed Janice the photo of the gravestone.

"May I?" she asked and took the phone. She zoomed in like Lucas had done, narrowing her eyebrows. She put her reading glasses on and nodded slowly.

"It's some kind of animal emblem? Maybe a coat of arms or crest?"

"Do you recognize it?" said Paul. "I did not."

"Maybe, but it's faint..." Janice said. "Perhaps when it dries from your cleaning and the rubbing is made, we may be able to digitally enhance it and clarify."

"I think it's eighteenth century," Andrea said, pointing to the dates.

"Yes, you're right. But I can't make out the other numbers. Have you tried to sort out the name at all? Did you show this to Sergei?"

"No, not yet. I can see a D," Andrea said. "But not much more."

"Well," said Janice, "this is precisely why we are doing this. The records for the cemetery were lost during the Nazi occupation of Leiden in the 1940s. It's a wonder anything survived, but the graves were less important to re-catalog than the other artifacts here."

"It's finally their turn," said Lucas. "Honoring the dead is important. Reminds us how far we have come and allows us to study the common man."

"Nicely put, Lucas," said Paul. "We have a responsibility to preserve history, and cemeteries are often the only place to acknowledge those who left no written record. We have a special job this semester."

Lucas swelled with pride. Andrea could tell this work meant a lot to him. It felt painful to think about the people in history who never documented their stories. What amazing things were never known because someone didn't keep a journal? What songs did they sing? What trials and tribulations did they face? Who were their friends and enemies and lovers? How could anything be known beyond dates on a tombstone...?

Preserving that past motivated Andrea to come to Leiden for this project. But it was hard for her to shake the feeling of that platinum ring on her finger. Now, the memory of it felt like a handcuff. Andrea wanted to stop thinking about him and the night the ring box flashed, his trophy animals staring. The easiest way to do that was to throw herself into this project head first.

It felt good to disappear into the past, especially with real things to preserve. Textbooks, photographs, and documents online were one thing, but genuine artifacts were another. Andrea could attach them to her catalog-like mind, recalling dates and personal objects along with the portrait of a historical person. The past felt so real it could be touched.

"Janice," she said. "Scroll to the previous photos?"

She swiped. A hand popped to her mouth.

"Andrea! Where did you find this?"

Chapter 10
Douwemout van der Meer
Calcutta, India

Douwe had to load the *Knappenhof* with trade goods for Amsterdam and South Africa. He was stocked with chintz, silk, anise, and cinnamon. The last months he had spent filling the storerooms at Fort William with his trade goods to satisfy the VOC officials, but he now had to adjust the weight of his load to accommodate a growing rhino and her food.

Douwe took Zubin and Clara back to Hirzet's with strict instructions that Clara should get milk every three hours unless she was sleeping and could eat hay, fruit, or vegetables. Clara was exhausted from the long walk to and from the stables, something she made clear with a dramatic heaving of herself on a bed of straw near the chicken coop. She curled up and dozed in a matter of minutes. Zubin made himself comfortable, and Douwe hurried off into the lingering evening.

He visited the VOC offices, gathering his papers and adding Clara's weight to his manifest. The crisp blue moon was waning, a sliver thinner than when he held Clara under the banyan tree in the garden two nights ago. On the walk back, he reflected. Divine intervention had come into play. He saved money for years—for what? He never married or owned property—why? For what purpose did he have access to a crew and ship to traverse the world?

Clara was his to save.

Douwe opened the gate to the yard near midnight and found Zubin there, sleeping with Clara. Douwe slid his hands under Zubin's small sleeping form. The boy grasped his neck, and Douwe carried him up the narrow staircase to their small, shared room. Douwe slid Zubin gently onto the blanketed mat and pried his coin-filled cap from his hands. He silently prayed for the boy and turned his face away from the moonlight.

Douwe shook off his salt-stained boots, laid his hat and papers on the mantel, and sat on the low cot. He wanted to watch the boy sleep but could not keep his eyes open. Cicadas lulled him fast to sleep.

The street below grew loud at dawn, and Douwe woke. The beamed ceiling was clean of cobwebs but not of geckos. Two lizards were statue-still in a beam of morning sunlight. He was pleased to be in this narrow cot and more pleased that Clara was safe outside. Zubin was on the straw mat next to him, soundly asleep.

The sounds of a waking kitchen, a busy street, and chickens in the yard pushed Douwe to the window that overlooked Clara's yard. She was awake, charging the chickens who flitted and clucked at her, then resumed their dirt-pecking. One white hen clumsily landed on Clara's broad back and picked at the folds of her skin. Clara ran a circle until the hen flapped off, clucking in disapproval. Zubin stirred.

"Morning, Zubin. Hope you slept well."

Zubin blinked and looked around. The lizard on the wall scurried to the windowsill.

"I've never slept in a room like this," he said. "I am so used to the stable and the yard." His knees were splayed out, and he rubbed his eyes.

The boy was a servant and had little to his name. Zubin's joyful reaction to the small and plain room was painful. Sichterman had no qualms about parting with him for money. The boy was nothing but property to him. To Douwe, he was so much more.

"Zubin, I hope you know I am excited for you to come to Leiden."

"Yes, sir," Zubin said. "I have no plans to leave Clara's side."

"That is what I hoped for, but it is your choice." He ruffled his hair. "Let's eat breakfast, and then we have several things to do. First mission of the day is to go get Betsy."

"Who is Betsy?" Zubin raised his eyebrows at Douwe. "A lady?"

"My lady cat," Douwe blushed. "She'll be joining us on the ship."

"I was silly to think you had a real lady."

"And why is that?" Douwe puffed his chest up. "You think I couldn't woo a lady?"

"Maybe a stinky one, like Clara," Zubin said. "Or a married one who is bored!"

Douwe threw his hat at Zubin. The two laughed, and Douwe helped Zubin to his feet.

"How much more coin to feed her?" Zubin asked. His cap was half full.

"I think we are set, Zubin," Douwe said. "The VOC always cares for livestock on its ships. We need things for you now."

Zubin stared, wide-eyed. "What do we need?"

"A few things for safety, some clothes," Douwe said. Zubin looked away, unreadable.

Hirzet wiped sweat from her brow as Douwe and Zubin strode into the hot little kitchen. Clara peered over the Dutch door. Zubin grabbed a handful of kitchen scraps.

"Ah, Zubin!" Douwe called. "Vegetables, please, not bread or cigars or anything else. Per Fateh's orders."

Zubin swept carrot tops and potato eyes into his hands. He shook the vegetables at Douwe, said, "Aloo," and held the potato aloft. "And this is gajar," he said, brandishing the carrots. He slid them over the half-door to Clara.

"Aloo, gajar," Douwe repeated. "I think Clara likes them both."

Hirzet screwed the lid onto Clara's pewter bottle and handed it to Zubin. He stepped into the yard, and Clara happily suckled. Douwe motioned to Hirzet.

"Hirzet, I am grateful for you." Douwe slid three silver coins into her hand. "We shall pay you in full for your kindness soon."

Hirzet looked puzzled. "So, the deal is on?" she asked, pocketing the coins without hesitation.

"I want to open the gate and show Clara to the passersby. They'll pay a pfenning to see her and a pfenning more to feed her. Half is yours." Douwe said.

"Done!" She rolled her "n," her Scottish accent audible. Hirzet grabbed a knife and continued chopping. "I'll let my customers know she's out back so they won't miss you, you ken?"

"You're a gracious hostess." Douwe bowed. "I shall set up Zubin and Clara and return to my apartment. Do you like cats, Hirzet?"

The knife smacked the chopping block, and Hirzet sighed.

Chapter 11
Andrea
Leiden, The Netherlands

Andrea's dorm room felt smaller with Janice, Paul, and Lucas inside. When they arrived at the door, Andrea's armpits prickled. Her suitcase and all of its contents were still strewn about the room. She definitely wasn't ready for visitors.

She managed to shove all the spilled contents of her suitcase back in with two sweeping armfuls, plopping it all on the tiny bed. Andrea laughed awkwardly and tucked strands of her dark hair behind her ears.

"It's been less than forty-eight hours since I landed, so I haven't had time to arrange everything yet."

"You're fine, Andrea," said Paul. "I've actually never been in one of these apartments, and I must say, I'm delighted."

"You are?" She was sincerely surprised.

"Yes," he said. "It's about twice the size of the men's dorm! Lucas, have you ever been in one of these before?"

"Once or twice," he said, leaning on the door frame with a smirk. Andrea stared at the upturned corner of his mouth, and heat rose to her face.

"Andrea, show us the discovery," said Janice, staring at the desk.

Andrea pulled her coat off before sliding to the ground. She reached under the massive carved claw foot, felt the metal button, and gently pushed it. A soft click sounded from above.

"Ooooh," said Janice and Paul simultaneously. They laughed lightly at each other. Andrea crawled up, and Lucas gave her a look that said how cute. She couldn't help but smile at him.

Andrea wiggled the hidden drawer forward and gently slid out the document. The three of them gathered in closer, and she uncurled it. Part of the linen crackled, and a corner piece crumbled on the desk. The warm-stone smell of old paper filled the air.

"Wait!" said Janice. She grabbed the leather tote she'd brought with her and sorted through it, pulling out what looked like a plexiglass cutting board. She slid the plastic over the page. The document was magnified and lay perfectly flat. It was like looking at a screen.

"Eighteenth century," said Janice. "German. Linen. Printer's ink. A rhinoceros."

"Yes," said Paul. "Andrea had all of those right. But I'm more curious about the backside."

"The backside?" said Janice. "May I?" She looked at Andrea, asking if she could flip over the document.

"By all means," Andrea said. "You're definitely better at this than I am."

"I am," she said. "But thirty years slaving away for the museum only means I've broken more artifacts than you."

Paul chuckled, but Lucas looked like a sin had been committed. Janice asked Paul to lift the plastic while she flipped it over. The other side was easier to lay flat because the document had been rolled up so long.

"This is so curious," said Janice. Her glasses slid down her nose. "A grocery list and a list of cities in French?"

"Prussia is listed, which means this handwriting has to be no later than 1870," Andrea said. She felt her history brain kick on, and her mind scrolled with facts about Prussia.

"Would someone write on a hundred-year-old document, though?" asked Lucas. Andrea's brain turned back off.

"No," Janice said. "It would have been hard to write on it anyway; linen gets crispy, and you wouldn't carry something like this around if it were already old. It would crumble to bits."

"Then we can assume the original owner of this document wrote on the back," said Paul.

"But who could that have been?" Andrea asked. "Who lived in these apartments, and better yet, why is this desk still here?"

"These apartments are 300 years old," said Paul. "Leiden University has been around since the 1500s, and with buildings this old, it's impossible to know who lived here in the past. Perhaps students, professors, clergy? Maybe for staff or travelers?"

"Instead of demolition, they renovated it to be women's dorms," said Janice. "In World War II, the city was under Nazi siege. They likely bolted it down permanently so it wouldn't fall into the wrong hands."

"I'm surprised it wasn't chopped for firewood," said Lucas. "Why leave it for the next eighty years?"

"I don't think it will fit through the door," Andrea said. Lucas stepped away from the door frame, sizing it up. He nodded.

"That's inconvenient," he said. "Every other room here has enough space for two beds."

"How do you know that?" Paul asked, grinning.

Lucas shrugged. "I know my way around campus." Andrea swallowed. Lucas was attractive, but if he knew the women's dorms like that, she wasn't sure about him. She guarded herself, crossing her arms.

"Have you looked at the desk more closely?" said Janice. "Usually, desks with one hidden drawer have more."

"No," Andrea said. "I didn't even think to check the rest."

"It's like a treasure hunt," said Paul, giddy. "This is the kind of stuff we professors dream of."

"It's the kind of stuff *all* us history nerds dream of," said Janice. "Start on the opposite leg. It's rare for things to be asymmetrical."

Lucas tried to fit his hand under the desk to check for another lever, but the opening was too small.

"Must be all that sandbag lifting from the summer, eh?" Andrea said. He smiled sheepishly and helped her to the ground. Her heart rate increased when his hand touched hers, warm and rough. She felt nervous, remembering the last time Jake pulled her hand, trying to get her to stay.

Andrea slid her hand under and felt around, ignoring the dust and cobwebs.

"There's another lever!" she said, face pressed to the tile. She pushed it. Nothing happened. "I think it's jammed. I need something to push into it."

Paul took an ink pen from his pocket protector, which Lucas ribbed him about, and handed it to her. She slid the cap onto the pen and pushed it hard into the lever. A rusty click sounded from above. The opposite side of the desk was ajar. Andrea stood up to pull the drawer from its slot. It was a second hidden compartment.

Chapter 12
Douwemout van der Meer
Calcutta, India

Sunlight fell in a curved arch on the floor of Douwe's apartment. Betsy lay in the warm patch, flicking her tail toward Douwe. Her ears pressed to her skull when he closed the door. She gleamed bronze in the sunlight, specks of golden dust illuminating her like a goddess. She tapped her tail, asking him where he had been.

"Aren't you in a dour mood," he said, scooping her up. She resisted momentarily but, with a few scratches under her chin, settled and purred.

Over a winter in Calcutta, Douwe put bits of his dinner into a basket until Betsy was used to being in it and even preferred it. She settled into the covered basket, the size of a large palm leaf, bribed with a piece of fish Douwe pilfered from Hirzet's kitchen.

He slid both the skeleton key and coins under the landlord's door. Part of him would miss the blue cream moon outside his window, the scraping palm, the geckos that decorated the ceiling. He did not plan to return.

Douwe's one last look was interrupted by a protesting mewl from Betsy in the basket. He tipped his tricorne hat to his former home and took to the dusty street, the late morning symphony of cicadas and green pigeons filling the air.

A substantial crowd was gathered around the tavern. Douwe entered through the front door and took Betsy upstairs. He opened the basket, but Betsy refused to budge, making a loaf of herself, black paws tucked under. She feigned sleep, and Douwe rolled his eyes at her. He left quickly to help in the yard.

Zubin was visible through the half-open Dutch door. Douwe grabbed carrot tops and leaped the lower half of the door. A throng of people with joyful faces greeted him.

"Douwe, she is loving this!" Zubin said. Clara trotted back and forth between peoples' hands, sucking fruit from their fingers and wagging her ears at them.

Her tail swung energetically. Zubin followed her, replacing a coin with carrots in an onlooker's hand and two coins with a banana. Clara eagerly followed the bananas, black eyes bright, squealing, and huffing.

"A crowd pleaser you have here, Douwe." Hirzet laughed from the Dutch door, wiping her hands on a rag. "I hav'na been this busy in years. Plum out of food and not just the bit that Clara's been eatin'."

"I'm not sure if I should say sorry or you're welcome!" Douwe laughed, watching Clara.

"Dinna fash," Hirzet said. "Tis been a true joy. The people love her."

Only some people produced a silver VOC coin. Hens pecked at copper pennies tossed in the yard. European ladies removed their gloves to feed her. A nobleman carried on a palanquin gave Zubin ten silver coins to feed Clara a bunch of bananas. A beggar sat, legs crossed, cane by his side. His black eyes sparkled as he watched Clara, his skin the same color as the dirt. He stayed for hours.

No one was excluded from Clara's joy. But the sun began to set, and the crowd thinned. Douwe allowed Clara a few more bananas and a bundle of hay and then closed the gate to the yard. Clara drank a bottle provided by Zubin. He rested on his knees while he fed her, exhausted by the day in the sun. Douwe's plan to go to market that afternoon was dashed, but he felt no real remorse.

"Zubin, that was remarkable," Douwe said, dusting his white breeches off.

"Can we take a break tomorrow?" Zubin said. Clara fought sleep as she drank. "She's tired."

"How much did we make today? Perhaps just a half day tomorrow if we have to?"

By the time they were through counting, night had fallen, and the fish stew Hirzet brought up was cold. They had more than enough to pay for a goat, bridle, and extra trade goods for Douwe to sell. He had enough to buy Zubin and himself new clothing. Betsy lapped at their dinner. Zubin picked her up and set her on the cot. She curled up and watched the coins clink.

"So, we give Clara a rest tomorrow?"

Douwe hesitated. He felt the coin on the table calling to him—he could make so much more. Perhaps enough to find lodging without trade when they arrived in Leiden.

"Listen, Douwe," Zubin said. "She's a baby still. She was tired today and ate a lot more than she ever has. I'm telling you, as her keeper, she needs a break tomorrow."

"Her keeper?" Douwe raised an eyebrow.

"You are her owner; I am her keeper. Makes sense, seeing as she would not be alive without me."

"Nor me for saving her from Sichterman."

"Sure, yes, you are right," Zubin sighed. "But she still needs a break."

"Then, by all means, Zubin," Douwe said after a beat. "I shall not challenge you when it comes to her care. You know her better than anyone. Tomorrow, she gets a break."

The morning dawned with crackling energy—dew dripped off the palm leaves, and the brown river roared with men entering port. Douwe counted three geckos on the ceiling before lifting himself from his warm cot. Zubin was asleep, and Douwe left him as such.

Downstairs in the empty tavern, a letter addressed to him and sealed with a red wax VOC stamp waited on a table. Sichterman's poor penmanship told Douwe that Johanna was recovering well and wished to bestow a parting gift. She would meet him at the dock on the morning of departure. Johanna's face played in Douwe's mind: the way the firelight caught her auburn hair, the smell of her powder at dinner.

Douwe folded the letter and went to Clara's yard. She was asleep, curled up, and stirred at his approach. Hirzet popped open the Dutch door, mixing something in a deep wooden bowl. Clara stood slowly.

"Mornin', Douwe," Hirzet said, smiling.

"Hirzet, I hate to ask, but do you think you could manage here for the day without us? I need to take Zubin to buy the boy some clothes."

"Aye. So long as no one comes into the yard, I'll manage fine."

Douwe heard several voices outside the gate, calling Clara. Hirzet gave him a worrisome look and pulled him close. The intoxicating scent of Hirzet's sweat mixed with herbs, onions, and sweet mint curled toward him. He forced himself to focus.

"I'm not keen to turn away customers, Douwe," Hirzet whispered. "And you shouldn't be either. I say we lock the gate and throw a basket down. People want to see her. They'll toss a few coins in and do so from the wall."

"They'll leap over!" said Douwe. "She could be hurt or fed something vile."

"Nah," said Hirzet. "I'll watch the gate and keep her in the paddock. Go do your business and get Zubin ready for travel. The lad's never seen past this part of the world, ya ken? You'll need to help him adjust to life at sea."

Douwe was worried about Zubin on the ship. Would the boy be seasick? Would he catch some kind of disease? Zubin coming to any harm made his pulse quicken.

He trusted Hirzet. He did not trust the slowly growing crowd. Douwe entered the yard, and Clara perked her ears at him playfully. He knelt beside her and cupped her face in his hands. The two locked eyes for a moment, and Douwe melted.

"You're in love, Douwe," Zubin called from the Dutch door. "Leave the girl be!" He shook Clara's bottle. She ran to her milk.

"G'morning, Clara," Zubin said to her. She nursed, Douwe and Hirzet looking on.

"I'll keep an eye on her," Hirzet said. The brass bell above the tavern door jangled.

"We won't be long, Hirzet," Douwe said. "Home by midday, I hope."

Zubin wiped milk off Clara's chin and slid the bottle back to Hirzet. He pulled his too-small vest over his skinny arms and followed Douwe through the tavern. Men from the docks were arriving now, clearly from all over the world. Different languages filled the air, and people of all colors and customs sat on the shallow stools. Hirzet was busy, rhinoceros in her yard or not.

On their way to the street lined with shops and stalls where Douwe could find things for Zubin to feel at home on the long sea voyage, he tried to warm the boy up to the idea of travel.

"Zubin, when we arrive in Amsterdam, we'll be landing in a port town called Rotterdam," he said. "We'll spend most of the winter on board the *Knappenhof* and land in Europe in the late summer. But we'll be traveling so far south that the seasons will change. We'll travel to summer, but it will be winter in your mind."

Zubin's eyes grew wide. "I don't understand. How can travel make the seasons change?"

"Well, I suppose it's difficult to understand how large the world can be..." Douwe hesitated. "Years ago, a Frenchman reported that the world is divided by a large invisible swelling—a line as such. Above it, where we are, it is fall, almost winter. Below the swelling, below the line, it is spring and almost summer. We will cross the line and enter another season."

Zubin stared at him blankly.

"You'll understand in a few months. In the meantime, you will need clothing for the voyage," Douwe said. "Both to grow into and to protect you from the elements."

Zubin shook his head lightly and laughed like he could not imagine any place but Bengal.

In the market town, Sutanuti, were stalls with trinkets and thread, silk and cotton, coarse cloth, chintz, indigo dye, peddlers and cobblers, farmers with wool and produce, and livestock of all kinds. There were Arabian horses, goats, sheep, camels, monkeys, parrots in cages, and green pigeons like the one that tormented Betsy. Not all of the animals were alive. The smell of blood and livestock mixed with the fragrant spices of India.

The skin of a red panda, a huge dead black crane, and elephant tusks were on display. Turtle shells and their tortoiseshell products were lined up, showing ladies where their combs came from. In one cloche, gleaming in the mid-morning sun, was a black and gray horn that could be from nothing else but an Indian rhino.

Zubin pulled Douwe toward the booth, gesturing at the cloche. He spoke with the shopkeeper in Bengali. Douwe picked up a few words but could not understand. Zubin's face became strained, his arm gestures more prominent as they spoke. Twenty seconds later, Zubin left the booth with a huff and a quick turn on his heel. Douwe followed quickly.

"What was that!?"

"That," said Zubin, marching away on his stick-skinny legs as fast as he could, "was the horn of Clara's mother."

Douwe stopped dead in the busy market. People streamed about him. He became a rock in a river. Bile rose to his throat, and sweat beads threatened to drop from his forehead.

"Douwe!" Zubin called, seeing that Douwe was no longer alongside him. "Douwe!"

Douwe was frozen. Clara's mother. If her horn was in that booth, the shop owner knew where she came from and who killed her. If her horn was in that booth, Douwe had to ask what had happened to the rest of her.

He turned before Zubin made it to his side. Douwe pushed through the crowd, stopping at the booth full of dead animals, and pointed to the rhino horn in the cloche. It sat on a far shelf. The merchant rubbed his fingers together, asking for proof Douwe could pay for the horn.

Douwe untied his bag of coins and dangled it in front of the man's face. The merchant turned his back to Douwe. Zubin pulled on his shirtsleeve, panting.

"What are you thinking, Douwe? It will take everything you have!"

"I need to know where he got it."

"He thinks you wish to buy it," said Zubin. "It is from a poacher."

"A butcher."

"Breathe, sir," Zubin whispered. The merchant approached with the cloche.

The black and gray horn, the length of Douwe's forearm, glowed dimly in the sun. He lifted the glass with a flourish and a salesman's smile. The horn was ridged, hairlike, but smooth. Douwe did not touch it. Heat rose to his face, his vision clouded. Clara's mother was attached to this horn. Killed for it. Clara was his because of it.

"He will force us to go if we aren't buying. He says there's a fortune to be made from it."

Douwe picked up the lid and closed it over the horn. He only wanted to escape and be with Clara, to protect her. Though Clara had not yet grown a horn, it was evident to Douwe that to many, she was worth more in parts than whole. She was in danger without Douwe.

Douwe turned to the crowd and the faces changed. Instead of the beautiful rainbow of humans moments before, each face leered at him, showing sharpened fangs. He heard whispers in his head: What calls your name in the dark, Dutchman? Hunters? Thieves? Butchers? People's eyes glowed red, bloodshot with the heat, sweat turned to blood dripping down their temples. The only sound was his heartbeat. The crowd noise, shouting of humans and braying of animals, clanking of crystal and brass, the chuff-chuff of the looms, the cries of babies... none could be heard for the ringing in his ears and the blood in his veins.

The market stalls closed in. The dirt road narrowed. The pulsing of the cicadas meshed with his heartbeat. The striped fabric of the market tents waved in the heat.

He did not come back to the scene. Zubin grabbed Douwe by the hand. Their skin melted together, sticky. Zubin led Douwe to the market's outskirts, handed him a tankard of ale and a heel of bread, and slapped him gently on either cheek.

The ringing in his Douwe's ears subsided. He drank. Zubin sat close, folded over in silence.

The hand of the devil lingered on the horn of Clara's mother. He foresaw Clara being butchered in the dusty streets of Calcutta; her parts strewn across the paths of parading noblemen on their palanquins. The vision was blinding, enraging. Douwe had to leave India, with Clara alive and protected, as soon as possible.

"Sir...?"

"I cannot let anything happen to Clara," Douwe said. "Help me get away from here."

"Let's go to the other market."

The other market was the Dutch Bankshall. Goods there were far more expensive. But nothing mattered more than getting away from the ghost of Clara's mother floating above the booths. Did Clara see, when it happened? Did her mother fight?

They walked to the other market silently. Douwe knew Zubin was worried. What child wouldn't be? Perhaps the boy thought this was a common occurrence. It wasn't. Douwe had never experienced anything like it.

Douwe and Zubin reached the market. It was prim and proper compared to the winding, crowded street they left behind. Douwe spotted a booth with clothing, and Zubin followed sheepishly. Douwe, still trembling, spoke with the vendor, and Zubin got measured. He bought tunics and breeches and a golden velvet vest with floral backing.

Zubin smiled. Douwe breathed a little easier.

At the next booth, Zubin's bare feet were measured, and he was fitted with soft brown shoes and a pair of sturdy boots. Zubin wiggled his toes as wide as he could, sending the leather rippling. Has he ever had shoes? Douwe thought.

Douwe smiled. Zubin breathed a little easier.

Zubin was sized for a tricorne hat that matched Douwe's. His gap-tooth smile widened. The milliner fashioned a new lead for Clara—a braided leather leash and matching soft suede collar. Douwe let Zubin pick it out.

The drama of the last market faded. Douwe was curious to know if Zubin would bring up what had happened. Zubin brought a sense of calm to him. He had a way of caring for those around him beyond the animal in his charge. Douwe felt as if he had never been without Zubin. He wondered if he'd have the courage to tell him as such.

He knelt beside the boy, checking the soles of his new shoes, and looked Zubin in the eye. Douwe opened his mouth to thank him but could not find words. Instead, he nodded curtly.

The boy beamed when Douwe bundled their parcels and placed Zubin's new hat on his head.

"I'm sorry, Zubin."

"For caring about the one thing I love more than anything, so much that you see her mother's ghost in the clouds?" said Zubin. "That is not a reason to be sorry."

"It's not something you should have to deal with."

"I would rather be with someone who would go to the ends of the earth to protect her than with someone who sees more value in her parts," Zubin said. Douwe nodded, unable to speak for the lump in his throat.

They made a handsome pair in their matching tricornes. Douwe and Zubin made the short, winding walk to Hirzet's, where Fateh waited for them near the intersection, fifty paces from Hirzet's tavern, a white goat by his side. He handed Douwe a letter of instructions for Clara's care.

"This is all I know about the genda. Add it to Zubin's experience, and you'll do fine for now. But as she grows, her care will change," Fateh said. The goat bleated. "This creature I am happy to part with. Consider it a farewell gift."

The goat chewed widely. Its long ears nearly touched its shoulders, and it had nubs for horns. It bleated, showing a pink tongue, its cry surprisingly human. The goat's udders were full of milk, and Douwe felt a wave of relief. Clara now had an unlimited supply for her bottles.

"Fateh," Douwe said. "There was a rhino horn in the market today."

Fateh's mouth dropped, echoing his long beard. His brows knit together.

"It was Clara's mother, wasn't it?" Douwe said. "I...I felt such anger."

"Her mother was killed, but you were given a blessing. Do not let the past haunt you. You were not there. You are here now to show this creature to the world."

Douwe nodded, setting his mouth in a thin line. The vision of the gray-black horn in the glass dome remained. He shook his head to clear the sight away. The goat bleated.

"Does it have a name?" said Douwe.

Fateh paused. "Bakari," he said.

Zubin laughed, doubled over, hands on his knees.

Douwe looked between the two and shrugged. "What does it mean?" he said. "Bakari?"

"Bakari," said Zubin, "means goat."

"Of course it does," said Douwe, shaking his head. "Goodbye, Fateh."

Bakari the goat continued screaming. Her udders were hugely swollen. Zubin turned the corner to the Apollo Tavern with her at a trot, eager to milk her and relieve her discomfort, but stopped suddenly in the dusty street, palm trees swaying above. A massive crowd surrounded Hirzet's.

The crowd did not want to part for them. Douwe pushed through to the tavern's front door. Inside, the place was packed with people. Beer and food lay on the tables where salt-stained boots were propped. Indian men in white tunics smoked hookah, European sailors smoked their pipes. Hirzet was nowhere to be seen.

Douwe sprinted up the staircase and deposited their parcels at the top. He hurried back down to the kitchen. The place was a mess.

Hirzet was outside, hands on her curvy hips, apron bulging with coin, holding a wooden bucket of kitchen scraps. Clara sat like a dog, observing the bucket. A coin was tossed into the dirt, pecked by a hen, swept up by Hirzet, and she placed a carrot or potato in a waiting hand. Clara devoured each piece from the strangers, who, after feeding her, melted back into the crowd to allow others to come forward.

Upon seeing the goat, Clara flicked her ears. The goat screamed. Clara replied. The crowd laughed. Hirzet shrugged apologetically at Douwe, who shook his head. She untied her apron and handed it to Douwe, leaving to manage her kitchen. The apron was heavy with copper and silver, plus a few trinkets, bags of herbs, spices, and a wooden figurine of a rough-cut rhino.

Zubin motioned to Bakari, who was still screaming. She needed to be milked, but someone had to manage Clara's crowd. Douwe straightened his tricorne and, heart pounding, fastened the apron around his waist.

By dusk, Clara was fed, the goat milked, Zubin bathed, and Douwe exhausted. They'd gathered much more money than the day before. Word had gotten around that the magical rhino from the forests of Bengal was giving blessings to passersby. Blessings meant whistles, ear flickers, and a few natural duties. But the people loved it, cherishing every move Clara made.

The goat quieted. She and Clara touched noses and seemed to enjoy each other's company. The paddock and yard were shut, and the chickens were put in their coop for the night. Soon, Bakari and Clara were fast asleep, curled into similar poses in the green hay.

At the end of the two-week stay at Hirzet's, Douwe counted the coin Clara had made, parting the pile. He gave Hirzet her silver. The following day, they were off to Fort William in preparation for boarding the *Knappenhof*.

"I am sad you're leaving," Hirzet said. "'Twas nice to have the company and the coin." Her blonde hair, covered with a bandana from the Indian market, was glowing honey-brown with sweat.

"Surely you'll come to Europe soon?" Douwe said. "How long will you stay in Calcutta?"

"Been here two years already. Seems like a lifetime. The journey home is a long one. Maybe a few years more, then back to Scotland."

"Stop in Amsterdam," Douwe said. Hirzet raised an eyebrow at him. "If only to see Clara's horn grown in." Hirzet was beautiful, but he could not imagine pursuing her bed in the dark of night.

"Aye," Hirzet said wistfully. "That will be a sight to see. There's always space for you here, too, Captain."

She looked away toward her work, her eyes hazed over. Douwe wondered what circumstances led a Scottish woman across the world to the East Indies. He didn't ask.

Zubin and Douwe settled for bed. Douwe dreamed of Clara's mother's horn floating on a toy boat around a curving river. Douwe swam after it. The current swept the boat away from his grasp, and soon, it was taken out to sea. The gray and white waves took the horn further away each time he got close. Soon, exhausted by his swim, Douwe sank into cold, black water.

In the morning, after breakfast, Douwe packed. Their older clothing he left behind, stowing it in the empty wardrobe in their room. Zubin wore his new clothes. Douwe went through the boy's things: a white tunic, faded with dirt and sweat, a small white cap, his too-small embroidered vest, one pair of pants. No shoes. In the pile was the wooden cup and ball game.

Douwe reminded himself that Zubin was still a boy. He picked up the game and put it in the inner pocket of his new emerald overcoat. He scooped up a purring Betsy from a pool of sunlight and placed her in her basket. Douwe was ready to leave Calcutta.

Zubin hugged Hirzet tightly. She smiled as she knelt beside him, telling him to behave himself. She looked at Douwe through downcast lashes. He grabbed her hand.

"Thank you, bonnie lass," he said. She blushed.

"Go on then, Captain," said Hirzet.

A carriage waited outside Hirzet's. Douwe loaded his trunk, Betsy's basket, and secured a leather satchel with his papers in the cab. Zubin loaded Clara's accoutrement and was set to walk behind with the two animals when Douwe hesitated. Clara attracted a lot of attention.

Douwe pulled the driver aside.

"Sir, you cannot be serious?"

"I am," said Douwe, sliding two coins into his hand.

Clara was hauled into the cab. She peered out the window, sniffing the air as they traveled the streets to load the *Knappenhof*. Passersby stared and pointed. On the back of the carriage, Zubin laughed, holding Bakari. Bakari screamed. Clara answered. Douwe smiled.

Chapter 13
Andrea
Leiden, The Netherlands

The narrow desk drawer was stickier than the first, and Andrea wiggled it back and forth like a loose tooth.

"What if it's empty?" said Lucas.

"Then it's empty," said Paul. "May I try, Andrea?"

He jostled the drawer. Dovetails emerged, then with a squeaking and a scratch across the desk's surface, it slid into his hand.

"Let me see," said Janice.

The drawer held at least five more documents. No one spoke as Janice pulled them out with white cotton museum gloves that ended at the wrist. The papers were all different but shared similarities. Honey-yellow linen, printer's ink in foreign script, and the big clue.

"They're all the same animal," Andrea said. "They all have the rhino." Goosebumps rose on her arms. Andrea would have to abandon this entire project if she wanted to escape exotic animals now. This rhino fell into her lap, forcing her to face the problematic memories she harbored from Jake's house. She felt dismayed and excited but hopeful. It was real history.

"An Indian rhinoceros. Her name was Clara," said Janice. Her eyes flickered with excitement. "Indian rhinos have one horn, unlike their African counterparts. Her story is amazing, if somewhat sad."

"Why sad?" Andrea asked. She couldn't take another blow—if the rhino was sold for her parts, her taxidermy body in some king's palace...

"It's not exactly the best-case scenario for an exotic animal from the tropics to be uprooted and taken to Europe," said Paul. "Not her climate here. But she made it to adulthood based on these images."

"Why would someone want to own a rhinoceros?" Lucas said. He stared at the rhino illustration under the plexiglass.

"It was the Age of Enlightenment," Paul said. "People were addicted to the exotic in art and culture. Curiosity ruled. This was the time of extravagance. People lived in style."

"Partly why the French Revolution took place," Andrea said.

"Not for another fifty years or so after Clara's arrival," Janice said. "But yes, some of the reason the world changed so drastically was because the wealthy, the one percent, lived so illustriously."

"The French Revolution wasn't the only upheaval in the eighteenth century," Paul said. "The American Revolution, of course, in the 1770s, Haiti revolted, and the British took over India from the Dutch."

"Didn't the Dutch focus more on South Africa after that?" said Lucas.

"They did," said Paul. "To the detriment of the native culture. Dutch colonies prevailed there and majorly influenced South Africa. Still do to this day. The conflict and cultural impact are palpable and irreversible."

"We're losing focus," said Janice. "If we think the owner of these documents wrote on the backs of them when they were produced, we're talking about the discovery of primary sources from a 1740s historical figure that haven't been seen in centuries. An animal like this in Europe would have opened the eyes of everyone around it. People would have realized the world was much larger, allowing the expansion of thought and the beginning of animal rights."

"Are we sure this is everything the desk has to offer?" Andrea asked, trying to change the subject. She feared that the trophy room would come bubbling to the surface.

Janice, Paul, and Lucas opened drawers and felt for hidden secrets on the desk. Andrea lay on the floor, feeling under each curve of the claw feet.

The desk had four more hidden compartments. An old ink pot, crusted with age and rust, came from one of them. Excitement faded when the other drawers were empty.

Janice produced sleeves for the documents and sealed them between plastic sheets. She placed them gently in her leather satchel and zipped it. The winter sky melted into an orange sunset when they left the dorm room. Their breath fogged.

Andrea's mind was a tangle of questions. If Janice recognized this animal and the museum had an entire exhibit dedicated to it, it must have been significant. But Andrea had studied early modern European history for her entire college career, and never in any classes or textbooks had she read anything about a rhinoceros in Europe. Maybe Clara didn't live long? Her trauma brain flashed images of her death, tortured and starved. But her history brain told her that she had to have been cared for if she was on a broadside. Andrea didn't know what to believe.

The snow on the ground and the icicles on the eaves made her think. A rhino needed a warm climate, and Leiden did not have one. She didn't know of any zoos in the 1700s that would have been able to keep one alive, either. But besides keeping it warm, how on earth did an Indian rhino even make it to Europe?

"Janice," Andrea said. She trotted to keep up with the curator. "How could someone have gotten a rhinoceros from India to Europe?"

"Good question," said Janice, staring at the pink streaks of clouds above. The bare trees shivered, and flocks of tiny birds hopped on the electric lines. "It was Napoleon's idea to make a cut through the isthmus of Suez in Africa."

Andrea knew this. "Napoleon had the idea in the late 1700s, but it wasn't until forty or so years later that construction began on the Suez Canal. Before that, there were only two ways to get from India to Europe. Overland or oversea."

"Yes," Janice said. "They would have had to go around the horn of Africa on a long sea voyage or cross the continent on foot."

"Someone made a rhinoceros walk from India to Europe?"

"It's possible. They'd walk through almost every climate on earth if they did: jungle, desert, the Taurus mountains. Hannibal in the Alps, remember? 200 BCE?" she said. Her boots scuffed across the cobblestone sidewalk.

"That's before my time of expertise," Andrea said. "I prefer a little more modern."

"What do you like to study?" she asked.

"The eighteenth century the most, I suppose. When humankind realized the world around them was bigger than what they saw daily."

"Enlightenment again," said Paul, tossing a snowball lightly at Lucas, who ducked and scurried to grab his own. He lobbed one at Paul, powder sparkling in the twilight.

"Hey!" Janice said. "No snowball fights while I'm hauling artifacts here!"

Andrea couldn't help herself—she laughed. They broke into a run to avoid the game. By the time they reached the museum, the sky was lavender gray. The smell of snow filled the air, but the storm clouds moved quickly to the east, revealing a creamy pink moon. Andrea wondered what city the snowstorm was headed to and reveled in the fact that she was breathing the air of Leiden, South Holland, on a cobblestone sidewalk outside a museum teeming with history.

Janice headed to a workroom where a document table waited. She unloaded the documents one by one, preparing them for digitizing. She delicately removed the documents from their plastic protectors with white gloves, barely breathing. Andrea was slightly mortified that she'd picked up the original find with bare hands.

Janice switched on a projector, and a monitor popped to life. The documents flickered on the screen, magnified and beautiful. They stared, enraptured, quiet, when a sharp knock on the door sounded.

Chapter 14
Douwemout van der Meer
Fort William, India

Fort William bustled with launch. Sailors and merchants hauled goods down the broad ramp leading into the tea-brown waters of the Hooghly, a delta branch of the River Ganges. The *Knappenhof* waited. The river's sandbars made navigation difficult as the underwater terrain shifted. Luckily, Douwe's maps were changed by whoever came in most recently.

The *Knappenhof* was ready—wind carried the flags flying over the masts atop the brightly colored ship. The stern boat was 130' long, capable of hauling 625 tons of trade goods. The crew was set at 170 men, plus a rhino and Zubin. They counted for the total weight, which Douwe needed to consider. By the end of the trip, he expected Clara and Zubin would grow significantly. Clara could weigh double when they landed in Rotterdam.

Clara was overly excited about her carriage ride. Zubin unloaded her, and she frolicked with the goat. The boy took her down the street to play while Douwe conducted his business. The passersby stared and laughed. The sailors were too busy to pay much attention, but they gave curious looks in Clara's direction.

Douwe watched the loading, ensuring everything meant to be on board was there. He pulled his papers and found again Sichterman's note about meeting Johanna. He had forgotten.

Douwe ran in the direction of the flagpole. Walking away was Johanna in a blue dress. He called her name.

She turned, her hair the color of golden hour. She shielded her eyes with a white-gloved hand and smiled. Perhaps the last one from her. Douwe's gut soured.

"Douwe," she said, curtsying lightly. "I feared I had missed you."

"I am sorry I kept you waiting."

They locked eyes, awkward in their silence. Johanna retrieved a parcel from her basket.

"I was so inspired by your little beast that I, well, I made you something," Johanna said, handing him the object. The parcel was no larger than Douwe's hand, wrapped in soft brown paper tied with a velvet ribbon.

"I feel silly. Maybe it's out of line."

Douwe shook his head as he untied it. "No," he said. "I feel I should give you something for your troubles."

"Troubles?" Johanna asked. "You mean our little incident in the dining room?"

Douwe nodded. "Are you well, Johanna?"

"Yes," she said. "Not many Dutch women can say they've been trampled by a baby rhino. I've been the talk of Calcutta. Calling cards by the dozens await me. Everyone wants to hear the story. I haven't been lonely, thanks to you."

Douwe unwrapped the package. It was a painted miniature on a thin bone disc with Clara and Douwe together on the green lawn of Fort William. Douwe held Clara's lead, painted with a single-strand brush.

"Johanna, how can I ever thank you?" he said. He reached into his inner jacket pocket and retrieved the wooden Clara carved by a guest at Hirzet's. Johanna held the trinket and smiled broadly, making Douwe's stomach clench.

"You'll always have Clara with you, in a way. Keep it."

"I have the feeling, Captain, that more art will be made from your beautiful beast," Johanna said.

"I hope so," said Douwe, tucking the miniature into his pocket. He longed to take her into his arms, feel her soft lips, touch the auburn curl that danced about her jawline. Instead, he kept a reasonable distance away, and though it was a yard, it felt like an ocean.

"Douwe," said Johanna. "If something should happen and my captain does not return—"

"You know the way to Leiden, Johanna."

She looked down. He was not sure that was the answer she wanted. The sun made mirages over the concourse.

The crew loaded the *Knappenhof*. Douwe was due on ship and had to find Zubin, Clara, and Betsy. There was beauty in the brown-tea water, the brightly painted hull, and the windows of his captain's quarters gleaming in the tropical sun.

He had a good crew: men from all over the world who had perfected their tasks. The cogs in his machine were set, the crew like the windmills in Holland. Each working part relied on the other, the machine more important than the piece. His job was ensuring each piece worked so the whole continued strongly. The *Knappenhof* neared readiness—dozens of men loaded spices, fabric, animal feed, barrels of water, and food all morning. The last thing to load was Clara herself. Zubin looked nervous.

"It's time, Zubin," said Douwe.

"Sir." Zubin swallowed, looking at his feet. "I am scared."

Douwe crouched beside the boy. Clara leaned into him, her favorite thing to do. Douwe wrapped his arms around her and spoke to Zubin.

"I will do everything in my power to protect you from man, sea, and wind on board this ship, Zubin," he said. "You are as precious to me as Clara, and neither of you will see harm while I am in charge."

Zubin gathered Clara's lead and handed Betsy's basket to Douwe. He sighed and pressed his hand against a nearby palm, a solemn goodbye to his homeland.

"Adventure is coming for both of us now," Douwe said. "I can't wait for you to experience the wonders at sea, Zubin."

They walked Clara toward the large ramp, but she would not budge from its edge. Her ears were perked, nostrils flared, eyes wide and bright.

Douwe gave Clara a tap on her rear, Zubin pulled her soft leather lead, and with great apprehension, Clara boarded the *Knappenhof*. Her round toes padded on the wood planks of the deck. She sniffed everything, including the crew, as they approached. Clara sauntered over to Bakari. Zubin did not leave her side. Her home for the next few months was a gazebo on deck reserved for royalty. On this voyage, Clara was queen.

"This," Douwe said to the crew, "is my personal companion and privilege on board the *Knappenhof*."

The crew stared at Clara with childlike smiles.

"I encourage you all to spend time caring for the livestock on this voyage," Douwe said. "When your duties are done, of course."

The men made a circle around Clara. A massive forecastleman, arms the size of Clara's thick legs, smoked a tobacco pipe. He knelt to let her smell it, blowing the smoke toward her. Clara drank the air with her lip and eagerly stepped toward the sailor. The crew laughed, barrel-bellied sailors and bone-thin boys alike were in awe of the rhino.

Zubin settled Clara while the men resumed their duties. He prepared her gazebo with straw and water and milked Bakari. Clara followed her bottles and reveled in the crew's kindness.

The captain's quarters were clean and plain, with desert-colored wood and handsome, crisp furnishings. Douwe's chair was padded with striped satin. Maps and books, precious objects, were stored on a small shelf to the right, navigation tools were on the left. When Zubin entered, he gasped.

Douwe opened Betsy's basket, and the cat, immensely irritated, mewed as she leaped out.

Zubin dropped his small parcel and spun around. "What a place to call your home!"

"It is temporary, Zubin, but it is comfortable. I shall not have you below with the crew. Your place is here." Zubin had a hammock, and Douwe picked up the boy to set him in. He swung, grinning.

"My work will keep me from you most hours of the day, Zubin," Douwe said, pushing the hammock. Zubin closed his eyes. "The most important job is yours, as you know."

"Tending Clara."

"Yes. We'll usually take our meals here, so the crew will not see how much I'm allotting for your food. They will not get as much as you."

Zubin sat up and rolled out of the hammock clumsily. "Where is Clara's food?"

"There are stores down below decks for all of the animals."

"All of the animals?" Zubin looked out the window at the commotion on the ship, where a sailor walked by with a goat that was not Bakari.

"Don't get too attached," Douwe warned. "Most of them will be slaughtered. A few are for milk, like Bakari, but most will feed us during our journey."

"And what of her?" Zubin asked. Betsy was cleaning herself on Douwe's small bed.

"She may be the most useful animal on this ship," said Douwe. "Vermin are here, even if we cannot see them. You'll hear them at night, and so will Betsy the ratter cat. With any luck, she'll have another litter on board, and we'll have kittens who love to hunt mice before the end of the voyage."

Outside in the hallway, a small closet held Douwe's captain's privilege. He opened it to place his black chest, not as full of silver as before he had purchased Clara. There was treasure from India in the closet: a jeweled dagger set with green and blue cabochon stones, a silver durbar set, ornate wooden boxes, a black chess set, a large bag full of nuts, and a bronze statue of a goddess.

Zubin gasped at the statue.

"Sir," he said. "Why do you have this?"

"I will sell it in Europe."

"This is a sacred thing," Zubin said. "Not for selling."

"This kind of thing will bring us a month's food for Clara," Douwe said. "Is this of importance to you?"

"This is the goddess Durga." Zubin picked up the statue. The goddess sat on a pedestal, her right leg stabilizing her, her left folded underneath. The statue's multiple arms held a sword, a shield, a trident, and a jewel. A row of skulls lay at her feet.

"She guards those who choose to do good," Zubin said. "She protects those who have come from nothing. She is the gatherer-up of treasures, the demon-slayer, the mother goddess. You cannot sell this."

"This is not my god, Zubin," said Douwe.

"She is mine," Zubin said, full of fire, clutching the statue to his chest. "She brings the oppressed out of their prisons, and that you have this is a sign from Durga that perhaps I am not chained."

"You are not chained," said Douwe. He knelt near the boy.

"Yet here I am, on this ship, with you and Clara," Zubin said. "I have no one else in this world."

"You have me, you have Clara, and you have a whole life ahead of you in Europe."

"I have gone from the baytar to Sichterman to you. Where shall I go next, after this?"

"After what?"

"After you are done with Clara and done with me."

"Zubin, I..." Douwe dropped his hands. He remembered the feeling Zubin helped him overcome in the market. "I won't be done with you, even if something happens to Clara."

Zubin loosened his grip on the statue and parted his mouth to speak but said nothing.

"If you need Durga to reassure you that you are no slave, we shall keep her. You are more than that. You're my friend."

Douwe grasped Zubin by the shoulders, took the statue with one firm hand, and embraced the boy. He breathed in the smell of a child, one he had forgotten existed. The *Knappenhof*'s crew signaled it was leaving. The sea waited.

Chapter 15
Andrea
Leiden, The Netherlands

"Hallo," called Sergei from the hallway.

"Ah," said Janice, rising and ditching her white gloves.

Paul, Lucas, and Andrea sat on tall metal stools, looking at the flat screen that was zoomed in on the backside of the first document. They were analyzing the brown gall ink, transposing the words, and measuring the six documents. Andrea rubbed the tips of her fingers together anxiously.

"Come in, we may have made a discovery," said Janice.

"I was just grabbing the trash. But I'll take a look, Janice."

Janice opened the door for Sergei. He was tall and massively built—thick arms and fingers, his bulbous nose still red with cold. He rubbed his hands together, warming them.

"Ever seen this?" said Janice, gesturing to the screen.

Sergei looked slowly from the screen to the documents on the table.

"Would you look at those," he said. "A rhinoceros?"

He exhaled sharply and reached out to touch the documents on the table. Andrea stood, taking two steps toward the artifacts.

"Careful," said Janice. "Those are not facsimiles."

He put his hands up and backed away a few steps.

"Sorry, just excited, like you all." Sergei leaned in, clasping his hands behind his back. "This reminds me of the exhibit from a few years ago."

Sergei's eyes shone. His face was inches from the crumbling documents.

"Janice was telling us about the exhibit, did you see it?"

Sergei nodded. "Many of the artifacts were borrowed. Nice to see one that maybe can stay in the archives here?"

"Certainly," said Janice. "We'll need to research it and see if we can figure out who wrote on the back."

Janice clicked the computer mouse and the back showed on the screen.

"Incredible," said Sergei. He narrowed his eyes at the screen. The room was silent for a moment until Andrea cleared her throat. Sergei grabbed the trash bag from the small can, still staring at the documents. He shook his head, seemingly in disbelief.

"See you tomorrow," he said, and left the room. The door shut with a mechanical click.

"Does he do that often?" said Andrea, letting out the breath she'd been holding.

"Sergei's perfectly fine," said Janice, slicing her hand through the air dismissively. "We couldn't do this project without him."

"He hangs around the cemetery while we work like he's waiting for something important," said Andrea.

"Of course he does," said Paul. "Sergei is our eyes out there, he knows every gravestone, every subtle change. Finding something significant would make this project even better for the museum."

"I'm sure he's helpful, Professor Hahn," said Lucas. He hadn't called him anything but Paul before that. "But how much training has he had with artifacts?"

"He doesn't need any," said Janice. "We're almost past the part Sergei needs to help with anyway. Once the digging is over, he'll return to his regular campus duties. When the remains are up, the project turns to just the museum staff and volunteers."

"Can we get back to the documents?" Andrea asked, desperate to reach out and reposition the camera to the next one. She wanted to stop her racing thoughts. The energy in the room calmed as each one of them took a deep breath.

Janice put her white gloves back on. "These are broadsides. Meant to spread news about something, basically a poster."

"Advertising an event hasn't changed much," said Lucas.

"Does this mean the animal was well cared for?" Andrea said. Lucas raised an eyebrow.

"Hard to say, Andrea," Paul said. "Seems to be a normal Indian rhino. It must mean something to you that it was well cared for?"

"I'm an animal fan."

"I hope we all are," said Paul.

"Some people don't care about that kind of thing," Andrea said, speaking quickly.

Paul and Lucas turned toward her, but Janice moved the camera over the second linen-backed document, and their eyes moved to the screen.

The documents were all roughly the same size, stamped on the front with printer's ink, still black even with great age. Individually, they featured the rhino and a small hunter with an arrow, a man in a cameo-like portrait, and the rhino in a pasture with two other animals in the background.

A few of them had handwritten notes in red iron gall ink. The handwriting was faded, but technology was able to enhance it. The darkened room and warm-lit screen with Clara's documents magnified felt like a blanket for Andrea's brain. Being involved in something specific felt good, and her mind couldn't wander.

"There's a name," said Paul. "Repeated on all of them. Douwemout van der Meer."

"That's a name?" said Andrea. Lucas nudged her.

"Douwemout is Dutch," he said.

Andrea rolled the name around in her mouth, testing it. The letters jumped out at her now, the same on each document.

"Could it be her keeper?" she said. No one replied.

After two hours, most of the documents were saved to a shared album. With a special app, they could zoom in, add filters, enhance the images, and use a notes section to share findings. Each document featured different dates, languages, and cities. They translated and transcribed them; soon, just one document was left.

"Hey, Janice," Andrea said. "Do you think this software could enhance the image I took of the gravestone from this morning?"

"It's worth a shot," she said. "Add the picture to the album."

Janice added a few filters and waved a special soap-bar tool over the image. In a few moments, the upper etching was noticeably more precise.

Andrea held up her phone to compare. The image from the broadside and the gravestone matched. "It's the same animal."

Her hands trembled. She was bringing this rhino back to life, one artifact at a time.

Chapter 16
Douwemout van der Meer
The Bay of Bengal

The water of the Hooghly River, richly brown, climbed Fort William's wide ramp in rapid white crests sent from the rocking stern of the *Knappenhof*. From the captain's quarters, Zubin sat, with Betsy on his lap, watching the Fort's Dutch flag grow small. The cat purred. The boy felt like his body had been laid in the Indian sun during a summer afternoon.

The ship was touched lightly by small waves of the wide river. Soon, they would reach the mouth of the Ganges, dump into the Bay of Bengal, and be swept to sea for two hundred sleeps before the shores of Europe greeted them.

Douwe led his crew from the deck. Clara was tied with a soft leather lead in her covered paddock. Clara made a squeaking noise, her lip curled, eyes bright. She was curious about the activity and sore about the lack of attention she received.

Douwe went to the paddock's edge and ruffled her ears. She searched his hands eagerly, disappointed when she came away with nothing. Even amidst the chaos on deck, he found her pewter bottles, shook one to ensure it was full, and fed her.

A crew member with a black bandana and ice-blue eyes approached.

"Captain! Shall I do this? Surely you have more to do than feed this babe?"

"Indeed, sailor," said Douwe. "Once I show you how it's done, you'll be Clara's favorite on deck."

"I always enjoyed the livestock. We shan't be eatin' this one?"

Douwe laughed nervously. "No, no eating her. She is going to Europe to allow the world to see the exotic and wild Indian rhino."

"Wild, eh?" the sailor gestured to the bottle. "We'll see how wild she is after being on board with us for six months."

"What's your name, sailor?" Douwe said, handing off Clara's feeding to him.

"Peregrine Snell." He didn't tear his eyes from Clara as he fed her. "From London, England, sir, formerly with the East India Company."

Douwe raised his eyebrows. The British East India Company was the VOC's rival.

"John Company and I saw eye to eye enough for me to leave before too much trouble brewed."

"I won't ask more questions, sailor, provided you do your work on board my ship with honor," said Douwe. He walked away, but Clara unlatched from her bottle and cried out to him.

"She prefers you, Captain."

"That she does," Douwe said with a smile, then grabbed the bottle and let Clara finish it. He told Snell of her needs, and Snell agreed to help when he could. Snell's smile faded when Douwe mentioned Clara's produce.

"If you perform your duties well, I'll see you get a share or two of her provisions," Douwe said. "When we make port in South Africa, we'll replenish. Until then, she gets the lion's share."

"Any chance I'll get a touch of her goat's milk too?"

"You ask a lot, sailor," Douwe said. He straightened. "Make sure she's fed properly."

Snell nodded, stroking Clara's ears. Douwe stepped away, ignoring her plaintive whistles. He should introduce Snell to Zubin. But the crew shouted that the river delta was near and needed Douwe to navigate. The sandbars shifted here, and there was danger of running aground.

The map was in the hands of his first mate, a Chinese man named Kang. He was short and blocky, with jet-black hair and sharp eyebrows. He was a no-nonsense kind of sailor, and Douwe had yet to sail a voyage without him in three years. Kang bowed lightly as Douwe approached and turned to make space for him while holding the map.

The narrow river was difficult to navigate, but Kang and Douwe had done it a dozen times. At its shallowest, it was three fathoms deep. At its narrowest point near Fort William, the river was nine fathoms. The winding channel thickened and flowed into the Bay of Bengal, but the sandbars shifted with every monsoon. They were drawn on the map like thick drips, waiting to catch ships like the *Knappenhof*.

Place names on the map spelled doom: *The Devil's Room, Buoy of the Broken Ground, The Kill.* The only way through was to drift—drive up with the tide, then use the wind to go back and forth across the current. The *Knappenhof* wound through like the letter Z, shimmying back and forth until the river's mouth opened.

"Where's our path, Kang?"

Kang drew a thick finger down the northeast side of the river.

"This will serve, provided we do not miss our turn south," he said. Douwe studied the path and shook his head.

"Too tight of a turn with this cargo," Douwe said. "Shouldn't we take the Sagor Road? Wider channel, deeper."

"Last time, it was barely three fathoms," said Kang. "We cannot risk that."

"Look at the numbers, mate." Douwe pointed. "We can drop the starboard anchor to slow us through the sand, nice and slow."

The map's numbers indicated fathoms last recorded. The names and dates of wrecked VOC ships were in the same curling script. Douwe's fingers skimmed over them and did not linger.

Talk of wrecked vessels and lost lives was taboo, though Douwe and Kang consciously noted them. It was best to avoid the areas and ensure the crew did not look closely at the maps.

Kang pointed to the script "Middle Channel," which was broader, deeper. At the base: "Passage Out." He smiled.

"That's a new one." Kang pointed at the neighboring channel, which said, "Old Passage Out."

Douwe took the map from Kang's hands and pressed it to his nose. It was perfect.

"Only at one spot is it three fathoms," said Douwe. "Broad enough. No sharp turns. We'll still drop anchor to dredge. Play it safe." No rolling script told of shipwrecks there.

In cursive were the names of ships that did not make it out: *Velserbeek*, *Prins Willem*, *Ceylon*. This was Douwe's last voyage. This vessel and its crew had a high chance of delivering the cargo safely, but adrenaline surged at the thought of Clara floundering in the fathoms. The ship must stay afloat.

"Let's make way, heading for the middle channel," Douwe said, pressing the map back into Kang's waiting hands. The men bustled to their stations, beginning the mechanical process of steering the ship.

Douwe gave the command to drop the starboard anchor. The helmsmen turned the massive wheel. One young sailor must have been fifteen or so, lithe, tanned, and blonde. He helped the lead helmsman steer, an imprecise art that sometimes took four men during challenging navigation.

Douwe helped steer the ship into port with the helmsman when they landed in South Africa, but for now, he trusted the cogs in the machine. The channels were serious business. They all longed to go home at this point—careening into a sandbar only miles from Calcutta would be disastrous.

Douwe wiped his forehead with a white rag. Sailors stripped away their tunics and worked bare-chested on board. Their bodies gleamed. All colors of man—pale Europeans, tan South Asians, brown and black Africans who joined the crew at the Fort of Good Hope. They worked, singing their hauling songs to keep the sails still, admiring the focus of the helmsman. Douwe momentarily forgot about Clara.

He had not heard her cries lately. He did not want to look panicked, so he walked calmly to her pen. Bakari roughly plucked green hay from a bale strapped to the wall. Despite the noise of the crew and churning river, Clara was asleep, feet out to the side, pebbled gray skin heaving with each breath.

Suddenly, scraping vibrated under his feet. He ran to the rail, clutching his tricorne. The ship should not have touched sand, not here. He yelled to Kang, who leaped off to the helm. Douwe followed. The wrong anchor had been lowered. The young sailor with pink shoulders was down, legs splayed, holding his elbow awkwardly. The remaining helmsman yelled: "HAUL!"

The ship listed, its direction changed by dropping the portside anchor and the apprentice helmsman's injury. Douwe and Kang grabbed the wheel and pulled, the slick wood bowing to them. The ship pulled heavily portside but slowly, and the hull sliced through sand. They were too close to the large sandbar on the starboard side. Douwe glanced at Kang, who nodded and hopped off the wheel. The wheel pulled hard, with just Douwe and one helmsman left.

Kang shouted to the crew: "ALL TO THE PORTSIDE! PORTSIDE!" The crew, as a stampede of wild horses, flew to action.

Smaller sailors clambered down the riggings like birds dropping to the ground. The carpenter and his crew emerged. The kitchen staff hauled up from the belly of the ship. A brass bell rang, and each time it did, the *Knappenhof*'s crew ran from side to side on the deck, sending the ship rocking.

One hundred sailors slammed to the rails. The sound of scraping underscored their shouts. The men gritted their teeth, ran, and wiggled the ship free from the soft, muddy sand of the riverbed. Douwe held firm the wheel, forearms near bursting, toes gripping the deck through his boots. Every muscle was contracted.

Kang held his hand up and motioned to small groups to slowly leave the rail. His black eyes flashed like a hawk's. He strode to Douwe once they were all released.

"To the cargo?" Kang asked, his body pointing in the direction of the hold.

"Immediately," said Douwe. "Find me relief. We go together."

Kang grabbed the second mate to replace Douwe at the wheel. Panting, Kang and Douwe dropped down the ladder to the vast underbelly of the *Knappenhof*.

"No water?" said Douwe.

"No," said Kang. "It's dry. The Ganges has a sharp scent."

"Indeed," replied Douwe. It was not the smell of the salted sea nor of Europe's clean, dark rivers. The Ganges had a scent of its own.

Douwe tightened his hat. Vermin lived here, leaping from man to man, creating a crawling hell of lice and fleas. Kang grabbed a lantern and strode forward into the night-like hold. Barrels of fresh water and weak beer were strapped tightly and strategically to balance the ship, undamaged.

Stacks of folded fabrics and jute sacks holding spices seemed untouched. Douwe rounded the corner where the animal feed was stored and gasped. Green bananas and dozens of vegetables he loaded for Clara were scattered across the floor. Douwe hurriedly gathered them.

The fruit crate was broken, having toppled from the high pile of barrels that held fresh water. This was not where he had put it. It was supposed to be near the hay manger. Douwe's mind buzzed—he had taken Snell down the hatch to show him Clara's produce.

Had the sailor moved her crate? Kang found rolling oranges and smashed bananas. Clara had to eat it today, or it would be rotten. The crate, which used to be brimming, was half-full. The damaged fruit did not account for the missing pieces.

Kang and Douwe shared a grim look. The lantern swung above them, illuminating the shadows under their eyes.

"Who?" said Kang.

"Snell," said Douwe. "I showed him how to feed Clara and where her food was stored."

"You're sure?" said Kang, grabbing the thick-glass lantern from its hook.

"I am."

"It wasn't your boy?" said Kang, his face lit from underneath.

"He has not left my quarters."

Kang stared at him, analyzing his answer. He made a decision, nodded sharply, and led Douwe up the narrow ladder to the crew's quarters.

Hammocks dangled and swayed, lanterns above. Kang and Douwe

asked sailors where they might find Snell. He quartered near the middle, a place of unremarkable dignity. He was not there. But under his hammock was a strand of orange pith. Douwe held it to the lantern, and Kang turned on his heel to climb the ladder.

"Sailor Snell!" Kang bellowed.

Snell stood by Clara's pen, feeding her hay. Clara flicked her ears at Kang and Douwe. Snell bristled at the shouting and slowly turned. His eyes narrowed like a bull, ready to charge. Kang gave the signal to gather. The crew lined up, stock-still and silent. Kang passed them, his thick-soled boots clacking. Douwe followed silently, raging. How much food remained for Clara?

"Sailor Snell," Kang said. The sailors watched. Punishment was always given in public. "You have stolen from the captain's privilege."

"The captain's privilege?"

"That produce was meant for my animal and no one else," Douwe said. "You have stolen from her. Therefore, you have stolen from me. Your punishment shall be three days on the masthead, given only bread and water."

Kang stared at Douwe, flaring his nostrils. The punishment was light as the Bay of Bengal was warm. Snell would not suffer much, but only bread and water after eating his fair share of Clara's food was cruel.

"You are not to go near my privilege again, sailor," said Douwe. He stepped between Clara and Snell. Zubin appeared from the captain's quarters. Betsy trotted ahead of him. Tail aloft, she headed into Clara's pen, mewing in response to Bakari's bleats.

"You are not to go near Clara," Douwe repeated. Snell cast his eyes downward.

This was the fiercest punishment. Animals gave great joy to the crew, and another Indian rhino was unlikely to ever sail on a VOC voyage. But Snell had made mistakes, and now Douwe was tasked with rationing Clara's meager produce for the remainder of the trip to South Africa. Luckily, they were on the shorter leg of their long voyage.

Zubin hauled himself over the top bar of Clara's paddock and grabbed her lead. Without a word to Douwe, Kang, or Snell, he unlocked the paddock door and took Clara out. She followed him with an eager joy. He held a banana in his hands, shuffling backward. Snell turned away, and Kang led him to the mast where he climbed a rope ladder to the top.

"We have to be careful with Clara on this ship," said Douwe to Zubin, kneeling.

Clara sidled up to him and, like always, leaned in. Her skin was dry and peeled near her armor-like plates' pink edges. The mottled surface moved like soft liquid suede over her muscles, soft as a moth's wing but tough like a canvas sail.

"What...what did he do to her?" Zubin was concerned.

"He stole her food, Zubin," said Douwe. "It may not be the last time, and we will have to ration her fruit for now until we get to the Fort of Good Hope. We can replenish her stores there."

"She can have mine!"

"No, boy, she cannot. She's important, but so are you. Without proper rations, you would not make it long on this voyage. You must promise me you will not give her your food, no matter how she begs."

Clara was begging. Zubin nodded at Douwe, eyes on Clara's gentle lashes.

"What do we do about her skin?" Zubin rubbed a flaking spot on her side.

"Remember what Fateh said? Fish oil. There are a dozen barrels in the hold, meant for the trade market," said Douwe. The barrels were stored near the freshwater supply in the hull.

"Can we use it?" Zubin asked, shielding his eyes from the bright sun.

"We must."

Fifteen minutes later, Clara glistened from the soft spot where her horn would be to the tufted tip of her tail. She shone and snorted, sneezed, licked herself, and flicked her tail wildly. Zubin laughed at her, shooing away a desperately licking Bakari. Clara's flaky skin was better, and the sailors passing by laughed at the oil-soaked rhino.

The crew had unfurled the sails to lead the *Knappenhof* west. The river dumped into the bright glass bay. Tendrils of ochre and brown stretched like flames into the crystal blue. The fathoms deepened; the ocean spread. Other ships, launched hour by hour, waited in the bay beyond for the fleet to assemble. They were all protected by a small, sleek black ship employed to keep pirates away.

The fleet of twenty ships was magnificent. The *Knappenhof* was the last, and cries from the other vessels signaled departure was nigh. They were ready to leave India behind. Kang commanded the crew to follow the fleet east southeast over the reefs.

Each ship was a quarter mile away, giving enough berth for maneuvering but allowing for communication with flags. His crew was busy, and Douwe found Zubin and Clara distracting.

"Back to her paddock for now, Zubin," Douwe said. He had to see where he was needed. He could not expect Kang to care for everything, though he knew he could. Although he was second in command, Douwe allowed Kang many freedoms. He respected the man. He'd been on more ships than Douwe could count.

Douwe shook his head, reminding himself Kang would not see his son until the voyage's end: 233 days. Clara would grow so much in that time. In sixty days, they would land in South Africa, replenishing their supplies and adding more to Clara's stores.

Lost in thought, Douwe bumped roughly into a short-statured sailor. Rubbing his shoulder, Douwe wheeled around.

"Watch yourself, lad!"

"Forgive me, captain," said the sailor, removing his brown cap. He could scarcely be twenty—a stubble-free face, delicate small ears, an upturned nose with freckles spurting across its bridge. His hair was cut clean to his scalp. The sailor kept moving, hauling rope to another crew member with abrupt speed.

Kang was suddenly at Douwe's side, hands behind his back, watching the workers.

"Small sailor, big hurt?" he said, smiling coyly.

"Something like that," said Douwe, watching the diminutive sailor and frowning.

"Luncheon, sir. I'll ring the bell. Gather Zubin and yourself in your quarters before the crew descends."

"Thank you, Kang," said Douwe. He went to Clara's paddock, where she and Zubin watched the chaotic maneuverings of the ship's deck. "Luncheon, Zubin!"

Zubin grinned and lifted himself over the wooden wall. Clara's paddock had narrow fence slats, a hay manger, a swinging gate, and an attached water bucket, readied by the carpenters in the days before launch. Clara made a squeaking noise, resting her chin where Zubin had disappeared.

"It's alright, girl," said Zubin, patting her neck. "I'll be back with your bottle after we eat."

In the captain's quarters, cheese, bread, honey, and two sausages were spread on a hammered silver platter. Thick silver knives and three-pronged forks were set on gold satin napkins. Silver goblets decorated with grapes were full of light ale, and a small copper mug held night-dark rum.

Douwe and Zubin ate, feeling the ship rocking underneath them. The movement was more prominent below the decks. Zubin kicked his feet; his toes barely skimmed the floor.

"Where are your boots, Zubin?" said Douwe. "It will not do to get splinters in your feet."

Zubin crossed his legs under him in the warm wood chair. He stretched a foot out for Douwe to see. It was dusty white on the bottom, tough and calloused. Rough like sandstone, thick patches of skin covered the bottom of each of his small toes.

"I am not yet used to boots," Zubin said. "I feel my feet have made their own shoes. Besides, the other sailors are barefoot, too."

"Their feet are even tougher than yours. When we get to Europe, it will be too cold to go barefoot all the time, son," Douwe said.

Son. The word startled him.

Chapter 17
Andrea
Leiden, The Netherlands

"It's completely identical," Paul agreed, holding his phone to the monitor. The screen was zoomed in on the faded grave, and the phone showed one of the broadsides. "What does this mean?"

"Janice, can you show us the archives?" Lucas asked. "Maybe our connection between these things is in the old exhibit."

"Yes," she said. "We keep records of each student project, from seniors who volunteered here. Let's see if we can find it."

She pulled off her white gloves and opened a door at the opposite end of the room. A sign read: Alleen Personeel—Collections Staff Only. It led to a windowless hallway lined with modern doors. Andrea pursed her lips into a sly smile. She was going into the collection.

"A few summers ago, we did a series of exhibits on obscure University histories," Janice said, pulling a ring of keys from an apron pocket. She unlocked the door at the end of the hallway. Paul, Andrea, and Lucas were close behind. Andrea felt claustrophobic and rubbed her fingers together anxiously. Janice turned on the lights, which flickered and struggled. She muttered under her breath; the only word Andrea caught was "budget."

Concrete floors, ceilings, and walls. No windows. The room was enormous. Rows and rows of shelving were to the left. Below the shelves were sliding drawers, pristinely clean. Andrea wanted to open them all. To the right were canvasses and framed art hanging on fifty or so racks that looked like sturdy chicken wire.

Artifacts surrounded her: marble busts, landscape paintings, flashes of gold, white bones, portraits. Andrea took a moment to soak it all in. She felt her knees get weak. There was taxidermy here, but her eyes opened to wonder instead of fear. Her fingertips stopped moving.

Paul sidled up to her, smiling, hands in his jacket pocket.

"Doin' okay, Andrea?" he asked, chuckling.

"Yep. Have I died?"

"Nope. This your version of the afterlife?"

"Yeah. Artifacts from heaven." An unexpected laugh escaped her.

"The exhibit records are over here," said Paul. "I helped advise this student on a few things with the VOC. Facsimiles of the documents we looked at should all be in the archive."

On the back wall, office boxes were lined up and labeled with exhibit names and dates. On the way there, Andrea stared steadily at each object they passed. Lucas caught up with her inches away from a bronze sculpture of the Goddess Durga.

"This has to be pre-1600s."

"Look at the sword and jewel in her hand," Lucas said, pausing with her.

"Look at the pile of skulls by her feet. How did this end up in a museum in Europe?"

"Is it Indonesian?" said Lucas. "Probably brought over by one of those Dutch trading ships."

"It could be," she said. "But the VOC in India could have brought it back too. Or maybe someone traded something for it. Or maybe someone in the 1970s found it at Goodwill."

"Goodwill?" said Lucas. "What is that?"

"Never mind," she said, laughing. "It's probably not from Goodwill."

"What did you find?" said Janice, coming close.

"Durga." Andrea memorized the sculpture, down to the delicate details of the Goddess's face and the skull under her foot.

"From Goodwill?" asked Lucas, raising an eyebrow.

Janice laughed. "Definitely not from Goodwill, Lucas. It's a 16th-century bronze. Let's focus now."

Paul approached, office box in hand, the label read: CLARA THE RHINO EXHIBIT, 2019. He unceremoniously opened the box on the concrete floor. All four of them peered eagerly inside. The box was empty, save three overturned photographs.

"That's it?" said Lucas, grabbing a photo. In the photo, Janice was smiling, a male student by her side. The exhibit could be seen, blurry, in the background.

"There should be accession records and facsimiles in here. Labels, a student paper," said Paul. He furrowed his brow and walked back to the boxes, running a finger across their labels.

Andrea looked from Lucas to Janice, who each held a photo. She reached in and grabbed the third. It was an image of one artifact on display: a model ship.

"Hey, Paul," Andrea said. "Is this what you advised on? The ship?"

Paul peeled himself away from the boxes and hustled over, exhaling. He took the photo from Andrea and nodded.

"My specialty," he said. "An East Indiaman was a massive ship used specifically for trade in the East. The Dutch had an advantage. Windmills chopped wood faster and in larger quantities than any other European country. The VOC became a powerhouse with those ships; fast, efficient."

"What happened to them all?" Andrea asked. She stored the information Paul gave her in a new slot in her brain, like an old-school library card catalog.

"Ships were recycled," Paul said. "Shipyards decommissioned them and used their parts on other vessels. Parts were used for hundreds of years. Last summer, I got to tour a restored one. They were painted in amazing colors. So beautiful! But the insides were questionable living. Tight, dark, stinky. They could lose twenty percent of their crew."

"Disease, right," Lucas said. "A diverse crew like that? Disease had to be rampant."

"Yeah, disease," said Paul. "And mutiny, deception, accidents, injuries on board. Anything could happen. The voyage from here to India could be over six months long, and then you have to come back."

"I can't imagine," said Lucas. "Some grand adventure. People unified with a single mission. Can you see it? Asian, African, Indian, Dutch sailors...all pulling their weight, moving the sails and navigating a ship bigger than a semi."

"Pirate stuff, Lucas? You a commercial historian?"

"C'mon, it's interesting!" he said. "Sailing without electricity, navigation tools, or ways to call for help."

"Actually," said Paul. He motioned to a gold instrument on a shelf not far away. "Their navigation tools were pretty sophisticated. We still use their ways of navigating longitude and latitude today, just with computers. They traveled by the stars."

The shelf held a chronometer, a brass telescope, and a bronze medal with the letters VOC stamped on it boldly. Andrea crept up onto her tiptoes to see.

"Cool, but what about the empty box of rhino stuff?"

Janice shook her head.

"Janice, would the archives be digitized?" asked Paul.

"Maybe," said Janice. "We have so many records, and I haven't the time to sort through them. It would take ages to find."

"I have the time," said Andrea. "Let me sort through and find it. Maybe the student in the photos has the archives saved as part of their project."

Janice turned to her. Suddenly, Sergei appeared around the corner. Andrea startled.

"Sorry, sorry," he said. "Didn't mean to scare you. I'm locking up for the night. That okay with you, Janice?"

"Just a few more minutes, Sergei," she said. "Andrea, I can give you PastPerfect access tonight. See if you can dig anything up. I'll keep looking, too."

Sergei gave a small wave and turned to leave the archives. In the back pocket of his dark jeans, Andrea saw a folded piece of paper. The unmistakable image of a black and white rhino peeked from the corner. He'd made a copy of the broadside.

Andrea opened her mouth to speak but was interrupted when Paul offered the brass telescope for her to see. She turned her attention to him and looked at the artifact with distracted admiration. Paul showed the rest of the navigation items to Andrea and Lucas, but Andrea couldn't focus. She kept thinking about the folded paper in Sergei's pocket.

On the way out of the museum, Janice handed Andrea a note with login information for the archive software.

"Janice, how long has Sergei worked here?" Andrea asked. She folded the note and put it in her coat pocket.

"Longer than me. He's the one who discovered the graves moving, insisted I get involved. He's highly invested," Janice said with firm determination.

Andrea pursed her lips in a half-smile and tilted her head lightly to the side. She wondered what a groundskeeper wanted with the documents, and why he'd made copies. She debated asking Janice, but the way Janice talked about him told Andrea she would get nowhere.

She exited the museum and Lucas walked alongside her for a few silent moments. Snow muffled the air around them, canals reflected the golden streetlamps.

"Amazing day," he said.

She nodded, turning to him. She shook the thought of the rhino peeking from Sergei's pocket from her mind.

"And tomorrow we'll have answers about what used to be in that box."

Chapter 18
Douwemout van der Meer
Indian Ocean

Douwe opened the creaking door to the *Knappenhof's* small surgery to check on the injured sailor. The young helmsman lay on the surgeon's table. His shoulder was dislocated. The surgeon, also the ship's husbandry man, was a Dutchman with a short brown beard and elaborate chestnut-colored wig. He was wrenching the shoulder back into place.

There was a pop and subsequent scream as the shoulder joint was reset. The surgeon's words were muffled through the thick glass windows. He bandaged the boy in a sling. Douwe had to talk to Kang about replacing the boy at the wheel. Douwe ducked under the low doorway to the surgeon's cabin and swept his hat from his head. The boy wiped sweat from his temples, shuddering in pain.

"How fares he, Dr. Wilhelm?" said Douwe.

"Fine for now, provided he keeps the sling on and rests," said the surgeon, folding the remaining cloth.

The walls of his cabin were lined with tinctures. Bottles clinked lightly with the ship's constant motion, labeled: liniment oil, mercury, bark, lard, arsenic. There was also a small barrel of fish oil, closer than the barrels in the hold for Clara's skin.

Instruments gleamed on the table beyond: saws, a vicious-looking corkscrew for removing teeth, forceps, scalpels, and wide, curved knives. The sea and the ship were brutal to men. Douwe hoped that the surgeon's quarters would be slow on this voyage.

"Forgive me, Captain," said the boy, scrunching his mouth tightly. "I nearly caused us to run aground."

"You are correct, sailor," said Douwe. "But we did not run aground. Still, I will not have a useless sailor. You'll help Dr. Wilhelm in the surgery until he says you are cleared."

Assigning this boy to the surgeon's side was a great honor. Douwe could have sent him to the kitchens, but there was something in this young sailor. Perhaps he likened him to himself at seventeen, eager to put his life on the line for the VOC.

"Captain," said Dr. Wilhelm. "I already have a surgeon's assistant."

"Take two then and pray you do not need them. I will need one to assist my cabin boy, Zubin, with the oiling of my rhino each day. We'll use your fish oil, if you don't mind."

"Very well, sir," said Dr. Wilhelm with a short bow.

Douwe nodded. As they rose to leave, the door slammed open, and Douwe leaped away. It was the same small sailor from above decks who ran into his shoulder. The knot on his back pulsed again with pain.

"Watch yourself, sailor!"

The sailor stopped, nearly toppled over, and gracefully caught himself before the pail of fresh water he carried sloshed over. He maneuvered around and set the water on the table near the instruments. Not a drop spilled despite the sailor's baggy clothing.

"Forgive me, Captain," said the sailor, bowing low. "I forget myself in my urgency."

"See that you pay attention. That's twice today," Douwe said, adjusting his blue velvet jacket.

"Yes, captain," said the sailor, still looking at the floor.

Douwe's nostrils flared. He was a forgiving man but easily irritated when the crew forgot how delicate a matter it was to be on board. One misstep in the rigging and disaster was imminent. He would urge Kang to watch this one.

"Ah, Lionel," said Dr. Wilhelm. "Captain, the sailor's shoulder injury might make it difficult to care for your animal. I think it best my assistant, Lionel, be trained to care for your beast, and the sailor can help me."

Douwe soured at the thought of having to train Lionel, whose missteps annoyed him.

"Very well," he said, gathering himself.

With Snell untrustworthy, he had to find a replacement for Clara's care. His own duties were too many, and Zubin could not care for her constantly. Douwe led Lionel to the bright deck.

Clara spotted Douwe and cried out. Bakari followed, and the crew laughed at her screaming. The lot brought joy to the ship. The chickens brought on board and stowed away during launch roamed the deck, pecking at insects and sprays of sea foam.

"Why do they not fly overboard?" said Lionel as a black hen clucked at him and flapped toward the rail.

"Common sense," said Douwe. "Animals are often smarter than men, you know. Clara's grown accustomed to the deck in just a day. It could take a man a week or more to grow comfortable on a ship."

Lionel laughed. "If they ever do."

Lionel dropped to his knees when they neared Clara. His wide pants puddled around him. Clara approached, her lip gumming his sea-calloused hand. Perhaps Lionel was tougher than first imagined despite his diminutive stature.

"This is Clara," said Douwe. "She's my privilege on this ship. The treasure I take back to Europe. I trust you understand her importance."

"I've never seen one," said Lionel, gently rubbing Clara's rough head.

Lionel grazed his fingers along Clara's black ear fur. Clara huffed, licking his other hand. Lionel smiled a half-smile. A gentler reaction than when Snell met Clara.

"She gets a ration of fruit and vegetables. I know exactly how many pieces remain," said Douwe. "It is hers and hers alone. Not for the goat or the chickens or you."

"I wouldn't dream of taking anything from this girl," said Lionel. "What else does she eat? What do I do with the fish oil? Why is her skin so pink in these crevices?"

Douwe hopped the short wooden planks of Clara's paddock and pushed Bakari out of the way as she let out a disappointed moan. He parted Clara's skin where her leathery plates met and sighed. She was red. She would need more fish oil than initially planned. He sent up a silent thankful prayer to whoever ordered a dozen barrels of fish oil from Calcutta. They would have to be content with eleven.

"She's sunburnt," Lionel said, delicately touching her skin. Clara flinched. "We have some herbs for this, a liniment, in the surgeon's quarters. I can mix it with her oil to see if it will help."

Lionel furrowed his forehead, making two lines between his brows. Douwe was surprisingly reassured. He did not want to like this crewmate but still accepted his help. Neither he nor Zubin could help her sunburn.

Clara gazed up at Douwe adoringly and leaned onto his right leg. She flicked her ears. He had not paid her much mind lately, and she seemed eager to remind him of such. She had grown much larger in the month he had owned her. Her weight nearly toppled him over.

"Yes, girl?"

He had stowed a crust of bread from his lunch in his breast pocket for her, and she eagerly found it with her long tongue.

"She eats mostly anything, then?" said Lionel, watching. "What does she drink?"

"Goat's milk and water," Douwe said, pointing to her bucket. It floated with chicken feathers, slime from Bakari, and hay pieces. "She's not supposed to eat everything, but—"

A sailor walked by, shouting to his comrades in the joy of fully unfurling sails, the open sea ahead. The burly man licked his fingers and tapped the horseshoe nearby. He held a tankard of ale aloft, and some of it spilled onto Lionel's bare hand. He flung it off in annoyance, and a piece of foam landed in Clara's pen. She bounded to it and licked the decking. The foam was gone, her wet tongue print remained, and Clara looked eagerly at Lionel, asking for more.

Lionel chuckled and held his hand for Clara to lick. It was soon wet from her mouth wrapping around his thin wrist. Douwe and Lionel were both thoroughly amused.

"Seems she might like a pint of ale, too," said Lionel. "Do you think it would harm her?"

"I can't see how," said Douwe, thinking of what the crowd at Hirzet's tavern must have given her in his absence. "It will allow us to save our freshwater supply as well."

"Indeed," said Lionel. "I shall go prepare her liniment. I must say, Captain, she is remarkable. But why doesn't she have a horn?"

"The baytar in Calcutta told us she may not have one until she's three years old," Douwe said, rubbing the spot where Clara's horn would grow.

"That's a good thing, sir, especially when we land at the Fort of Good Hope," said Lionel, rising and dusting his too-large pants.

"Why is that sailor?" Douwe said, hopping over the paddock rail.

"Rhino horns are magic, sir. Ground up, they're used to, er, uhm..."

"Get it out," Douwe said, genuinely curious.

"Help with the impotent gentlemen, sir," Lionel said, turning crimson.

Douwe pursed his lips. Clara's life was much more valuable than a nobleman's sexual escapades.

"Thankfully, she does not have her horn yet," said Douwe.

"I understand, sir, but sometimes a lord making an heir is worth all the trouble in the world," said Lionel. "Even if she does not have her horn now, any man with that knowledge may try to steal her from you anyway."

"How do you know this, Lionel?"

"I have been to the markets, sir, where horns hang waiting for their buyers," said Lionel.

Douwe's mind's eye flashed with the teeming crowd of people at the Calcutta market.

"Even more reason to protect her," Douwe said, heart beating fast in his chest.

"I am with you," said Lionel. Douwe believed him.

Lionel darted off to make the liniment. Snell sat on the mast above, staring down. He had been up there for close to a full day now. His legs dangled from the crow's nest. Douwe wondered if Snell had heard their conversation. He turned and headed to his quarters.

His quarters were empty, save Betsy, who lounged on Douwe's bed, black tail flicking. She mewled, showing her pink tongue. Douwe put a hand on her belly, which was slightly swollen, and felt a kitten kick. Betsy's second litter would be born on the *Knappenhof* after all.

He picked up his ledger, recorded their launch story, and then flipped to the store list. He took parchment and quill and headed below decks. The crew usually checked the stores, but he had to oversee them after the incident with Snell. The sailors below were counting in Dutch, rearranging things in the hull. He dropped down the dark ladder.

The salt smell of the bilge water, of sweating man, remnants of sausage from luncheon, sweet, pungent tar, and the earthy smell of the hay stores were familiar, comforting. It pulled him back in time, on board as a young man, and the memory made him close his eyes.

"Ahoy, Captain!" said an older crew mate with sinewy muscle and fairer skin than those who worked on deck.

"Good day," said Douwe. "I'm here to help you inspect the stores. I had an incident earlier and want to ensure it was isolated."

"Aye, Captain." The crewmate pulled out a ledger book and held it to the lantern above. His handwriting was neat and orderly.

"Everything accounted for, then?" Douwe said as they compared notes.

"No, sir. Sorry to say we're missing a barrel of fish oil for a London trader and a crate of fruit from your personal privilege."

Douwe nodded. "We are in alignment. Both of those are accounted for. The oil is with Dr. Wilhelm, and the fruit is now in my cabin, though it is not as full as when we began our journey."

"Is that so? Who do I need to watch?"

"Snell," said Douwe, closing his book.

"Aye, sir," said the sailor, bitterness creeping over his features. "I have always watched that one."

"You have two more days of him on the masthead," Douwe said. "Clara's stores are precious, and I cannot afford to lose anymore until we get to the Fort of Good Hope."

Douwe climbed the ladder back to the deck to find Zubin. The day was fading. They would follow the coast for several more days until the Bay of Bengal slowly became the Indian Ocean. The green coast blocked the sunset, and the sky turned tangerine. The crew split into their two watches for the night.

The first watch worked in the quickening twilight, watched the stars brighten, and made for their beds at midnight. The second watch started its shift under the brilliant Milky Way, which kissed the black sea to the east. They switched shifts the next night and the next, and despite the crew above shouting orders and bells ringing every half-hour, hammocks still lulled exhausted sailors to deep rocking sleeps below.

The bright stars guided them onward, comforting in their familiarity. A map home to Holland could be drawn by these stars. The day's brilliant blue or stormy skies held heavens that revealed themselves only in darkness. The dusty-dark cloud of the Milky Way spilled itself like cream on silk taffeta into the shining sea. It was only possible to see as far as the moon allowed, illuminating only what was directly important. Night felt calm most times. It was reassuring that the celestial heavens did not change and always revealed themselves, no matter the day's challenges.

Douwe found Zubin feeding Clara with the pewter bottle. Bakari nodded asleep. The chickens, like the ones at Hirzet's, found Clara's paddock comfortable. Zubin had moved their wire crates inside. They clucked and rocked with the motion of the ship.

"I think, sir, that I like the sea," said Zubin, staring at the reflection of the close moon on the water.

"She has her glories but is not to be trusted."

"Why is that?"

"These are calm waters," said Douwe. "When we go further south, we may find danger. But when we get through it, we shall rest in a good place for a month. We'll moor in South Africa, where we'll get more food for Clara. We'll see if your shoes still fit you by then."

Zubin gave a half smile and wiggled his toes in his boots. Douwe was proud of him for trying but wondered if he'd wasted his money. The boy might be barefoot like the other crew by journey's end.

"Why do we stay for a month? Can't we keep going?"

"You'll see soon enough," Douwe said to the boy who spread Lionel's liniment on Clara's peeling skin. "After a few more weeks on board, you'll long for solid ground beneath your feet."

The days grew monotonous, the horizon of endless sea unchanging. Zubin and Lionel cared for Clara, who drank ale from sailor's tankards and loved Kang's pipe, lifting her lip and inhaling deeply. She pressed against the wooden enclosure, which Zubin reinforced. Clara ate less than planned, as they had to ration her food. She was given treats and kitchen scraps meant for the pigs on board. Douwe chastised Zubin when he caught the boy feeding her from his dinner plate.

Zubin's ribs no longer showed through his skin. His hair grew longer, and Dr. Wilhelm, also the ship's barber, trimmed it. He practiced the sailor's accents, played card games, and learned bawdy songs about ladies, belting raunchy words to the heavily pregnant Betsy.

Lionel did not grow tired of the work and became invaluable. Daily, Clara was exercised on deck by Lionel, Douwe himself, or Zubin. She lunged at them, played with pieces of rope, and tried to move chains with her nose. When Lionel walked her, the sailor sang a sea shanty about an Amsterdam maid, usually portrayed as Clara.

The crew belted the chorus:

"I'll go no more a-rovin' with you, fair maid
A-roving, A-roving, since roving's been my ru-i-in
I'll go no more a-roving with you, fair maid!"

Clara was friendly with most of the men on board, constantly searching for food with her ever-moving mouth. After escaping the near disaster at the river delta, the sailors considered her a good-luck charm. The Atlantic neared and the smoothness of their voyage, regardless of the rocky start, was praised.

But they had yet to face the Cape of Good Hope. Kang licked his fingers and touched the horseshoe. It felt best to talk of smoothness only after the hard part was over.

The Cape of Good Hope was called such because when ships finally made port there, it seemed celestial hands lifted them out of the darkest seas. The currents produced by the colliding Atlantic and Indian Oceans sank ships. Good Hope was restful after storms, hundred-foot waves, and uncontrollable oceans.

The sea rocked Douwe's cabin as they grew closer, and Zubin swayed in his hammock. Rain pelted the windows. A storm brewed.

"How long 'til it's over?"

"We are nearly there, Zubin. This is the hardest part," Douwe said. "The storm tonight may be frightening. But we'll make it through. Try to get some sleep."

The next day marked sixty days at sea. The coast of South Africa awaited them, as did the treacherous Cape. The crew was managing—but Zubin's restlessness grew. To a boy and a landlubber, sixty days was a lifetime. Douwe stroked Betsy's pregnant belly for luck and met the crew as the bell rang for the midnight shift. The sea was roiling, black, angry. The wind picked up Douwe's tricorne hat, which he caught as it lifted off his head. He braced himself and pushed toward Kang, directing the sail crew.

"How long 'til it blows over?"

"We're going to sail through it!" Kang yelled against the wind. "No visible cloud wall. We'll keep going!"

Douwe had sailed around the Cape many times. But the growing waves and violent sky were ill omens. In Clara's pen, Lionel stacked chicken coops on each other to be moved.

"Wave comes, they're all overboard!" he shouted to Douwe, thrusting the cages his way.

Douwe clambered below with the cages, where most men were awake from the storm. The chickens squawked. The men slid on their boots at the sight of the captain in their quarters.

Lionel ran with Bakari in his arms. The brown goat was not happy being carried, and Lionel handed her down the narrow ladder shaft to Douwe. He tied her to a pole that held a sailor's hammock and hauled himself back up the ladder.

Clara was too heavy to carry, and Lionel yelled for help. The ship tilted dramatically portside, and Douwe struggled to keep his feet under him. The *Knappenhof* was nearly keeled over. Waves crested over the rail.

Clara screamed.

Lightning flashed, illuminating the lucky horseshoe. Douwe ran on the slippery boards and slid into Clara's enclosure. Lionel could not get her to move. The whites of Clara's eyes showed. Her mouth was open, chest heaving as she made a guttural, primitive noise—pure fear. Douwe slid his hand under her belly and shouted through the spray for Lionel to do the same on the other side. They hauled Clara through the gate of the paddock. Lightning flashed again, outlining a figure near the door to Douwe's quarters. Over the rail of the *Knappenhof* was a rogue wave.

It towered, black, crest unseen, water casting a shadow from a solid wall of rippling water. Within moments, it would crash on the *Knappenhof*. Kang shouted. The crew responded, and the outlined figure sprinted from the door frame. It was Zubin, banana in hand. Clara, Douwe, Lionel, and Zubin collided. Water sprayed them as Zubin slid to Clara. She was on her side, leveled by the uneven deck and slick surface. Douwe grabbed her leather lead.

Clara slid fast, weighing more than all three sailors combined, but still they hauled. Zubin pushed her from the belly up. Screaming at each other, Lionel and Douwe hauled Clara to the door frame. Clara kicked wildly, eyes rolling, staring at the rogue wave.

Zubin shouted her name in the dark, thunder behind his voice. She turned to him and was suddenly on her feet. He scrambled to the door. Clara followed, pushed by Lionel and Douwe. The crew turned the *Knappenhof* against the wave. The four skidded as the wave crested with a sickening crunch, flinging the *Knappenhof* right side up. Douwe's cabin door slammed shut.

Chapter 19
Andrea
Leiden, The Netherlands

The workspace of the museum hummed with activity. Lucas, Andrea, and Paul shed their coats well before opening hour and, with steaming cups of hot coffee set far away from the artifacts, clustered around the artifact box from the rhino exhibit.

"I think it's mostly ephemera," said Lucas, studying the photos with a magnifying glass.

"Sorry, I'm not following," Andrea said. "Ephemera?"

He handed the glass to her, and she bent close. She could see a glistening coin-like medal, several documents, and one small sculpture. A large framed portrait of a rhino hung in the back of the exhibit.

"Like keeping ticket stubs," said Lucas. "They seem special because they hold a memory, but their face value is minimal."

"The broadsides, the medals, even the art?" she said. "All ephemera?"

"Not the art," said Paul. "The art tells a story of a different time. To art historians, this stuff is pure gold. The artists, the paint used, the techniques employed, the finished or unfinished product—it tells a story within a story."

Andrea handed the magnifying glass to Paul, who paused, squinting.

"Wait, I recognize this one," he said. "I think it's still in hanging storage. Hey Janice?"

Janice came over from her office. She grabbed the glass from him and nodded slowly.

"We have so many pieces like this one, I didn't recognize it," she said. "Come with me."

A row of hanging canvases and art in archival storage were dated from the 1740s. Framed broadsides were hung and labeled, and one had a near-identical image of Clara. Janice grabbed her laptop bag and powered on her MacBook.

"I haven't been back here to look at these properly in years. I would have recognized yours, Andrea, if I paid more attention to these. This one is from a wealthy couple who donated the broadside sheets in the 1960s," she said. "They bought them at a charity auction the decade before; before that, the provenance is unknown."

"Is there anything besides paper that remains? What else was on display?" Andrea asked. She couldn't stop thinking about what could have happened to the rest of the archive. It should have been kept safe here if it was a piece of campus history. She shuddered at the thought of Clara's remains somewhere in this building. She wasn't ready for that, even though Clara's past felt brighter, different, than those hunted animals that haunted her.

"Many things," said Janice. "I wish I could remember specifically what was on exhibit. I know a few other museums that specialize in porcelain sent some on loan. The packing process was tedious."

"Porcelain," Andrea said. "Wasn't porcelain made in China?"

"There was one factory in Europe that made fine porcelain then," said Janice. "Remarkable how they devised the formula. It was a huge trade secret for decades."

Lucas pointed to the background of the photo. Behind the smiling Janice was a glowing statue the size of a kitten.

"Janice, where else could the documents be?" Andrea said. "This one piece you have, this broadside. I can't help but notice it doesn't look like the ones I found."

"You're right," said Lucas. "That looks like Albrecht Dürer's rhino."

"Albrecht Dürer, born May 21, 1471, in Nuremberg," Andrea said. It was like her mouth worked without her asking it to. "Died April 6, 1528, one of the greatest artists of the Renaissance. His theories on art, proportion, and beauty are still studied today. He was a master."

Lucas and Andrea got closer to see. It was striking—a horned beast facing right, splayed toes firmly on the ground, armored plates, and sharpened horns. The animal's skin looked like the craters of the moon. Below it in Olde English printed font was a long paragraph in German.

"Yeah, you nailed it," said Lucas. "This says 1515. Five hundred years ago. This image changed the way animals were viewed in art forever. But the kicker is that it's completely wrong. Albrecht Dürer never saw a rhino."

Andrea relaxed. Lucas didn't say anything about her spouting out facts. He accepted her vast mind for what it was. His eyes creased at the corners when he smiled and spoke quickly. She'd never met someone who openly accepted her gift or anyone her age who engaged in historical conversation with such passion. It felt like her brain was getting a very warm hug.

"Dürer drew this from a description that someone else gave him," he said. "The man was an absolute master. His art was so realistic for the sixteenth century that even today, I look at his work and wonder if it's a photo or pencil."

"You're missing a crucial piece of this story," said Paul. "Do you know what happened to Dürer's rhino?"

Lucas nodded. "I do," he said. "Died in a shipwreck off the coast before it even reached Europe. But years later, another rhino arrived, right Paul?"

"Clara?" Andrea said, hopeful. Her stomach knotted again, thinking of the horror of a rhino in a shipwreck.

"No," said Paul. "Abada the rhino belonged to Portuguese kings, maybe sixty years after Dürer's rhino was immortalized in art. They routinely removed Abada's horn, and rumor is they purposefully blinded it to make it tamer."

"That's horrific," Andrea said. "I don't understand why people treat animals so cruelly."

"Most people back then didn't realize animals could actually feel things," said Janice.

"That's still the case today," Andrea said, sighing. "So many killed, for what?"

"Listen to that passion," Paul said. "Humane treatment is a modern phenomenon. People showed great wealth by owning exotic animals in historic times."

"People show great wealth today by hunting them for trophies," Andrea said. "I think I'd rather live back then."

"The problem with that, is that eighteenth-century animals weren't purposefully mistreated. It was a product of the times. Mistreating them by today's standards was unfortunately common," said Janice. She eyed Andrea cautiously. "René Descartes had this idea that animals were closer to machines in the early 1600s and performed experiments to prove his point. Unfortunately, the idea stuck around for too long. Animals today have much better care."

"That was Europe, though," said Paul. "In Greece, Japan, and India, people have long been vegans and advocated for the humane treatment of animals. Europe was late to the party."

"Where did Clara's owner stand in all of this? Who was he?" Andrea asked. If Clara's owner mistreated her, she didn't want to know any more of this story.

"There weren't any journals left behind to know," said Janice, shaking her head. "We can draw some conclusions based on evidence."

"That evidence is all in the exhibit notes," said Paul. "We can't do much without the research that was done. And if it's gone, it means someone might have misplaced it."

Lucas nodded his head in agreement. He was thinking deeply, bronze hand on his strong chin. His full lips were slightly parted. Andrea felt heat rise in her belly as she watched him.

"One conclusion," said Lucas. "Clara had a lot of art made from her throughout her life, which means she had to have been well cared for if she made it in front of all these artists. They depict her as a full-grown, healthy-looking animal. If she were thin or sick, they'd have painted her that way, as she was their only sight reference for a rhino model. We can look at this portrait and conclude that she was healthy in appearance, at least."

"Conclusion three," Andrea said. She felt buoyed by Lucas's remarks. "Someone took a baby animal away from its mother and homeland to cold Europe for entertainment. How can you safely take a rhino on a ship like that? How did anyone know what she was supposed to eat? Did she receive vet care? And what did they do in the winter?"

"There go the warm fuzzies," said Paul, a sad smile crossing his face. "But you're right, Andrea. Any animal displaced and taken away from its natural habitat forces us to question the motives of the people behind it. I'd like to think there were extenuating circumstances of her removal from Bengal."

"Me too," Andrea said. "But it's impossible to know, isn't it?" Her mind was swimming with emotions—sad, confused, betrayed. But those emotions belonged to her, not to Clara or Douwemout.

"Unless we turn up that exhibit archive or more primary documents," said Janice. "Which is possible with what we've found today."

"Imagine if a journal does exist somewhere," Andrea said, looking again at the single-framed broadside. "What kind of stories would we know about Clara and her life on the ship or at the University?"

"What would you memorize? We can only dream about that," said Lucas. "If her owner left a journal, a lot more art would be made from her. Movies, books, children's toys. She'd probably still be the most famous rhino ever."

"She's up there," Andrea said. "I can't personally think of another rhinoceros."

"Just Dürer's," said Lucas. "But that one was a figment of his imagination."

"Ah, PastPerfect dug up one item we should see," said Andrea. "Janice, do you know where this is?"

Andrea turned her computer screen to Janice, who read the listing and walked to the shelving units. She raised on tiptoe to grab a catalog box at the opposite end of the cavernous room. The others followed. She donned her white gloves and produced a tiny porcelain disk carefully wrapped in tissue.

"This is Charles Joseph," said Janice. "Maria Theresa's favorite son."

"Amazing," Andrea said, daring to breathe around it. "Look at the detail, look at his little mournful face. Maria Theresa was the Habsburg empress, one of the most influential women in history."

"Such bright blue eyes," said Lucas. "Look at the book he's holding."

Paul brought out the magnifying glass. In the book in his hands was a blurry but unmistakable rhino. The group lingered in silence around the miniature. The boy only lived to be sixteen. Sadness clouded Andrea again. It looked like he could laugh or cry, even painted on porcelain. His life was short, but moments like seeing Clara had to have brought him great joy. She was an animal worth celebrating. Andrea stored the face of Charles Joseph in her mind.

"How has something like this survived?" Andrea said, breaking the silence.

"How could it not have?" said Lucas. "It's alive, isn't it?"

Andrea looked at him, taking in his black shirt and raven hair. What a miraculous thing to say. He was right. This item felt alive.

"We should find that archive," said Paul. "We have too many unanswered questions, including why an entire exhibit report is missing."

"Yes," Andrea said. Spell broken.

"Janice, who can we report this to?" said Lucas. "It's pretty serious to disturb your archives."

Janice put the disc back in its wrappings.

"Unfortunately," she said, "I am the only full-time employee, and many volunteers, docents, and students come through. It's possible the archive was never fully completed, which means the student in charge of the exhibit shouldn't have passed that class. But we can look in a few other places to see if we can find it."

"None of my students would have passed without completing the archival part of the exhibit," said Paul. "We'll find it; it's likely misplaced, in another box."

"I hope so," Andrea said, imagining Clara trundling through an eighteenth-century village. "I'm beginning to think no one really knows what life was like for her."

Chapter 20
Douwemout van der Meer
Fort of Good Hope, South Africa

Douwe woke to the smell of rhino dung, pulse pounding in his temples. He was in the surgeon's cabin. He touched his head, fingers becoming sticky with blood. He was bandaged. His clothes were damp. Bright light streamed in the windows; the *Knappenhof* had made it through the wave.

He tried to stand, but the room spun. Silver sparks dusted his vision.

"Ho there, Captain," said Dr. Wilhelm. "Not too fast. You've got a bump on your head."

The wooden beams on the ceiling waved. Douwe closed his eyes.

"What happened? Where is Clara?"

"She's in here with you if you couldn't smell her." The surgeon forced Douwe's eyelids open and humphed. "All four of you survived the colliding oceans, as did the *Knappenhof*. Though not without injury."

Douwe faded.

He opened his eyes several hours later, and the ceiling was still. He wondered how long he'd been asleep and took deep breaths before attempting to sit up again. He touched the bandage, and his hand came back dry.

"Douwe!" Zubin's voice. Douwe smiled. The boy was at his side, Clara's leather lead in his hand.

"Zubin. How long have I been asleep?"

"Long enough to miss docking at the Fort of Good Hope, sir."

"We haven't docked. I always lead the ship into port."

"You haven't this time," Kang said. "Sorry, Captain, I did as our chain of command calls. The crew has left for mooring."

Douwe gently swung his legs around and stood. Clara was beside the bed, shaking her ears. Zubin had a purple black eye and a cut above his eyebrow.

"You're fine, Zubin?" Douwe said. He brought Zubin closer, running a hand over his hair.

"I'm alright." He waited for the examination to end.

"And Clara?" Douwe knelt beside her, rubbing and holding her face close to his. She flared her lip at him and huffed, sending spittle his way. He wiped his face and sighed.

"She's fine, too, but was not happy staying the night in here," said Zubin.

He motioned to a nest of bandages in the corner that made her makeshift bed. Zubin had slept beside her.

"Lionel?" said Douwe, looking at Kang.

"Lionel was injured as well," Kang said. Douwe furrowed his brow.

Lionel was not in any of the beds. He looked back to Kang, concerned.

"Lionel deceived us," said Kang. His eyes were on the floor. "Lionel's real name is Lonnie, captain."

"Lonnie?" said Douwe. His pulse quickened in his temples. His hands grew hot. "I am not following you, Kang."

Kang glanced at Douwe and looked away quickly, letting out a sharp breath.

"Lionel, Lonnie...is a woman."

A woman? Douwe's mind whirled, thinking of everything he had told Lionel, all he had trusted the sailor to do. How was this possible? The baggy clothing, soft features, beard-free face, thin wrists. He shook his head. Of course, Lionel was a woman. How could he have missed the signs? It was easy—he trusted her.

"Is he...she... alright?"

"Yes, but she's been court-martialed. She's awaiting trial in the Fort," said Kang.

"For what?"

"Lying, falsifying documents, deception," said Kang. "Punishable by death, captain."

He slid on his salt-crusted boots and took Clara's lead, ignoring the red-hot pulse that fired in his head. Zubin looked so happy, considering the many complications now presented to them.

"Why the smile, Zubin?"

"Betsy's kittens, sir," he said. "They've arrived."

"How many? Where are they?"

"Five," said Zubin. "She gave birth in your bed."

Douwe sighed and closed his eyes. Blessed Betsy.

"We must hurry, Zubin," Douwe said, ushering the boy out the door. "Trials are open and closed in minutes, and I'm afraid he...she... Lionel is in danger."

Quickly, Zubin, Clara, and Douwe made their way into the Fort. The ship was in her mooring position where she'd be for four weeks off the coast, sails pinned, rocking with the tide. Zubin and Clara wobbled on their sea legs. Douwe had experience with unsteady legs, but his raging headache made it more challenging. Clara's weaving was concerning. Zubin stopped, dizzy, and wretched by a palm tree.

The poor boy had not been seasick once, then set foot on land and lost his lunch. Clara flattened her ears against her head. She was much larger than when they left Calcutta. Her shoulder was now at a man's hip.

Zubin was weak and needed water, but they had to hurry through the Fort's lemon-yellow walls and gain entry to the jail where Lonnie was held. The Fort was star-shaped, like Fort William. Locals called it the Castle. It had a large bell tower at its entrance, and Zubin stopped momentarily to catch his breath in the shade.

Douwe and Clara stood and waited, passersby commenting in many languages terms of endearment toward her. Zubin was jealous of the attention and grabbed Clara's lead from Douwe, introducing her though still green-faced and dizzy. They found the yellow jail. Douwe told Zubin to stay put. He hoped that Lonnie had not yet faced her punishment.

The jail was stiflingly hot, a novelty that Douwe still marveled at. Late January was icy and cold in Europe. The jailer was not there, empty cells were easy to see, and the display of prisoners made an example to the public.

Douwe strode out of the jail and turned on his heel. Zubin and Clara bounded up beside him and followed him to the courthouse, where the governor presided over criminal cases. It, too, was yellow.

"Why is everything banana colored?" shouted Zubin as they ran.

The gates of the courthouse were open. Zubin and Clara followed, panting. The door to the courtroom slammed open, and Clara heaved herself onto the cool stone floor. The room became silent. Douwe removed his hat, forgetting his bloody, bandaged head. The ladies in the crowd gasped and fluttered their fans dramatically. Zubin, still dizzy, vomited on the floor.

The governor sat in his white robe and wig at the bench, looking dour. On the stand was Lonnie, dirty and forlorn, a sling tied close to her body. In the slant of her eyes, her slender body curved in the right places, the delicate bones of her wrists—it was evident she was a woman.

Douwe stepped toward the governor and bowed low, his bandage slipping. It landed on the floor with a gentle whisping sound, and Clara picked it up with her lip. Zubin, still delusional, snorted back a laugh. Douwe grabbed the rags from Clara's mouth and shoved them in his coat pocket, sweating profusely.

"Governor Swellengrebel," Douwe said. The judge stared open-mouthed at the trio. "I apologize for my appearance. I am Captain van der Meer of the *Knappenhof*. That is my sailor on your stand. I am here to make a statement."

"Captain van der Meer, your statement has already begun."

"This sailor has fulfilled the contents of their contract upon my vessel with flawless execution," Douwe said. He stepped toward the bench. Clara followed, leash trailing on the floor.

"I gave this sailor access to my personal privilege, which follows me now."

Clara sat like a dog by his side. "She cared for my animal and helped in the surgeon's quarters. I have no complaint against her. I ask you to release her."

Lonnie's face was white. She looked anything but fragile. Her eyes were locked on Douwe. Clara flicked her ears at Lonnie and let out a low moan.

"I appreciate your statement, Captain, but you have revealed the problem. You ask me to release *her*."

Douwe shook his head and began to speak, but Swellengrebel held up a hand.

"She falsified documents stating she was fit to serve in the VOC," said Swellengrebel. "This offense is punishable by death."

"Provided the captain agrees to the punishment," Douwe said quickly so he could finish. "Which I do not."

Lonnie looked to the judge, hands bound in black chains. Her small wrists were red.

"Then what do you propose we do with her?"

"You cannot expect me as captain to care for this animal alone, can you? Surely you see my position."

"I see something, Captain van der Meer, and I am certain a creature like that has never been in this courtroom before." The judge motioned to Clara.

"Nor anywhere else. It's crucial I bring this animal to Europe, with my sailor's help. This is one of God's most special creatures, your honor."

Clara flapped her ears and sighed. The judge pursed his lips and tugged at the neck of his robe, looking from Lonnie to Douwe and back again.

Twenty minutes later, Douwe, Zubin, Lonnie, and Clara sat under a coconut palm, scraping white meat with their teeth and pouring coconut water into Clara's mouth. Lonnie got off with a heavy fine, paid with coins and a ruby withdrawn from the seams of her baggy pants. She was banned from the VOC.

"Thank you again," said Lonnie. "I can't ever repay you."

"You can tell me why you did it," said Douwe. He sucked coconut flesh from his thumb.

"I wanted to see the world," Lonnie said. "Make my own way, have an adventure. Not be judged by my sex or married off to make babies and live my life for some man. I don't always love being a woman."

Douwe raised his eyebrows.

"So instead, you signed an illegal contract with the largest man-ridden organization in the world? I am surprised you did not get caught sooner."

"I was careful," she said. "You did not suspect a thing. You would have protected me if you had been awake when Kang found me. Instead, he threw me off the boat."

"I would have protected you?"

"Of course. Right?"

"I believe I would have," Douwe said. He fed coconut meat to Clara. "As soon as I heard from Kang, I raced to fix this."

"I'm grateful," Lonnie said. "I wonder how I'll get back to Amsterdam."

"We hire you to care for Clara," Zubin said. "Under the captain's personal employ, right Douwe?"

"It's not that simple, Zubin," said Douwe. "Women on board are bad luck. The men would never allow it. It's too dangerous for her."

"How many know I was outed?"

"The whole courtroom," said Zubin.

"None of our crew was in that courtroom," said Douwe. "They're in Cape Town. Kang and Wilhelm are the only ones who know. Did any see you taken off ship?"

"They saw me in men's clothes. They don't know why I was court-martialed."

Keeping Lonnie to care for Clara was smart. He did not want to risk another Snell situation. Her sex could be the best-kept secret on the *Knappenhof*, but he had to convince Dr. Wilhelm and Kang.

"Let me see what I can do," he said.

A few hours later, Douwe and Zubin were settled into a first-floor room at an inn in Cape Town. The innkeeper was more than happy to rent the space to them with the promise of ten percent of Clara's earnings. Granted, the crew members in Cape Town would not pay a penny to see their shipmate, but the other twenty VOC ships in the fleet had only caught glimpses of Clara from their decks. The coin started flowing right away.

Clara was happy with crates of fresh fruit and vegetable scraps from the inn. She'd lived on hay alone on the *Knappenhof* for the past week. Based on what Snell had stolen, her supply should have run out much sooner. It was uncertain who contributed to Clara's diet with their own ration of beans and mushy peas, but Douwe and Zubin both noticed.

Douwe loaded the ship for the last leg of the voyage and planned his conversation with Kang. Kang could be found in a small tavern at the edge of the compound, avoiding the rest of the crew. The pub was near farms that bordered the city.

"What's become of Lionel?"

Douwe was not surprised Kang brought it up immediately. Kang strictly abided by the code of the *Knappenhof* and the VOC, and violation required discussion. "Lionel is Lonnie, as you said."

"Still is? I thought the punishment would be carried out by now."

"Lonnie is still alive and paid a heavy fine. I would like to continue their employment as Lionel, to care for my privilege under my personal protection."

Kang rubbed his forehead. "It is bad luck to have a woman on board. The crew will know. I cannot protect her, and neither can you."

"Lonnie protected herself and kept her secret for four years with the VOC. You, Zubin, Dr. Wilhelm—we're the only ones who know," said Douwe. "When we get to Europe, you'll never see her again. I will pay her with my own coin. You'll keep her secret. I'll use her to care for my animal. She serves a purpose."

Kang was silent.

"I do not give you many orders, Kang, but this I demand of you." Douwe's mind flickered to the VOC charter he was commanded to obey. The VOC only employed men. Clara did not belong to the VOC, and by asking an illegal sailor like Lonnie to stay to care for her went against his role as Captain. He was asking Kang to violate the law that governed them on the sea and risk his career.

"Very well, Captain," said Kang. "If she is found out, see my hands are not dirtied."

"We shall not speak of it," said Douwe. "Your reputation will not change in the eyes of the VOC." But Douwe could not guarantee this, and he dropped his voice low to hide the quiver in his words.

The month spent in Cape Town was a fever dream. Clara and Zubin ran the beaches and picked fruit from the trees. Clara rolled in the sand, covering her rough body. She played in the waves, splashing about and trotting back and forth with Douwe, who rolled up his breeches and stripped his shirt.

Clara wallowed, her stubby legs in the air, flipped on her back, and Zubin did the same, mocking her. They played like the children they were. Lonnie and Kang joined them on the beach, and while Zubin's bare skin shone in the sun, Lonnie stayed in her baggy clothes, cutting strips of coconut to dry. Kang did not say a word to Lonnie. Douwe imagined how Lonnie's shirt might cling to her slender frame if she dove in the waves with him.

"I like it here," said Lonnie. Douwe shaded the sun with his hand.

"I do, too. Not like Europe."

"No, it's not. Though my part of Europe might be a little nicer than yours."

"Is that so? Not much beats spring in Holland."

"The coast of France does. My family is still in Biarritz, minus my father. His whaling ship did not come back when I was eleven."

"Is that why you left? Sought the VOC?"

"Partly," Lonnie said, gazing out to sea. "And partly because the time to make my own happiness is short. Maybe someday I'll take you to Biarritz, and you can bathe in the sea there. You won't want to leave."

"If you wanted to leave, I imagine I would too."

Lonnie turned to Douwe. Freckles blossomed over her upturned nose which crinkled when she laughed. Her blue eyes were bright, intelligent. She was hauntingly beautiful, with close-cropped hair and sailor's hands. They returned to the beach day after day until the month was up.

Douwe replenished supplies and negotiated terms with the farmers and merchants. More treasures filled his chest, and Clara got a larger collar from the tanner. He wondered how much longer she would need it. She had begun to follow Zubin when he called her name.

After their month-long furlough, the bell of the *Knappenhof* rang, and the crew assembled. The ship was restocked. Clara's food was stacked in the corner of Douwe and Zubin's cabin instead of in the hold. Betsy's kittens opened their eyes, safe in Douwe's cabin for their first month living. Four kittens were as black as Betsy; one was steel gray, a perfect match to Clara's cobbled skin. Zubin gathered the kittens on his lap, seeming content in the captain's quarters.

Douwe pressed his nose into Zubin's hair, happy to see him enjoying the kittens. He absorbed his warm-salt boy smell and sat at his captain's desk. The bell rang again, and Kang commanded the crew. Douwe tended to the ledgers. *February 27, 1741, the* Knappenhof *departs from the Cape of Good Hope.*

Lionel resumed his regular duties with Clara's fish oil the next day. Douwe told Zubin about Lonnie's wishes—"call him Lionel, use male pronouns." Zubin understood. Douwe had not spoken to Dr. Wilhelm. He waited as Wilhelm stitched a sailor's fleshy thumb in the surgeon's quarters.

"Captain," Wilhelm said without looking up. His half-moon glasses slid down his nose. The surgeon finished and wiped his tools, back turned. The sailor left.

"Dr. Wilhelm, I need to speak with you about Lionel and why he was court-martialed."

His glasses fit perfectly into a wrinkled crease on his nose. "What kind of surgeon do you make of me that I should not know?"

"A good one," said Douwe. "We have not lost a sailor to injury."

"Indeed," said Wilhelm. "If you think I did not know of Lionel's predisposition before Kang found him out, you have forgotten who I am."

"And your plan?"

"To keep Lionel as the helpful sailor he is and introduce myself to Lonnie in Amsterdam."

A beat passed in silence.

"I am in your debt, Dr. Wilhelm." Douwe tipped his tricorne.

"You're a good captain, Van der Meer," Wilhelm said. "The decisions you make and the secrets you keep impact us all."

Douwe stiffened. Bringing Clara on board did not feel selfish in the moment. But now that he risked Zubin and Lonnie's safety, and the livelihoods of Wilhelm and Kang, a small black ball of worry grew in his gut.

The following week took a dramatic turn. Sailors caught a wracking cough in Cape Town, and fever swept the crew's quarters. A dozen times, bodies were taken from the sailmaker's workshop wrapped in cloth. Douwe whispered a silent prayer for each one, and Dr. Wilhelm crossed himself as the black ocean swallowed them. In the ledger were each crew member's names and death dates who found everlasting rest beneath the waves. The crew grew restless and anxious, though Douwe did his best to maintain decorum.

On a no-moon night, after the midnight bell signaled the shift change, there was shouting outside the captain's cabin—Kang and Snell. The door burst open, and Kang threw Snell into Douwe's room by his shirt collar. He hit the floor near Zubin's hammock. Zubin sat up. Douwe was on his feet.

"It's Lonnie," said Kang. He breathed heavily, pointing at Snell. "She's been found out."

"Where is Lionel?" Douwe said.

"Surgeon's cabin," said Kang. Snell whimpered in pain. Douwe commanded Kang to keep him there. Zubin rolled from his hammock and exited. The kittens darted to hidden corners.

In the growing distance between the rooms, Snell's muffled cries echoed as blow after blow hit his body. Douwe was relieved that Zubin left. At any sign of danger, he tended to head straight to Clara. Douwe opened the door cautiously to the surgeon's quarters, only to have it slammed shut.

"Who goes there?" came Dr. Wilhelm's panicked voice.

"Your captain," Douwe breathed through the crack.

The door opened and closed abruptly after he entered. The lantern-lit room glowed gold, the black sea shining through the windows. Lonnie was on the table on her side, back covered in red welts. Douwe reached out, but Dr. Wilhelm grabbed his wrist, stopping him. The surgeon shook his head.

"Do not touch her now," said Wilhelm. "Let her be."

"What happened?" said Douwe. He could hear little but the beating of his heart.

"She crawled here," Wilhelm said. "I found her in front of the door. Snell attacked her after she fed Clara her last bottle. He saw when she was rewrapping her bandage from the rogue wave accident."

"And he...?" Douwe could hardly breathe.

"She fought." Wilhelm's half-moon glasses reflected the golden light.

Lonnie lay shivering on the surgeon's table. The welts were darkening. Her slender neck transitioned gracefully into her shaved head. The freckles on her shoulders gained from days in the South African sun were blurred by a hand-shaped mark. Douwe wanted nothing more than to hold her, but instead, he stood. Had he not insisted, had he honored the charter and rules of the *Knappenhof*, she would not be here. The black ball of guilt in his gut fizzled.

Hands balled into fists, he strode across the deck. Clara watched, chin resting on the wooden beam of her pen. Zubin crouched beside her, fingers curled around the rung below. From the Captain's quarters came Kang's deep voice and muffled words from Snell.

Douwe flung the door open as Kang landed another blow, seized with fury.

"I told you it was a bad idea to keep her on board," spat Kang. "Now what?"

"The sailor has committed two crimes under my command. According to the VOC charter and the code of the *Knappenhof*, he shall receive the highest level of punishment."

"You'll hang him, then?"

Douwe felt fear creep up his back. If Snell was executed publicly, Douwe had to reveal his crime. To reveal his crime revealed Lonnie to the rest of the crew. Mutiny would follow.

Mutiny meant Clara could be thrown overboard. Zubin and Douwe, perhaps even Kang, would be set adrift to perish at sea. He could not prevent the sailor from revealing Lonnie's secret. He could not keep the sailor from harming her again. He could not keep himself or those he cared for safe.

Snell lay prone and coughed a bright spray of blood onto the wide-planked floor. Kang stood back, ready for command. Douwe turned to the narrow closet that held his privilege. Inside, the jeweled dagger waited.

Douwe stepped between Snell and Kang. He held the dagger in his right hand and knelt beside Snell. Kang backed away.

Snell looked up at Douwe.

"Please," he said, holding his hands in front of his bloody face. Was his smashed nose from Kang or Lonnie? Douwe hoped the blow that broke it came from Lonnie's fist.

"You cannot be trusted," Douwe said.

"Neither can you, *Captain*."

Douwe clenched his jaw and set his mouth askew. With a swift, sure motion, he grabbed Snell by the hair. The jeweled dagger cut into his thick neck. Kang rushed forward, but it was too late.

Snell screamed, gurgling. Blood pooled. Douwe took a step back, adrenaline and fever-hot anger coursing through him. He wiped the dagger clean on the crimson sash around his waist. Hands trembling, breath steady. The green and red jewels gleamed as he replaced the blade in his closet, locking it with a click. His mind was on Lonnie, and the secret that nearly undid everything, now hidden again.

"Douwe—" Kang started.

"Don't," said Douwe. "Say nothing, Kang. I cannot command you to help me, but I ask you anyway." Douwe's breath quivered through his nose.

Kang let his arms fall to his sides and blew out his cheeks.

"After this, I keep no more of your secrets, Captain."

Douwe's body shook. He signaled to Kang to grab Snell's arms, and the two turned him over. His lifeless face was locked in a frown. The cut on his neck carved a second mouth. Kang grabbed Snell's legs. The two descended with the body to the sailmaker's workshop. Blood stained the deck of the *Knappenhof*.

Kang said nothing as he sewed thick stitches into the sail that covered Snell's corpse. Douwe leaned against the table, considering all that could have happened that did not. He considered the risks he took by keeping secrets. The shrouded body hit sharp waves and sank as pink dawn greeted the remaining crew.

Douwe marked in his logbook that they were as far west as they would go: *I expect we shall never see the coast of South America, but we are as close as we would ever get today, April 30, 1741.* He made no remark about the death of Peregrine Snell.

Chapter 21
Andrea
Leiden, The Netherlands

It was past dark when they stopped for the day. Andrea was still jet-lagged and absolutely starving. The cafeteria was closed, but Janice gave her a cup of ramen from the office. Andrea heated it up in the shared kitchen in the dorm and thought about the grave while it was cooling. She was glad for the distraction, especially while alone. She was used to being with Jake every night and was grateful now for something else to occupy her time.

The documents were definitely tied to the grave, but how? The rhino emblem might have been a popular symbol. It was clear Clara was famous if there were posters and art about her. It could be a coincidence, something the gravestone carver had done a hundred times. Why was the archival box empty? It felt like a shroud had been pulled over her, and she desperately wanted to remove it.

Andrea turned on her phone to pull up the document picture again—the notifications gave her a gut punch. Text messages from Jake.

"Hey" 11:30 a.m.

"We need to talk" 2:40 p.m.

"My family was embarrassed by what you did" 3:15 p.m.

"There's no excuse for your behavior. My father legally paid for every animal in that room" 4:10 p.m.

"It's not doing you any good to ignore me, Andrea. You freaked out for no reason, but you'll come around. Let me know when you get over your holier than thou attitude and see common sense. No one cares about you like me." 6:22 p.m.

All she heard was the booming of blood in her ears. Being busy with this project kept her mind off of Jake, but she had to face the past.

Andrea could not believe her sweet Jake, who held doors open and gave her roses on actual dates, was responsible for the demise of rare beasts, now dead on his parents' walls. He made Andrea think she was special by asking about her past and future, laughing with glee while she spouted out her precise knowledge of historical figures. All his talk about caring for her was hiding a dark, dark piece of his history.

No, not his past. His present. His real life was a family who paid to kill big game and lived on a former plantation. How could she have been so naive?

Andrea's phone rang, snapping away the memory.

"Hi, Ma."

"How's Holland, sweetie?"

"It's... It's great, Mom." She smiled and looked up, taking a deep breath to shed the flashback. "This project feels important, and I feel like we're about to uncover something big. Mom, I found these documents in a hidden drawer in the desk in my room. The museum thinks they might be important, and we got to explore the archives."

"Well, breathe, girl! I haven't heard you talk like this in a while." Her mother laughed; a clear-bell sound that often filled Andrea's good dreams.

"I wasn't ready for happiness, Mom, not while I was still dealing with Jake."

"I know. You've been through a lot, but you made a good decision. You're on the right path."

"I can't help but wonder, though, Mom... Would someone else have looked the other way? Said yes to marrying him despite it all?"

"It doesn't matter what someone else would have done. You did what was true to yourself. You could not have been part of anything like that, and you know it."

"But—"

"No buts. The wealth? The big last name? Worth nothing. Baby girl, I raised you better."

"You raised me in poverty, Mom."

Andrea exhaled deeply. She didn't mean to make her mom feel bad, but she fell hard for Jake because she could tell he'd never gone to bed hungry.

"I did raise you in poverty. And look at you now. You're headstrong and resilient, and you know right from wrong. Money can't buy those things, Andrea. Money can buy you comfort and less worry but can't guarantee happiness. You just discovered that, didn't you? What do you want—a ring on your finger and a life like Jake's or a semester in Holland and a historian's paycheck?"

Andrea paused and drummed her fingers on the desk.

"I'd rather have you and this semester. If I'm lucky to be hired anywhere, that historian's paycheck would be nice, too."

"Tell me about your documents," she said.

The grave, the documents, the hidden drawers. It was a joy to tell. She told her about Clara and Douwemout, Janice and Paul, who Andrea suspected were secretly in love. She told her about Sergei and the missing archive. And she hesitated but told her about Lucas.

"Oooh, he sounds lovely, Andrea!"

"He loves history, and he's so smart."

She squealed.

"Calm down, Mom. You know I'm not ready for anything dealing with love."

"You're finding love in the work and in yourself."

Andrea paused. She wasn't ready to admit to loving herself. Truthfully, Andrea felt anxious. She couldn't help but think she was in danger every moment, even half a world away from Jake.

"You feel safe there?"

She avoided answering. "I know you were scared about me coming alone."

"You're a pretty, young woman thousands of miles from home, but I trust you, and you're smart."

"No one's messed with me, Mom," she said. "I'm fine."

"I love you, museum baby."

The ramen was ready, so Andrea said her goodbyes and hung up, feeling cared for.

She wished the feeling would have carried into her dreams, but she had nightmares. She dreamed she was on a big painted ship on a black sea and woke up when a giant wave swept the deck and took her overboard.

Chapter 22
Douwemout van der Meer
The Atlantic Ocean & The Netherlands

Lionel slept in a corner in the surgeon's quarters. The bruises turned purple, then green and yellow. Zubin provided Douwe with updates. Douwe could not bring himself to visit her, knowing that forcing himself to see the sailor Lionel would not work. He had killed for Lonnie, he told himself.

Lionel returned to his duties shakily, mostly helping Zubin care for Clara. His demeanor changed. The sailor was jumpy and tinged with sadness but smiled still with Zubin and Clara.

Each morning, Zubin and Clara played fetch with a leather ball made in Cape Town. Clara pushed it across the rolling deck with her nose, using the spot where her horn would grow. She trotted and chased the chickens, played with the kittens, and grew accustomed to ale pails.

Her true vice was Kang's pipe: she cried out to him when he passed, hoping for a puff of tobacco smoke to be blown in her face. He did not oblige as much as she would have liked. The black tufts of fur on her ears and tail lightened to chocolate brown. Lionel ran a curry comb through them to keep them free of debris. The sailors greeted Clara by name and walked her on the deck while Lionel taught Zubin to read and write.

By mid-July, Douwe felt satisfied when the *Knappenhof* entered the English Channel, and he could see Europe on both sides of the ship. With help from the calls from the navigators, Douwe steered the ship into port at Rotterdam on July 20, 1741, wearing a green velvet coat and salt-stained boots.

Douwe visited the underbelly of his ship one last time. Soon, it would be filled with the same trade goods and the same rolling sea underneath, but the captain and crew would be different. Most of his life was spent at sea, the *Knappenhof* his only true home. He closed his eyes, breathing tar, stinking sailor, and the faintest whiff of cinnamon and clove. His last voyage was over.

From above decks came Zubin's laughter and Clara's whistling noise. Douwe licked his fingers and tapped the horseshoe one last time before ascending into the bright summer sun.

"Douwe," said Zubin. "Are we ready?" Clara and Bakari were both on leads. The two animals were unhappy with stillness.

"Yes, Zubin, we are," said Douwe. Their chests were loaded into a large carriage for transport to Leiden, where he would arrange a place to stay. Betsy and her five kittens were in one of Clara's fruit crates. Bakari was tied to the back, and Zubin walked alongside leading Clara, now on the eve of her first birthday.

"Wait!" Douwe turned, halting the carriage. It was Lonnie's voice. "Wait!"

The crew had unloaded the ship the day before, and Douwe and Zubin were the last to leave. Douwe did not know where Lonnie had gone. He tried desperately to treat Lionel as the sailor he knew, but Lonnie the woman was impossible to ignore, despite the disguise. He could not meet the gaze of the sailor whose secrets he guarded. He did not tell her goodbye.

Zubin crossed the busy street trailing a trotting Clara, who ran to Lonnie. A horse reared, tossing its rider. Clara startled and bolted, jolting the lead from Zubin's hand. She ran. Douwe leaped from the carriage box, but Lonnie was ahead of him. Clara wove in and out of traffic, lead dragging behind her. Lonnie grabbed the lead, running beside Clara. She touched her shoulder to slow her down, and Clara tossed her head, startled again. Carriages and draft horses skittered out of the way, causing chaos on the cobbled street. People cried out at the sight of a nearly grown rhino running between the carts.

Lonnie kept a grip on the lead and slowed Clara to a walk. She pulled her to a side street, where Zubin and Douwe caught up, breathless. Zubin was wobbly on his sea legs and vomited on the corner of a building as he had done in Cape Town. Passersby stared—a rhino, a woman with close-cropped hair, and a vomiting Indian boy made quite a scene.

The city was startling to Clara, used to the sea and sailors and sounds of an East Indiaman. Douwe and his odd assembly took a moment to gather themselves as Clara calmed. Zubin sat leaning on a brown-brick wall, steadying himself before standing to a spinning world.

"Lonnie, I..." Douwe began, not sure of what to say. "I'm sorry for what you endured, sailor."

"I endured nothing, Captain. I fought it."

Douwe nodded. "I am not a captain anymore."

"And I am not a sailor anymore," she said, indicating her brown dress and cream-colored apron. Her waist was cinched in, a low-cut neckline revealed a slight curve of bust.

"I am still Zubin!" shouted Zubin from the ground.

Douwe snorted, and Lonnie fought a smile. He faced her, truly looking at Lonnie and not Lionel for the first time. She darted her eyes away and he felt his gut churn. Would she ask him why he killed Snell? He had rehearsed uncountable answers.

Her nostrils flared lightly. Her chest expanded. She looked him in the eye. There was a specific pain there—one of curious sadness, an infinite number of questions. But instead of asking him anything, she turned to Clara.

Clara pulled on the lead, ears raised, listening to the whinny of nearby horses. Lonnie shushed her and spoke gentle words in her ears.

"Lonnie, come with us to Leiden," Douwe said. He did not want her out of his sight.

"What will I find there?" Lonnie said. Her pale lashes draped downward. "A European town with nothing for a woman to do but marry and grow old."

"Clara," Douwe said. "We have plans for Clara, and you know her so well. You can be Lionel or Lonnie. It makes no difference to me."

"For now, I'm Lonnie," she said. "I've no place to go."

Clara snuffled in Lonnie's hand, and Lonnie sighed, agreeing to join them.

A few hours later, Bakari, Clara, shaven-head Lonnie, five kittens, Betsy, seasick Zubin, and Douwe had made it a measly five miles. Leiden was twenty away, and they already had to find beds for the night. The inn fussed about Clara startling the horses and forced Douwe to buy out the entire stable. Douwe and Zubin stayed the night in the stalls. Lonnie slept in the carriage with the cats. Clara ate her way through hay meant for three horses, and Douwe paid out loads of coin before they even made it to Leiden.

The next day, they left early and arrived before nightfall with a dramatically exhausted Clara. Leiden felt like home to Douwe, with its brick buildings with red-orange roofs illuminated by the setting sun. The University's church spire was visible in the distance. They crossed under the Zijlpoort, the city gate.

The gate's spire touched a fresh summer moon in the still-blue sky. Zubin led Clara across a red-brick bridge where her feet padded softly on the cobbles. Douwe had passed through the gate a hundred times. But this was absolutely the first time an Indian rhino had done so. He memorized the scene.

A driver led their carriage to the University, where Douwe would meet with the anatomy department. Known for corpse dissections, the anatomists had changed medical care with precise illustrations and diagrams of the human body. It was impossible to unsee the opened bodies drawn in the books displayed in the windows of the shops. Doctors owed many advances in medical knowledge to Leiden.

Ahead lay the Burcht, a ruined round castle, close to five centuries old. Clara had some freedom to roam there while Douwe made a plea at the University. The gate to the castle was a sandstone archway, above which a carved lion held a sword aloft. Zubin and Clara both stared at it as they passed underneath. Douwe and Lonnie followed.

A set of steep stairs on a grassy hill led to the castle walls. Zubin pulled while Lonnie and Douwe pushed, but Clara would not climb the narrow stairs. Instead, she pulled loose from her lead and grazed on the hill in dimming daylight. Enormous chunks of grass were ripped by the root.

"Head on," said Lonnie. "Zubin and I can take care of her."

Soon, a crowd gathered. Clara lifted her head to greet the newcomers, searching for food in their hands. Lonnie slipped her collar back on and stood alongside her. Passersby stared at Lonnie's bare head and Zubin's brown skin, but they stopped when they locked eyes with Clara.

Douwe slithered through the crowd and hurried to the University, a good ten-minute walk. The black stone floors of the church shone, flat-fronted buildings singing songs of his past. He was home, certainly, but the place had changed. He hurried through the cavernous church to the anatomy theater.

The straight sidewalks of the university common were checkered with palms and herbs. There, the Hortus Botanicus garden drew hundreds of visitors. Scientists studied plants and herbal remedies for medicine. Alongside the anatomy theater, no place in Europe had changed medical care more than Leiden.

It was a curious place, set up in the round with a large table in the center. Surrounding the many benches were cabinets full of specimens, several large animal skeletons looming. A fully articulated horse was in the room's far corner, nothing left but bones. It had a crimson halter dripping with gold tassels. On its back, a human skeleton wore a plumed helmet that must have been three hundred years old. A pitted sword hung on its side, gleaming in the golden light of the setting sun.

Mounted deer and cabinets full of skeletons and specimens lined the walls. Taxidermy and bones towered. Douwe compared the place to the market stall where the horn of Clara's mother haunted him. Perhaps it is different here, he thought. They were supposed to study, not sell, these animals.

A slight cough echoed from a man in a white wig arranging a display. In front of him was a shining human skull, brown from age, and several vertebrae.

"Excuse me," said Douwe. Even though he whispered, his voice felt too loud.

"Mmm?" said the man, not taking his eyes off the skull.

"I'm seeking someone to speak with about a rare species."

"Rare species, you say?" said the man, still focused on his work. "What is its scientific name?"

"It does not have a scientific name yet. It is a rhinoceros from India."

"A rhinoceros?"

"Yes, in Leiden."

"In Leiden?" The man shoved a bone deep into the pocket of his black robe.

"I left her grazing at the old castle hill," said Douwe.

"Her? Grazing? Is it alive?"

"Her name is Clara," said Douwe. The man's erratic energy was startling

"Clara! I must see her," said the man, flourishing a notebook pulled from another pocket of his billowing robe. "What is your name?"

"Douwemout van der Meer, former captain of the VOC," said Douwe, bowing. "I have just returned from Bengal."

"Bengal indeed! I am Bernhard Albinus, Professor of the Practice of Medicine."

"The anatomist? Your books, Professor, they're everywhere."

"One and the same," Bernhard replied. "Though I do not draw the illustrations for publication. I arrange the specimens, and my friend Jan Wandelaar draws them. We have never drawn a rhino."

He paused, his fingers scratching his remnant of a beard.

"I am not sure of the last specimen drawing of a rhino since Dürer's in 1515... Show me your animal, Captain."

"Call me Douwe," Douwe said, offering his hand. Bernhard shook it wildly, leaving charcoal smudges on Douwe's wrist. "I'm in a bit of a predicament, professor."

As they walked quickly back through the linear gardens and echoing church where the black slate floors gleamed like the sea, Douwe told him that they needed a place to stay.

He explained Clara's mother's demise, the macabre booth at the market, and the horn. Bernhard asked how long the horn was—a foot, said

Douwe, who felt nervous speaking of it. He did not want Clara's worth to be deemed by her parts. Bernhard brought out his notebook. The Professor wrote down what she ate, how old she was, and that she had no horn, a point Douwe made several times. He described the color of the folds between her plates, the liquid-leather look of her skin, and her sunburn on the *Knappenhof.*

"And her dorsal horn? Has it appeared yet?"

"Dorsal horn? She does not have a dorsal horn."

"Dürer's rhino had a dorsal horn," said Bernhard. "Surely your rhino does, too."

"I'm not sure. Perhaps Dürer's rhino was a male?"

"Possible, possible..." Bernhard muttered.

As they neared the castle, the hill and stairs were full of people. Children pulled on their mother's arms to look closer at Clara, who still grazed. Lonnie's soft, fuzzy head bobbed near Clara's shoulder. Zubin cupped his hands around his mouth.

"Clara the Rhino!" he cried. "Apples, fruit, bread, and beer! A copper for us to give her your food! Two to feed her yourself!"

The crowd pressed forward, coins shining in their hands. Heels of bread and apples waited for Clara. Zubin grabbed the patrons' money and wrists, thrusting those with two coppers in front of Clara. She sucked dark bread from their hands and crunched apples. Children squealed, and she snorted at them, resuming her grazing once more. Lonnie kept the crowd at a distance.

It was by far the largest crowd Douwe had ever seen gathered around Clara. He glanced at Bernhard, who was staring open-mouthed. Douwe took the Professor by the shoulders and navigated the throng of people, who parted at the black robes of the University titan.

Bernhard approached Clara slowly as one would an unbroken pony, with both hands in front of him and steady steps. She did not flinch and continued to chew whatever the last patron had tossed to Zubin. Her ears flicked forward, the fur on them now an inch long, and she blinked at Bernhard. He bent low to make eye contact with her, five feet away, whispering to Zubin if she was dangerous.

"Sometimes," said Zubin, thinking of Sybilla Sichterman's dinner party. "And sometimes she is gentle as a lamb."

Clara whistled on cue, sending a ripple of laughter through the crowd. She needed a stable soon. The streetlamps were lit, and Clara's eyesight was poor in the dark. Douwe stood in front of Clara and thanked everyone. With his eyes on Bernhard, he told them to spread the word that the University was hosting Clara for the foreseeable future and public gatherings would be scheduled. The crowd slowly dispersed, a few hangers-on lingering.

Lonnie swept her hand over her shaved head and lowered her eyes as she met the Professor. She was clearly uncomfortable, and Douwe did not know if she would be better off with a bonnet or back in men's clothing. Professor Albinus paid Lonnie little mind. He was focused on Clara.

"May I?" he asked, holding his hand out to take her leather lead.

Lonnie stood at Clara's shoulder while Bernhard looked her over. He ran a hand down her neck. Clara flinched as if ridding herself of a fly. He removed his hand and backed away a few steps. Bernhard watched her heaving sides and flared nostrils. He curved around the back of her to see her flicking tail; she bent to rub her head on her leg, and he startled. The Professor and the rhinoceros regarded each other.

Douwe took the lead and raised his hand, motioning for Bernhard to stay. He walked Clara down the hill to show how her skin shifted over her bones, muscles rippling like curtains. She descended, hit the bottom of the hill, and trotted a few steps onto the road. Her rounded feet squished as she moved. Zubin went ahead, coaxing her with a heel of bread.

A flickering candle-lit lantern was above them, the moon the same cream blue from that fateful night in the garden of Clara and Douwe's first meeting. Bernhard's eyes shone, on his face a broad smile, a look of complete and utter wonder.

Hours later, Clara was stabled in a horse stall near the University. Bakari was curled up beside her, and Douwe locked the half-door with an iron padlock.

Bernhard arranged an empty campus apartment for Zubin and Douwe, and a kitchen room for Lonnie, who looked off-put. The fourth-floor apartment held only a new, sizeable, ornate writing desk with hinges and carved lion's feet. Zubin was fast asleep on a cot within minutes, but before he closed his eyes, he asked if the room would constantly be spinning. Such little time had passed since disembarking the *Knappenhof*. Douwe collapsed onto the small feather bed and dreamed of Clara, black stone floors, and human skulls.

Chapter 23
Andrea
Leiden, The Netherlands

In the morning, Andrea was eager to get going and rubbed the scratched surface of the desk before she closed the door. The remnants of her nightmare lingered. She craved coffee and, surprisingly, conversation to rid herself of the feeling of cold waves pulling her downward.

She stopped by the student center for a black coffee and turned the corner. Lucas was waiting for her, wearing the same black pea coat.

"This is a much more pleasant way to run into you."

"No kidding," he said. "My shoulder has a knot in it from you."

"Sorry. Didn't realize I could pack such a punch. Heading to the cemetery?"

"Yes," said Lucas, gesturing. He had on fingerless gloves and black slim-cut jeans. His raven hair shone in the morning light, contrasting with the white fog that left his mouth when he spoke. He waited for her, and he didn't have to.

They walked together, and he pointed out the historic buildings on campus. Andrea stopped to pet a black cat with amber eyes near a massive greenhouse.

"Do you know what this is?" he asked.

"A greenhouse?" The cat wove between her legs.

"One of the oldest in Europe," Lucas said. "The Hortus Botanicus opened in 1590."

"Can we go in?" She brightened. It was teal-glassed, glowing.

"Of course. They've been bringing plants from around the world for hundreds of years. I'll give you a tour. I come here all the time."

The place was warm. They shed their coats at the front. Lucas wore a European death metal band tee. She felt comfortable with him, eager to talk about history and plants. Andrea had never felt a brain-match like this but was cautious. She was skeptical and worried he harbored deep, dark secrets. She wondered if she'd ever lose that feeling. They walked the paths of the Hortus Botanicus, and he translated the Dutch signs.

"This one says that this fern was brought here in the mid-1700s from a VOC journey."

"This fern?" Andrea said, pointing at the massive plant. "This fern is three hundred years old?"

"Give or take. Pretty wild."

"Think about all the things this plant has lived through," she said, picking up one of its fallen leaves. "Revolutions, wars, kingdoms come and gone."

"There are beautiful things in history, too," Lucas said. "Think of all the art it has lived through—Rembrandt, the Rococo period, Monet, Picasso."

"I didn't take you for a romantic," she said, handing him the leaf. He put it in his pocket.

"I can surprise people," he said. He opened the door to the next exhibit, full of cacti.

Lucas read the signs to her. His accent was mesmerizing, and she was unwittingly staring at him instead of the cacti.

"What is it?" he said. "Do I have something in my teeth?"

"No," she said. "I'm sorry." She blushed.

"Why are you apologizing?" he said. He smiled, walking through the exhibit to a giant cactus covered in blooms.

"I shouldn't stare," she said. Lines formed between his eyebrows, and he looked away.

"You...you have someone back home?"

Andrea took in a big gulp of air and started walking, dreaming of changing the subject.

"I did. But it's over."

"Not a movie script ending, then?"

She snorted. "No, definitely not. But honestly, good riddance. I'm here partly to get over what happened."

Lucas paused.

"Fair enough," he said. "I'm glad you spilled your coffee on me."

She didn't take her eyes off him. He looked at her like she was art. She put her hands in her jean pockets and looked down, feeling something undefinable. Perhaps contentment, flattery? It felt...good.

An hour later, they'd traipsed the entirety of the Hortus Botanicus. They were extremely late for their morning session in the graveyard. Nearby was the vast church Andrea saw yesterday. She told Lucas how much she loved the massive black slate tiles on the floor, and he asked if she'd like her picture taken in front of it.

"Yes!" she said, handing him her phone. She posed, her Doc Martens squeaking on the slate floors.

She checked the picture and smiled.

"Is Jake your ex?" Lucas said. "He texted you."

Her heart was in her throat. "I haven't been responding to him."

"You probably should," said Lucas. "He said he's boarding a flight."

"What?!" She swiped to check the messages. Goosebumps rippled up her arm. "I gotta call him. I'll meet you there."

The phone went to voicemail.

"Damnit!" He could not be here. He could not ruin this good part of her life. She texted her mom but knew she was still asleep. It was predawn in the States. She ran to catch up with Lucas, fearing being alone.

"Everything okay?"

"No," she said. "I left him a voicemail, told him I don't want him to come. But I'm afraid now it's too late. I seriously cannot see him."

The panic in her voice was clear.

"Whoa, Andrea," said Lucas. He gently grabbed her shoulders. She buried her face in her hands.

"What did this guy do to you?"

She shook her head wordlessly, hearing the memory of braying hunting dogs. She tried to stop the past from emerging, but it was vivid and palpable.

"There's no way he will find you. Campus is big, you can stay in your room or maybe Paul's office. We can call the police."

He believed her, without context, that trauma clouded everything.

"We have hours before he gets here. What do you say we get to work, tell Paul what's up, and go from there?"

She wanted to get to work. She needed the distraction. Pacing her dorm would have done no good. She couldn't stop a transatlantic flight, either.

"Want to work on that grave with me? Test your theory that it's important?" Lucas said. Andrea nodded, finding her breath though her body trembled.

Five minutes later, he opened the gate to the cemetery. She was silent the walk over. "Show me the plot. Let's forget Jake and whatever it is that happened."

"I don't know if I want Professor Hahn to know," she said.

"Alright. But if I need to tell someone, you should give me permission to do that."

She nodded, looking up at him with trusting eyes. "Yes, if it comes down to it. I'll accept your help."

Lucas greeted Paul with a quick wave.

"Morning, you two," said Paul, looking at them quizzically. It was clear their conversation had been intense. "Off to the mystery grave?"

"Yes," she said, grabbing a bucket of supplies. She had to shrug off the fear. "I'm hoping it's dried overnight."

They walked to the far corner where the graves leaned back toward the river like they were pulled with an invisible rope. Andrea spotted freshly turned dirt at the base as they neared the gravesite. She started running, the fear rippling once again. But this time, it felt more significant.

"What's happened?" said Lucas.

"It's been dug up!"

The headstone was dry. Her work yesterday had paid off—the stone was bright white marble, veined with black. The carving was clearly Clara the Rhino. She laid the rubbing paper over it and grabbed a teal crayon, rubbing furiously. The image became crystal clear.

"Douwemout van der Meer," Lucas read out loud. He translated the next part from Dutch: "VOC Captain. Rhino Keeper."

"1705 to 1775," Andrea read. She took in a sharp breath. "The Rhino Keeper—this is Clara's owner!"

The grave dirt was partially overturned. Black earth was in a pile beside the stone, but the frozen ground prevented whoever was digging from going deeper. Thoughts of Jake on the flight to Amsterdam vanished. Andrea's scalp prickled. This was Douwe's resting place, and it was disturbed.

Lucas shouted for Paul, who came running.

"What is this?" Paul said, dropping to his knees to peer into the hole. It was two feet deep. "We aren't supposed to start digging until next week!"

"Someone wants whatever's in this grave," she said. "Look, the headstone is clean, and it's definitely Clara's owner."

"What a find," said Paul. "This changes history. Who would have done this? What were they looking for?"

"The frost stopped them," said Lucas. "We have to exhume this grave today."

"Yes, we do. I'm calling Janice," said Paul. "The museum may not be ready for this, but they don't have a choice."

Twenty minutes later, Janice had a flat-bed pickup truck and shovels onsite. She briefed them on how to dig without damaging the site. She set up a digital camera on a tripod.

"We must be careful," she said. "It's possible the casket is softwood and decayed, and we do not want to damage whatever may be inside."

Andrea held a shovel in her gloved hands, not believing that she was about to dig up a 250-year-old grave. She took a deep breath, and the shovel hit the dirt. As Jake's flight grew closer, so was bringing up whatever lay below.

Chapter 24
Douwemout van der Meer
The Netherlands & Berlin

Douwe and Zubin left the University, headed for a coachbuilder's shop outside of Amsterdam. It had been nearly a year since he, Zubin, Lonnie, and Clara took residence at the University of Leiden. Lonnie was pulled away on a VOC journey where she gathered botanical specimens for the Hortus Botanicus. Zubin perfected his reading and outgrew his clothes. Douwe negotiated, with fine terms, Clara's likeness in an anatomy book. She was the focus of many students in the anatomy theater, with the nub of a horn showing in their sketches.

To their chagrin, they had to stay the night in Amsterdam. Douwe and Zubin had never had a night away from Clara. Zubin commented that Clara could not have fit in the inn's narrow horse stalls. Douwe agreed, but neither of them slept much. Douwe had a nightmare of returning to find Clara's bones on display in the anatomy theater.

The morning dawned cool with a low-hanging fog that made the boats in the harbor look as though they had clouds for sails. Douwe and Zubin knocked on the door of the coachbuilder's home before the lanterns were lit. The builder, named Verheul, answered the door in his linen nightgown, bags under his eyes. They walked into the workshop twenty minutes later with steaming ceramic mugs of potent tea and stale biscuits.

Clara's coach was enormous: thirty feet long and twelve feet tall, wheels six feet in diameter. It was light wood, finished with dusty gray paint to blend with the dirt of the roads. Two small windows were on either side of the wagon at the rear near the top. Clara would have to strain to see out, and the windows were out of arm's reach from the ground. On the left side, a covered window could be lowered by removing a plank of wood. Clara could be fed safely by patrons there.

"Why such small windows?" asked Zubin.

"I don't want her to startle," said Douwe. "We never know what we may see on the road. But I want people to see her at the same time, hence the small window. She cannot be fed without us near."

Verheul opened the rear for them. A shallow, wide ramp led inside where there were troughs for food and water, a large hay manger at the front for storage, and a wide bed. It was large enough for Clara to lie down.

Zubin wandered inside, smelling fresh wood and testing the hinges of the hay manger. He nodded his approval and leaped up to hang from the window. His nose poked out the other side.

"Bigger than her stall!" he said, his voice echoing in the empty carriage.

"You'll need six horses," Verheul said. His voice was deep, gruff. "Or four draft."

"Hear that, Zubin? Horses," said Douwe. "We can drive the carriage back to Clara this morning."

Verheul nodded and instructed them on how to hitch the horses. Zubin sat in the box, daydreaming and dozing, while Douwe learned about the wagon.

"If I need repairs...?"

"Pray the nearest coachbuilder has a workshop large enough," said Verheul, shaking his head. Clara's coach was the only piece in the building. "I have not built a thing like this since the *Knappenhof*."

Zubin turned, startled. Douwe smiled at him and put a finger to his lips.

Douwe procured four Ardennais draft horses and hitched them to the carriage, which wobbled wildly on the cobbled streets while empty. Soon, the horses stomped and snorted as the stable boys met them at the University stables. Never before had such a large carriage been drawn through the streets of Leiden. Zubin darted inside to see Clara, barely letting the carriage stop before leaping from the box. Douwe parked and placed coins in the hands of the stable boys.

He was also anxious, but Clara's whistles greeted them, and Douwe marched toward her stall, sighing happily. She was fine. The stable boy who cared for her was grinning at Zubin, overly proud.

"Clara, ready for an adventure?" said Zubin, scratching her neck. Clara huffed at his hands, demanding fruit. Zubin obliged, slipping Clara an apple. Douwe rubbed in between the folds of her skin, and she leaned into him. He braced himself, worn boots digging into the earth. She had grown.

Douwe and Zubin had to introduce Clara to the draft horses, careful that the animals were amiable. They planned to take it slow before picking up Lonnie from the docks. She'd been gone six months, and they were ready to welcome her back.

On the morning of their departure to meet Lonnie, Douwe stopped dead in his tracks in front of the window of the University's bookshop. Through the paned window on an easel was the engraving of Clara by Jan Wandelaar. Douwe could hardly breathe. A lump formed in his throat. Inside, in the hands of patrons, were copies of the engraving. They were purchasing the image of Clara. The shop bell clanged above. The shop-keeper smiled and announced him.

"The Rhino Keeper!" he shouted. The patrons turned and murmured amongst themselves. Douwe picked up a copy of the engraving and put two copper pennies on the counter. The same amount people paid to feed Clara at Hirzet's.

The engraving didn't leave Zubin's hands for the twenty-mile ride to find Lonnie. Douwe tried to keep his pride in check, but many people now owned a copy of Wandelaar's version of Clara. In the flesh behind them, Clara huffed her dislike for the jostling carriage. Zubin turned around and shoved a tiny window open. His voice calmed her, and she was eating when they arrived in Rotterdam.

They pulled up to the same docks where they had last seen the *Knap-penhof*. The bustle of the ports felt like a homecoming to Douwe, who strained to see Lonnie.

"Want to try to gather a crowd?" said Zubin, motioning to Clara. He had a burlap sack of red apples.

"Why not," said Douwe. He hopped from the carriage and removed the board holding the feeder window. Clara immediately craned her neck out, swiveled her ears, and opened her mouth for food. She was irritated and wanted out. Zubin rounded the carriage with the bag of apples and began his call.

"Clara! Apples for Clara!"

Clara peeped in response, her call mixing with the bells and sounds of port. A line formed to pay two coppers to feed her. Sailors nudged each other with elbows, wobbling on their sea legs to watch. They stood on tiptoe to see Clara. Her soft, fish-oiled armor glowed in the sunlight. She raised her lip to the sky, showing two short ivory teeth on her bottom jaw, begging for food. Merchants left their wagons, careening their necks around the crowd to catch a glimpse of what took their patrons from them.

Clara's fans left with slimed hands and smiles. Zubin was out of apples and had a full coin pouch in a few hours as the sailors and merchants went on their meandering ways, whispering the word *rhino* to anyone they passed.

"No more apples, friend," Zubin said to an approaching shadow. "If you have your own, I'll charge you half price."

"Half price?" It was Lonnie. Zubin popped up and threw himself into her arms.

Lonnie wore tan skirts and an olive-green bodice. Lean muscle showed on her upper back, sprayed with freckles. Her hair was still short but had grown in honey-brown curls that framed her small ears. Douwe felt his heartbeat quicken when she smiled at him.

"Welcome back, sailor," said Douwe. He had never seen Lonnie look as feminine as she did, and he hesitated to embrace her but longed to. "A skirt and bodice?"

"You're used to me in my breeches in the gardens while I work. But on the ship, as an official member of the University's botany department, I had to dress the part. It's not my preference, but I could keep myself a rung above the common seaman."

"You were safe, then?" said Douwe, thinking of the black pool of blood in his captain's quarters.

"I kept to myself and helped Dr. Wilhelm," said Lonnie. "I am grateful he was aboard. I have many specimens to deliver to Leiden."

"We'll take you back, and then we're ready to depart," said Zubin.

"Depart?" said Lonnie. "To where, lads?"

"We're ready to show Clara to Europe," said Douwe. "The broadsides of Wandelaar's etching are selling. She's growing her horn. Look at her, she's huge! Far too big for the University's stables."

"Are you sure it's Clara who's eager to leave, or is it you, Captain?" said Lonnie, rubbing Clara's neck. "I understand the need for adventure as a sailor moving from port to port. Is Clara your new *Knappenhof?*"

Douwe scoffed and shook his head. He had a duty, a calling, to present Clara to Europe. It was not a wild adventure, as Lonnie suggested. Zubin nudged him in the ribs, smirking.

"She has a point, Douwe," said Zubin. "Clara would be content to graze the pasture near the University the rest of her days."

"Then the world would know nothing about her," said Douwe. He pictured Clara in a pasture as Zubin said. His imagination showed him a warm house and green farmland, but he shook the thought from his head. Clara deserved more than that. She deserved the fame she attracted.

"I know your purpose, Douwe," said Lonnie. "But I won't be going with you."

How could she abandon them? They needed her. Clara's liniment and Lonnie's knowledge of herbal remedies were important. So was Lonnie's care of Zubin and her presence. Lonnie had been there for Clara,

Douwe for Lonnie, and both adults for Zubin. They all trusted each other. And yet, Douwe could not convince her. She was her own person, and he admired that. Lonnie's satchel was flung over her shoulder, over-stuffed with dried plants in jars. She had found her place, and he could not take her from it.

"You're staying at the University?" he asked, sadly. Lonnie nodded. "I cannot fight you. I've already taken one fair lady from her home, which has proven the most difficult thing I've ever done."

Clara snorted. Lonnie approached, and Clara focused her small eyes on her. Both of Clara's tufted ears were pressed forward in a warm embrace. Lonnie placed her hands on either side of Clara's broad face, feeling the rock-warmth of her skin. She rubbed the place where her horn would be, scratched under her chin, and backed away.

"Everyone loves you, Clara," she said. "As do I."

"I have something for you," Lonnie said to Douwe, removing her satchel. Inside was a large leather envelope fastened with a wooden button. "It should be helpful. These are the ingredients I use for Clara's liniment."

Lonnie showed Zubin sachets of dried herbs and tiny glass vials labeled in Lonnie's winding script. She told them which herbs would relieve their pain if chewed, which would help with fever, and which would soothe a burn. At the bottom of the envelope was a leather pouch.

"This is rare and valuable," she said, pouring the contents into her hand. A round brown stone rolled out. "It's a bezoar. A remedy for any poison. Mixing it with milk works best."

"How do you know this?" said Douwe, buttoning the pouch.

"I have seen many things on my voyages now, Douwe," said Lonnie. "Dr. Wilhelm has taught me well. I hope you never have to use it."

"Will you do me a favor, Lonnie?" said Douwe. "Betsy and her kittens are still at the University. Will you see to them? And Bakari, too?"

"Of course," said Lonnie, kneeling by Zubin. She wiped his tears with her thumbs, held his face as she had Clara's, and brought the boy close. "No tears, Zubin, you've an adventure ahead of you."

Little good her words did. Zubin cried. Douwe lamented the loss, not because of the help she provided, but because he realized at last, through the tightening of his chest as she walked away, that he loved her.

Four draft horses led Clara's gray cart to Hanover the following week. The crew stopped along the way to graze in the greening pastures nearby. Zubin took to finding Clara warming farm ponds. He tested the water first, submerging his arm. He shook his head and moved on if it came back covered in gooseflesh.

But when a warm pond was found, Clara submerged herself except for her fringed ears and the highest part of her back. She blew bubbles in the water and emerged when satisfied, moving into her crate for bread and spring produce from the village carts. They wanted to make it to Hanover by mid-April, and when they rolled into town, the first stop was the local printer.

"How many?" The printer wrote in his ledger book.

"One thousand," said Douwe, placing his coppers on the wooden counter. "To be distributed from here to Berlin."

The broadsides Douwe printed featured Clara, illustrated.

It read:

All animal lovers are informed of the arrival of a living rhinoceros to your town, which many believe to be the Behemoth of the Book of Job, Chapter forty, verse ten. It was caught in Asia, in the realm of the Great Mogul, 4,000 miles distant from here. This incredible animal is dark brown, like the elephant it has no hair, except for hair on its ears and tail. The skin looks as if it is covered with shells overlapping each other, about two inches thick.

The leaflets were distributed by messenger boys who traveled the towns. Soon, the hamlets near Berlin tacked up broadsides of Clara. *She's coming!* The people whispered. *The Behemoth of Job in the flesh!*

When her caravan rolled through a village's narrow, muddy streets, the townsfolk were ready. Children gripped their mother's skirts as the feather-footed horses pulled Clara's cart. Clara's nose or a flickering ear emerged, and Douwe scanned the streets for people's reactions, waving all the while.

A thin, dusty-cheeked peasant boy, feet bare on the dirty cobbles, heard the rumbling of the large cart. He turned, holding the shoe he was mending, as the towering structure blocked the sun. The boy assumed the cart housed the emperor.

Clara set her nose through the barred window, and the boy gasped. The cart rolled past him. He dropped the shoe and ran. The boy followed Clara's wagon to the edge of town, where an inn's large paddock draped with calico banners awaited.

The boy watched the unhitching of the horses from behind the inn wall. He approached Clara's carriage, clambering up the six-foot wheel and balancing, brown toes curled over the massive wheel. Clara snorted at him. The boy yelped, hit the ground, and sprinted homeward.

"Why did you let that happen?!" Zubin asked. "That boy will say Clara is dangerous."

"We'll have the biggest crowd of our lives tomorrow, boy," Douwe grinned. And they did.

Clara mouthed the calico banners flapping in the breeze. She perked her ears at the early-morning crowd, gathering as Zubin threw down a handful of green hay in the rough-hewn manger. The paddock was muddy, and Clara's three-toed, wide feet made large pock marks where brown water pooled. Dozens of people lined up, trading coins for apples as Clara heaved herself onto her side in the mud.

Mothers and their children laughed as she flailed her large legs in the air, showing her strange, small navel. When she righted herself, she was caked in cold dirt. Her eyelashes were covered, and when she took fruit from the hands of the thin-wristed children, muddy splatters scattered their tunics.

"How many, Zubin?"

"I cannot count past one hundred yet, Douwe, but the apple sack is empty."

Douwe ushered Clara inside to a stable stall where she had just enough room to turn around. She lifted her lip at him, ears pressed forward, and he rubbed between a fold of her skin.

Copper and silver coins jangled in Douwe's corsair chest. He snatched a wind-blown poster of Clara's off a tavern wall and folded it neatly. He placed it in his pocket with Johanna's miniature of Clara. That night at the inn, he made a list on the back of the places he longed to be: Berlin, Vienna, Dresden, Leipzig, Versailles. Onward they went. Berlin waited for its animal queen.

In the center of Berlin was a market—the Spittelmarkt. Douwe and Zubin desperately needed to reach it. Clara was out of fish oil. While her wallows in the mud and farm ponds were helpful, Zubin needed to keep her clean for her crowds, and her skin cracked and dried in the April sun. Fish oil was not available in large quantities in the countryside, so they navigated the narrow streets of Berlin with Clara's carriage.

News of Clara's arrival spread throughout the city. Her cart was unmistakable. The boys who distributed the fliers through the cities cried 'A rhinoceros comes! In the biggest carriage in the world!'

Soon, word reached a kitchen boy who worked in the Berlin Palace, who told the cook. The cook mentioned it to the butler, who told a maid, who told the Queen of Prussia's maid. And the Queen of Prussia's maid told the Queen everything.

Within an hour, Douwe and Zubin found the fish market and the oil, paid the bill, loaded the cart, and perused the fishmonger, debating whether they should buy lunch here or at the tavern when a court party unexpectedly descended upon them.

A herald announced the party, informing the crowded market that the King of Prussia Frederick II and Queen Consort Elisabeth had arrived. A quiet hush swept the place. The hollering salesmen were still, silver-scaled fish shining in their hands. Patrons swiveled, pausing their conversations. Douwe and Zubin, caught unaware, stepped toward Clara and stood still as trees.

A gold and white coach was drawn by two white horses, and a footman opened the gilded door. Queen Elisabeth emerged first, dressed in white and pink. Her tiny sateen shoe squelched in the mud. The crowd bowed in unison. King Frederick appeared next. Seeing the King and Queen together was rare, and applause followed a deep collective bow.

Clara's nose stuck out her wagon window. Douwe stopped clapping and bowed deeply, grabbing Zubin down with him. Was the arrival of royalty happenstance? Or were they here for Clara?

"Rumor has come to the palace that the Behemoth of Job is in this carriage," said King Frederick, tapping the wheel with a walking stick.

Douwe stood, white-faced. King Frederick was there to see Clara.

"Yes, Your Highness," he said, smiling, though his stomach turned. "This is Clara, the Indian rhino, all the way from Bengal."

Clara flexed her lip and showed her pink mouth through the bars of the carriage window. Frederick approached her, and Clara lowered her ears at him, listening for the rustling of Zubin's apple bag. Zubin tapped Douwe lightly on the elbow and cast his eyes to the bag of apples. Douwe nodded.

"I have never seen such a beast," said Frederick, standing on tiptoe. Queen Elisabeth approached, her ladies holding white parasols above her.

"Queen Elisabeth," said Douwe, bowing low again. "I am Douwemout van der Meer, and this is Clara. Please, allow our guests to give Miss Clara what she wants, Zubin."

"What does she want, Mr. Van der Meer?" said Queen Elisabeth with a pleasant smile. Clara opened her pink mouth.

"Apples, Your Majesty," Douwe said. Zubin opened the sack, and Clara snorted. The Queen pressed a gloved hand to her face and laughed. King Frederick smiled broadly and stepped back, avoiding Clara's spittle.

"I shall show you; if you like, you may give her one as well," Douwe said.

Douwe took a small apple from the sack and showed Clara. Her eyes fixated on it, ears swiveling forward, brown tufts floating in the wind. She scooped the apple in with her lip, using it like a finger. She crunched noisily and begged for more with eager eyes.

The royal court drew nearer the carriage to watch. They applauded with delight and made joyous noises. Zubin readied the apple sack and asked who would like to feed her. Douwe got a crate from a nearby stall so they could easily reach the window. Zubin did not think to charge this crowd.

The bolder gentlemen and servants fed Clara first, and then a lady's maid, and then attention was turned to the King and Queen. Douwe scarcely breathed. If royalty fed Clara, every person, rich, poor, or otherwise, would long to do the same.

Queen Elisabeth was known for being a monarch of the people. She held court more than her husband and made far more appearances than King Frederick. Douwe fully expected her to delight in feeding Clara, and he was correct. She removed her pearl bracelets, at which Zubin dropped his jaw, and took two apples from the bag.

Standing on the fish-market crate, the Queen of Prussia held both apples simultaneously. Clara whistled joyfully and took them one at a time, crunching madly. A fine spray of apple juice and rhino slime spattered the Queen's gown. Queen Elisabeth grinned and slapped her hands together. The crowd applauded. Elisabeth rubbed Clara's heavy, cobbled neck with her pale hand.

King Frederick stood to the side, hands behind his back. He was tall and white-haired, blue-eyed, serious. He looked as if he had a million questions, so Douwe stepped a little closer.

"How old is she?"

"Two, Your Majesty," said Douwe.

"Where's her horn?" said the King.

"Growing slowly, your majesty."

"No dorsal?" said the King.

"You must know Dürer, Your Majesty," said Douwe. "No dorsal horn. He may have been mistaken."

"Remarkable. And she can live to be one hundred?"

"If she does, I'll never know," said Douwe with a half-smile. "She'd outlive me."

"And the boy?" said King Frederick, gesturing to Zubin.

"He and Clara were attached. I have no plans to separate them. He is like a son to me."

"You are remarkable, Mr. Van der Meer. I can see you keep this animal held in high regard."

"I am honored to hear your words. The truth is that Europe knows nothing of her kind, and I have a unique position to bring wonder and educate at the same time."

"I can think of nothing better to do for the people," said King Frederick. "May I feed her?"

"I'd be honored if you would."

Douwe walked to Zubin and took the sack. King Frederick withdrew a dull farmer's apple and held it in his palm for Clara. Clara ate from the King's hand, and the fish market cheered. King Frederick smiled and shook off the slime. Clara huffed for more.

Before the procession left, and the golden door to the carriage closed on the King and Queen, a servant dropped a black velvet cloth in Douwe's hands. It held twelve gold ducats.

The herald called: "The King and Queen of Prussia extend their favor and goodwill to Clara and her keepers and wish to present the animal to the public tomorrow at the palace grounds. All are welcome!"

Douwe kept calm, bowing low. But Zubin, who was still just a boy, hopped into the air and let out a whoop, startling Clara, who thundered in her carriage to the crowd's amusement. The royal procession pulled away in its glittering glory, starkly contrasting with the dull, muddy fish market. Douwe's heart soared.

That night, Clara's wagon was driven to the palace. The gates swung open. They were expected. The palace yard was mostly stone, with nowhere for Clara to graze. Nevertheless, the royal stables were plentiful with hay, and the kitchen had a bucket of vegetable scraps set aside for Clara. She ate well and slept in a large stall, her legs curled under her like a cat.

Zubin and Douwe took the opportunity to clean out Clara's carriage. Zubin wrapped a kerchief around his face and scrubbed with a rough bristle brush. Her straw bedding and droppings were removed, and soon, the flies were less. The carriage needed daily cleaning, and Zubin claimed the task.

The April morning dawned clear and blue in Berlin. Douwe and Zubin woke in the servants' quarters. Zubin knocked Douwe on the shoulder, and they went directly to the stables. Douwe spoke to Clara in soft tones until she stood, yawning. Zubin grabbed a carrot, and Clara followed him into the empty courtyard.

Clara and Zubin made circles, chasing each other in the palace yard. She needed no lead and was not keen to go far from Zubin, who produced delicious bites from his pockets. Clara clearly loved the boy and answered to her name when he called it. She trotted to him, he sprinted away, she snorted, and he returned, putting a carrot in her open mouth.

For all of the worries she brought, Clara had also brought them to the Prussian King's courtyard. Zubin had no idea how incredible this was. Douwe must explain European royalty to the boy so he understood the miracle in the fish market. Doors were opening for them to complete Douwe's mission—to show Clara to all.

Servants meandered through the yard, and Zubin led Clara back to her stall where she ate more hay and another bucket of kitchen scraps. Douwe rubbed her with fish oil, forever smelling it and Clara's earthy, warm stink no matter how much he scrubbed. The staff prepared a makeshift paddock for Clara, and within a few hours, the gates opened.

Clara was shepherded to the paddock, where she had a wide manger full of green grass, a large bucket of water, and a barrel of produce outside the fence. The townspeople flooded in, paying their two copper pennies to feed her. Clara took most of the food from peoples' hands but was more interested in the green grass in the manger. By lunchtime, the staff excused the common folk and closed the gates.

The royal procession was coming. Frederick and Elisabeth emerged from their square, gray palace. Their court followed, settling in for luncheon nearby. Douwe recognized royalty, artists, and a curious, long-faced man who introduced himself as the philosopher Voltaire. Tables were laid with fish and bread, and they ate while Clara ate. She emptied her manger, and the staff refilled it. Two men argued in front of Clara's paddock. Douwe prepared Clara's fish oil and listened.

"I'm certain you cannot be serious, Pierre," said Voltaire. "The mere existence of this animal does not guarantee a creator. Just let this animal exist."

"Existence of this creature, Voltaire, signals divine purpose," said the rounder, squatter man. "Look at the folds of its skin! The ripples, the creases, the bubbling rock-like surface. How could it be random? Surely you see, sir, that Clara holds a mathematical exactness in her very hide."

Voltaire's wig hopped as he laughed. He patted Pierre Maupertius on the shoulder and turned to Douwe.

"This animal of yours, sir, does she prove God exists?" Voltaire said with a weasel-like smile.

Douwe paused. Clara's existence proved something. Clara proved that life can unfold unexpectedly and that people can come into life exactly when needed. Clara proved that joy was the same, regardless of a person's status or rank. Clara proved that animals and humans shared a bond of trust and equal admiration. But God? Did Clara prove God existed?

"All I am certain of, Mr. Voltaire, is that Clara's existence has true and deep meaning, at least to me," Douwe said. He had not felt like this about any living creature, person, or animal. It felt good to admit his fondness. "I do not consider her life a random occurrence."

Maupertius stared at Voltaire. The two walked away arguing, and Douwe gave Zubin a look from the corner of his eye. A philosophical debate about Clara was certainly unexpected.

King Frederick approached while Douwe and Zubin were oiling her. The white-wigged King asked more questions like he had at the fish market: how much she ate and drank, how her feet were cared for, and what her teeth were like. He asked if they'd ever tried to ride her (no) and what she was like as a baby. He asked about her oil and ear tufts and how much her carriage cost. Douwe rubbed his hands clean on a rag and told him. The team of horses and her custom carriage were all he had left from his VOC payout.

The King reached into his pocket and pulled out six more gold ducats, pressing them into Douwe's fishy hand. In the background, Voltaire and Maupertius still argued, pointing at Clara. The ladies resumed feeding her apples, holding their parasols overhead and giggling at Clara's swiveling ears. Zubin held the bag for them, expertly talking about her. Douwe bowed, holding himself together, and pocketed the coins. They clinked into the miniature Johanna gave him.

Douwe and Zubin were invited to spend the summer there. They accepted, setting up a paddock in a field near the city's outskirts where a steady stream of visitors saw Clara. She grazed and submerged herself in the farm pond. Birds landed on her back and pecked at the folds between her skin. She rested in the calm summer evenings of beautiful Berlin.

Chapter 25
Andrea
Leiden, The Netherlands

They dug for hours. Frost glistened when the sun hit the hole, and they spoke of it as if it was sent by whatever god looked out for archaeology expeditions. The digging was challenging, but by mid-afternoon, Paul's shovel hit something with a thud.

"Stop!" cried Janice. "That's it!"

Paul and Lucas dropped into the hole with brushes and small trowels and cleared the top of a flat wooden casket. Andrea's palms tingled. She was thrilled and terrified at the same time. Her stomach dropped, and her adrenaline pumped. Here we go, she thought. Her breath was shaky.

"You good?" asked Lucas, studying her face from below. She nodded, unable to formulate words. He was asking for more than one reason.

"Everyone out," said Paul. They muddied their clothes climbing. He carved out a little platform for himself beside the casket so he could stand and then knelt beside it. Using gloved hands, he felt around the rim of the coffin and lifted it slowly.

The grave was muddy, and black dirt walls threatened to push in. If the ground wasn't frozen, it would have collapsed completely. No one above could see anything until Paul hauled the lid off. If there were ever hinges, they were long decayed.

Lucas slid down the muddy embankment, dirtying his jeans, and helped Paul. It was small but dense, and the two men struggled to lift it out of the hole. People were shorter back then, and the casket was small. Janice and Andrea pulled, Paul and Lucas pushed, and the lid was on the grass in moments.

Janice and Andrea slid the lid out of the way and sprinted back to the hole. The wind picked up as dirt fell inside. Peering back at them under the brilliant blue sky was a perfectly intact skeleton.

Chapter 26
Douwemout van der Meer
Europe

Clara's wagon was shoveled out of muddy, early fall roads in front of an orangery in Breslau. The green glass building was fogged over, and the caretaker saw Clara as a good omen. The estate owners were gone to Greece for the winter, and he was happy for the company. Douwe paid six ducats to spend a few months there. Clara stripped leaves from the orange trees and thumped down the steps of a tiled indoor pool where she flickered her ears in joy. Zubin hoped they would never leave. But their coffers could use filling, and Douwe, like the captain he was, set his sights on the horizon again.

Two more draft horses and eight swordsmen led Clara in the most elaborate procession yet, and they entered Vienna on October 30. They headed for the Freyung, a public square surrounded by homes of the elite. A large cathedral towered over the flat-fronted houses. Zubin led Clara out of her carriage, flanked by the swordsmen, to a hushed and entranced crowd. Clara pranced.

Her temporary paddock was set up, and Zubin's calls rang for coin in exchange for feeding. This time, three coppers fed her instead of two. The city bustled with oxen pulling carts, beautiful horses and homely donkeys, vendors hawking their wares. Tall brown church spires seemed to reach the tops of the ever-moving clouds, blocking much of the sky.

People of all kinds mingled on the first day of their arrival. Paupers gaped from the alleyways. Affluent ladies draped their bare elbows out of windows and fanned themselves in the warm October afternoon, watching. Douwe hoped they would capture the attention of Maria Theresa, the Habsburg Empress.

"Three coppers!" yelled Zubin. "Feed the Behemoth of Job!"

He pulled copper coins in exchange for fruit from the Breslau orangery. Clara ate through the paddock rungs. Her horn shone like a lightning-filled thundercloud, and Douwe felt grateful for the eight swordsmen lined up around the paddock. The horn was six inches long now, thick and rough, and as the crowd's press grew, so did Douwe's anxiety. Her horn was magic to some. How many people thought of Clara's worth in parts?

A Catholic priest, dressed in all black, stood on the steps of the cathedral. Mass ended, the bells echoing in the Freyung. The priest's congregation exited the church and milled to Clara's paddock. Copper coins flashed in their hands. Douwe saw the priest strain to see what they gathered around, watching the crowd, money, and smiles, slowly meandering toward them. A man in all black was a rare sight to Douwe, whose native Netherlands was a country of mostly Protestants. Zubin elbowed Douwe and gestured to the priest, who stood on the fringes of the excited crowd.

Douwe gave him a short wave. The priest approached the paddock, hands behind his back. His congregation parted for him, offering polite smiles. He nodded back, but his focus remained on Clara.

"Hello, Father," said Douwe. "Care to feed her? The Behemoth of Job?"

The priest came closer. He was tall; his robes barely reached his ankles. His long face was drawn but the corners of his mouth upturned. His smooth face made it impossible to tell his age. His dark hair ruffled in the fall breeze. The swordsmen lowered their weapons.

"The Behemoth of Job...in the flesh," the priest said, raising his eyebrows. He held his gaze on Clara, standing with his body pressed to her fence. "How did you acquire this creature?"

Zubin clambered up the post, answering with a rehearsed speech that he took great pride in reciting. Douwe watched, mouthing the words in perfect cadence along with Zubin.

"She comes from the exotics of Bengal," Zubin said, leaning toward the priest. "My homelands, where many gods are worshiped and unnamed beasts roam the wilds. We tamed her after her mother was slain, and she is our bonded creature. Rarest beast in all of Europe, Clara the Behemoth." Zubin's wild hand gestures caught Clara's eye. The priest showed straight teeth in a smile and leaned in, gently grabbing the back of Zubin's neck. Zubin stiffened.

"Where many gods are worshiped?"

Zubin looked at Douwe. "Yes, sir."

"And the Christian God? Were you guided by Him?" The priest let his hand fall.

Zubin hesitated. Though he had attended services with Douwe infrequently, he did not know enough to tell this priest what he wanted to hear. Douwe saw his panic and stepped forward.

"This is why we call her the Behemoth of Job, Father. A true marvel of creation, don't you think?"

The priest stared at Clara, and Douwe handed him a dirt-smeared carrot. "Perhaps you'd like to feed her?" The priest took the carrot, and dropped his jaws to say something, but quickly closed his mouth.

He smiled, pursing his lips together, and held the carrot to Clara, who huffed and slimed his hand. The priest shook his hand off abruptly and stared at his dirty palm. He stepped back, gently greeting his congregation members with hands on their shoulders and whispered words. In contrast, the look he gave Zubin held a tinge of sorrow.

"I try, rhino keeper," he said, "to show God to my flock in the same way—by immense wonder through words spoken in that cathedral behind us. But you've done it in the flesh of a rhino."

"I do not claim to show God to people. Just wonder," Douwe said.

The priest turned an ear toward Douwe. "Yet you call this animal the Behemoth of Job as if you know it for certain it was sent by God?"

Douwe inhaled and held his mouth open, unsure of what to say.

"I see your confusion, sir," the priest said. "Such a perfect vessel to prove the existence of creation in this world of turmoil. Perhaps we misunderstand each other. I am glad you are here to show the creature."

People waited behind him, nodding and bowing at the priest, coins shining between their fingers. The man closest to Clara cried: "I wish for a strong harvest!" Then licked his fingers and touched her horn.

The priest looked from his outstretched hand to Zubin's bulging apron, then backed away cordially and walked to the cathedral. Douwe watched him go. He was unsure what the priest thought of Clara.

As evening fell, the onlookers faded from the square, and Zubin prepared Clara for stabling. Whispering words of love into Clara's ear, Zubin rubbed the folds between the soft, warm armor plates of her neck. He left her with kitchen scraps, an apple, and a loaf of stale brown bread. Douwe met him in their room upstairs with dinner on pewter plates: sausage, potatoes, and the same bread as Clara's, just less stale. Zubin sat on the low-slung bed to eat.

"Did I upset that priest today?"

"I'm not exactly sure, Zubin," replied Douwe, removing his boots. "He doesn't seem to like her. He doesn't seem to like..." He stopped himself. He got the feeling that Zubin's speech about other gods and exotic worlds stoked a fire. But he did not want to tell the boy.

"Does not like what? He was nice enough to his church goers. Maybe he needs to feed Clara again, or see her play?"

"Perhaps," said Douwe. "He was kind to others. Maybe we're too close to the church for his liking. I'll go in the morning and speak with him."

"Can we keep the swordsmen for now?" said Zubin through a yawn. He lay back on the straw mattress, feet dangling.

"I don't think we need swordsmen to protect us against him," said Douwe. "But if it makes you feel better, I will count our earnings."

The familiar clinking of coins sent Zubin straight to sleep. When Douwe finally slept, he dreamed of a hooded figure in Clara's shadow.

The next morning dawned cool, frost clinging to the cobbles. Douwe's breath fogged as he strode across the Freyung to the grand cathedral. Candles were lit, but it was empty. His footsteps echoed in the sanctuary. From the first pew, he sat gazing at the crucifix. He heard nothing but his own breathing for several moments until the clicking of a side door announced the priest, carrying a silver tray.

At the sight of Douwe, the priest stopped short. His mouth curled at the corners, but Douwe could not call it a smile.

"Good morning, Father," said Douwe, rising.

The priest nodded and set the tray on the altar, back to Douwe. The longing eyes of Christ stared down at the two men.

"What did you think yesterday, watching your congregation near Clara?" Douwe asked. The priest did not turn.

"So many of my flock were present. Seeing your beast, they seemed... bewitched," he said.

"Most people are, having never seen such an animal. But I couldn't help but notice some...discomfort, Father."

"Discomfort. Yes, I felt discomfort. I have had a night to think. Your Behemoth is enchanting, you have a full coffer no doubt." The priest turned and stepped slowly down the dais stairs.

Douwe clasped his hands behind his back.

"I am glad you can see her for what she is—a creature that helps us see the world beyond what is right in front of us. She is a wonder."

"Enchantment is not wonderful," said the priest, putting a hand on Douwe's shoulder. "Do you not see? You've created your own temple. You call the people to give you offerings. You show the animal like an idol. Surely you see the sin?"

Douwe felt the weight of the hand. The priest's eyes reflected the red candlelight, and he laughed gently, his smooth cheeks unmoving. The church echoed as Douwe stepped back. Shadows leaped onto the priest's face from the stained-glass windows.

"Surely you see the problem here, rhino keeper?" the priest said, drawing closer to Douwe. "You've been enchanted, like you said. Misled. Perhaps those gods the heathen boy worships have infiltrated your Christian heart. I can help cleanse you of those thoughts, guide you back homeward."

"Father, this is not home," Douwe said. "Zubin is not a heathen. Clara is not an idol."

The priest smiled and pulled Douwe closer to him.

"God wants to help you, if you'll let Him. He wants you to distance yourself from the boy. Rid yourself of the temptation of the beast's magic."

Douwe backed away. The priest's hands fell, then rose in a sign of piety. Douwe's chest rose and fell rapidly. The priest's pale palms glowed, his expression softening as Douwe continued to back away. Douwe reached the last pew and turned on his heel, taking the steps two at a time. The white morning sun had melted the frost, though patches still shimmered in the darkened corners of the Freyung.

Clara's paddock was empty. She remained in the warm stable, asleep. Douwe picked up the fence posts and moved them far from the cathedral. He chose a spot closer to the road, where passersby in carriages and carts would see her. He refreshed Clara's straw and went to wake her.

Douwe paused before opening the stable door. The priest's words frightened him. He had not expected anyone to think Clara was an idol. Was he genuinely leading people to sin? Had he himself fallen into sin?

Please be well. He said this every day as he brought out Clara. He suddenly longed for the protection of the statue from Bengal, the one Zubin kept in their apartment at the University. He found his mind tangled. He did not know which god to pray to, but he knew it was not the priest's.

Clara was alert. He grabbed her rations and led her out into the frosted morning. She flickered her ears, took in the scene, and followed Douwe's bucket and armful of hay to the new paddock location. The sun shone brightly now, and a few citizens on their morning walks paused in awe of Clara devouring her breakfast.

Douwe let them touch her rocky skin while she ate. Clara did not mind, gentle creature that she was. Her legs were thick as timbers now, her three toes larger than teacups. She was magnificent. After his confrontation with the priest, Douwe felt particularly protective of her.

Zubin joined him shortly, running out of the inn like he was late. "Where were you?!" he cried.

"I spoke to the priest," said Douwe.

"Oh, good," replied Zubin, applying Clara's fish oil.

"It was not," Douwe said, shaking his head. "He thinks Clara's patrons are worshiping her like an idol."

"An idol?" said Zubin. "What is this?"

"An idol is something other than the one God that he worships. Any other god, or image or statue, or in this case, Clara."

"I worship many gods, and it is not sinful," said Zubin. "Why is he angry?"

Douwe sighed. Explaining theology to Zubin was not on his agenda today.

"I think he's angry that we set up right in front of the church and made people pay to see Clara. He thinks they're worshiping her, that *we* worship her."

"People kind of do worship her," said Zubin, pulling a piece of hay from the corner of Clara's mouth. "What did he say about us, then, Douwe?"

Douwe could not answer without damaging the boy.

"We should make the most of our time here. We've moved the paddock. We'll keep our distance and move on."

Douwe paid the swordsmen to stay for two more days. They stood like soldiers around Clara's paddock, and word reached the outermost corners of Vienna that the rhino on the posters paced the Freyung.

Douwe saw the black-robed priest on Thursday and immediately hopped the fence to Clara's side. It was noon, a time when passersby with their mid-day meals loved to share their food. She declined meat, munched on baked goods, and licked salt from children's hands with her narrow pink tongue.

Those who did not approach Clara's paddock lingered, watching her meander. The priest drew closer and closer until he was next to the paddock, gently smiling.

Douwe prepared to defend Zubin and Clara when the priest began a sermon.

"People of Vienna, hear me clearly! You kneel before a false god and give it a crown, giving it offerings like the pagan ancestors you denounced generations ago. This animal, this so-called Behemoth of Job, is a test of your Christian nature. I see you pray to its horn, this idol, for a miracle. You cannot fathom the harm of worshiping such a thing. Instead, I beg you, worship the creator. Do not become weak animals yourselves. God does not conceal himself in this creature. You confuse God with an animal."

Douwe was white-faced. The priest continued, words echoing in the suddenly silent square.

"Confession, my friends, is open to you. These deniers of God are here to mislead you, to condemn you," he said, raising his eyes to the sky. He gestured toward the crowd. "Your coppers belong in the church, your food belongs on the tables of your households. Do not be led into temptation by this Behemoth, not of God."

The crowd began to disperse, murmuring and spitting on the cobbles. Some headed straight to the church, others exited the Freyung quickly. A few stepped forward.

"Father Gregor," said an old woman. "I will wait for you in the sanctuary."

The priest, Father Gregor, dipped his head low and grabbed her hand.

"You are being tested," he said, his eyes filling with tears. "We will not replace God with this falseness." The woman kissed his hand and turned to the cathedral.

Douwe, wide-eyed, stared at the old woman, who walked toward the church wiping her face. Zubin hopped up onto Clara's fence. Douwe caught him by the shirt collar and met Zubin's eyes, giving him an almost imperceptible shake of his head.

"Father, we mean no harm," said Douwe. "Perhaps it is divine that this animal is here in front of you, reminding you of what God can make."

The priest lowered his gaze to Douwe's clothing, still smiling. Douwe itched suddenly, his velvet overcoat felt ostentatious, bizarre next to the plainly dressed onlookers. Gregor took slow strides toward Clara at the paddock's edge. She shook her head at him, stamped her front feet, focusing on the priest's billowing black robe. Gregor raised his eyebrows and sighed, turning to the dwindling, silent crowd.

"We are not ignorant peasants," he said calmly. "We are the creation of God, made in his image, unlike this beast, made to distract us from the one true creator."

He walked away; the remaining patrons followed. The swordsmen looked around warily. Though they said nothing, their shifting feet and clinking weapons on stones were loud with discomfort.

Clara's crowd diminished. Word traveled fast; if the priest had considerable influence, their time in Vienna would be cut short. Douwe's plan of garnering the attention of Maria Theresa, the Habsburg Empress, was in peril.

Paul and Lucas cheered. Andrea felt tears on her face and wiped them away with a soil-smudged hand. The release felt good. Janice removed the camera from its tripod and handed it to Paul.

The camera snapped, and Andrea looked at Lucas, beaming from six feet below. She smiled back and sighed. This was the kind of life she'd dreamed of—making historical discoveries of great importance. In a few minutes, they were ready to haul the remains out.

"The casket is completely decayed on the bottom," called Paul from the hole. "Slide me a board from the flatbed, and Lucas and I will secure it."

Lucas and Paul slid shovels under the casket to make room for a one-inch board. Janice and Andrea analyzed the pictures on the screen.

"What's he holding?" Andrea asked, zooming in. She got on her hands and knees and looked into the casket. "Hey Lucas, what's in his hands?"

Lucas shed his coat. His band tee clung to his body. His face was muddy and sweaty, and his hair had dirt clods. He was kneeling, trying to shove the board under the casket.

"Can I look in a moment, Andrea?"

"I think it's Clara's horn," said Janice. "Look."

She zoomed in on the screen. A dark object, roughly a foot long, curved at the end in the curled skeletal fingers. It was dirty. Andrea peered over the hole when she lost her balance and tumbled in.

"Shit!" Lucas said. "You okay!?"

She tumbled in face-first but managed to turn sideways. She was lying right next to the remains.

"Damnit," she said softly.

"The jostling got the board under," said Paul. "Great job."

Andrea rolled away and kept low, staring at the skeleton. Golden brown bones were articulated beautifully. Nothing had touched these remains since they were placed there in 1775. Pieces of cloth were wrapped around the body, remnants of a fine article of clothing. They were deep teal, like the edge of the sky at dusk.

"Hey, Janice, toss me the camera."

She dangled it by its strap, and Andrea took up-close photos of the fabric scraps. She snapped a picture of the hands, and her jaw tightened. They were indeed wrapped around a shining horn. Clara's horn. She couldn't take a deep breath.

The trauma from the trophy room at Jake's house was entangled with the history she discovered. This felt impossible. How could she feel admiration for one kind of man who kept a wild animal out of its habitat and hatred for the one who killed them?

Her conscience answered that question: One of them kept the animal alive.

"Can I move the hands?" she called up to Janice. She wanted to see the horn, to see part of Clara. To feel its weight in her hands and know that her predictions were accurate, that she was loved.

"Don't disturb the remains. We can analyze them when we return to the museum today, but nothing will be moved onsite."

Andrea nodded, frustrated. She understood. It was better to preserve everything for documentation and respect this person who was once alive. She took a moment down there in the pit. Memorizing. Douwe lived at one point. He breathed and ate and loved people. He was someone's friend. She wondered what clothes he wore and what his voice sounded like. She wondered what color his eyes were and to whom he told his secrets.

Warm tears streamed down her cheeks while she stared at this human who was no more, who loved an animal so much he rested with her. He did not expect to be dug up and studied, and here she was, violating his eternal rest.

Lucas touched her shoulder with his dirty hand.

Andrea sniffled. "He was a person. And he loved Clara."

Paul nodded sagely. "Enough to be buried with her. That's the tough part, Andrea. History is easy when it's on the page or in a movie. But when you see it right before you, you sometimes forget it is real. We're fortunate to know anything about these people who lived before us. There are so many historical figures that we'll never know. We're lucky to meet Douwemout van der Meer today."

Paul and Lucas helped Andrea out of the hole. Janice prepared ropes to hook around the board. Once everything was secure, a pulley system helped them move the casket out of the pit. Water poured in from the back. The river had made its way into the grave of Douwemout van der Meer.

Chapter 28
Douwemout van der Meer
Vienna

A chill draped Vienna, and people hustled to their destinations. Few stopped by Clara's paddock, especially with Father Gregor nearby, ushering would-be patrons to the cathedral. Douwe felt ripples of unease.

Clara was content enough. She did not care that her crowds diminished, but Douwe did. He made plans to move on. The sun poured from the clouds on Sunday. The church bells rang out and echoed through the square. Zubin yawned and rubbed his eyes, organizing the fruit and vegetables for the day. Clara watched the early horses and carts with interest.

Douwe settled his balance with the inn when he heard trumpeting from the narrow street connecting the Freyung to the city. The instruments were close, signaling the arrival of royalty.

Douwe ran outside, tossing his coins on the inn's counter. Empress Maria Theresa's carriages were parked directly between Father Gregor's church and Clara's paddock. Zubin's mouth was open. Clara was on her feet, tail twitching, ears pointed at the trumpeters.

The carriage was so ornate that it must have dropped from the Milky Way. Gilded, carved, and painted with a heavenly scene featuring cherubs, it was light on its wheels and pulled by four white horses with plumed headdresses. Tassels dripping with pewter beading swung from the coach and sparkled in the sunlight.

The inside was upholstered in blood-red velvet, and visible from the window was the soft profile and coiffed hair of the Empress herself. Sweat gathered on Douwe's calloused palms. He straightened his navy jacket.

"Your Majesty." Douwe bowed as a footman gave Maria Theresa a hand. In her right arm was a small squirming white and red dog. Its ears were like Clara's, feathered and turning at every noise.

Maria Theresa's powdered face was round and cheerful. Her hair was translucent, star-white, though she was youthful. She wore braids and curls; large pearls dripped from her ears. Her gown was rich teal, the color of a predawn sky. It was lace and silk taffeta, with the textured slubs of Indian silk, the fabric from the trade goods in the *Knappenhof*'s hull.

The world came full circle. Fabrics made where Clara was born dressed the Habsburg Empress. Douwe smiled, bowed, and swept his hand grandly to Clara's paddock. Maria Theresa's maids and several party members exited the other carriages, chattering like birds.

Clara turned her ears their way. People meant food, and her eyes were bright. The dog stared at Clara, a low growl rumbling. One last carriage was left to unload, and Maria Theresa turned around, watching.

The footmen opened the door. Francis emerged, wearing black shoes with silver buckles and white stockings. His pantaloons and a brocade jacket were the same rich teal as his wife's gown. His hair was perfectly curled, a teal bow held his ponytail.

He sniffed loudly and smiled, taking his wife's arm and patting her hand. The dog squirmed out of Maria Theresa's arms. It ran toward Clara barking, silky tail wagging furiously.

"Oh, Phalene!" the Empress called, signaling her many servants to go after her.

Clara lowered her head as if to charge. The dog slipped between the paddock rails and danced around Clara's feet. Clara shook her head playfully at the little dog, nudging it with her dull, short horn. The dog continued barking and circling, then dropped into a playful posture, wagging her tail, licking Clara's face.

The audience awww'ed, and Zubin gestured to see if he could pick the dog up to remove her from the pen. Maria Theresa nodded and opened her arms to receive Phalene. The Empress's double chins pressed against her milky-white neck. Her cheeks were pink, full and round. The dog licked her, leaving a streak where her powder smeared.

Clara stomped playfully, staring at Phalene. She wanted more of the little dog.

"Captain van der Meer, I presume?" Maria Theresa said.

"I am," Douwe replied, bowing again. "Clara would like to play with your dog, Your Majesty."

The Empress smiled, and the pearls in her ears swung lightly. With delicate, slippered feet, she moved toward Clara. Her blue eyes were kind.

"I have come to see if this animal is as real as the rumors," she said. "Though no one said how absolutely majestic she is."

Douwe felt like leaping into the air, but instead, he picked up Clara's fruit bag and held out a carrot to Empress Maria Theresa. She took it with a gloved hand and gently pressed the dog into Douwe's arms.

The Empress held out the carrot to Clara, who opened her pink mouth and partially wrapped her lip around it, slurping it in. Her gloves were sticky with rhino slime. Maria Theresa clapped her hands and reached into the bag to get more. Douwe held the bag open with one hand and Phalene in the other.

The tiny papillon stared at him longingly, slowly wagging its tail. He could not put Maria Theresa's dog down. Zubin let out a bubbly laugh as he took the bag of produce and ensured each royal court member retrieved a treat for Clara.

Douwe shifted Phalene the Papillion from arm to arm. The dog's tiny paws dangled in the air. Zubin showed each person, from the coach driver to the emperor, how to feed Clara and where she loved to be petted. He opened the small jar of fish oil and let Maria Theresa sniff. Zubin told them of Calcutta and the dense jungle of Clara's birth. He told them about her horn and how it was not done growing.

"She may even live to be one hundred," said Zubin, scratching between Clara's armored plates. Douwe held Phalene all the while watching Zubin talk with royalty about their beloved animal.

"Thank you, Your Highness," said Douwe, eventually handing Phalene back to Maria Thersa with a ceremonious bow.

"Captain, I would like to invite you to stay at the palace with us through the end of the month," said Empress Maria Theresa. "My children are due home soon from the countryside. They would delight in your animal."

Douwe was exuberant but kept his calm demeanor and agreed. Zubin scratched Phalene under the chin to Clara's chagrin. She huffed behind him. The carriages trundled off and left Zubin and Douwe to gather their things from the courtyard. They made no delay and began the journey to the palace.

Douwe shifted his gaze to the cathedral, but he saw no movement. Despite the stillness there, a gripping fear rose in his throat.

Chapter 29
Andrea
Leiden, The Netherlands

The flatbed truck drove slowly back to the museum. Andrea was seated on the bed, holding down the straps of the coffin. Lucas and Paul were there, too. Janice drove. The campus sidewalks were too narrow for the truck, so they went roundabout to the museum's loading dock.

Andrea's heart pounded like crazy. This part of the project felt unstable. She didn't have control. She wanted to get the casket and remains safely inside. It felt like all hands on deck once they parked at the loading dock.

"I feel like I'm working on one of those East Indiaman ships," Andrea said to Lucas, who pulled the straps off the casket. He nodded, still covered in dirt, sweating.

"Twenty more feet, team!" shouted Paul. He and Lucas grabbed the inch-thick board under the casket. Janice unlocked a wide garage door.

Andrea ran inside to grab the lights. Lucas and Paul slid Douwemout van der Meer onto a large dissection table, and Janice closed the garage door.

"Listen, I know we are all eager to document our eighteenth-century friend here," said Janice. "But we absolutely have to clean up. This is a delicate project, and he's dirty enough already. We'll break for an hour, clean the dirt from our nails, and meet back here at 3 p.m."

"Got it," said Lucas. He held his arms up like a swamp thing. He was filthy.

An hour later, Andrea was showered, hair washed, fingers scrubbed, cleanly clothed, and ready to document Douwemout van der Meer. She made a point not to look at her phone. She was avoiding. Andrea didn't want to break the spell of her current life for the destruction barreling over the ocean. She ran back to the museum, meeting Lucas on the way.

"Hey!" Lucas shouted, hair still damp. "Did you get a hold of Jake?"

"No," she said. "I didn't try."

"If he's on his way, you have to do something," he said.

"I want to focus on Douwe right now."

"I get it, but tomorrow—"

"Is tomorrow," she said. She didn't want to deal with it. It felt more terrifying to face than she was willing to admit. Lucas shrugged, but she could tell he was worried. They went through the museum's front door through the exhibits, and something caught her eye.

"What's this?" she said. A room to the right showcased an exhibit full of skeletons and taxidermy specimens. She took a deep breath.

"This stuff freaks you out?" said Lucas.

"Yeah, it does," she said. "My ex...he...his family..."

Lucas narrowed his eyes, trying to read her.

"You can tell me, Andrea. We're friends."

"I know we are," she said. "His family were trophy hunters. I didn't know. I thought he was different."

"Trophy hunters? Like safari shit?"

She nodded. "They had all but the rhino, I think, for the big five."

A look of distaste grew on Lucas's face. "That's not cool, especially knowing how much people pay for something like that. Innocent animals killed literally for thousands."

Andrea nodded again, her mouth salty and dry. She had a choice. She could walk through this place and try to undo the trauma of the trophies, educationally seeing taxidermy. These were museum specimens, not rich peoples' status symbols.

"Are you alright?"

"I'm not, but I will be," Andrea said, determined. She stepped into the room.

Anatomy jars lined the shelves, clearly old, full of amber and greenish-gray liquids and floating things.

"Leiden used to have a huge anatomy theater," said Lucas. "They would dissect people and animals for students to watch. Gruesome, but it allowed for advances in science and medicine. No one knew what the human body was like inside until they cut it open."

They walked through the exhibit, examining the artifacts. Bones, saws, and a sketchbook. She leaned in to see the book—it was crisp like a leaf.

"Hey, Lucas," she said. "Look."

Lucas came close. She could smell the cool scent of his freshly showered body and inhaled. He cupped his eyes around the glass.

"That looks like a rhino without a horn," he said. "It's so faded. Kohl on parchment does that after nearly 300 years. The exhibit notes said no other rhinos in Europe except Clara existed. That has to be her."

The sketchbook was open to a page where Clara's face was the focus, a nub of a horn showing. It showed her textured skin and one padded foot with three toenails. The artifact card read: *Jan Wandelaar Sketch Notepad, ca. 1740-1760.*

"It looks like someone's work in progress. But why is her horn gone?" she asked. "Is that normal for rhinos?"

"You're asking the wrong person," said Lucas, shaking his head. "But as an art person, I can tell you Wandelaar was one of the best anatomy illustrators in history. He drew the human body down to sinew, muscle, and bone like never before. Learned it through dissection."

She shivered. "How did they get the specimens to dissect?" This was worse than trophy hunting.

Lucas shrugged. "Maybe donated? But I wouldn't be surprised if the anatomy school paid for some, and if that's the case—"

"Graverobbers," she said.

"Yeah," Lucas said, leaning toward a pen and ink drawing beside the notebook.

"It feels weird that the same thing is happening now," she said.

"It feels very coincidental, too," said Lucas. "That the box and the grave are both disturbed."

"We'll figure it out."

Andrea kept walking, leaning in to see the glass cases. A framed illustration on the wall showed the anatomy theater: a round room, skeletons set up in the corners, bleachers surrounding, and a table in the middle. In one corner, a fully articulated horse had a human skeleton rider.

"This place you say helped advance science? What happened to it?"

"Says here it closed in 1821 after dwindling popularity," Lucas read the placard near the framed print. "Look at the table."

Andrea got closer and grimaced at an illustrated corpse, belly splayed open on the dissection table. All she could think of was a rhino in the room, audience members gathered around, watching its horn being sliced from its face.

"You don't think they cut off Clara's horn in that room, do you?"

"I don't think so," said Lucas. "I think someone would have drawn that. Art loves gore."

"We gotta get to Douwemout before that graverobber does. They're bound to return to the cemetery and know we've taken him up. Especially if the empty box is their doing, too."

"I didn't think about that," said Lucas. "But I bet Janice hasn't left his side."

"Let's make sure," she said, grabbing his hand and heading toward the back.

They wound through the exhibits, and Andrea began to realize her mindset shift. The specimens on display here were for education. Progress comes with a price, and that price shouldn't be tens of thousands of dollars to kill an animal. It should be to preserve the historic ones that still existed, whether as specimens, documents, or just in memory.

Douwemout and Clara's horn in the back room propelled her onward. The metal door to the prep room was heavy, and Lucas pushed it open.

Pure chaos awaited. The fluorescent lights above were dangling as if struck by something heavy, sending shadows swaying on the floor of the dissection room.

"Oh god! Paul!"

Paul was on the floor, not moving. Andrea rushed to his side and grabbed his hand. Lucas put his finger to his mouth, beckoning her to be quiet. Whoever harmed Paul could still be in the room.

She took his pulse and checked his breathing. He was alive but unconscious. Andrea grabbed her phone from her coat pocket to text her mom. She did not know how to call for help in the Netherlands.

Send help, 911, she texted her. *Professor hurt. Ambulance and police, Leiden University Museum. I am not hurt. Cannot answer your call.*

The phone made a swooping noise as the message was sent, and she cursed herself for not putting it on silent. Lucas was slowly casing the room, seeing if they were alone. Douwemout van der Meer's casket was open on the table above.

She got to her knees slowly and peered inside. Panic swept her. The skeleton was still there, draped in its teal scraps of fabric. But the horn was gone. His finger bones were broken. She made a silent promise to see his bones repaired herself and conjured their positions from the perfect picture stored in her mind. She searched the casket for the horn.

It was gone—the horn, gone! Panic crept into her limbs. The graverobber's target was revealed. Rhino horns were extremely valuable on the black market, and she couldn't imagine what a famous rhino horn like Clara's could bring. She looked around for Lucas. He lingered by the door that led to the archives.

Another wave of panic hit her. The artifacts were at risk. If the graverobber knew the horn was here, they knew other valuable things were in the next room.

"Lucas," she whispered. He crouched down and came over, eyes still locked on the door.

"He alright?"

"I don't know," Andrea said. "I texted my mom to call for help, I don't know how to do it here."

"It's 1-1-2," he said. "Go out and call. I'm going to check the archives."

"That's not a good idea. We should stay together. The horn is gone, Lucas."

"The horn...?" he said. "Of course it is."

"They made the connection before we did that it was likely Douwe-mout van der Meer buried there. Stole the archival box to make certain. Probably guessed there'd be something of value in his casket."

"How could they have known?" Lucas said, still watching the door. "The only people who knew about the documents in your room and the archives and the grave were me, you, Janice, and Paul."

She shook her head. "You're forgetting Sergei."

"Oh, shit," said Lucas. "Sergei. He was at the grave and tried to pick up the documents last night."

"Yeah. And he knew exactly where the archival box was stored. Maintenance guy—he had all the tools to dig up the grave, too."

Lucas crossed his arms over his chest, exhaling loudly. His jaw muscles tensed. He stood, looking into the dark archives.

"Hey Andrea, where is Janice?" Lucas asked.

Chapter 30
Douwemout van der Meer
Vienna

Douwe and Zubin loaded their trunks and harnessed the team. The horses blew steam, stamping and shaking their heads. They were eager to pull after days without work.

Clara was loaded into her carriage, hay manger full. The horses strained, their muscles rippling with every slow step. The going was slow through Vienna. Zubin counted the gargoyles on the towering, flat-faced facades. He asked Douwe which each creature was. Dragons, dogs, lions, griffons, and the ones he could not identify, he called demons.

The chilly November morning blossomed into a bright blue day, and Schönbrunn's lemon-yellow facade glowed before them. The palace grounds boasted 400 acres, gardens, fountains, and forests full of wild game. The wide, wild grasses on the outskirts of the property waved.

The team of horses pulled to the stables where servants waited. The stable hands stood in a military-like line, wearing tan uniforms. They methodically unhitched the team, and a tall, slender man with bony hands approached.

"Hallo!" he called with a smile, showing horse-like teeth. "I am Karl, the head groom here. I understand you have quite an animal in this box." The wagon dwarfed him.

Clara stuck her nubby horn out the barred window and flexed her lip toward the man. They dropped the ramp. Clara's three-toed feet padded onto the soft gravel. The first rhino ever there. Her column-like legs were rough and pebbled, a stark contrast to the shining coats of the strong draft horses that pulled her.

Clara unloaded into a vacant pasture, butting up to the long stables. She dropped her head and grazed for the first time in a week. Douwe felt relief wash over him and began telling Karl about her care.

"Fish oil?" he said.

"Or mud, if you have it," shrugged Douwe.

"We have a pond here," Karl said. He motioned to the back of the golden fall pasture where ducks swam, bobbing their heads under.

"She may destroy the banks," said Douwe, concerned about the beautiful grounds. "It may be too cold, besides."

"She is the Empress' special guest," said Karl. "Do not worry while you are at Schönbrunn. If she needs fish oil, she gets fish oil."

Sculptured pines framed the walkways of the gardens, fountains gurgled, and servants bustled about. In the stables, dozens of stalls waited. The horse team was groomed, and a more oversized stall nearest the pasture was set up for Clara. Fresh straw was tossed down for her, and a hay box packed full.

They were taken to the palace. The compound was more extensive than entire hamlets they had visited. The Schönnbrun was glowing like an enormous lemon-yellow pearl. Every inch was decorated inside—the corners ornate, walls covered, even the ceilings carved to beautiful effect. Zubin spun in a circle, then uncharacteristically grabbed Douwe's hand, nervous.

The servants showed them to the guest quarters, where their chests were delivered. The walls were cream with bronze wainscoting and gilded bows. The furniture was toile printed, delicate-legged and exquisite. Quite different from the inns they frequented.

There was a deep bathtub, and warm water was brought in. Douwe and Zubin turned the water brown and dressed for a special audience in the clothes they bought in Calcutta. Zubin's jacket looked tight. Douwe straightened Zubin's lapel, and the two were led to court.

The prospect of a formal meeting with royalty made Zubin extremely nervous, but a room was full of children connected to the garden. A table layered with fruit and cakes was set for them, and the room was full of toys. Dogs barked and darted about. Zubin's face glowed.

"Behave yourself, Zubin, and eat all you can," Douwe said. "I'll find you after court, but if you grow tired, ask the servants to take you to the apartments. I am unsure if we will be asked to dine with them again. It is a great honor, my boy. Enjoy it."

Zubin cracked a smile, hugged Douwe, and ran into the room. A boy no older than three toddled up to him, and Zubin accepted the ball he offered. Seeing Zubin content, Douwe strode toward the large open room where court was held.

Maria Theresa was seated at the end of the elegant ballroom. Phalene the Papillion was in her lap. Another golden, curly-haired dog sighed at her feet, clearly irritated that it was not in Phalene's spot.

The day was warm for November, and large windows streamed with light. The walls were deep teal, not unlike Maria Theresa's dress the day before. Douwe waited while a few friendly merchants showed the Empress their wares. He remembered the dinner at which he first met Clara years ago. Formal, but Sichterman's home paled in comparison. He wondered what Clara would do in this enormous room.

He conversed quietly with the men around him, conscious of his out-of-date fashion and fascinated by the many comings and goings of court. He was the last to be presented. A herald announced him as Captain Douwemout van der Meer, the Rhino Keeper. Douwe bowed and thanked the Empress for having him.

"I hope you and your children can find time to spend with Clara while we are your guests, Your Majesty," Douwe said.

"The children would like nothing more, Captain," said Maria Theresa. Her gown was navy blue. Douwe stared at the bright sapphires on her necklace.

Though he was a commoner, she was polite to him, and her kindness extended to everyone she met that day at court. Phalene was asleep, her tiny paws dangling off the Empress' lap, when a knock on the window came.

It was Karl, the head groom, smiling in his long-toothed way and leading Clara, who had a collar not unlike an ox, except it was festooned with flowers. Douwe had never seen anyone, but he, Zubin, or Lonnie, lead Clara. He was shocked. Members of the court let out pleased noises and chattered amongst themselves. The merchants raised eyebrows and spoke in hushed, excited tones.

Phalene the Papillion woke, startled by the sudden movement at the window, and began barking. The little dog leaped from Maria Theresa's lap, and the Empress rose. Douwe paused to compose himself and darted into the garden where Clara waited. Karl nodded and winked. Douwe took a breath and smiled, his palms damp with sweat.

"Your Majesty, may I formally introduce you and your court to Clara." Douwe swept his arms toward his animal.

Clara recognized Douwe and stepped toward the door, swiveling her ears and chomping at her floral collar. Karl held her back a bit. Clara was attached to a black leather leash. Douwe had not collared her in at least a year as she had outgrown her equipment, and he burned to ask if he could keep this new set.

But his goal right now was presenting his masterpiece to Empress Maria Theresa and her guests. She was suddenly by his side. He could smell lavender water and the sharp scent of her face powder. Douwe turned into a showman.

"Clara is the only rhinoceros in Europe, Your Majesty," he said. Maria Theresa and her court followed him. A gaggle of tiny dogs pattered out, and Douwe wondered where they had all come from. They circled Clara, yapping, and one by one were scooped up by their owners, mainly the court ladies.

"Clara is coming into adulthood. Her horn is stubby now, but it will grow large. It is said that rhinoceros horns have magical properties, and while that may be true, I have no desire to let anyone test the theory on my beast," Douwe said. He rubbed Clara's nose, and the Empress laughed.

"Though you likely learned while studying Pliny the Elder that rhinoceros are vicious and dangerous, I have not seen that side of her," Douwe said. Clara licked his hands like a dog.

"She is more like the little animals you hold right now, ladies. Spoiled, hungry, and affectionate," Douwe said. Laughter rippled.

"It is said she may live to be one hundred. I suppose we shall find out in 1840," Douwe said. Again, the court laughed.

"It is said her natural enemy is the elephant, so we may be traveling to Versailles to find out." Douwe laughed this time. The ladies fanned their faces, and Maria Theresa gave a loud guffaw.

"Clara travels with my assistant and me in the largest animal carriage yet created, pulled by draft horses," Douwe said. "She eats a bushel of hay daily, drinks water and ale alike, but will eat about anything else given to her."

"Is there any food she doesn't like?" Maria Theresa asked.

"Radishes, Your Highness," he said. "Too spicy for her delicate disposition."

Clara bobbed her head at Phalene, who mouthed her horn playfully, and the audience laughed again.

"Is she truly armored?" asked a merchant.

"Touch her and feel for yourself," said Douwe. "She's like a rock, a warm one in the sun. Let me pick up this little one before you do." Douwe bent and picked up Phalene, who danced at his feet. The little dog licked his chin as she had done to Maria Theresa. Douwe tucked her under an arm, his mouth curved into a prideful half smile.

The merchant raised a shaky hand and rubbed Clara's neck above the grand collar. Clara paid him no mind. She was more focused on the fact that Douwe was holding a different animal. After the merchant backed away, she huffed.

"Oh!" said Maria Theresa. "She is much like a dog, jealous of others and possessive of her owner! How absolutely fascinating, Captain."

Douwe handed Phalene to the Empress and went to make amends with Clara. As she had done so many times, Clara relaxed her ears and leaned into Douwe. He braced himself and rubbed her neck. The audience burst into applause.

Suddenly Maria Theresa was searching for a lady's maid and urgently whispered in her ear. Douwe pulled a flower from Clara's collar. She ate it. A few court members approached, wanting to feel her rock-like skin and ask questions. Moments later, the glass door opened.

"Announcing the royal children, as requested, Your Majesty," said the herald.

The children politely lined up with their nannies in tow. Douwe searched for Zubin. He was the last to enter. His thin tawny ankles showed as he walked, pants several inches short. Zubin smiled at the sight of Clara in her decorative collar.

At the sight of Zubin, Clara gave a soft whistle. Zubin met Karl, took the lead, and rubbed Clara's flank, taking his place between Clara and Douwe. The children's mouths opened in awe.

"Mama!" said the eldest girl. "What a wonder you have brought for us!"

"Now, Maria Anna, she won't be staying forever," Maria Theresa said. She scooped up the girl's hand. "She is a guest in our home for a few weeks. Perhaps you could learn more about her?"

The girl nodded, bright blue eyes shining. She asked what the rhino's name was, and Zubin answered her. The children took timid steps toward her, asking Zubin all kinds of things. He crouched, telling them baby Clara traveled for six months at sea and drank goat's milk. He told them she had cat and goat friends. He taught them what Bakari meant, and the children laughed.

Clara was a star, standing still and observing the people around her with little care. She was more concerned about Douwe and Zubin than the strangers, though she longed to play with the dogs.

After an hour, she presented an enormous dropping pile to the great amusement of the children, who were promptly led inside. Douwe's face hurt from smiling. He and Zubin went with Clara and Karl, who suggested she graze for the day. Clara strode, now collar-free, into the wide grassy field as the golden rays of sunset descended upon Vienna.

That night, Douwe and Zubin retired to the apartments, fighting the urge to check on Clara. Douwe reassured Zubin: far too many people were invested in her care in this place for anything to go wrong. But they slept fitfully, both waking to see if the sun had risen long before dawn. Douwe's dreams were of Clara's horn and Father Gregor.

Unseen to Douwe in the belly of the palace, Maria Theresa descended a hidden staircase in her bed chamber to a sanctuary. She woke in darkness, stars dropping into their final places before they faded in the blue light of morning. The room, dimly lit by red candles and the gray promise of the day, was hers and hers alone until the priest arrived.

Father Gregor performed mass for her daily, leaving before the household woke. Maria Theresa was a devout and earnest Catholic. She took messages from God to her heart each morning. She listened closely for signs of Him—flickering candles and whispers of the vapors in the fire became the syllables of words.

She asked questions of God and received answers in the form of future plans: How can I serve my people? And the answer came: Marry your children to countries with the necessary resources. Your people will be provided for. And so she planned to. She asked: How will I know what my people need? And the answer came: Invite them to your palaces and ask them. And so she did.

When Father Gregor arrived the morning after Clara's court debut, he spoke of the Behemoth of Job.

"You've heard of this creature," he said to Maria Theresa, "invading the minds of your loyal citizens. They're driven to sin by an unrepentant man. He believes he has something worth worshiping. I remind Vienna that idolatry is a sin against the very foundations of the church. There is but one God and all others must be forsaken."

Maria Theresa considered carefully the priest's words. She understood his duty to protect her from sin, yet she was reminded of the feeling of lightness she felt around Clara. The woman glowed, fire in front of her, like a celestial being. Her silver gown shone. Gregor was dull in comparison—sallow-skinned, dressed in black.

"Father Gregor," she said, touching his cold wrist. "Have you considered the wonders of God in animals?" She spoke to him as if he were a child.

"This is not a wonder of God," Gregor said. He moved his hand out from under hers. "It is a creature worshiped by more of my congregation than Christ inside the cathedral. Anything that pulls us away from God must be stopped."

Maria Theresa straightened in her chair. Gregor had forgotten much power she had. She smiled.

"Father Gregor, when I look in that creature's eyes and at her broad, strong legs, I do not see sin," she said. "I see a miracle. Proof that God exists—how could he make my dear sweet children, you, and a beast like that?"

Maria Theresa gazed up at the ceiling. She had in her mind the faces of the two children she had buried. Their bow-like cherub mouths faded to blue so quickly. Gone, swift as bird wings.

Her children's wrists still held the fold of fat from babyhood. Instead of wrapping those small arms around her neck, Maria Theresa folded her two babies' arms over their hearts. They never lived long enough to see the wonders of this world.

"I see joy, Father Gregor, when I see my children and that Behemoth. And I see a God whose creations cannot be anything but intentional," she said. Maria Theresa blinked. She pushed their cherub faces to a far corner of her mind.

"Have you considered, Your Majesty, that the devil lures with the promise of a miracle and instead is tempting you with idol worship?" he said. "Do not be fooled when joy comes so unexpectedly. Your time should be spent in prayer and with your duties, not allowing a beast to take the attention and money of your subjects as offering."

"Your opinion is your own, Father. You are spoiling your congregation's happiness. You've become a little dog, yelping when you hear a loud bark. I have special intentions for the owner and the animal. I shall not have you interfere."

Father Gregor's angular, clean-shaven face was cast in shadow.

"Special intentions, Your Majesty?"

"My plans are my own, Father."

The priest turned his face to the fire. The hair on Maria Theresa's arms prickled.

"You have been my priest for three years now," she said, blue eyes burning. "It may be time for you to move. I've been in correspondence with the archbishop."

Maria Theresa held her arms out to the staircase, ushering the priest in front of her.

Father Gregor hesitated, staring. He had always let her go first. Maria Theresa gritted her teeth and extended her arms again.

"Go, Father Gregor," she said. He went. Maria Theresa's heart pounded. She followed him and locked the door.

Night withdrew its blanketed hold on the palace. Douwe woke to shouts outside as the pale walls grew bright with sunrise. He shook Zubin awake, and they pulled on their boots.

"Fire!" They heard from the mouths of servants. "Stables!"

Douwe and Zubin locked eyes and ran, marble floors shining

beneath them. They slid out the nearest door and flew over the steps onto the gravel paths. Smoke poured from the stables, a gray mar on the autumn sky. They ran faster. Horses galloped past, saddle-less and panicked, the whites of their eyes rolling.

Zubin yelled, spotting one of their draft horses with a herd of royal war horses cantering ahead.

"Leave it!" shouted Douwe. The stables windows poured smoke, the smell of burning hay acrid in the chill air.

The closest stall to the hay meadow was Clara's. Douwe headed to the far end of the long, pearl-yellow building. Black smoke gathered around them, and Zubin tried to wrench the stable door open, but it was locked from the inside. Douwe bid him back up and kicked hard.

The door splintered, Douwe's leg puncturing the wood. Smoke billowed out in a gasp, sending Zubin coughing. He waved his hands before his face while Douwe wrenched his boot free and ran inside. Clara was in her paddock, lying down. Zubin yelled to her.

"Clara, up!" He hurled open her stall door. The fire was nearest the main entrance. Hot orange flames jumped the stall walls. Clara's eyes rolled back. Douwe tossed a bucket of water on the closest flames and grabbed the floral collar that hung outside the tack room. He flung it over Clara's head and pulled the lead. She stood.

Tears streamed down Zubin's face—smoke, fear, both.

Clara moved, panicked, feet splayed underneath her. She reared her head. Above them, the wooden beams blackened with flames. They were not long from collapse. Zubin pushed Clara's massive body out the stall door, and the crackling of the wood above them grew louder. A pop sounded and the stall frame collapsed as Zubin skittered underneath it.

Douwe pulled. The fringes of Clara's floral collar were singed and smoking. Blessed blue sky waited outside if she'd only move, but the rhino refused. Zubin cried out, pushing hard against the debris, coughing. Douwe pulled hard, and Clara's front legs slid from under her. Douwe ran using the momentum from her near fall, allowing Clara the space to do the same. Zubin followed closely behind into the hay meadow beyond.

The stables erupted into flames, smoke rolling out the remaining windows. Clara ran, her smoldering floral collar flung to the ground. Zubin let her go and collapsed to his knees, coughing until he gagged. Douwe sat, chest heaving, watching Clara run to the hay meadow with dozens of loose horses.

The stable hands and servants ran buckets from Clara's farm pond and fountains to extinguish the fire until a wagon rolled up with massive wooden water barrels to extinguish the flames. The Schönbrunn's stables were gone.

Douwe and Zubin let Clara run. The hay meadow was fenced, and she was terrified. The horses fueled her anxious energies, and Karl agreed to leave them all be. His staff, soot-faced and weary, ensured every animal was alive and accounted for.

"We'll find a place to house them," Karl said. "But I am not sure what to do with Clara."

"She can stay in her wagon for now," said Douwe. "Our time here is nearly done. What happened, Karl?"

"The night stable boy saw a man in black carrying a lantern this morning," said Karl. He shook his head as the horses trumpeted nearby. "Perhaps it was the devil in his dreams before the fire broke out."

Douwe ears rang. In his mind's eye was Gregor, hands curled around a flame, staring at Clara. Surely, the priest was miles away at the cathedral. But fear lingered.

In the following days, as makeshift stables were created, Clara traveled to various sites on the property for audiences with the Empress and her guests. Douwe answered questions and showed the parties how she knew her name. His hair still smelled of smoke.

The family was largely unaffected by the fire. The workers of Schönbrunn had to deal with the livestock, and though the stress did not change the family's routine, it changed everyone else's. The family's children played in the courtyard each afternoon, where Douwe attended to Clara. She had little rest as Douwe didn't want her locked in her wagon. The children made up Clara songs:

Lovely little Clara always wants to play
Lovely little Clara eating through the day
Lovely little Clara, larger than a cow
Lovely little Clara, never pulls a plow

During one of these play dates, Maria Theresa came up to Douwe with a gentle smile and Phalene in her arms. The dog was nodding off.

"Douwe," she said. The skirt of her golden gown shimmered in the sun. It was cold but bright, and she wore a black fur bolero that rippled in the wind. Douwe felt very aware of his jacket that had singe marks and smelled of smoke, but he did not own another.

Douwe bowed and smiled. "Empress, how may I please you today?"

"My son," she said. "He has taken ill. His one request is to see Clara."

"Of course, Your Highness. We can position Clara outside the boy's room, perhaps open the window for him?"

"He wants to touch her horn," she said, blue eyes sharp and keen. "He remembers what you said, that it has magic properties."

"Some believe that," Douwe said. "Did the boy understand that many people believe those powers exist only if the horn is severed from the animal and ground into a fine powder?"

"He missed that part of your lesson, Captain," Maria Theresa said. "But I still believe seeing Clara would make him feel better."

"Then, by all means," Douwe said.

"I shall speak to Karl and the head of my household. They will accomplish it within the day."

Douwe nodded.

"There is one more thing," said Maria Theresa. Her bright eyes caught the light. She seemed far away. "Do you believe the animal is sent from the devil to tempt us? An idol we are worshiping?"

Douwe's stomach dropped. He inhaled sharply through his nose and sighed. The wind ruffled his auburn hair. Maria Theresa straightened her bolero and furrowed her brow, now looking directly at Douwe. Her eyes held the weight of sadness he could not have defined before being here in this grand place.

Despite the trimmings and ease of living, the people to help her, all of the money, treasure, food, power—anything that she could need at her fingertips, this woman had great and terrible pain. It was there in glimpses when she watched her children play.

"Your Majesty, if I may?" Douwe offered his arm to her. She put Phalene down. Douwe walked up to Clara, grazing on the short, manicured lawn. The palace glowed lemon yellow behind them, and the noises of children and dogs surrounded them.

Clara glanced up as they neared, taking a few padded steps toward them. She huffed, waving her head back and forth in her special greeting. Phalene trotted to her on tiny feet, and Clara bent, ready to play. Despite their size difference, the two took to the open yard and soon ran circles around each other. They ended back at the water trough when Zubin whistled for Clara.

Maria Theresa and Douwe stood silently.

"She is a marvel," said Maria Theresa. "I cannot see evil in her, Captain."

"Neither can I," said Douwe. "We have seen evil, you and me. We have faced demons in the flesh. Even here, in the fire. You cannot tell me after all you have endured, and pardon me for mentioning, but the loss of your children, that this animal is evil."

Maria Theresa drew back and pursed her pink lips. She picked up panting Phalene, whose tail wagged wildly.

"Life is brutal enough to deny one the joy your animal brings, Captain," she said. "I am grateful for your kindness, especially to my children."

Later that day, Clara donned a new floral collar, and Zubin and Douwe led her to a wide bay window on the first floor where Charles Joseph waited. The small boy was almost three with dusty blonde hair and lake-blue eyes that matched his mother's. He wore a white nightgown and stood with a nurse by his side. His cheeks were flushed with fever. At the sight of Clara, he dropped his nurse's hand and pressed his nose to the thick glass.

Douwe and Zubin walked Clara in front of the window. Zubin had her sit and lie on her side for a belly rub. Then she was up on her feet, stretching the folds of her neck to grab an orange from Douwe. The boy clapped and grinned, showing his small baby teeth, talking joyfully to his nurse.

Douwe heard Charles Joseph's muffled voice through the glass but could not understand him. Clara fogged the window. Zubin pulled her back, and she turned in a circle on her leash. Douwe smiled and nodded at the nurse, who picked up the child. It was clear the boy did not feel well. He put his head on his nurse's shoulder and popped his thumb in his mouth. His fluttering eyes closed. Clara was taken back to the large pasture behind the ruined stables. Charles Joseph did not touch her horn.

Clara lived out the month in the pastures and gardens of Schönbrunn, and on their final day, Maria Theresa called Douwe and Zubin to the throne room.

Maria Theresa was dressed in teal silks. Her husband matched her, and the children stood in an orderly line, each with something in their hands. They stepped forward and presented Douwe and Zubin with gifts.

The eldest, Maria Anna, presented two matching embroidered overcoats in the same rich teal that Maria Theresa favored. Joseph Benedict presented them with a fine, strong leash and a large, embossed collar for Clara. Maria Christina had a single orange in her hand and told them with a short curtsy that one hundred oranges awaited them in Clara's cart. Maria Elisabeth gave Zubin a new cup and ball game. Charles Joseph waddled up with a basket full of brown bread. The baby, Maria Amalia, held in a nurse's arms, had a small bouquet of flowers.

"Captain Douwemout van der Meer of Leiden," said Maria Theresa, rising. "I, Maria Theresa, Queen of Bohemia and Empress of the Holy Roman Empire, hereby name you on this day, the twenty-sixth of November, a Baron of the Holy Roman Empire by my decree."

Douwe's mouth slightly parted. Zubin grabbed his arm. A royal title. Douwe could scarcely breathe. He mouthed a breathy thank you and dropped to one knee. Zubin followed. Maria Theresa smiled grandly. Her children gathered around her, and Douwe memorized the scene in his mind.

After Clara left Vienna, a miniature was painted of young Charles. He talked non-stop about the rhinoceros, and to his delight, his mother requested the artist draw Clara in his portrait in the book in Charles's lap. The porcelain miniature was perfect if flawed, as the boy never actually held a book featuring Clara, but certainly had dreamed it.

Chapter 31
Andrea
Leiden, The Netherlands

Paul stirred, moaning and grabbing his head.

"Hey, hey." Lucas knelt beside him and touched his shoulder. "You okay, Paul?"

"Oh, gosh... Lucas," Paul said, breathing heavily. He removed his glasses and pinched his nose. "I'm not sure."

"Stay put," Andrea said. Her phone buzzed. It was a Dutch number. She answered it, whispering hello.

The dispatcher spoke in Dutch and Andrea panicked.

"There's been a break-in at the University Museum. My professor, Paul Hahn, is hurt," she said, praying the dispatcher spoke English.

The dispatcher responded in English that the campus police were informed, and the city police and an ambulance were on their way. Andrea returned to Lucas and Paul, then dropped her phone in shock.

Sergei was there, shovel in hand.

"Sergei," Lucas said. "Put the shovel down."

Sergei was red-faced and screaming in Dutch, pointing to the archives. Andrea couldn't understand him.

Lucas popped to his feet and responded, motioning to Paul and the casket. Sergei furrowed his brow—angry, confused, both. He got close to the remains, and Andrea ran toward him.

"He doesn't have the horn," Lucas said. "He's asking where it is."

"Three hundred thousand on the black market," Sergei said, pointing at them. "One of you has it!"

Sergei wheeled, shovel in hand. Andrea and Lucas held their hands up, jumping back from the dirty tool.

"Sergei, we don't have the horn," Lucas said, pulling out his pockets and patting his coat.

Sergei's chest heaved with breath, and he rushed to the silver table where the skeleton lay, jostling the remains.

"No! Get away from it!" Andrea yelled.

Sergei narrowed his eyes at her and spun away, shovel dangerously close to her head. He ducked, looking under the table, and saw Paul. Sergei stood quickly and turned to Lucas.

"What did you do?" he said.

"What did *you* do, Sergei?" Lucas said.

Sergei's face went pale and with a metallic thud, the shovel hit the concrete floor. He ran into the connected archives. Lucas grabbed Andrea and they followed, leaving Paul and the skeletal remains behind.

The lights were off. Emergency floods spotlighted macabre artifacts in their glass cases. A wave of adrenaline pumped through Andrea. Another nightmare room. They followed Sergei, but the room was too dark to track him closely. Andrea ran by the drawers where the miniature of Charles Joseph was stored, out of breath, hearing the gentle tinkling of glass.

"What do we do now?" she cried to Lucas, who fumbled with his phone's flashlight.

"We follow," he said.

Chapter 32
Douwemout van der Meer
Europe

S pring storms rumbled, sending torrents of rain down the glass walls of a Breslau orangery. On warmer days, Clara grazed in the tan fields near the property, huffing steam from her mouth and nose. To her delight, she ran alongside the horses, covered in cold mud. Gentle rainstorms sent her playing in the yard. The orangery kept warm enough that fruit blossomed year-round, and they had to keep Clara from stripping the leaves from every low-hanging branch.

"Dresden," said Douwe to Zubin. In March, the trees outside the orangery blossomed and fruited, beckoning returning birds. They hovered over a map of Saxony. "To the porcelain factory."

"You want Clara to go to a porcelain factory?" Zubin asked as Clara tried to rear up on her hind legs to grab a particularly tempting pear.

"Not inside, Zubin," said Douwe. "Have you ever heard of King Augustus?"

"No," said Zubin, who clambered up the tree to save Clara from the strain. He landed gently and dangled the fruit in front of her. She stretched her neck and grabbed it with her lip, spraying juice on Zubin's tunic. He rubbed her neck and smirked.

"His legacy is an entire menagerie made of porcelain," said Douwe. "A life-size one."

"Oh, so, we are to let them make Clara?" said Zubin. "Can you imagine her encased in glass?"

"A pure white, clean version of her, remade in many sizes for all of those who value Meissen porcelain," Douwe said, pointing to the map. "We'll pack up and stop along the way where we wish. At Regensburg, then on to Freiburg on our way to Dresden."

"Shall we create another broadside?" asked Zubin. Clara's horn had grown significantly over the winter, and Zubin often had to dodge it when she nuzzled him. She looked different now than from the broadsides printed last summer.

"Yes," said Douwe. "I'll go into town and speak with the printer."

Regensburg's narrow, muddy thoroughfare was clogged with people—even the old, whose ancient knees creaked as they stood shoulder-to-shoulder with the crowd. The one-ton queen of Europe, the rough-skinned and stinking marvel of the world, exited her carriage. The picky eater, the toe-trodder, the crowd bringer. The money giver. The rhino, who snored as she slept and smelled worse than cattle, but whom everyone loved regardless. Douwe's livelihood was both a gift and a joyful burden. The crowds cheered.

"Is she lonely, Douwe?" said Zubin after their show. He rubbed Clara with fish oil.

"She has us and the horses," Douwe said. "Do you think she misses Bakari?"

"Yes," said Zubin. "Shame we can't get another rhinoceros."

Douwe introduced a squat, round-bellied goat to Clara the next morning. The goat and the rhino stared at each other, and Clara tossed her head, her signal to play. Zubin clapped Douwe on the shoulder.

Douwe's sights were set on Dresden, though he wanted to spend more time in the beautiful city of Freiberg, where the buildings were red, pink, and yellow with brown roofs. They looked like tropical birds, a comparison Zubin and Douwe alone shared. The new goat, named Maria Bakari, bleated constantly from the carriage it shared with Clara. A week in Freiberg doubled the money in the black corsair chest.

The spring roads were bumpy after winter's thaw, and Dresden was hundreds of miles away. The carriage stopped along the mountain cities. Zubin gathered snow for Clara to eat, and they all drank snow melt, savoring the sweet water. The snow-capped peaks touched the sky, and the sight of Clara grazing on white spring flowers and baby grass by the roadside stayed with Douwe for many months. Her mottled skin matched the Alps. She and Maria Bakari ran through the open fields midday when the carriage grew too hot. They clambered onward.

With wheel repairs made at Zwickau and a few nights gathering copper to pay for it, the unusual crew of draft horses, a white goat, and the only rhinoceros in Europe rode into Dresden on April 4. Douwe sought the porcelain factory.

They parked Clara at the inn near the city's center, where thousands walked by. Douwe questioned the locals, asking where the porcelain factory was located. Greeted by royalty, mayors, and local leaders at each place he brought Clara, Douwe was puzzled by the lack of presence of the world-famous artists. The townspeople furrowed their brows each time he asked where he could find them. Then, finally, a break. A man with a hawk's beak for a nose told Douwe he could take him to the factory for a price one rumbling stormy evening.

Douwe paid, leaving Clara and Maria Bakari in their wagon and Zubin at the inn. A carriage took Douwe northwest to Meissen. The rain pelted them as the man led him to the bottom of a steep hill and pointed upward. Lightning flashed, and a castle showed itself against the dark-cloud sky.

"Albrechtsburg," said the man, black hair shining like oil. "Ask for Hao, the guard."

Douwe climbed the hill, pounded on the door, and stood under the wide stone archway, wetter than he'd ever been at sea. The door remained closed. The rain let up, and he pounded again, thinking perhaps his fists on the door were mistaken for thunder. The door creaked open, black rings jangling. An Asian man looked about warily.

"Good evening," said Douwe. He stepped from the archway, dripping wet. His suede jacket clung to him, sticky and hot. "I'm looking for Hao."

"That's me," said the thin man at the door.

"I am Baron Douwemout van der Meer," he said. "I have a proposition for the master of porcelain. I have in my possession a rare animal for him to sculpt."

Hao's eyes grew in surprise while Douwe spoke. He gave a curt nod and slammed the door. Minutes passed.

Douwe sat under the archway, waiting. He watched the post-storm moon, guessing an hour came and went. He would wait until dawn if he had to. He peeled his jacket off, leaving it inside out, and tried to rest. Two more dark hours passed when he was startled awake by the creaking wooden door.

Hao was back, this time with a friend dressed in fine but thread-bare clothing. He was medium height, with a double chin and strawber-ry-blonde ponytail. His green eyes were friendly despite the dark half-moon circles underneath them. His hands were filthy. His fingernails looked painted gray, coated in clay.

"Good evening, sir," said Douwe. "I appreciate you letting me in, as the night has grown cold."

The two men did not move aside. Hao closed the door behind them. Douwe hesitated. He felt uncomfortable but swallowed his pride and proceeded.

"I...have an animal in my possession and find it most prudent for you to sculpt it," said Douwe. "Your depiction of her kind is incorrect."

Hao watched the newcomer's reaction. The larger man stayed still.

"It's a rhinoceros," said Douwe. "So rare there is no scientific name yet. Only one in Europe."

The rounder man stepped forward, rubbing his hands together. They made the same sweeping sound as a hand on Clara's flank without her oil—dry.

"Alive?" said the man. His voice was high-pitched and breathy.

Douwe nodded. The man looked at Hao. They stared at one another for an unsettlingly long time. Douwe looked down the hill, wondering if he should go back.

"Look, come to Dresden tomorrow morning," he said. "My rhino will be outside the Red Stag Inn at dawn. It is a long walk. If you let me stay here tonight, I will charge you half price for her sitting fee." He exhaled heavily, frustrated.

"I cannot let you in," said the larger man. "But I can let you borrow a horse. We will see you tomorrow at the Red Stag Inn. We will pay you in full for your sitting fee."

Douwe nodded and followed Hao to a stable where he saddled a black mare. Douwe nodded, drowsing on its back. What would he give to be asleep in Lonnie's small cot instead, warm, dry, and unseeking? By the time he reached the inn, purple dawn threatened.

Douwe slept briefly, then told Zubin of the strange events over breakfast.

"Of all the people in the world we have encountered, these cannot be the strangest," Zubin said, breaking apart a stiff pastry. "Think of what will come from Clara being made into porcelain."

Douwe ushered Zubin outside. They opened Clara's wagon, and Maria Bakari darted out, bleating. Clara backed herself out slowly. She could no longer turn inside her wagon. Douwe filled her hay trough, and she ate furiously. He tossed her a piece of pastry and leaned against the fence, searching for the two men from Albrechtsburg.

Zubin locked Clara's ramp door as the men arrived. Hao drove a black carriage, and the larger man poured himself through its small door.

"Baron van der Meer," said the larger man. He bowed lightly. "I apologize for the lack of hospitality last night. I am Johann Kaendler."

"Mr. Kaendler, your reputation precedes you." Douwe bowed back at the porcelain maker. "Are you eager to see my animal?"

Kaendler flashed a genuine smile and motioned for Hao, who hauled over a small trunk. Kaendler followed Douwe toward Clara's paddock. She trotted up, ears swiveling, skin rippling. He stopped a dozen paces from the paddock.

"Shwew!" he whistled through his teeth. "Baron, the Meissen factory prides itself on anatomical correctness. And either your animal is an anomaly, or Dürer was wrong."

"Dürer was wrong, Mr. Kaendler," said Douwe. "You see now the true worth of this animal? She will correct the European history of the rhinoceros. Every royal household will desire a Meissen rhino cast in porcelain. Imagine adding her to your employer's menagerie."

"My employer does not know I am here," said Kaendler. "I do not leave the factory. What he does not know will not kill him…" Kaendler hesitated. "Though it might kill me."

Douwe gave the man a puzzled look. "Mr. Kaendler?"

"I am not to let any of the secrets of our craft escape the castle walls," he said. The dark bags under his eyes crinkled as he smiled. "Therefore, I cannot leave the castle walls without explicit permission."

"How did you explain a new species to your master?" said Douwe, rubbing Clara's neck as she leaned into the sturdy brick posts of her paddock.

"He is always eager for more," said Kaendler. "He will be glad to add such a rare animal to his porcelain menagerie."

"We are here for two weeks, Mr. Kaendler," said Douwe. "Is that long enough?"

Kaendler shook his head. "Not long enough to make the final porcelain sculpture, Baron, but long enough for the mold. How much will you charge?"

"What will this entail?"

"I shall sculpt your animal from my sketches," said Kaendler. "The mold will be in the Meissen factory in perpetuity. All Indian rhinos made with the Meissen crossed swords emblem shall be made of your rhino's likeness. I will pay you for the model I observe to make the molds, which will be mine. You may have a sketch or two to keep or sell. But today, and every day I can, I need to draw her."

"Your price is ten ducats," said Douwe.

Kaendler snapped fingers at Hao, who popped open the trunk. Inside were tools of Kaendler's trade: a sketchbook and kohl, clay, smooth knives, and instruments for carving. At the bottom was a fat coin purse. He counted ten gold coins and pressed them into Douwe's waiting hands. Kaendler asked for a stool and unfolded an easel. He began to draw.

The crowd milled in and out, paying to see Clara. Kaendler did not move from his spot. As he sweated, his pink scalp showed through his roan ponytail. Clara did simple, crowd-pleasing tricks, wallowed in the dirt, and Zubin applied her fish oil. Kaendler stayed rooted to his stool, and when Douwe went to offer the man bread and cheese at midday, his sketchbook was full.

Clara's hide was drawn in kohl, as were sections of her flank, the unique and strange folds of her neck, and her small, kind eyes. Kaendler drew pieces of her as if he were piecing together an elaborate puzzle. Douwe asked if he could see more, and Kaendler handed him the pages, taking a long drink of dark ale.

Kaendler captured Clara in a way Douwe had never seen. Each ripple of her skin was there, each bump and tender flesh fold. Her facial expressions were sincere on the page, and Douwe's mouth curved into a small smile as he thumbed through the thick parchment.

"I shall need a few more days," said Kaendler. "I sculpt in the round, Baron. I need to see the animal's underside in more detail."

Douwe motioned for Zubin, who was straddling the paddock, teasing Clara with bits of his lunch. He hopped down and sauntered over, always prideful after a successful show.

"Oh, Kaendler, you've done so well." Zubin clapped the man on the back. Kaendler looked startled. It was clear he had not spent much time around boys.

"He needs to see Clara's belly and chest, Zubin," said Douwe.

"After the crowds go home," said Zubin. "Clara will love to show you."

Kaendler nodded, finished his cheese and bread, and took back the sketches from Zubin. His next focus was Clara's ears. Zubin remarked on the artist's blackening hands and small, clever kohl strokes.

"May I be taught this?" he asked, pointing a brown hand at the white page. "If you have the time?"

Kaendler's eyes crinkled in a smile. There was pain there, and he did not look at Zubin when he answered.

"If I have the time, Zubin," Kaendler said. "Then yes, I shall teach you."

That night at the inn, Douwe found Kaendler alone in a darkened corner, a glass of amber liquid in front of him.

"May I?" Douwe gestured toward the seat.

"By all means, Baron."

"Tell me, Kaendler, why are you held captive in the factory?" Douwe accepted a wooden tankard from a barmaid.

Kaendler sipped his liquor, pursed his lips, and smiled at the darkwood table.

"Baron van der Meer, I possess the only formula for priceless porcelain outside of Asia," Kaendler said. He avoided eye contact. "My employer has trusted me to create objets d'art the way no European person can. It is not unlike you and your own captivity."

"My captivity?"

"Your existence is controlled by Clara, is it not?" He sipped again. "Every moment she is awake, you tend to her needs. Protect her. Make sure she is safe and unharmed. Your one job in this life is to protect the only representative of her kind on this continent."

The half-moon circles under Kaendler's eyes were gray-purple in the golden lantern light of the Red Stag Inn's bustling tavern. Douwe and Kaendler were alike, though Douwe hesitated at the connection. He had to admit its truth.

"I, too, protect something utterly precious," said Kaendler. "I must admit my envy of you, Baron."

"Your envy?" Douwe drank the foam of his beer.

"To be locked in a cage is one thing," he said. "To be locked in a carriage is another."

"I get to see all of Europe," said Douwe. "And you do not."

Kaendler nodded. "You have seen the world, my friend. I have seen scenes of it, painted on Chinese porcelain I am made to copy."

"What of the menagerie?" said Douwe. "Your life-size sculptures cannot be copied."

"They cannot. They are my greatest pride. They are my escape, you see. I cannot bring a stork or a rhinoceros inside the factory."

"You're allowed to leave if a specimen presents itself."

Kaendler tipped his glass to Douwe. "Precisely, though at some risk."

"We are alike, in a way," said Douwe. "Prisons or none, we are creating something everlasting."

"Yours is more fragile than mine, Baron," said Kaendler. "My porcelain, with all good fortune, will last generations. Unless war or mishap shatters it, of course. Your rhino will not live forever."

"In a way, Kaendler," Douwe said. "You allow Clara to live forever, as long as your art survives."

Kaendler's eyes twinkled, and a genuine smile crossed his face. He raised his glass to Douwe.

"That, my friend," he said. "Is worth celebrating."

They drained their glasses, and two more full of amber liquor were set before them. Kaendler drank heartily, but Douwe let his sit, hearing more of Kaendler's story. The man was indeed a prisoner—his master's every desire met with this collection of white glass.

"Why is this so important to King Augustus?" Douwe asked, hands wrapped around the chalice. The liquor was the color of a dying fire, and Douwe smelled it. It was strong.

"No one else has one," said Kaendler, red-faced. "That is the appeal of everything now. That is why your rhino is invited to the royal palaces and paraded in front of citizens and earls—because she is singular. The same goes for Augustus and my work. Only in China is porcelain made like this. I am the only one who can do it. It brings me many enemies."

Douwe considered Kaendler's words and nodded. He was right. The trend of the times was individualism. Everyone wanted the one thing that didn't belong to anyone else. Kaendler, Clara—they were the same. One of a kind. Douwe picked up his glass and drank.

His throat seized shut. Douwe felt the liquid hit his stomach, burning. He rose from the table, clutching his chest. Kaendler stared at him in confusion. Douwe stumbled through the inn's tables, knocking into patrons who cursed at him as their drinks spilled over their hands. Empty chairs overturned, and sparks filled Douwe's vision.

Kaendler rose, sniffed Douwe's glass, and chucked the remaining liquid on the wooden floor.

"Poison!" Kaendler shouted. He grabbed him and forced Douwe toward the door.

Zubin appeared on the stairs, drawn by the noise. Kaendler led Douwe outside, and Zubin took the stairs two at a time, barefoot, to catch them.

"What happened?" Zubin shouted, grabbing Douwe by the arm. Douwe was white-faced and collapsed to his knees to vomit.

"Poison," said Kaendler. "No doubt meant for me, damnit."

Zubin blanched. "Poison!" His mind went to Lonnie's satchel with the bezoar stone. He left Douwe and Kaendler. Douwe wretched again, and Zubin sprinted to Clara's wagon.

Zubin pulled the satchel from under the seat. It was covered in road dirt and muck. He yanked it open and rifled through. Underneath Lonnie's sachets and glass vials was the bag holding the bezoar.

"Milk!" Zubin shouted as he slammed open the tavern door. "Milk!"

The bewildered barkeep filled a tankard, and Zubin popped the bezoar in. He ran, followed by hollering patrons craving visuals of the action. Douwe vomited again as Zubin slid to him on his knees.

"Drink, Douwe! It's Lonnie's bezoar."

Douwe drank, gagging as he did. The milk slid down his face and onto the dirt, covering his shirt. The bezoar clinked against his teeth, and Douwe released the contents of his stomach. The bar patrons moaned their disgust and hollered for more milk from the bar. Zubin and Kaendler stayed with Douwe, grim faces set.

"It was meant for me," said Kaendler. "I should not have left the factory."

Zubin shook his head. "You cannot know that. Clara is as desirable as your formula."

Kaendler forced Douwe to take the second glass of milk, bezoar rattling at the bottom of the tankard. Douwe vomited again, straight white, and curled onto his side.

"Let's get him inside the stables," said Zubin.

Kaendler and Zubin hauled Douwe into an empty stall. Zubin stayed with him through the night. Douwe had nothing left in him by dawn, but he was alive.

Kaendler shook them both awake the following morning. He had bread and ale, at the sight of which Douwe gagged. He had no more to vomit, though his face was still pale.

"Douwe," said Kaendler. "I am sorry. I know well that was meant for me."

Douwe shook his head, throat so scratched he could not speak. He took the bread and soaked it in ale, eating slowly. Zubin and Kaendler watched, ready to put the bezoar back in his mug. But Douwe smiled lightly and sighed, grabbing his head in relief.

The bags under Zubin's eyes matched Kaendler's. The two tended to Clara while Douwe slept upstairs in the inn until early afternoon. When Douwe emerged, he and Kaendler sat with the barkeep. Douwe's glass was still on the table, empty after Kaendler loosed the contents on the tavern floor.

"The bottle came from Vienna yesterday," the barkeep told them. "I thought it opportune to entertain the two of you. I had no idea it was poisoned. Your drink was the last of my own bottle, Kaendler. The other was from the new one."

"There's a priest by the name of Gregor who thinks Clara is an idol," said Douwe.

Kaendler looked at him quizzically.

"My enemy has caught up with me."

"I must admit relief that the bottle was not meant for me," said Kaendler. "Will you stay? So, I can immortalize your animal in porcelain? Or must you flee?"

Douwe looked at the barkeep. "Who delivered this bottle?"

"A boy," said the barkeep. "He had a dozen more. I sent my son this morning to all the taverns in the city to tell them to destroy it."

"So, Gregor doesn't truly know where I am," said Douwe. "He's guessing in a broad circle."

The ten ducats were too valuable to give up, and he desperately wanted to see Clara in porcelain. Kaendler waited.

"We'll stay," said Douwe. "But one more breath of trouble, and we'll be gone."

Kaendler sketched. Douwe found Zubin by his side, attempting to draw Clara. He was no artist but produced a likeness well enough that Douwe recognized a rhinoceros. Kaendler told Zubin it was excellent and tucked Zubin's drawing into his notebook.

When the crowds dispersed, Zubin and Kaendler went into Clara's paddock. Zubin helped her sit, then coaxed her down to her side to be petted. He scratched the deep, warm pits under her leg joints. Clara lay, legs straight, her head on the ground. She flapped her ears, still and calm. Zubin motioned to Kaendler to join him, and the artist timidly rubbed her belly.

"Like stone," he said, a smile on his face. "I did not know she was so warm. I could remove my calluses on her hide."

"Why do you need to sketch her like this?" said Zubin.

"I cannot tell you, Zubin," said Kaendler. "My process is a secret."

"Well..." Zubin said. "I don't know any other porcelain makers."

Kaendler shook his head and stood, tightening the leather strip around his ponytail.

"I make my largest pieces in sections, Zubin," he said. "For Clara's, I will make her belly separate, her legs separate, her head separate. When the porcelain is fired, it will be less likely to crack."

"How big will you make it?"

"My master wants his menagerie to be life-size," said Kaendler, arms crossed, staring at the snoozing Clara.

"Life-size?" said Zubin. "How could you move it?"

Kaendler paused, a look of distress crossing his face. "I do not know, Zubin," he said. "I have made life-size birds, goats, and other beasts, but not one as large as Clara. I will do my best."

"I'd like one I could put in my pocket and take with me everywhere I go," said Zubin.

"Don't you take her everywhere you go already?" said Kaendler.

"Yes," said Zubin. "Perhaps one day that will change, and we can be somewhere forever."

"Where would you choose to live forever?" said Kaendler.

"A place where winter isn't too cold. Where Clara can graze all day in a field of goats," said Zubin.

"Forever is a long time, Zubin," said Kaendler. "Goats, eh?"

Zubin shrugged, and the two walked toward the tavern where Douwe ordered dinner. "She loves goats!"

Douwe and Zubin only drank what the barkeep made himself. They watched closely who came to see Clara. There was no sign of Gregor. Perhaps the priest believed his mission was accomplished.

On a breezy Sunday morning two weeks after Douwe was poisoned, Hao's black carriage pulled up to the Red Stag Inn. Kaendler's notebooks were full. Every angle of Clara, front and back, belly, tufted tail, and bulging armor drawn to full detail. He had a small, rough clay model and a thin square of clay that he'd warmed between his hands and pressed onto the bumpiest part of Clara's skin. An imprint.

Douwe and Kaendler shook hands and clapped each other on the back. To Kaendler's great surprise, Zubin gave the man a child-like hug. He fed Clara a carrot, scratched her behind the ears, and blew a puff of tobacco smoke near her. She enjoyed all three. While Kaendler loaded his things, Hao handed Douwe a thick, cream-colored envelope.

It was official correspondence from the King of Poland, Augustus III, Kaendler's patron, requesting a private viewing of Clara. Douwe was torn. His friend was essentially held captive by the man. He had no desire to spend time with him.

"He has an ailing son, Douwe," said Kaendler. He read the letter over his shoulder. "He is not a bad man, just a protective one. See him. He will want more sculptures of Clara if you do."

Douwe considered. Another king under his belt was good for his prospects.

"Kaendler," Douwe said. "I feel I have made a true friend."

"That you have," said Kaendler. The bags under his eyes were lighter, and his skin was not so pale. "I must admit I am jealous of your animal and your life, Captain. Enjoy it. Take care of each other."

Zubin and Douwe waved as the carriage door closed. Kaendler settled back onto his seat. Douwe wondered when the next time the porcelain maker would leave his palace of glass.

Douwe wrote back to King Augustus, and the next morning, a royal carriage arrived with Augustus and his son, Albert. The King wore a white wig, burgundy velvet breeches, and a blue satin sash. His eyebrows were thick and animated. His son was thin and pale, dressed in matching burgundy.

Douwe and Zubin led Clara out of the stable, and the boy gasped, applauding. Clara ate an apple and crusts of bread from Albert's hands. He looked no older than six, but Zubin asked, and the boy answered in a small, sweet voice that he was nine. The second sick boy Clara gave joy to. Douwe made sure Albert touched her shining horn.

Several gold ducats richer and another royal singing their praises, Douwe and Zubin closed the carriage door on Dresden.

Chapter 33
Andrea
Leiden, The Netherlands

Floodlights streamed from the archive corners, reflecting on statues and glass cases. Andrea couldn't tell what was moving and what was long dead. A taxidermy tiger made her scream. The tinkling of glass surrounded her. The loud click of a door handle sounded.

"He's out the door," Lucas shouted. "Into the museum!"

Andrea forced herself forward. Lucas caught the door before it closed and ran into the hallway. She followed closely behind, and saw Sergei run to the end of the hall and out the entrance to the employee's only section of the museum.

They ran down the carpeted hall, past Janice's office and the empty cubicles. Sergei was far in front of them, but Lucas caught a surge of speed and left Andrea behind. "Stop!" she heard him cry.

But Sergei was too far. Through the glass doors leading out, Andrea saw him turn the corner past the statue of Rembrandt and run out of sight.

She caught up to Lucas, who held his hand to his chest, breathing wildly. Her eyes widened with fear, thinking of why Sergei ran from them, why he ran from Paul, clearly hurt. Lucas gathered himself and pulled her down the hallway into Janice's office.

"There's only one more person who knows we found that rhino horn," he said.

"Janice," Andrea said. "And we haven't seen her in hours."

"What happened when Paul arrived, just before us?"

"I don't know. It was almost like Sergei was accusing us." She bit her lower lip, mind torn between helping Paul and chasing down the horn.

"He may not know what happened, either. Is it possible the horn is in this office, right?" Lucas started pulling open desk drawers.

"It's possible," said Andrea. "Or it's possible it's long gone."

Chapter 34
Douwemout van der Meer
Leipzig

Douwe and Clara arrived at night to a city ablaze with color. Lanterns and torches lit the way to Leipzig's fair where vendors clogged the streets. Tents were set up along the cobbled stones, boasting goods from around the world. Douwe felt a memory overcome him—he had not seen a market like this since Calcutta.

Food, fur, baskets, books, jewelry, toys, maps, art—spread a half-mile deep through the main road and the side streets. Bright colors flashed in the firelight, contrasting the deep shadows tucked in pockets between the booths. In an alley, a carnival exhibit boasted a fish-man, an alligator, a fat lady, and a stuffed giraffe. Zubin gasped and pointed at every new sight. At night, primarily men roamed the streets. Greeks, turbaned Turks, and English dandies perused the goods and made their way to the tented carnival.

Douwe and Zubin followed the crowds, cursing the narrow streets in their massive wagon. The going was slow, and Clara stuck her nose out of the barred window, sniffing the roasting meat, tobacco, and exotic burning spices. The torches blazed, sending smoke trails and casting yellow light on the rainbow tents. The place was a jewel box.

In the center of the carnival was a large paddock for Clara. The Easter Fair crowds would wake to the only rhinoceros in Europe. Douwe and Zubin settled in the upstairs room of an inn where, from the window, Douwe could see both paddock and wagon. Clara's carriage was locked for the night. Maria Bakari bleated as he fell asleep.

The morning dawned clear and warm, a true harbinger of spring. The sweet scent of new grass and roasting meats, livestock, and leather from the tanner's booth filled the damp morning air. Douwe tapped Zubin awake and pulled on his cream-colored breeches, sliding his waistcoat over his sea-trained shoulders. Even though he hadn't been on a ship for years, Douwe still had his trim figure to show for decades at sea.

He slipped a tricorne hat on his head, ducked under the short stairway's door frame, and grabbed a fresh biscuit and a steaming peppermint tea. He slowed to take in the sights. He had never shown Clara in a place like this, and by the poster nailed to the inn's door, he could tell they were the main attraction.

LEIPZIG EASTER FAIR! FEATURING CLARA THE RHINOCEROS, BEHEMOTH OF JOB! LIVE IN THE FLESH FOR YOUR VIEWING, 2 COPPERS PER PERSON. CARNIVAL ROW.

An illustration of Clara with the floral collar she wore in Vienna took up half the page. Douwe smiled and reached for it, but it was the fair's first full day, and people needed to see the broadside.

Zubin was slow-moving but made his way downstairs, honey-dripped biscuit in hand. He yawned and shoved the whole thing in his mouth, holding it with his teeth. He needed both hands to get Clara out of her wagon. She backed out, Maria Bakari darting between her feet. Her paddock was wide and shallow. Zubin readied his bag of apples and carrots provided by the inn. They took ten percent of Clara's earnings at the fair in exchange for the room and food.

A steady crowd moved in, line-by-line the same reactions: exclamations and gasps, young ones pulling on their mother's hems begging to be picked up, men debating her species and the reason for a rhino on this earth. Douwe let the words roll, absorbing each one. Zubin gathered the coppers and answered questions, straddling the fence. He was a showman.

The fair dazzled. Turbaned Turkish men sold Ottoman spices, silks, and tobacco, their jewel-colored tunics sparkling in the April sun. There were Greeks whose olive oil and wine created long lines at their booths and Chinese traders whose porcelain reminded Douwe of Kaendler. He wished he were here to examine its quality. Poor farmers and their brood came in threadbare clothes, having saved their coin for Leipzig once a year.

He breathed it in, the crowd representing Europe and the places it touched. A pauper traded a trinket with Zubin to feed Clara, as princes had traded gold before him. It did not matter who these people were. It mattered more that they possessed the same eager curiosity.

Clara did her regular thing: swallowed vast mouthfuls of hay, guzzled ale from a large bucket brought by a nobleman, wallowed in the dust, and when the time came, stood still as a statue for Zubin to reapply her stinky fish oil.

The crowd loved her, and the other carnival acts nearby were enhanced by her presence. At the end of the day, Douwe and Zubin locked

Clara in her freshly cleaned wagon, left Maria Bakari in the paddock (to her chagrin), and paid the street booths a visit.

Pockets bulging with new coin, the two spent their money with relish. Zubin got a new pair of pants and a fine leather belt from the tanner whose booth smelled of sweet, soft hides. Douwe purchased a yellow feather for his tricorne and had his boots polished. They ate excess hot fried pastries from a cart, oiled bags dripping. A booth full of prints had Clara's anatomy picture, a broadside from Leiden with her image, and a new pamphlet contradicting her existence as the Behemoth of Job. Douwe purchased them all, rolling them to slide into a leather tube. He had dozens of Clara's broadsides.

A horse race earlier in the morning resulted in the crowning of a black Arabian. It wore a floral collar with white daisies, clearly picked from the roadside. The cattle lined up in temporary pens, and Zubin was taken with a milk-white calf with long dark lashes. The fair buzzed with patrons even after dark, and the torches along the road were lit once more. Late-night tavern goers sloshed sour beer, singing raucous songs and clapping each other on the back. Zubin and Douwe headed to the inn and ate one more roast chicken and fish pie before turning upstairs.

In the morning, the mayor was waiting downstairs at the tavern.

"I have an idea," he said. "We have a grain scale to weigh farmer's crops. We want a raffle to weigh Clara. The winner takes half the pot. You and Leipzig take the rest."

Douwe and Zubin agreed, and the mayor ordered his chorus of heralds through the town, announcing that the weighing of Clara would commence at eleven in the morning. The sundials near the roofs had never been stared at more than they were that day. People lined up along the thoroughfare, waiting for Clara to pass by.

Zubin dressed her in a collar from Vienna festooned with flowers and filled his satchel with apples and tobacco from the Ottoman traders. Clara followed him, slow and steady at Douwe's request, through the cobbled streets of Leipzig. People parted for her like Moses and the Red Sea, and crowds gathered behind her as she went. Her feet rolled over the uneven street, and Douwe made a mental note to check them.

They made it to the scales where a bookkeeper had gathered money and guesses on her weight all morning. His book was full of names and numbers. The raffle players stayed put, waiting to see if they'd won half the pot. The mayor arrived, smiling broadly, with a crimson sash and pewter scepter in hand.

"Baron van der Meer and his rhinoceros Clara!"

The crowd roared, sending Clara stomping and swiveling her ears. Zubin palmed an apple into her mouth. The crowd cheered at her arrival, and Douwe made a spectacle of her stepping on the scales, feigning that the grand scales of Leipzig were not enough to hold her. He stood there with her momentarily, weighing the scales more to increase the suspense.

"We weigh the Behemoth of Job at the Leipzig Easter fair! Guesses have been recorded all morning. The closest guess wins half the pot!" said the mayor.

The crowd cheered again, and Douwe stepped off the scale after a dramatic pause. The merchant calculated quickly, sweat dripping. Clearly, he was terrified his scales would break under Clara's immense weight.

"Four thousand five hundred and eleven pounds!" shouted the merchant. The crowd roared. Douwe balked. He could not believe how large Clara had gotten. The bookkeeper scanned his pages, searching for the winner.

"The winner!" The mayor shouted. "With one hundred percent accuracy! Is Captain X. Kang!"

Douwe's mouth fell open, and he looked at Zubin in astonishment. The crowd waved forward. A black-headed, short man with sharp eyebrows hopped onto the stage. Kang. Douwe's face hurt from smiling. They embraced, for the first time, Douwe realized, and said hello.

Hours later, after Clara's joyous parade back, Kang, Douwe, and Zubin were situated in the inn, reminiscing over a mug of black beer and hearty stew. Douwe had not dreamed of seeing his friend and first mate again, and here he was in the flesh, ripping brown bread with his sea-calloused hands.

"What do you think of Clara?" Douwe asked.

Kang shook his head. "I did not think she would live this long. I knew she would be large, but my guess on her weight was exaggerated."

"I am glad you won," said Douwe. "And even more glad Clara is still alive. Would you have found us without the broadsides?"

"No," said Kang. "Though I did not know if she was still yours, as it listed you as Baron van der Meer." Kang raised his glass.

Douwe gave him a half smile and raised his mug to Kang's. "I have Empress Maria Theresa to thank for that," said Douwe. "Clara has opened many doors for me. Without her, I do not know where I would be."

"Probably on a ship," said Kang. "Without the Behemoth or the boy."

Kang, Douwe, and Zubin talked long through the night. Kang remarked on Zubin's growth, and Zubin showed Kang three tiny whiskers growing from his chin. Douwe smiled sadly, not having noticed them himself. He remembered the small boy he met at Clara's stable in India. What change had swept them all.

The fair was much the same the next few days, and at the end of the week, a parade closed out the ceremonies with great fanfare. Douwe, Clara, and Zubin trundled out of town, their team of six great horses leading Clara's wagon. People threw flowers in their wake, stems catching in the massive wheels of Clara's wagon. Zubin sang with the crowd.

A group of black-clad priests were in the crowd. Douwe was waving, and many of the priests waved back. Then, Douwe locked eyes with Father Gregor.

He slid his hand onto Zubin's knee and pointed. Zubin looked, gasped, and looked away. Clara's nose stuck out the window, and she moved from side to side in her wagon. There was no way to hide, and their slow-moving team could not move faster in the heavy crowd. Father Gregor left the other priests, a steady-moving black column, faster than Clara's wagon. He disappeared in the scores of people.

Soon, the carriage was outside the city gates, with Gregor close behind. The crush of people swarming around them slowed them down.

Douwe hopped down to ask the people to back away and a hand grabbed his upper arm. He wheeled about, expecting to put a fist in Father Gregor's face, but it was a portly blonde man, not the black-clad priest.

"Baron!" he huffed, out of breath. "I'm glad I caught you."

Douwe panicked, searching to see if Father Gregor was close. He swallowed his fear and smiled at the man. Zubin craned his neck in search of Father Gregor.

"Douwe!" Zubin cried.

"One moment, lad," said the blonde man. "I need to speak with your master."

"How may I be of service?" said Douwe. "We need to make haste out of Leipzig, sir."

"I can see that," said the man. "I am Frederick, Landgrave of Hesse-Kassel. I had an audience with Empress Maria Theresa, and she told me of your time in Vienna. I'd like to extend an invitation. My home for the summer with Clara? I'll make it worth your while."

The man smiled with bulging pink cheeks. Douwe had no true plans after Leipzig, and now that Gregor was on his trail, he had to find a place to disappear. Indeed, nothing could be better than a nobleman's summer home. He glanced at Zubin, who scanned the city gates. Father Gregor was not there.

"I would be honored, Sir Frederick," said Douwe. "Shall we follow your party out of the city?"

"Head on!" said Frederick. "I'll round up my group."

Frederick gave Douwe directions and told them another orangery waited for Clara.

As Douwe and Zubin urged their team onward, Father Gregor stood under the medieval city gate, fading from view.

Chapter 35
Andrea
Leiden, The Netherlands

Andrea's mind was tangled—where was Janice? Her thoughts flickered back to Paul, injured on the floor near Douwemout van der Meer's remains.

"Sergei dug up that grave and was promised money," she said, thinking out loud. "Rhinos are an endangered species, and that horn is worth a fortune. Whoever gets their hands on it will want more after they have one. Trust me, I know the type."

Lucas shook his head. "Andrea, you didn't get the vibe from Sergei that he was just as concerned as we are?"

"No," said Andrea. "He seemed angry, didn't care that Paul was hurt."

"I think he panicked. I think he's going wherever he thinks the horn is."

"You have a lot of trust in him."

"Hard for me to believe that someone who's worked on this project for years would want to ruin it."

Andrea considered. "I...I have a hard time trusting people lately."

"Will you trust me when I say we're going to find it? And that it's all going to work out?"

"You don't know that."

"I can believe it, even if I'm unsure. Try it for the next five minutes while we search. No thinking about Sergei, or Janice, just searching this room."

She stared at him, his sharp-jawed face serious and calm. A lock of his night-black hair fell onto his forehead, and she swallowed. He lifted a corner of his mouth to her, gestured to the room, and raised his eyes gently as he nodded.

"We can do this, Andrea. Let's find that damn horn."

She took a long exhale and returned his nod, then filtered out the noises in her mind and focused.

"Her laptop is gone," Andrea said, showing Lucas the remaining cord. "Her purse, too."

"It doesn't look like theft," Lucas said.

"Drawers closed, nothing else missing, no papers rifled through," Andrea agreed. She narrowed her eyes at the case on the back wall. "Even the valuable artifacts are still here."

She opened a desk drawer and gasped.

"Lucas," Andrea said. "I just found all of Clara's archives."

Lucas turned fast around the desk. Andrea pulled out a disheveled stack of papers, stapled with glossy photos of Clara's artifacts. There were dozens of items listed, the exhibit report pulled straight from the archival box. Entries about broadsides that matched the description of the ones Andrea had removed from the desk were circled in red colored pencil.

"Wherever Janice is, she has some explaining to do," Lucas said.

The printer whirred. "Must've been another delayed signal."

"What did she say? Two hours later, it prints?" Lucas asked, waiting for the page.

"Something like that."

"It's a one-way ticket," said Lucas, reading over Andrea's shoulder. "To London."

Underneath was another page.

"Lucas, how clearly do you remember the broadsides we found?"

"Very," he said, checking the flight on his phone. "Why?"

"This one was not on our app," she said. The page in the printer was a copy of a document. The rhinoceros emblem at the top of the page matched Douwemout van der Meer's gravestone. It was in Dutch; she handed it to Lucas for fast translation.

"Oh shit, Andrea. It's a draft of a will."

Lucas scanned the page, mouth parted in astonishment.

"Everything we need is here."

"Except Janice and the horn."

"We can find her, if we hurry. We need to talk to Paul."

The faint sound of sirens filtered in.

"I think I know where she's going," he said. "Let's check on Paul and ask him our questions, then we're outta here."

Andrea grabbed the stack of exhibit notes and the one-way ticket, and they ran.

Chapter 36
Douwemout van der Meer
Europe

May was vibrant, a month of white clouds and blossoming countryside. Douwe was grateful but anxious waking in the gardens of the seat of the Landgrave Frederick II of Hesse. The elaborate fountains and bridges allowed plenty of exercise for Zubin, who helped the gardeners and watched the fair young ladies promenade. Douwe kept a wary eye on every guest, watching for Gregor.

Clara stayed inside the orangery, which was unbearably hot to most animals. She thrived, forgoing her daily fish oil and submerging herself in a tiled pool. She ate her weight in fruit and fogged the windows of the structure, which was three times as large as the orangery they'd taken respite in last winter. The comings and goings of Frederick's court determined their schedule. They were observed but not overly worked, and each meeting was one that Clara enjoyed as she grazed in the manicured gardens.

After weeks with no sign of him, Douwe felt wholly removed from Gregor. But in the dead of the night, Douwe woke from nightmares. He dreamed of Gregor preaching from a pulpit dripping in black flames. In his hand, stretched out to the crucifix, was Clara's shining horn.

Summer came and went, and Douwe and Zubin considered where they should go for the coming fall and winter. Zubin longed to go back to Leiden. He missed Lonnie and the cats and their university apartment. Though Douwe felt the road compelling him onward, pushed forward by the praises they received in each small town, he paused those thoughts when a letter from Lonnie revealed their apartment was vacant and waiting. September arrived with the pink skies of early autumn. Douwe told himself a stay in Leiden was temporary, and the promise of new cities in the spring allowed his wandering thoughts a place to go.

Leiden looked the same, and Douwe smiled as Clara's wagon crossed under the city gates. The residents knew Clara's wagon, and excitement followed. They were greeted at the University with joyous faces. Douwe felt like he was home for the first time in a long time.

Lonnie waited for them on the black slate floors of the church. Zubin ran to her and, after a moment of hesitation as she realized he was now the taller one, collapsed in a deep embrace. Lonnie pushed his head down to kiss his black hair, pulled into a ponytail, and wiped her eyes.

Douwe's stomach jumped. More freckles had bloomed across the bridge of Lonnie's nose. Her hair was pulled into a thick plait that lay loosely on her left shoulder. Ringlets escaped it, golden blonde, shining in the fall sunlight. She was plainly dressed in olive green homespun and wool. A cream-colored apron stained with soil wrapped around her waist. She wore short leather boots and had a trowel in her pocket. She was as warm as the afternoon sun.

"Lonnie," said Douwe. His heart beat rapidly.

"Baron," said Lonnie. She dipped low into a curtsy. A curl fell in her eyes, and she moved it, her hands showing many hours in the dirt, with green-tinged fingernails.

Douwe wanted to do as Zubin had done and embrace her. He had not gone a day without her face in his mind's eye. Her quick smile, the curve of her jawline turning into her freckled shoulders—she was beautiful. He offered her his arm, and they walked to their apartment.

"I spent most of the afternoon cleaning this place," said Lonnie. Warm light came through the single window, and the beds were made with fresh linens. The ornate writing desk glowed with new oil in the corner. A quill, ink, and parchment waited next to a stack of letters. Douwe recognized the hand of the first on the stack from Johanna. He felt a twinge in his gut and prepared to open it when a mew sounded.

"Betsy!" The black cat wove through his legs. He put the letter down and picked her up. "I cannot believe it."

"What else would you think?" said Lonnie. "I was commanded by my captain to keep her safe. You'll find Bakari in the dairy barn and Betsy's kittens all over campus."

Zubin took Betsy from Douwe, and the black cat purred. She had a notch out of her ear and a scar on her nose. Zubin flopped loudly on his bed and sighed.

"I'm glad to be back here," he said.

"Douwe," said Lonnie. "May I show you my work?"

Douwe nodded, eager to be alone with Lonnie. He wondered if she felt the same. "By all means, Lonnie," he said. "Coming, Zubin?"

Betsy made circles on Zubin's bed, preparing to nap. "Later. I want to sleep in my old bed."

Douwe followed Lonnie out of the small curved door, leaving Johanna's letter behind. They strolled by the canals toward the Hortus Botanicus to see Lonnie's collected specimens.

"I've managed to help describe a dozen species unknown to the professors," she said. "And keep them alive, at that. I must show you my new fern."

The greenhouse was lush, the gardens in the courtyard beyond heavy with the grandeur of autumn's harvest. There was a banana tree, cacti, tropical palms, and many plants Douwe could not identify. He reached out to touch a glimmering bloom when Lonnie put her hand on his wrist.

"Please," she said, removing his hand gently. A shiver ran through him. "Leave the touching to the bees."

"All of the touching?" said Douwe, eyes steady on hers.

Lonnie intertwined her fingers with his. He leaned closer, smelling the rich earth of her skin, the sharp-sweet smell of the liniments she made, and the warm honey smell of her braid.

She brushed her soft cheek against his. He had days of stubble, and her skin on his felt like draping silk on Clara. He grabbed her small chin with sea-strong hands and looked at her pink mouth, partly open. She kissed him hard. Douwe grabbed Lonnie's waist, then her braid, and suddenly his hands were everywhere.

She led him to the shed that was her home. Lonnie and Douwe made love in a way Douwe had never experienced with his youthly adventures at whatever port the VOC bid him go. The windows of the shed fogged. Pots of dirt and baby plants awaiting care surrounded them. Lonnie explored every inch of Douwe, enjoying the salt-sweet skin of the rhino keeper, and when they were through, they found night had fallen and chose to sleep together in Lonnie's small cot, intertwined.

Douwe rose before dawn to sneak back to his apartment. He worried what Zubin might think. He slunk, keeping to the shadows, watching the bright moon dance with the clouds. He wound around the writing desk in the dark and slipped into bed. Douwe closed his eyes but did not sleep. If he stayed in Leiden, would Lonnie end up sharing a bed with him permanently?

Fall draped itself in a deepening chill. Clara was regularly on display in the anatomy hall. This time, the resident anatomist Petrus Camper sculpted and drew her. Clara was content enough, though she genuinely disliked being cold. She played in the snow a few times with Zubin, who took up reading and sketching again. He attended lectures and helped Lonnie in the greenhouse, where she and Douwe rendezvoused many times.

"There's a brown brick manor nearby," Lonnie said to Douwe one evening. "It's been vacant for months. We should see it."

"See it?" Douwe said. "What do you mean?"

"It would have enough space for Clara," Lonnie said, drawing a finger down his bare spine. "And you and Zubin and me."

"Us. What a dream that would be."

Douwe saddled a draft horse in the morning and hauled Lonnie up behind him. They rode two miles, pressing into each other as the landscape unfolded. Bare trees, windmills, rolling golden grass.

The home was handsome: brown brick with a five-horse stable and acres of land. Douwe wandered the property with Lonnie, who spoke of the south-facing windows where sunlight could fall on her tropical plants, shifting her leather satchel from one side to the other. They smiled and laughed, breath fogging the air. There were no worries of harm here—Gregor or drama on the road.

What would it be like to spend the coming spring here? Douwe could offer the money he made on Clara for the place and set up a regular viewing area like his own menagerie. Clara would never have to move again. The rhinoceros would love the pasture with a muddy pond and willow tree. Head full of dreams, Douwe and Lonnie returned to the University to a crimson-sun dusk. Zubin was curled up in the shallow, small bed. Douwe furrowed his brow. It was unlike the boy to go to sleep early. He knelt; Zubin's breathing was shallow and rapid.

"He's burning up," said Lonnie, pressing the back of her hand to his neck. "Has he ever been sick before?"

Douwe shook his head. His stomach roiled. "Not like this," he said. He rose from the floor, clicking the small brass knob under the claw-foot leg of the ornate writing desk. He slid broadsheets of Clara into it for safekeeping, cleaning off the desk's surface to make room for Lonnie's satchel, full of medicine.

Lonnie peeled back Zubin's damp sheets and dropped them, hand rising to her face in shock. Red lesions covered Zubin's neck and face.

"Douwe. This is smallpox."

Douwe rushed to Zubin's side, turning the boy's face to the light. Zubin was covered in pox, his face pale. He was fire-hot and sweating but shivered. Douwe looked to Lonnie, who had spent years in the surgeon's quarters of various VOC ships.

"What do we do?" he said. Smallpox killed people. And Zubin, unlike Douwe and Lonnie, had not been exposed to it early in life.

"Keep his fever down as best we can. I have the medicines to help. But we'll get the University doctor's help and pray that he makes it. He'll scar, Douwe, permanently."

"Is there nothing to make it go away?" Douwe was on his knees at the boy's bedside.

The last sliver of golden light had left the room. Lonnie lit a candle and placed it on the writing desk.

"All we can do is pray and wait," Lonnie said. "Hopefully, it will be mild. With all the oranges this boy eats, it may not hit him as hard as it could have."

"If we wouldn't have traveled so much, he might not be sick."

"You're right," said Lonnie, arms crossed before her. "You should stay put for a while."

Douwe turned to look at her, but she'd already turned to gather the supplies from her stores. He knelt by his boy's bed.

The next few days were frightening. Zubin woke confused, calling the names of people Douwe did not recognize, and Gregor's. Zubin could not tell Douwe from Lonnie. His skin was ember-hot; Douwe could scarcely bathe his gray-tinged body. Sores spread, pustules forming and bursting.

Zubin scratched himself. Lonnie put mittens on the boy so he could not pull the heads off his wounds. They fed him broth and oranges meant for Clara. His black ponytail was cut so it would not stick to his neck where the worst of his sores were.

After five days, Zubin sat up. Douwe was wary. Was the worst over? Or would the boy's fever return? Zubin was not lucid, and the first thing he asked was if Lonnie and Douwe were married. They blushed and shushed the boy, spoon-feeding him more broth and slivers of orange. On the tenth day, Zubin stood, trembling, and sat back down.

His wounds wept, bloody, and hard balls formed under his skin, worst on his back and arms. His face was mostly untouched, save a few spots across his cheeks. His legs wobbled beneath him, limbs limp, feet unusable.

The cats were too heavy for Zubin's lap, and he could not enjoy their company. He could not sit up long enough to attend classes. And worst of all, he was too weak to help with Clara. Long months of recovery awaited the boy. Douwe made arrangements to stay through December in Leiden.

He and Lonnie discussed the brown brick house and how easily they could move Zubin there. But the same day Douwe was to make a trip to the landowner's office, the University doctor recommended that Zubin be taken south.

"South?" said Douwe. Lonnie cast her eyes to the floor.

"His strength will grow with warmer climes, with warm sea water nearby," said the doctor, packing away his instruments.

"How could we get there? He cannot travel in Clara's wagon. The boy can barely sit up for an hour, let alone weeks in the carriage." Douwe lowered his head. What should he do? Stay with Lonnie, or heed the doctor's orders? He had to decide.

"I would employ the barge, Baron," said the doctor. "Follow the coast to the Seine. It will provide easy transport to warmer climates."

Douwe slept fitfully, Lonnie's face combining with Zubin's in his dreams. Visions of the brown brick manor, crumbling and old and empty, haunted him. How could he choose between both places he called home—the manor, or Clara's wagon? He woke with his stomach in knots. The decision he made was solely for his boy, whose sails had lost all their wind. Douwe secured passage via a swift ship to deliver himself, Clara, and Zubin to the barge. The barge could take them from Leiden to Paris, and Douwe made plans for Rome. Lonnie shut herself in her small shed. Douwe knocked on the door when the stars emerged overhead and let himself in. The growing fog on the windows that night was evidence of a different level of passion.

Of all the places Douwemout van der Meer imagined himself to be, it was not on a ship's deck with Clara again. But there they were—Clara sniffing the sea air, Zubin in the surgeon's quarters accompanied by Dr. Wilhelm. Douwe and the surgeon from the *Knappenhof* embraced warmly and spoke of Lonnie and Kang. Clara's empty wagon and six draft horses were onboard. Douwe was not captain, for which he was grateful. The crew grumbled about the heavy load.

Three days later, Douwe woke to the vessel docking at the port city of Le Havre. Zubin slept. Douwe spoke to Dr. Wilhelm in hushed tones outside the surgeon's quarters.

"He may never fully recover, Douwe," said Dr. Wilhelm, shaking his head.

"Surely it's worth trying to return to our normal lives," Douwe said. "Maybe it will invigorate him."

"The barge ride is another day from Paris," Dr. Wilhelm said. "Make sure he sleeps and apply his poultice twice daily."

"From there, we go to Italy," said Douwe. "To the Mediterranean. Clara will love it there, and Zubin will be better."

Dr. Wilhelm gave him an uncertain look and patted his shoulder.

Douwe loaded Clara and Maria Bakari into the wagon, the horses were hitched, and Zubin was seated, leaning, next to Douwe. They were bound for Rouen, where a barge would take them to Paris. Before they loaded, Douwe found a messenger and, for the first time, used his royal title to send a letter to the attention of Versailles.

The wait near Rouen was long. Douwe kept Clara in her carriage. They were not the only patrons using the barge. A brewer and his casks waited, as did a load of soft, fine wool laid in sheets. The crew loaded the barge and approached Douwe's wagon last, not knowing what was inside.

The bargemen stared open-mouthed at Clara, who shoveled green hay into her mouth. They'd hauled heavier loads before but were nervous Clara would panic and topple overboard into the Seine, taking the barge with her. The length of the carriage and horses would not fit on the barge together, so Douwe had to unhitch.

Douwe reassured them that Clara loved being aboard a ship—a barge could not be much different. He hoped. Douwe loaded the wagon, locked the wheels, and sat Zubin in the front. Zubin was wrapped in his teal coat and smiled weakly at Douwe, who loaded the six horses, and Maria Bakari.

Clara was last. The thin boards of the loading ramp curved underneath her as she clambered aboard. She turned her ears and sniffed the air, curious. The crew was uncertain and kept their distance. Clara had no lead.

A team of draft horses pulled the seventy-foot barge from both shores. The bargemen realized that Clara was extraordinarily tame and, one by one, approached to pat and feed her. Clara spent the day drinking beer from bowls and eating bread.

They landed in Paris and paid a heavy fee. Douwe helped Zubin to the carriage and tossed a few coppers to a boy nearby, who helped him harness the horses and get Clara aboard. The boy gawked more than he helped, and Douwe had a pit in his stomach. Though Zubin was still with him, he was not the same.

Zubin was asleep as the carriage rolled into Paris the second week of December. Douwe drove the team to an inn where he was expecting a message. He stepped inside, leaving Clara in her wagon, hoping to depart immediately for Versailles if the right kind of letter awaited him.

The innkeeper handed him a crisp brown envelope sealed with the royal insignia of Versailles. Douwe ripped it open, placed a coin on the counter, and ran out the door. Clara had an open invitation. Zubin smiled when Douwe told him of the menagerie.

"What waits there?" he asked. "Another rhino?"

"No, Zubin. Clara is still the only one in Europe."

"I wonder if she hates that."

"Hates what?"

"Being alone."

Chapter 37
Andrea
Leiden, The Netherlands

The ambulance loaded Paul, his head wrapped like a mummy. The medics assured Andrea and Lucas that he just needed a few stitches and he'd be fine. Andrea asked what Paul was hit with, figuring it was the shovel.

"We aren't exactly sure," said the medic. "Likely a small, dull object with extreme force."

"That doesn't sound like a shovel," she said. "That sounds like a rhinoceros horn."

"A what?" said the medic.

"Never mind," she said, turning to Paul. "Paul, do you know who attacked you?"

"No," he said. "I was bending over to look at the skeleton, and realized the horn was gone and I was struck from behind."

"We think it's in London. Janice's heading to a museum there. We're gonna figure this out."

"I have a colleague at the Natural History Museum," Paul said, grabbing his phone. He shared the contact with Andrea. "Maybe he can help."

Andrea nodded, holding his hand gently. His words were slightly slurred, his eyes unfocused. Lucas leaned in close to her ear.

"He looks dazed."

The medics signaled they were ready to go.

"Be careful," Paul said.

"We will," Andrea said. She didn't want to tell him everything yet— that Sergei didn't have the horn and Janice had the archival documents stashed in her desk drawer. She had a phone call to make. She cringed, seeing a dozen missed calls and thirteen text messages.

"Mom!"

"Andrea, my god!" her mom answered, huffing. "I've been worried sick! You can't send a text like that and not call me!"

"Mom, I need two plane tickets to London. It's an emergency."

"First, you have me call the police, and now you need plane tickets!? What is going on!?"

"For me and Lucas. Someone's stolen the rhino horn, and we're going after it."

She wrote down her mother's credit card number, promising to pay her back, and got on her phone—the tickets were only $100 each. She shook her head. Europe.

The soonest flight was in three hours. It took off at 8pm, landing in London by 10pm.

"Let's get our stuff," Lucas said. "I'll meet you back here in fifteen, okay?"

"Lucas," she said. Her hands trembled. She'd remembered Jake's plane, and the nightmare that waited if he found her. "I don't know if I want to be alone right now."

Lucas grabbed the back of her arms and pulled her close.

"This is the only time I'll leave you," he said. "Get your things and meet me right back here, okay?"

"What if Jake comes?"

"He won't. Go, I promise I'll be waiting for you."

She sprinted back to her dorm, lungs burning in the chill air. Throwing a change of clothes, cell phone charger, and her retainer in a bag, Andrea was nearly ready. She changed from boots to sneakers and pulled her hair tightly into a magenta scrunchie. Andrea didn't know what they would face in London, but safety felt closer with Lucas leading the way.

Lucas waited beneath the streetlight in front of the museum with a black backpack over his shoulder. They booked an Uber to the airport and sat close. It felt good to have her leg pressed against his. She trembled. The canals sparkled with white streetlights, and the stone buildings and bridges made Andrea feel like, for a moment, she was in 1740. They passed under the Ziljpoort city gate and onward toward the airport.

The car dropped them off at the terminal, and as soon as she shut the door, she heard:

"Andrea?" It was Jake.

"Oh shit," she said under her breath. She shrank behind Lucas.

"What the hell is going on?" Jake said, gesturing to Lucas. "Who's this?"

Jake looked exhausted and concerned. He wore a pair of wrinkled Chinos and a striped button-down. His curls glowed in the fluorescent lights from the terminal behind him. Andrea's stomach clenched. The noise around her deafened. She took a big breath and chose to stare at him.

"I'm Lucas," Lucas said, extending his hand. Jake did not shake it. Andrea's heart pounded.

"Okay, Lucas," said Jake, mocking his accent. "Where do you think you're going with my fiancé?" He motioned to her overnight bag.

"Fiancé?" she said, stepping forward, finding courage. She could not let him claim that. "No, Jake, I did not say I would marry you."

"Yes, you did, Andrea, before the embarrassing stunt you pulled at Thanksgiving. Just because you're high and mighty on your animal rights horse doesn't mean you can walk out on me like that. You're committed to me. You made a promise to me."

"You lied to me, Jake. You never told me you lived on a former plantation, that your family spent a fortune hunting animals for fun."

"I didn't have to tell you those things, Andrea. You love me. Hunting trophies can't change that."

She balked. "Yes they can."

"Just because you don't like it?"

"Yes," she said. "Just because I don't like it. I never will. It will always disturb me, and you're not in charge of those feelings. You cannot change my mind."

Lucas inched toward her, putting himself between them.

"You're confused. You saw something you didn't expect, which scared you a little. I know the lions can be intimidating at first, but—"

"No, Jake, no. It's not that I didn't expect it. It's that you have no respect for other living things. Caged dogs, safaris, shoving Primrose. And here you are, telling me I don't have to worry because it's not my business? What happens when I introduce you to my mom and her service dog? Will you treat her like a piece of trash, too?"

"I don't treat those animals like pieces of trash, Andrea. I treat them like animals. People are more important."

"We are equals. People and animals share this planet. We live because of each other. Those animals deserved better, and so do I. You do not understand me, and I am done, Jake."

Jake laughed. "You're delusional. You'll regret this. You're giving up your whole future, girl."

"I've always hated it when you call me girl. You don't get to do that again. I've chosen where I want to be, Jake, and it's not with you."

She turned to Lucas and grabbed his hand. Jake pointed and stepped forward, but Andrea put her palm up, refusing him. She walked into the airport, her mind leaving Jake's trophy room and focusing on Clara's horn.

"Are you okay?" Lucas asked. They spoke to each other in the security line. "You handled that well."

"I think I will be," she said, holding her passport to be scanned. Truthfully, she was shaking like crazy, feeling out of control but simultaneously solid.

"I can see how you got caught up in his spell. He's manipulative, coming all the way here. You're better off without him. I'm sorry you will never be rid of his memory."

"Maybe I will be someday," she said, sliding her bag onto the conveyor belt. She knew she was genuinely okay without Jake.

"What did you mean, you've chosen where you want to be?" Lucas asked, pulling his shoes off.

"I mean here. I mean...with you," she said, stepping into the body scanner in her sock feet.

Andrea felt the skin on the back of her neck grow hot. What if Lucas didn't like her like that?

He sidled up next to her. His black socks contrasted her pink unicorn socks.

"I like you, too. We click." Lucas grabbed her shoes, and she grabbed his, offering them to each other and sliding them on. They hauled their bags from the belt and ran to the gate.

They walked onto the plane as the last boarding passengers. Once they were seated, entirely out of breath, Lucas produced the facsimile of Douwemout van der Meer's will. As the flight took off, Lucas translated the document.

"This handwriting is nearly impossible to read. I don't think it's a final copy," he said, pointing to a line written in brown iron gall ink.

"What kind of property did he have?"

"A manor and a hundred acres north of the University," he said. "I think it's been developed, but it was prime real estate back then."

"Who was that supposed to go to?"

"It says Zubin, his son," said Lucas. "That's not a Dutch name. That's a name from my ancestry."

"Zubin? What else does it say?"

"Clara's remains were given to a museum in London," said Lucas. "It's all here in the exhibit notes."

Andrea took out the papers documenting the exhibit. Each detailed artifact entry described the items and their provenance. She read it out loud to Lucas, whispering over the sound of jet engines.

"Albrecht Dürer's woodcut, 1515," she said, breathing deep into her gut. "A goblet made of a rhino horn. Unpainted Meissen porcelain by a man named Johann Kaendler. A portrait of a man named Jan Sichterman. The Trading Post of the Dutch East India Company in Hooghly, Bengal, oil on canvas. The loading list of the *Knappenhof*, compiled by the VOC upon the ship's departure from Hooghly. Sketches by Petrus Camper, an engraving by Jan Wandelaar of a man and rhino, and a handwritten advertisement featuring Clara, and her paintings from Vienna, Paris, and Venice. A small portrait of Charles Joseph, Maria Theresa's favorite son. A clock, a dozen medals, Douwemout van der Meer's signature."

She found herself wiping hot tears from her face. Her throat grew tight and whisper thin.

"We know so little about her, yet look at what remains," said Lucas.

"I understand now that I will never know or love her like this man did." Andrea flipped through the small photographs that accompanied each listing. The signature of Douwe was last. Scrolling, red with age. She paused at it.

"I can't help but feel strange that he left us so little, and she left us so much."

"It answers my question," said Lucas. "Why would Janice, Sergei, or whoever took the horn go to London? Wouldn't they head straight to China to sell it?"

"Because Clara's horn is worth real money because it's hers, and so are the rest of her remains," said Andrea.

"We can't let anything happen to her. She's too important for them to grind her horn and bones to bits."

"I don't think that's the plan," said Andrea. "Not for this rhino."

"Then what is?"

"Selling her to the highest bidder."

"The last line of his will says that he's to be buried with his most prized possession and Zubin was to place it in his hands," said Lucas. "He had so many other objects made of her likeness, but he knew her horn was most important. This proves the horn is Clara's."

"What did he do after Clara's death? Did he get another animal?" Andrea said after a moment.

"No," Lucas flipped to the end of the papers. "After Clara died, Douwemout completely disappeared from the historical record until his death in 1775."

"You're telling me he made a fortune showing her around Europe and did nothing for the rest of his life?"

Lucas nodded. "Sure, he made his money, but there's something larger here."

"What's that?"

"He showed her to people who wouldn't have ever seen a rhino. He opened their minds to things beyond their small worlds."

"And somehow, he lost her," Andrea said.

Chapter 38
Douwemout van der Meer
Versailles

The fountain in front of Versailles was void of water. Douwe wished for summer. The true majesty of the place was lost in the cold. Douwe's job was to get Clara out of the biting wind. He and Zubin followed a path to the gold-and-black gate of the menagerie.

The menagerie's building was gray stone with arched windows and a hexagon-shaped multistory viewing area. Guests walked out into the structured paths that butted up to animal enclosures. The entire place was topiaries and evergreen. Each wall had missing patches of vegetation from grazing creatures.

Animals rustled beyond the building. A low, breathy roar startled Clara, and Douwe popped onto one of the enormous wheels to rub her horn and reassure her. Lions in France. Of all the places Clara could be, none was more perfect, despite the lions. The staff here knew how to care for exotic animals.

A keeper greeted Douwe with a deep bow. He was black-haired with brown eyes and a ready smile. He wore wheat-colored breeches, a dark waistcoat, and a white blouse. A long brown overcoat and a fur hat guarded against the chill.

"Baron van der Meer," he said. "It is a pleasure to meet you. I am Andre Jardin. I've heard many stories of your magnificent animal."

"Please, call me Douwe." He hopped from the carriage box. Zubin shivered. "May we speak indoors?"

Andre ushered Douwe and Zubin inside, leaving a huffing Clara in her wagon. Steam poured from her windows. Douwe left Zubin by a fire, cross-legged on the floor. His pock-marked hands were extended in front of him, wrist bones prominent.

Douwe followed Andre to the viewing room, explaining Zubin's condition in hushed tones. Andre nodded. No one in Europe was alone regarding smallpox—children were lost to the disease in every kind of family.

"Ah, poor boy," said Andre. "I will arrange a handsome apartment near the kitchens so his meals might still be hot by the time they are delivered. He will get plenty of rest at Versailles if he chooses to."

"What animals are in your care here, Andre?" Douwe asked. He peered out the window of the viewing chamber. The enclosures were still, the cold forcing the animals into their sheds at the back.

"A camel, a seal, a pelican," said Andre. "Two lions and two tigers. A gaggle of birds. Particularly impactful is the ostrich. Have you ever seen one?"

He shook his head and asked Andre questions about the cats—how did he manage to feed them?

"Hunting, small farm animals, donations," said Andre with a slight smile. Douwe gestured to the art on the walls. Enormous oil paintings of jungle scenes depicted the creatures held there. Douwe asked if Clara would be included in the paintings next, even if she was a guest.

"Oh, perhaps. Louis loves adding to his collection. I have an enclosure for Clara near the camel who shares her kind of food." Andre pointed to their right, where a camel's hump was plainly visible, though its face was buried deeply in a hay trough.

"She may enjoy the company," said Douwe. "Clara loves other animals. We do have a goat with us as well, Maria Bakari."

Andre assured Douwe that the goat would be well tended to.

"What does your Clara eat in a day?"

"Seventy pounds of hay, twenty-five pounds of bread. She drinks at least three gallons of water daily, plus her preferred treats of fruit, particularly apples, and she usually consumes at least two tankards of beer."

"Very well then," said Andre, whose eyes grew large. He looked around for something to write on. Douwe produced a folded broadside of Clara. On the back was a list of dates and places now in the past. He added the list of Clara's food with Andre's quill.

He passed the note to a groom who stood near the gate. "King Louis is pleased to meet your animal's needs. Let's get Clara situated."

Clara's wagon was taken back. Her area had not been inhabited by an animal in a long while. Wild grasses were up to a man's thighs. A few black-capped cranes hopped over the enclosure walls when Clara's wagon approached.

She backed out unceremoniously, irritated and frustrated with the cold. She did not want to follow Douwe and instead looked around, swiveling her ears, searching for Zubin.

Once Clara entered her new temporary home with many corrections by Douwe and help from Andre, she set to grazing. She angrily ripped chunks of grass, trotted to the enclosure gate, huffed, and ran away. She was pacing, anxious. Douwe had to tell Zubin how important it was that he was around for Clara's unloading.

Clara had a lean-to shed to protect her from the elements. The evergreen walls blocked the wind. Douwe set Maria Bakari inside the enclosure, and the two grumpy ladies chased each other. Douwe parked the wagon near Clara's pen, and the horses were taken to the stables with a thousand stalls. Douwe sighed—at least he had no worries about the animals.

Andre showed Douwe and Zubin to the apartments. It was a long walk, and Douwe was pleased that Zubin needed little help. Perhaps he was getting his strength back.

Their apartment was warm, furnished in yellows and creams. A crackling fire and tea service awaited them. Zubin slept most of the afternoon. Douwe had an audience with the King that evening back at the menagerie. He weighed his options: Should he wake Zubin? Clara was much easier to work with when the boy was around. Or should he risk the chance of her wildness and let Zubin sleep?

He woke Zubin as the last rays of winter sun touched the palace, turning the whole place into a pink pearl. He helped Zubin dress in their matching teal coats, though the boy's was short on the wrists. They walked to the menagerie, puffing steam clouds from their mouths.

Andre waited with a set of servants. Chairs were brought to the viewing area, and Zubin and Douwe were asked to parade Clara at close range in front of the King. Douwe felt the bite of cold and shoved his hands in his pockets. When they arrived at Clara's enclosure, and Zubin hollered her name, Clara sprinted toward him.

Zubin grabbed her head and rubbed her nose. Clara's lip gummed his hands, clearly relieved that Zubin was in front of her. They fastened Clara's collar around her neck, and Zubin shuffled backward with a handful of apples, enticing Clara forward to meet Louis XV.

Louis and his entourage were seated inside the warm viewing area where a fire cast lively shadows. The King was surrounded by people. A woman who was not the queen was closest to him.

A herald announced: "King Louis XV and his companion Madame de Pompadour. Introducing Baron van der Meer and his rhinoceros Clara."

Madame de Pompadour clapped her leather-gloved hands politely. Serving staff carried trays of hors d'oeuvres and petit fours for the group.

He grabbed a tray of food from one of the waitstaff and held the tray aloft in one hand. He pulled a dessert off for Clara, showing her the treat between his fingers held high in the air. She reared up briefly, causing the crowd to gasp. Zubin rewarded her.

Madame de Pompadour grabbed King Louis's arm and grinned. Zubin ran around the courtyard with Clara following, her tail straight out behind her. Each time he darted away from her, and she turned, he fed her another dessert. Soon, the tray was empty, and Clara heaved with exhaustion.

Zubin was out of breath and shaky, but the audience was on their feet. Douwe grabbed the boy by his arms to steady him and hugged him on the side. The royal party came forward, removed their gloves, and fed Clara hay from a sack. Clara was delighted by the attention but stayed focused on Zubin.

King Louis was more interested in Madame de Pompadour's reaction to Clara than in the animal herself. Pompadour wore a white fur hat and a powdered face. Gooseflesh rose on her long, pale neck as the breeze whipped. She was all smiles, ungloving her hands to rub Clara's horn and neck folds. Louis' eyes did not leave Pompadour.

Zubin and Douwe took Clara back to her enclosure where she and Maria Bakari bedded down for the night with a fresh layer of straw in their lean-to. Andre assured them after Zubin expressed concern about the cold. After all, the camel was fine, and the lions were as well. Zubin looked back at Clara once more. She stood staring, ears pressed forward eagerly.

Douwe and Zubin caught a carriage ride back to their apartments. Douwe pondered—what would it be like for Clara to be stationary for an extended period? What would it be like to have many animals to care for? He was glad to be in this place but even more pleased that Zubin was returning to his usual self despite the scars that covered his body like deathly constellations. With Zubin well, their plan with the manor in Leiden seemed possible.

The mornings in Versailles showcased blossoming frost. January was harsh, though little snow fell. When it did, it was a gentle dusting, and Clara and the camel spent those days in the large indoor arena at the stables. The thousand horses there whinnied and stomped as Clara and Zubin ran. Douwe scraped snow from the corners of buildings and presented it to Clara in a wooden bucket. She sniffed, scooped at it with her lip, and ate it all.

The camel did not care for Clara, spitting at her constantly. Andre helped Douwe keep them apart. Clara was genuinely curious about an animal as tall as she was that was not a horse. Life felt settled at Versailles.

Andre was aspirational to Douwe—he knew the ins and outs of animal husbandry and had questions that embarrassed Douwe. Douwe did not know a lot about Clara's species. Douwe shared everything with Andre, including that Clara was temperamental when things did not go her way and how food prompted her to do almost anything.

One evening, as Douwe and Zubin rode in the carriage back to their apartments, Douwe began thinking out loud.

"Zubin," he said. "Do you think Clara is happy here?"

"I do. She has other animals, and she does like Andre. Her enclosure is big. She hasn't even grazed the whole thing, and we've been here a month already. She likes it here."

"What if she stayed?" Douwe said. He rested his hand on his mouth.

"What?"

"What if she stayed here at Versailles?"

"And us?"

Andre might ask them to stay on and help with the menagerie with Clara as a new addition. Douwe would consider it. He enjoyed the care of the animals, but when he slept, his dreams were of Lonnie and the fogged windows of the Hortus Botanicus.

"Perhaps we stay, perhaps we move on," said Douwe.

"It's too cold here for her," said Zubin.

"It's cold in Leiden, too, Zubin. It's Europe."

Zubin nodded. "But what will become of her if we leave her?"

"I know she is dear to you. The fear of having to care for her without you was burdensome. She loves you, Zubin. You are her person."

The carriage stopped. The two of them were silent, walking inside. The gleaming mirrors of Versailles reflected the dirt on their faces from a day working at the menagerie.

Zubin took his boots off slowly and sat cross-legged by the fire. His legs were longer than Douwe's now. He was no longer a boy.

"Zubin, is this the life you want? To be with me always? Clara always?"

Zubin did not speak. He stared into the dancing flames and hugged his knees to his chest. Douwe watched him. The boy's face was a mixture of fear and sadness.

"I have never imagined anything but what is right before me. Future is a word, not a thing I dream of."

Douwe sat next to him on the hearth rug. This boy from India, who left the shores with his first pair of shoes at age ten, made Douwe's life have true meaning beyond the animal that bonded them. Douwe felt like wrapping the child in his arms, though the child was no longer there. In front of him was a young man.

"I think I would like to have a family of my own," said Zubin. "A place in the countryside for animals and a few crops. A garden like Lonnie's. A way to make money without moving from place to place."

"Can I tell you what I see?"

"Yes," said Zubin, not looking at Douwe.

"I see the brown brick manor in Leiden, covered in ivy in the spring-time. I see ducks and cats in the yard, windows full of Lonnie's plants," Douwe said. "I see Lonnie and me and you."

"Yes," said Zubin. "And when I am old enough to have my own wife, I will be in the cottage by the pond, where I can watch Clara wallow."

"If we sold her to the king, we could buy the brown brick manor."

Zubin hugged his knees, rocking lightly. He wiped his nose and buried his face.

"I don't know."

"I don't either," said Douwe. "But if we get the right amount, we can be free of the worrisome question we ask every morning."

"Is she alive...?" said Zubin, rubbing his eyes. "It is my first thought."

"Mine, too," said Douwe. "She would be well taken care of here."

"She would never forgive us."

Douwe nodded. "She would have Andre and Maria Bakari. She may not know we're gone."

"Or perhaps every morning, her first thought would be: Are they coming today?"

Zubin looked at Douwe, red-eyed.

The next morning, Douwe arranged for an audience with King Louis. He entered the throne room in the teal jacket presented to him by Maria Theresa. He had an amount in his head and a sickening feeling in his stomach.

The heralder introduced him: "Presenting the Baron Douwemout van der Meer, the Rhino Keeper!"

He bowed to the King and his consort, Madame de Pompadour, who sat to his left, fanning herself. Douwe's polished boots clacked on the marble floor. Cherubs stared at him from every corner. The walls crawled with design. Douwe longed for a blank space. He could not find one.

"Welcome, Baron," said King Louis. "To what do we owe your visit today? Certainly, the menagerie is up to your standards?"

"It is beyond my wildest dreams, Your Majesty," said Douwe. He felt sweat drip down his back despite the chill of the large room. "I have come to present an offer to you, if I may."

"Let's have it then." The King crossed his legs in amusement and grabbed the hand of Pompadour. She looked at him through downcast lashes and fanned herself.

"I offer you the option to own Clara the Indian rhino, the only one of her kind in Europe. She has taken a liking to her quarters at Versailles, fit for a royal menagerie such as your own."

"You offer me the option to own Clara?" said King Louis. "I am surprised, Baron. I thought you were making a handsome sum with her."

"Indeed, Your Majesty, I do not want for much," said Douwe. His next words surprised him. "But the prospect of belonging to a place permanently has become a dream I cannot abandon. As does a woman to make the house a home. I am certain you know of what I speak." Douwe nodded at Pompadour, who nodded back demurely.

The King shifted in his seat and considered Douwe's words. Douwe's heart beat so loudly he worried Louis might hear it. Pompadour whispered to him behind her fan, and Louis uncrossed his legs and leaned forward in his gilded throne.

"What is your price, Baron?"

Douwe took a shaky breath. "One hundred thousand ecus."

The throne room was still as a painting. The hum of the court ceased. The ladies' fans stopped. The King inhaled and exhaled loudly through his nose. One hundred thousand ecus was enough to live off of for fifty years.

The King turned to Pompadour and spoke to her in hushed tones. The conversation was exciting. Sweat dripped into the waist of Douwe's pants.

"I have told Madame de Pompadour that she must choose," said the King. "I have been hiding a secret from her. She may choose Clara the Rhinoceros or a new palace made for her in my gardens."

"And what has your fine lady chosen, Your Majesty?" said Douwe. His stomach churned.

"She chose the palace, Baron van der Meer."

Clara remained his.

"We shall call it La Petit Trianon, and it will cost considerably less than the price of your animal. I bid you farewell and thank you for the highly entertaining time you have allowed us here at Versailles."

Douwe did not remember leaving the throne room or returning to his small apartment. He sat on the ornate bed. Through the window, snowflakes fell in the black evening sky. Clara was still his. He sighed in relief, yet anguish swept him when he thought of the brown brick manor.

"Well? Douwe!?" Zubin said.

"He said no," said Douwe, staring at the wall.

"He said no?"

"He said no. Clara is still ours," said Douwe. "We will leave Versailles."

Zubin nodded, pulling a hand through his short black hair, the hand continuing to the absent ponytail Lonnie chopped when he was sick. He breathed deeply and settled into the chair near the fire, stoking the thin, dead embers.

"Where to, then, master?"

"Venice," said Douwe. "Let's get there by Easter."

"Warmer climates," said Zubin. "Clara will love it. Douwe?"

"Yes, Zubin?"

"Let's not tell her."

"Tell her what?" asked Douwe, finally looking at his companion.

"That we nearly let her go."

"Never."

Their last morning in Versailles gave an inkling of spring—one of those too-warm February days that set the birds singing early. Andre helped load Clara and Maria Bakari. He gave Douwe and Zubin ample supplies, and when Douwe tried to pay him, he declined, saying Louis would never know. He slipped the broadside of Clara back to Douwe.

Grooms and dozens of horses lined the long path. In the distance, Clara's enclosure was empty. The camel leaned over the stone wall. Clara's pond was thawed at the center, completely free of weeds. Clara was not particularly happy to be back in her rolling cage and made Douwe and Zubin laugh at the multitude of noises she made. They were gone from Versailles, despite Clara's protestations.

News reached Paris about Clara. Douwe stayed months in the city, showing Clara at street fairs and meetings of the minds. He found an empty alleyway that needed only one section of fence. They dressed it with a blood-red tent and took hundreds in admissions.

She prompted several artists to visit, though Douwe's favorite was Jean-Baptiste Oudry, who insisted on painting Clara life-sized. The canvas stretched the entire wall of his studio. He studied Clara daily, and when Douwe came by his workshop to see the finished product, he was brought to tears. He had not seen such a likeness. With the payment from Oudry and the alley showcase, they made enough for Douwe to purchase passage from Marseilles to Naples in three months.

It was in Marseilles that Zubin picked up a curious bit of news. The rumors in lavish Paris, where the latest trend was a hairstyle called Le Rhinoceros, manufactured that Clara went on a rampage and escaped her pen. Apparently, Zubin read aloud, she trampled five people to death before the Paris city guard shot her dead in the street. Douwe startled and jerked the reins when Zubin read that Clara was dead.

"It will be a miraculous recovery when we reach Venice," Douwe said. "I wonder who came up with such a thing."

"It says a local priest witnessed it all," said Zubin, scanning the words.

A prickle rose up his spine. "A priest? By what name?"

"Gregor."

Chapter 39
Andrea
London, England

The flight was quick, and Andrea pulled up her Uber app. It was nearly midnight.

"Where to?" she asked Lucas.

"Small problem," he said, examining the document. "Douwemout's will doesn't say which museum took Clara's remains."

"Okay, let's go to the big one," she said, shrugging.

Lucas let out a short "ha!"

"What's so funny?"

"There are like 150 museums in London, Andrea. How can we know which one has Clara's skeleton?"

"We have Paul's friend."

"It's late but try to call."

It rang through to voicemail. Andrea Googled London museums. Tons of listings popped up quickly, but when she added "rhino," things changed.

"We have two good bets. The first is the Natural History Museum, where Paul's friend works, and the other is the Grant Museum of Zoology."

"There's no way anyone will let us in tonight," said Lucas. "We'll find a place to stay and go first thing in the morning."

"In the morning?" she said, seriously concerned. "Clara's horn could be on a plane to China by then."

"Without knowing which museum the thief is heading to, we don't have a choice," Lucas said. "We'll head to this hotel right by the Natural History Museum, and at dawn, we'll go to the staff entrance and tell them everything. We know Clara's skeleton has to be somewhere in the city, and that's where the thief is heading."

"Yep, let's find it."

The one thing Andrea didn't consider about Lucas's plan until they arrived at the small hotel was that they'd stay the night together. Andrea's heart pounded as she read her mom's credit card number to the front desk staff. She was grateful they spoke English—she stuttered over the numbers. Lucas swiped the keycard to a third-floor room with two beds overlooking the museum's steps.

She closed the curtains, and Lucas shed his leather jacket and boots. She shrugged off her canvas coat and cream-colored sneakers.

"I'm going to shower," he said. She nodded, finding her phone charger and pretending to be busy as he pulled his vintage t-shirt over his head. She listened to the water and couldn't help but imagine him in there.

He emerged, black hair wet, loose pajamas on. She patted the bed beside her, and he narrowed his eyes, cautiously sitting.

"Thank you," she said. "For taking care of me, this rhino horn, and my problematic ex. I ...thanks."

He took her hand and smiled gently. "You did the right thing by leaving, Andrea," he said. "Even if you did leave a family heirloom ring behind."

She laughed. "It was a pretty ring."

"You deserve pretty things," he said. "And people who care about every part of you, not just the surface stuff."

"Lucas?"

"Yeah?"

"Will you kiss me?"

Lucas gave her a half smile. "Only if you're okay with it. I don't play games, and I must admit I like you. A lot. But tonight, it's just a kiss, okay? And we're in separate beds, or whatever makes you feel safest. I want that for you, forever—safety."

Her eyes welled with tears. He brushed them away with rough thumbs and gently grabbed her face. He kissed her, and she kissed him back, tears like rivers down her cheeks. The last hold of fear anchored in her heart by Jake slipped away like a tide.

The next morning, their alarms buzzed, and they popped up in opposite beds like they promised each other. It felt good to take things slow.

"We gotta go," Andrea said, feet hitting the floor. Lucas shook out his black hair, his back to her. He was truly gorgeous. She tossed his shirt to him, and he pulled it on while she checked her phone.

"Hey," she said. "I have a message from Paul."

"What's it say?" Lucas grabbed his jeans and slid them on.

Andrea, don't trust Janice, she read. *There are ulterior motives at work, and money is involved. You need to come back to campus.*

"We're in too far for that," Lucas said. "Ulterior motives and money mean criminal activity. No one will believe that Janice is involved unless we catch her. We've removed all of the evidence from her office."

"How do we know it's entirely Janice, Lucas? Remember Sergei?"

"There's no answer right now."

"We have to get to the museums before she does and warn them. I think I know what she's after."

"Clara's entire skeleton?"

"Yes. Reunited, the identified remains of Clara's skeleton and horn together would be worth hundreds of thousands."

"She's better off to take the horn and run. No one in the museum world will trust her once we've told them what happened," Lucas said, pulling the sleeves of his jacket over his gloves.

Their breath fogged in the winter air, and pink dawn barely skimmed the rooftops as they made their way to the Natural History Museum staff entrance. It was a massive, church-like building made of terracotta bricks. Andrea gazed upward, hoping they could make it through security.

A guard at the door stopped them, and Andrea took a deep breath, ready to explain everything, when Lucas spoke up.

"Hallo," he said, his Dutch accent thick. "We have a meeting with Alfred Brewer. We're Professor Hahn's students from Leiden University." He popped out his student ID to show the guard.

"Ain't no meetings today, to my knowledge," replied the guard, full Cockney on display. Lucas shrugged at him. The guard sighed and got on a walkie-talkie. The voice on the other end sounded agreeable.

"Alright, you two, go ahead," said the guard. The door buzzed open, and he followed them inside, leading them to the education offices.

"Straight ahead and to the left," he said. "Don't go anywhere else, got it?"

The education office doors were dark, save one. They knocked. An old man waved them in, reading glasses perched on his nose. His shock of white hair sprung up, waving like it was pulled by a helium balloon. He was dressed in suspenders and a plaid shirt, which hung loosely over a once-rugged frame.

"Guard said I had unexpected visitors. Come in, come in."

"Hi, I'm Andrea. This is Lucas. We're kind of in trouble, sir."

"I'm Alfred Brewer. American? You're Paul's students from Leiden?"

"We are," said Lucas. "She's studying abroad."

"Sorry," Andrea said. "We have to tell you what's going on." She handed him the printed facsimile of Douwemout van der Meer's will.

Alfred read, mouthing the words, removing his glasses to replace them with a second pair that dangled around his neck.

"Douwemout van der Meer? It's been a long time since I've seen that name."

"You know it?" Lucas asked. Andrea realized this meant Alfred hadn't heard from Janice.

"Indeed. The Rhino Keeper. Like I used to be." Chills covered Andrea's body. Used to be?

"I volunteer here now," he said. "But years ago, I was the curator of a small museum attached to a university. The Grant Museum of Zoology."

Lucas gave her a knowing look. "We've heard of it," he said. "Is that where Clara's skeleton is?"

"I always said so," said the man. "But there was never any proof. The records were destroyed during the Blitz eighty years ago. The skeleton we had was in poor shape, and it was old. It was my task decades ago to clean it and remount it."

"Could you tell us, Alfred, does the skeleton have its horn?" she asked. If it did, there was no way it was Clara.

"You'd be hard-pressed to find an old rhino skeleton with a horn intact," he said. "Thieves strip taxidermy and skeletal rhinos of their horns in museums all the time. They're ground up to make medicine. Most museums choose not to put them on display."

"We think we found her horn," Lucas said. "Clara's horn."

Alfred's eyes shone behind his glasses.

"I knew she'd lost it. Though I can't dream of how. Her later portraits show Douwe holding it, you know? It might still fit on that skeleton. We could match the diameters. We could prove that skeleton is the most important rhinoceros in history. Where is it?"

"We don't have it," Andrea said. "It was stolen. We're going to get it back."

Alfred held the facsimile in his hand and breathed deeply.

"Would you like a copy of that?" Lucas asked.

"Yes," said Alfred. "I would."

"Alfred, how do we get to the Grant Museum of Zoology?"

Chapter 40
Douwemout van der Meer
Italy

Clara boarded the schooner bound for Naples as if she'd lived on a ship her whole life. She eagerly swung her ears toward the sailors with pipes, hoping for a puff of smoke in her face.

"She remembers," said Zubin. "Remarkable."

"Indeed," said Douwe, eyes closed to the sea breeze. He felt he was back on the *Knappenhof,* leaving South Africa for Leiden. It seemed long ago. The voyage was easy enough in comparison, and Douwe and Zubin made it to Rome in June.

The holy city was abuzz with her arrival. On top of the rumors that she was dead in Paris, it was now rumored that the schooner capsized on the journey from Marseilles, and Clara sank to the bottom of the Mediterranean. Douwe's dreams were haunted by the image of her heavy body beneath the waves, mouth open in fear. But Clara was alive, kicking at her cart door and fighting to graze as they neared her temporary home.

The Largo di Torre Argentina awaited. The square was home to a large opera house, and across the square were ancient ruins dotted with columns and steps where cats lingered in the bright sun. There once was a rhinoceros destined for Rome in the papal gardens. The poor animal died in a shipwreck near Lisbon, never setting foot in Europe. Douwe owned the only rhinoceros ever in Rome.

A roomy display pen awaited Clara in the square, dotted with spindly olive trees in large planters. Clara made a spectacle positioned near a large fountain. Lines to see the twice-dead rhino were hours long. Douwe and Zubin hired several helpers, primarily young boys who milled around helping for free before they were hired. The boys gathered coins and distributed souvenirs: tin medals and posters of Clara. Douwe was pleased to use one of Oudry's detailed sketches. The crowds could not resist the ephemera.

Douwe leaned on a fence post, watching, the same tricorne hat he wore on the *Knappenhof* shading his eyes in the summer sun. The money rolled in, but Douwe felt restless. What was Lonnie's life like this summer without him? He daydreamed, picturing the draping willow near the brown brick manor, planning the paddock for Clara's enclosure.

One particularly warm morning, the crowds were sparse. It was humid, and the air hung heavy around the city. The cats in the ruins beyond lay splayed out and panting. Clara's favorite weather. She spat sprays of water from her pink mouth. Zubin and Douwe served the meager crowd, dismissing the street boys for the rest of the day.

A group of ladies approached, parasols in hand. They were dressed more formally than locals.

"Welcome, ladies," Zubin said, removing his hat and bowing deeply. He winked at them, the sun too bright to see their faces. "Let me introduce you to my companion, Clara."

The ladies gathered near the fence, talking amongst themselves. Douwe gave them space and stayed behind them. Zubin walked the paddock, cleaning Clara's droppings and laying fresh straw and hay for her. Douwe unloaded fresh fruit and bread for Clara, stored in her carriage nearby. One of the women wore a shining olive-green dress.

Zubin dumped his stinking load outside of the paddock. An olive farmer nearby offered Douwe a nice amount for Clara's droppings. The man happily hauled it off for fertilizer every few days. Zubin grabbed a basket of small bread loaves meant for Clara. He skipped to the ladies at the fence, ever the showman, and handed each of them a loaf.

"Let's see if we can get this lady away from her trough," Zubin said. He called to Clara, her ears turned toward him. She did not budge.

"Is your name Zubin?" asked a lady in green.

Zubin smiled at her, his teeth bright against his summer-tan skin. His hair was longer, and his scars, though still visible, were less noticeable in the sun.

"You've heard of me," said Zubin, bowing deeply in a show. The ladies fanned themselves and giggled.

"How is it you know his name, Johanna?" asked a woman in a white gown.

"Because," said Johanna, "I knew him as a boy in Calcutta."

Zubin turned white and dropped the basket of bread. Clara clambered over, dripping water from her mouth, and as only a rhinoceros can, snuck up behind Zubin and consumed the bread from the ground.

"Johanna?" said Zubin. He climbed the fence.

Johanna nodded, flushing, and smiled brightly. "You've grown, Zubin. And so has Clara!"

Zubin grabbed Johanna's hand and kissed it, then spun. Douwe was marching back to the opposite side of Clara's paddock with bags of apples, muscles straining, when he heard Zubin shout his name.

"Douwe!" Zubin said. "It's Johanna!" The young man held both hands out toward Johanna, who sheepishly curtsied.

Douwe dropped his sacks. Johanna. He had long forgotten the un-opened letter he left behind in Leiden and forgotten, too, her face. He cursed himself for that. She was stunning: aquiline nose, auburn hair, eyes that danced between amber and green. Breathtaking. He looked at the ground, their kiss years ago fresh again, tingling on his mouth.

"Douwe," said Johanna. "I did not expect to see you again."

"I am beyond words, Johanna," said Douwe. "I am glad to see you."

Johanna's friends were bewildered. It was apparent Johanna did not tell them she knew Douwe and Zubin, let alone Clara. The woman in white waved Johanna close with her fan, and furious whispering began.

"My friends would like to invite you to luncheon," said Johanna. "Would you like to join us? Both of you?"

"Are you leaving Clara out?" said Zubin. He leaned on the fence post. One of the younger women stared at Douwe from behind her paint-ed fan, eyes flirtatious.

"I have dined with Clara once," Johanna said. "I have no desire to do so again."

Douwe shook his head, remembering how terrified he was for Jo-hanna at Sichterman's. Clara was a little thing then. Now, she was taller than he was. He could not imagine the destruction she would cause in a dining room today. They agreed to dine with the ladies, Zubin more excit-ed than Douwe. He was apprehensive, his heart in his throat. Did he feel this way when he first met her? He could not remember.

Douwe paid one of the street boys to stay by Clara's paddock for the afternoon. He was an honest kid, and Zubin trained him well. With the heat, Douwe doubted many would come by. His mind was on lunch and Johanna. At sunset, they would return to guard Clara. As they left, a gaggle of young priests in black headed toward the paddock. The sight was common in Rome, but Zubin pulled Douwe's shirtsleeve and motioned to the crowd.

"It's fine, Zubin," said Douwe. "Our worker can handle them. It's likely the same group from three days ago."

Zubin glanced back again, studying their faces. They had not seen Gregor in months, but Zubin looked closely. He pursed his lips and caught up with Douwe.

Johanna sat next to Douwe at a long table in an open-air courtyard of an inn. She explained that the ladies were on a trip to the Holy City to see the sights. He asked after her husband.

"He caught a fever on board during his last voyage," she said. "He did not survive."

"I am sorry, Johanna."

"It has been years," said Johanna. "My children cannot remember his face. I wrote to you to tell you. But I didn't get a response."

"I never got your letter." The truth, that Douwe left it unopened, was left unsaid.

They talked of her life in Holland and how her children had grown. Douwe told her all about their adventures with Clara: the sea voyage, the towering rogue wave, Clara's time in the anatomy theater, her wagon, his title from Maria Theresa, the orangeries, Versailles.

He did not tell her of Lonnie. But his heart felt a nagging pull back to her—to her small shed in Leiden with the soil-covered floor. He could smell the rich earth and honey of her. He longed to feel her working hands on his skin, fingernails permanently stained with dirt.

In front of him was the rose-sweet Johanna. Her bronze hair was perfectly curled, carefully modeled around her small ears. Her hands were delicately pale and clean like they were carved from ivory. Johanna's cream-blush bust rose and fell in her corseted bodice, and when he took his eyes to her face, he found he could only focus on the slight pink curve of her lips. She smiled.

"Where will you go next, Douwe?" she asked. "On to Turkey? Or Greece?"

Douwe shook his head. "I am not sure," he said. "Wherever the road leads us. I may write ahead and see which royal household wants us next. They tend to feed her well."

"What a life you lead," Johanna said. She touched his knee. "One of adventure. I cannot imagine the people you have met and the things you have seen."

Douwe's mind flickered to the porcelain maker, the Empress, the stable boys, the peasants. The printers and the carriage maker. The kings and their sons, the clinging children of peasants and royalty alike. He smiled and told Johanna more. She fluttered her eyelashes at him, nearly crying when Douwe told her of Zubin's illness.

"Johanna," Douwe said. "May I show you something?"

Douwe pulled the miniature out of his pocket. He always carried Johanna's gift with him. It was tinged with grime from his hands, usually slimed from Clara's mouth. She gasped.

"You kept it," she said. "After all this time." Johanna smiled at him and remarked how much Clara had changed.

Johanna's friends pulled her away to freshen up. The night was falling, and Zubin told Douwe they should get back to Clara. Douwe agreed and made his way to bid farewell.

He found her leaning over the balcony of an upper terrace, a view of the city in front of them. A fresco behind her was intricately tiled in reds and golds, and a fountain burbled. A breeze picked up, and Johanna's hair was loosed from its pinnings, tumbling to her waist. She leaned over the plaster railing, her curved, delicate frame outlined.

Her back was to Douwe, and he put a tanned hand on her creamy shoulder.

"Douwe," she said. "Or should I call you Baron van der Meer?"

"You may call me whatever you like, Johanna," Douwe said. She turned and slid Douwe's hand from her shoulder to her waist. Douwe wanted to back away, but he stayed. She grabbed his white tunic and held her face inches from his. Johanna leaned in and kissed him. She tasted of sweet Roman wine. She breathed heavily and pulled him close, her rose perfume clinging to the air. But Douwe found it cloying, heady. It was all too much.

Zubin cleared his throat from behind them.

Douwe and Johanna separated. Zubin was irritated.

"Pardon me," he said. "We have a rhino to tend to."

"Baron van der Meer," said Johanna. She curtsied a goodbye.

"Goodnight, Johanna," Douwe said. "Do not trouble yourself with worry. Zubin is not one for spreading rumors."

"This is a rumor I would not mind spreading," Johanna said. "I give you permission to call on me, Baron." A sickening feeling rose in his gut. He thought of Lonnie; her laugh echoed through his mind. He felt the whisper of her freckled hands on his chest. He knew that he would never call on Johanna.

The walk back to the gardens was lit by a crescent moon and lanterns from narrow doorways. Zubin chattered about the frescos and tile work at the inn, and when the conversation became one-sided, he paused.

"Baron van der Meer," he said, waving his hand in front of Douwe's face. "Why are you quieter than Clara tonight?"

"I made a mistake, Zubin."

"With Johanna?" said Zubin. "Only she could distract you from our rhino."

"Johanna is beautiful and desirable. But I think I know where my heart belongs."

"In Leiden?"

Douwe nodded. He looked at Zubin and grabbed the boy by the shoulder, bringing him close as they walked. He made a decision on their next destination.

"Leiden, Lonnie," he said. "The brown brick manor."

"Can we afford it?" Zubin said. "You say we're dropping anchor for good?"

"Yes," said Douwe. "We can make our way back. We can live a long and happy life with the admission we charge and the souvenirs we sell. By winter, we'll retire Clara permanently."

Zubin leaped into the air and let out a yelp. At the same time, a group of priests rushed around the corner. The narrow alleyway wasn't large enough for them all. They were sprinting away from something. Far in the distance, Douwe heard the unmistakable screaming of an Indian rhinoceros.

Chapter 41
Andrea
London, England

Alfred walked Andrea and Lucas to the main entrance of the museum. A massive blue whale swam through the rafters. He showed them the few taxidermy rhinos they had on display, but they weren't Indian rhinos like Clara. A sign below said their horns were replicas. Andrea did not cringe at them like she would have a week ago. They were for education, Alfred explained. Without them, people would have no idea what a rhino was like, minus pictures or TV. The displays made these animals accessible, especially the rarest species on display: Javan and Sumatran rhinos, far smaller than imagined.

When Andrea asked him where the specimens came from, he said most came from the zoos around Europe over the last hundred years. Once, the specimens were precious animals, loved by zookeepers, who were not destroyed in death but made, in a way, immortal. Andrea's chest rose and fell with a deep breath. Her fingertips tingled with the desire to touch them, and instead, she painted permanent pictures of them in her card catalog memory.

"Clara's not here, is she, Lucas?"

"I don't think so."

Alfred told them goodbye. They hopped another Uber, the Natural History Museum fading behind them. The Zoology Museum wasn't slated to open for another half hour, and traffic was tight. London unfolded in a curling fog through the car windows.

Lucas held her hand, sitting forward. Andrea was nervous. They pulled up to the Museum, mist clouding the windows. It was much smaller than the Natural History Museum, more like a small-town Carnegie library in the States.

The door to the museum was ajar, and Lucas put his finger to his mouth. Voices sounded inside.

"That's Sergei's voice," she whispered to Lucas. Another voice entered the conversation, but it wasn't recognizable. Then, Janice's unmistakable Dutch accent.

Lucas pushed the door open, and Andrea felt like a doll in a macabre eighteenth-century curio cabinet. The museum was one room. Warm wood cabinets filled with specimens loomed. From the balconies, articulated skeletons stared.

Skeletons of animals were positioned inches away from each other, creating layers of bones, impossible to discern one specimen from another. Claustrophobia kicked in, and Andrea's veins pulsed with adrenaline. At the center tables, Janice, Sergei, and a man sat, leaning over an object. The man had a jeweler's loupe on his eye, examining the horn.

"Janice!" Lucas called. "You don't have any right to that horn!"

Janice turned, puff of red hair cascading above her. She smiled, sickly sweet. It made Andrea's stomach flip. The horn sat on a velvet cloth on the table.

"Oh, Lucas, Andrea," said Janice coolly. "I can't believe you're here, how silly. These are my interns, likely overthinking everything."

"You shouldn't have taken it, Janice," Andrea said. "Even as interns, we know this isn't right."

Janice laughed, and Sergei rose, arms crossed. The curator at the table looked confused. He put his hands up, showing he was not touching the horn.

"Janice," he said. "What are they talking about?"

"She stole it," said Lucas, striding across the room to the end of their table. Sergei took a step between Lucas and Janice. "She stole that horn from Douwemout van der Meer's grave."

"Stolen?" said the curator. "You told me you'd been searching for it since I helped with that exhibit years ago, and that you finally uncovered it yourself."

"You were the student curator?" Andrea said, turning to him. "She's been setting this up since I discovered documents with Clara on campus. She stripped your archive to prove this was Clara's and dug up Douwemout's grave herself. Then she assaulted our professor, Paul."

The curator balked and stood abruptly.

"You discovered those documents? An assault? Janice, you told me this was your biggest achievement. Surely these students are mistaken?"

"This is *my* discovery," Janice said. "It doesn't matter who *found* the pieces. I work night and day for that institution, and for what? Pennies! Hundred-hour work-weeks, no recognition, no funding. My dreams have been trampled! I can't even get a new printer, goddamnit! I deserve better, and you're not taking this opportunity from me." She began wrapping Clara's horn in blood-red velvet.

The curator backed away, heading to a phone at a nearby desk. Lucas stepped closer to Janice, reaching for the horn. She twisted her body away from him, elbowing him in the chest. Lucas stumbled and hit a table on his way to the floor, sliding it into the display cabinet nearby. The glass shattered, and the curator cried out.

"No!" he said, running toward the display. Specimens in liquid spilled onto the tile floor. The smell of formaldehyde sharply stung Andrea's nose. On his knees, Lucas covered his head with his arms as glass fell from the tall cabinet. Sergei met him halfway as he tried to stand, pulling him to his feet and out of the way as the skeletons inside loosed from their bindings. Janice bundled Clara's horn and prepared to put it in her coat pocket when Andrea clenched her fists and ran toward her.

"That's not yours. It's Douwe's!" said Andrea.

She ripped Janice's hand from her coat pocket, sending the velvet-wrapped horn flying through the air. Andrea slipped on the liquid on the floor, head hitting the corner of the table. Silver stars dotted her vision, pain blossomed over her face. The horn landed with a dull thud near a glass case where primate skulls loomed.

Andrea scrambled to get to it, but Janice was faster. Andrea crawled under another table, head pounding, and reached out to the velvet cloth under the horn. Janice slipped on the formaldehyde. Andrea pulled the horn toward her. In what seemed like slow motion, Janice fell into the glass case with her whole-body weight. It careened backward, the skulls inside sliding.

The case wobbled, unsteady, and fell, sending the museum's first floor displays crashing in a domino effect. Glass shattered, the sound deafening. Cases and tables fell, and amidst the chaos, Andrea grabbed Clara's horn, lay her body on top of it, and curled around it like a fierce mother cat protecting her kitten.

Andrea heard shouting as glass continued to shatter. An alarm sounded, sprinklers sprayed water. Sergei hauled an elephant tusk away from the water. The curator shouted orders, grabbing whatever he could, arms full of specimens. Andrea's bloody hands, cut from the glass, grasped Clara's horn, and sirens blared outside.

Lucas pulled her out from under the table. He gathered her up like a child and carried her outside. She dripped with water and formaldehyde. Sprinkler water sprayed onto the displays. Unharmed, standing tall in the distance was the articulated skeleton of a hornless rhinoceros. The last thing Andrea saw before she blacked out were piles of wet white bones.

Chapter 42
Douwemout van der Meer
Rome

Douwemout van der Meer stumbled up the embankment, fire in his lungs. He was too late—Clara's screams told him so. How badly was she hurt? He ran. The last time he coaxed his sea-strong legs to move like this was across the deck of his broad ship to join the crew in stripping down the rear sails of the *Knappenhof* during the storm at sea. This storm was a different kind. It felt like the devil was there, hands clasped around his lungs—shortening his breath and stride. But the screaming did not stop, and neither did he. Clara was in danger, but she was still alive.

Zubin was ten paces behind him, breathing heavily and yelling.

"Go Douwe, go!"

Douwe and Zubin found the winding, narrow streets made no sense and took wrong turns. Clara screamed and screamed, her voice growing hoarse in the distance. Finally, the Largo di Torre Argentina opened up before them, and they sprinted.

There were two figures in Clara's paddock and a third on the ground, undoubtedly the street boy they'd left in charge. A priest had a large swath of fabric pulled tight over Clara's eyes. He strained, and she fought. The other priest used a surgeon's saw to remove her horn. It dangled by a three-inch strip.

"No!" cried Douwe, leaping the fence. The man with the saw turned and swung at him, blade flashing in the crescent moon. Douwe ducked and tackled him, taking his legs out from under him. They crashed to the ground, and the commotion startled Clara out of her shroud. She violently reared.

The priest covering her eyes was flung into the air, and Clara charged, her horn bending as she collided with the man. A crunch and gurgling, wheezing breath sounded. Then, the solid, unmistakable noise of Clara's feet on flesh. The man under Douwe stirred, still brandishing the saw, and Douwe pinned his hands to the ground. He turned his face to Douwe.

"Gregor!"

"Remove the desired object, remove the lust," Father Gregor said. He pushed Douwe hard, and both men were on their feet. The silver saw he held was covered in dust from Clara's horn, and bits of Douwe's precious rhinoceros were flung through the air as the saw swung at Douwe's arm. It made contact and bit through his shirt.

Zubin grabbed Gregor from behind, wrenching the priest's arm back in an unnatural position. Gregor yelled and Clara charged, startled and angry. The five-thousand-pound animal turned on a dime. Gregor's accomplice beneath her feet was no longer recognizable, trampled.

Clara charged, and Zubin darted, sliding hands-first under the paddock. Douwe leaped over as Clara slammed into Gregor. The saw clattered to the ground near the fountain. Clara backed up and charged again, aiming at Gregor. Douwe watched. Her broken horn caught Gregor in the neck.

Douwe crawled to Zubin and covered the boy's eyes. The torches near Clara's wagon flickered. All was silent, save the heavy breathing of their animal, who successfully defended herself.

Douwe stayed on the ground, covering Zubin until Clara approached, trotting. She made sad, funny noises, pleading at them. Douwe sat up and brought Zubin with him. Zubin was alright. Douwe's arm was bleeding, his hand red with his own blood. He stood slowly, shaking, and went to the paddock fence. Clara shook her head, defensive from the terrifying events. Zubin stood, his legs trembling, using the paddock fence for support. Clara came up slowly to them, and Zubin cried out.

Clara's horn dangled, careening to the right off her rough face. Zubin covered his mouth with his hands, dropping to his knees. Douwe balled his fists, teeth clenched. He wanted to scream but did not want to upset Clara further. She collapsed to the ground.

"Zubin," said Douwe. "We have to finish it."

"Wh...What?"

"We cannot leave her like this," said Douwe, ripping his shirt sleeve off to bandage his wound. "We must take her horn off. Can you please help me, Zubin? We must!"

Zubin gagged. He nodded and stood, then slowly, weaving, went to Clara's cart. He grabbed her a fresh pile of hay, apples, and the teal jacket Maria Theresa had given him.

They calmed her in the unique way only a human who truly knows an animal can. Zubin draped the Empress's gift over Clara's eyes. Her sides heaved. Douwe retrieved the bloody saw from the fountain. Clara wheezed a high-pitched squeal. Zubin did his best to hold her still. A vibrating, swift cut and Clara's horn was in Douwe's hand. Zubin let her go, and she ran, bewildered, to the back of the paddock. They exited quickly, reminded that, at her core, Clara was a wild animal with the tools to protect herself.

The bodies in the paddock would have to wait. Douwe stood there, Clara's horn in his hand, too shocked to move. Clouds moved over the crescent moon. Zubin dropped to his knees.

They slept that night in Clara's wagon, fitfully listening to her rub her stump of a horn on anything she could. The noise was sobering. Douwe woke before Zubin to drag the bodies from the paddock. He clambered out, a knot in his neck and shoulder pulsing up to his temple and was glad to see the street boy sitting up against the fountain, awake but dazed.

"Boy," he said. "What happened?"

The boy spoke in Italian, and Douwe's limitations were frustrating. He caught some words: priests, a hit across the back of his head, and blackness. He held the small boy's face and examined him like Dr. Wilhelm aboard the *Knappenhof*. The boy had a large bump on the back of his skull, but he wasn't bleeding, and his eyes were clear. He let the boy sit and grabbed him an apple meant for Clara.

Douwe shaded his eyes from the coming dawn to observe the two mangled bodies in Clara's paddock. He made sure they did not move. Clara had indeed trampled them. She was asleep, legs pushed to one side, near the paddock's edge. He hopped the fence, and her eyes flicked open. For the first time ever, Douwe was frightened of her. He braced himself. She slowly rocked to her feet, and he considered sliding through the paddock posts.

Clara walked to Douwe. He stood still, making ticking noises, heart hammering. She flapped her ears at him, acting like her regular self. Clara sidled up close to Douwe and opened her pink mouth. He showed her empty hands, and she took a few steps closer. Douwe's adrenaline pumped, and he put his hands out to brace himself. One foot was pushed against a sturdy fence post. Clara leaned in to Douwe as she had when she was small. He rubbed her rock-soft skin.

Douwe managed to drag the two bodies outside of Clara's closure while she ate. He had no earthly clue what to do with them. He covered their faces with their black clothes. The crumpled forms of their bodies were turned in ways bodies should not turn. Zubin woke a few minutes after sunrise and did exactly what Douwe had done: checked on the street boy. Douwe watched him sit next to the child and reassure him. He brought him a mug of ale and a stale piece of Clara's bread.

"Zubin," said Douwe, crouching next to them. "I have to get help. Clara may be in trouble. I don't know what the loss of her horn means for her, and she has killed these priests."

"She killed Gregor, who tried to kill her in Vienna. He did not deserve anything less. I am glad it was not you who did it. I have an idea," said Zubin. He stood and pulled Douwe away from the boy. "Let's change their clothes. If no one knows they were priests, they will be unrecognizable. We can claim them thieves, wishing to do Clara harm."

"It is not a lie, exactly," said Douwe. "And may buy us Clara's freedom. I do not know what would become of her in Rome if it was made known that she killed two priests."

"Two evil priests," said Zubin.

"They thought they were serving God, Zubin," said Douwe, shaking his head. "Protecting their beliefs. Ridding people of temptation."

Zubin's eyes spoke volumes as he turned to Clara, who rubbed her stub of horn on a fence post in her paddock. Zubin pushed his mouth into a thin line.

"Let's get to work, Zubin."

It took great effort to change the priests, whose black robes clung to their mangled bodies. Douwe threw their bloodied clothing in the pile of Clara's droppings. The olive farmer would buy the lot and never know the difference. No one would look twice.

Douwe told Zubin to stay behind with the street boy, and he went to find help. Douwe showed soldiers the bodies, Clara's horn, and the saw. He showed them the cut on his arm and the knot on the back of the street boy's head. The soldier and his partner nodded in agreement. A crime had been committed, and Clara's rampage was justice served.

In his broken Italian, Douwe asked the two men where he could find help for Clara. He did not know what would happen to her now that her horn was missing. They consulted amongst each other, speaking too quickly for Douwe to follow. Their conversation ended abruptly, and they bid Douwe follow.

They took Douwe to a nearby farrier, newly open in the bright blue morning. The dark complected farrier ducked under the doorframe. Draft horses lined up for his services, stamping their impatience. The Dragoni partners spoke to him in drum-beat fast Italian, and the farrier listened intently, brows furrowed, tying a leather apron around his waist. He looked at Douwe and nodded.

The farrier was in Clara's paddock in twenty minutes, speaking softly as he checked her dinner-plate feet. Zubin fed apples to her for each foot the farrier lifted. At last, he came to Clara's horn stub. She shied away, tossing her head. The farrier backed off and asked Douwe for the horn.

The farrier held it aloft to the sun to see its density, scraped it with his fingernail, and smelled it. He nodded and returned it to Douwe, brushing rhino dust from his hands. He slowly approached Clara once more and felt the rough spot of her horn base. She allowed it, mainly because Zubin was at her ear, rubbing her neck folds.

"I shall need to file it," the farrier said slowly so Douwe could understand him. "This smells like a horse hoof."

Douwe nodded, and the farrier took out his tool. Clara balked as the soldiers came close, and Douwe's heart beat wildly. The men joined Zubin in steadying Clara. She calmed, and Douwe and Zubin spoke in her swiveling ears, whispering their love for her.

The farrier filed. Zubin fed her apple after apple. The uneven mess of Clara's horn was rounded in a minute, and when Douwe and Zubin released her, she did not leave. Clara braced herself, sides heaving, leaning into Douwe. The farrier backed away, dusting his hands. The soldiers darted from the pen. Clara watched the farrier leave and stood upright. She walked away slowly, and Zubin and Douwe exited the paddock, walking backward. They were both slightly wary of Clara.

Douwe considered his next move. Rome was no longer safe for them. He did not know what the street boy remembered, if the boy would stay quiet despite the large sum of money he was paid. He witnessed Clara's rampage and knew full well priests were involved.

Douwe and Zubin cleaned Clara's horn. It was a foot long, black-tipped, dense. Douwe held it to the sun, and it glowed. The thing that made Clara a true rhinoceros. Clara's mother was killed for this very thing. People from all walks of life saw magic in her horn, now a palpable object in his hand. It felt more precious than gold, not because of its supposed powers, but because it was hers.

"Zubin," he said. "We're taking a break."

"Good," said Zubin, sweat dripping down his scarred arms. "I need one, and so does she."

Clara paced in her paddock. Maria Bakari, who had all but disappeared the night before, chased her. It was clear they had to leave Rome. Douwe and Zubin loaded the fence posts of Clara's paddock, her food, her buckets, and their belongings. They rolled into the countryside. The wagon made it outside the city of Arezzo, where a willing vineyard owner met their needs.

In the following weeks, Douwe focused solely on Clara's care. He did not go to their scheduled appearances in Florence. He wondered what rumors swirled. Perhaps of her death? Or of his? Or maybe the rumors had caught up to them all, and authorities were sweeping Italy looking for the murdering animal and her keepers. His mind was wild—arrest, public execution? Had his own past come to haunt him?

Clara's breath did not slow. Douwe pointed it out to Zubin, who suggested she was still recovering. She rubbed her horn on everything. Perhaps the stress of her new habit made her tired. Douwe longed to speak to the baytar in Calcutta. He told Zubin of his fears.

"She's breathing so heavily, Zubin."

"She is," said Zubin. "But she's fine, yes? She has Maria Bakari and us."

Douwe never let her horn out of his sight. Death was strong in his mind, and he feared what would happen if Clara were left without him. He took a broadside and wrote his wishes on it. His throat still burned from the poison many months ago; the healing wound on his arm reminded him of the dangers he had faced.

Douwe led a team of borrowed oxen into the vineyard a week later. Zubin cheered, and the oxen lowed, too broad to fit properly on the long drive of their temporary villa. Douwe allowed the oxen a night's rest before beginning their journey. Zubin bid farewell to the horses, which were traded for their stay.

If Clara had been sold to King Louis, they would have avoided this entirely. But at that thought, the word *alone* flashed through Douwe's mind. He pushed it aside. He had Clara. He had Zubin. And he had Lonnie, despite the many worlds away she was.

Chapter 43
Andrea
London, England & Leiden, The Netherlands

The London police had difficulty believing their story. Still, Janice was in jail after Sergei spoke against her, finally clued in to Janice's deception. Andrea produced cell phone evidence of Douwemout van der Meer's damaged gravesite, broken fingers, and Paul's assault. Andrea thanked whatever gods watched out for her that she took photos of everything she'd done. Her mind's eye kept it, too.

Janice's attempt to prove herself undid her, but her desire for notoriety saved Clara's remains. Luckily, Janice craved recognition, fame, praise, taking the horn to a museum instead of the illegal trade rings. Clara's horn would have been turned to dust before they arrived if she wasn't so deeply attention-seeking.

With many apologies, they were allowed into the Grant Museum the next day. Most of the specimens at the Grant Museum were fine, minus the unfortunate formaldehyde-bottled ones. The Natural History Museum offered to help put the place back together, and Alfred was there to care for Clara's horn.

The police didn't want anyone to touch it, but Alfred convinced them that before the horn was returned to Leiden, it must be verified. If it fit the old rhino skeleton in the Grant Museum, it proved that the skeleton was Clara's.

The rhino skeleton towered over Andrea, who said wow about a dozen times until Lucas grabbed her bandaged hand and shushed her. She didn't feel nervous at all, a contrast to the nightmare events that led her here in the first place. She touched the rhino's bones with shuddering breath.

"Alfred," said Lucas. "The horn?"

Alfred grabbed the horn from an evidence box a policeman held. With shaking hands in white museum gloves, he raised the horn to the correct place on the white skeleton. He rotated it a few times. He had Andrea take his picture. She took two: a still frame in her mind and a cell phone shot.

He measured the base of the horn and its spot on the rhino's face. They were a perfect match.

"Could it be a coincidence?" she asked. But Alfred's eyes were filled with tears.

"Hey, Clara," Andrea said. Goosebumps rose on her arms.

Back in Leiden, Paul waited. The police brought the horn to him, and with his goofy smile and Chuck Taylors, he posed for pictures for the local newspaper.

"HISTORIC RHINO HORN FOUND IN LEIDEN GRAVE-YARD," read the headline.

"What do we do now?" Andrea asked Lucas. "The horn is import-ant, but so is Douwe's final wish."

"Why do you call him that instead of Douwemout?" Lucas asked.

"Douwe? I don't know. Feels right."

"We have a big decision to make," said Paul. "The university has lost its museum curator. We're charged with figuring out what to do with this horn."

The following month, they walked into the newly renovated first floor of the Grant Museum of Zoology. In a glass crypt in the museum, next to Clara the Rhinoceros, lay Douwemout van der Meer's skeleton, complete with remnants of his teal jacket. Like Andrea promised, she used her memory and photographs to repair his fingers. A full display of art, porcelain, and Clara's life was on permanent exhibition. Clara and Douwe were together, teaching people that relationships with animals are everlasting. CLARA THE RHINO, the sign read. A SEA CAPTAIN'S REAL TREASURE.

"I feel bad," said Lucas, gently rubbing his jaw. He stared at Douwe's skeleton, complete with Clara's horn in his hands. "He said Zubin was supposed to put the horn in his hands."

"He did once," she said. "We just helped this time. I can't think of a better place for Douwe to be than right next to Clara," she said. "So, are we applying for that museum job?"

"Of course. You saved Clara, Andrea."

"She saved me," she said.

Chapter 44
Douwemout van der Meer
Europe

Douwe drove the team of borrowed oxen into Venice. Zubin complained about their slow pace. They crossed the city gates, where waiting crowds were enraptured. What could twelve oxen be pulling?

Douwe stood in the carriage box, brandishing Clara's severed horn and crying: "Clara the Rhino! Alive and visiting Venice for two weeks only!"

The people stirred, crowds thickened, and rumors of Clara's arrival spread through the city on the winding water canals. Douwe delivered the borrowed team where they were promised after depositing Clara's wagon near the port. He now had the task of getting Clara to the city's center via barge.

Clara was wary, stubborn to board. Her armored sides heaved, and she peeped, a child-like sound. She shuffled down the ramp where brown water lapped, following Zubin. Zubin found a basket of bananas at the market. Douwe did not ask him how much they cost. With them, they convinced Clara to step onto the barge.

Each heavy foot made the craft jostle in the canal, and the workers nearby stopped, holding their breath. The barge settled as Clara situated in the middle. Douwe scrambled aboard, Zubin let Clara have her banana, and the oarsmen launched.

Clara wobbled, and Douwe and Zubin attempted to steady her with promises of bananas and bread. She settled, and Zubin began his cries to the people on the sidewalks: "Clara the Rhinoceros!" he called, cupping his pock-marked hands around his mouth. "In Venice for two weeks only!"

Zubin called to each group of denizens, remarking to Douwe about their ceramic masks. Black porcelain disks held between their teeth hid their faces. A chill clambered down Douwe's spine.

Clara and the crew meandered the canals of Venice, crowds pulsing forward when she rounded corners. A barefoot boy in brown breeches ran along the canal chasing the barge, weaving through legs and around merchant carts. He stopped, hands on his knees, path ended by leaning alabaster buildings. Clara's barge moved on to its destination: the red brick bell tower Canpanièl de San Marco.

The barge slowed and stopped, sending Clara weaving. Her eyesight was poor, but she spotted her exit and suddenly darted from the vessel onto the ramp. She slipped, and Douwe's breath caught in his chest. Clara slid both feet into the water and fell to her knees, sliding backward into the canal.

Zubin and Douwe yelled orders at the oarsmen—within moments, Clara had a rope around her massive belly. They hauled. She let out a noise like a screaming sigh, and with ten men pulling and Zubin showing her the entire basket of bananas, Clara clambered out from Venice's canal.

The people erupted into applause when she stood, swaying. Douwe sighed heavily and clapped Zubin on the shoulder. They gave each other wary looks—they almost lost her. Her path to the paddock in the gray brick square in front of San Marco was ready, but Douwe felt unsafe. It looked so similar to the paddock in Rome.

A crowd gathered, many members wearing masks for carnival. Clara swiveled her ears, curious about the night-sky faces. Once her paddock gate was shut, Douwe reached into his leather overcoat and held her horn aloft.

"Welcome, Venetians!" he cried above the din. "Meet the only living rhinoceros in Europe!"

Zubin shouted the prices to feed her and sliced bananas in two, their value apparent. Zubin's small leather pouch on his belt was soon full of jangling coins.

Patrons asked what happened to her horn, and Douwe dramatically told the story: "Thieves attempted to take her precious horn from her! She trampled them, defending her own life!"

He did not mention that the thieves were priests. Zubin cast a worried look at him and frowned. Douwe shrugged and sat straddling the paddock, waving her shining horn in the air. He felt he had nothing to lose. The church bells rang noon, sending flocks of pigeons wheeling overhead. Clara glanced at the sky. Douwe wondered how far she could see.

The crowds diminished come sunset, and Zubin led Clara to a stable for the night. Douwe and Zubin slept in the stall across from her on low-slung cots. Neither one of them was willing to leave her alone again. Her heaving breath kept them from sleeping soundly. Douwe placed her horn under his coat nearby and dreamed of Clara sinking to the bottom of the canal.

Two weeks passed slowly; every coin counted was crucial, and Douwe was eager to leave. He longed for the black slate floors of the church in Leiden. Several Venetian artists paid him handsomely to paint Clara, wealthy families sketched into the backgrounds. Douwe and Zubin were invited to see the art before they left. They followed a pigeon-filled street to a small studio, crumbling and damp.

A large canvas showed Douwe to the left, Clara's horn in his hand. Clara stood in her paddock, eating in front of a family of regal, masked Venetians. Even her droppings were painted, at which Zubin smirked. Douwe thanked the artist, who dropped a sachet of coins in his hands.

On their last night in Venice, a parade of partygoers circled the square. The torches and glimmering gems on the masks of the crowd frightened Zubin, who chose to stay in Clara's paddock rather than join the fray.

Douwe ventured out, hands in his pockets, a simple white mask tied across his eyes. The procession circled around the carnival acts in the square: a tightrope walker clad in fire red balanced above, twirling flaming batons. Puppet theaters pulled easy laughs out of children seated on their mother's laps, fidgeting with their own small masks. The canals were full of gondolas, lanterns swinging and reflecting on the black water.

Denizens of Venice waited in line for the opera and for Clara. Zubin fashioned a mask for her and draped it over her face gently. He cut a large square so her eyes were out. It was tied in a silver bow around her ears, but she shook it off. The crowd threw roses in her pen. Clara tossed her mask away after Zubin's many attempts, and he eventually tossed it into the crowd. A cheer erupted, and many hands reached for it. The victor held it aloft and waved it wildly. They sold out of commemorative Clara medals that night, lightening their load and deepening their pockets.

The bright colors of the carnival played out in front of Douwe like his own life: saffron and magenta, the colors of India. A contortionist bent like Zubin's goddess statue. Though their vessels were much smaller than his beloved *Knappenhof*, the sailors on the canals reminded him of his loyal crew. The black water lapped the stones, mimicking Snell's dark blood that stained his captain's quarters.

People of all kinds wandered the plaza, dazzled by the fireworks and lantern-lit booths. All of them were masked. All of them were equal. Clara did not care who fed her apples.

The night ended, stars wheeled overhead, and when the last fiery torch was extinguished, and the carnival ended, Clara was asleep, legs folded under her, Zubin by her side. Douwe let them sleep and stared at the stars with her horn in his hand, feeling the rough grooves of it under his palm. He took comfort in the bright cream-blue moon, the same light by which he saved baby Clara in the garden in Calcutta. He longed to be in the garden of the Hortus Botanicus. He wondered if Lonnie had any new plants from Bengal. Clara would love to eat them.

The next morning, Clara loaded onto the barge, and Venetians pressed inward, waiting to see if she'd fall into the canal again. There were mixed reactions when the rolling vessel steadied under her feet, and the oarsmen pushed off. Both cheers and disappointed noises sounded from young children who longed to see Clara swim in the black canal waters. Douwe held steady next to her. Zubin was on Clara's opposite side.

When they reached the docks, Clara's wagon was already boarded onto a vessel. By midmorning, wheeling gulls replaced the pigeons whose cries made Clara twist her ears to the bright sky. Venice faded into the background, masks and all.

Douwe and Zubin were eager to return to Leiden. The ship was slow, and they spent time caring for Clara, telling stories to the crew, and playing card games. The black corsair chest was full of coin, and the key Douwe wore around his neck felt heavy. He was ready to cash in his fortune for the brown brick manor. Clara breathed shallowly. She had changed since Rome.

Douwe pointed as they passed through the Strait of Gibraltar with Africa on their left.

"Zubin," he said. "That is Africa, and likely the closest Clara will ever come to seeing another of her kind."

Zubin leaned over the ship's railing, black hair ruffling, and squinted into the sun. He was taller than Douwe now. The wind caught his words as he turned.

"She'll never come here again, will she?"

"No," said Douwe. "She won't."

Clara raised her lip to the wind and sniffed. Zubin set her cask of fish oil nearby and doused her. She lifted each foot for him, and he praised her in simple words. The crew watched. Douwe felt for Clara's horn. It rested in a deep inner pocket of his coat with the miniature from Johanna.

Douwe and Zubin enjoyed the two-week voyage, and the seasons changed as they sailed farther north. Winter pressed its chill upon them. A storm was visible, rolling in from the Frisian Islands, blocking their route to Rotterdam. Their course had to alter.

"We're diverting," said the captain to Douwe. "We cannot risk it and have no need to. London is a few hours away. We'll wait a few days and set sail once conditions are favorable."

The ship turned north, leaving Leiden farther away yet closer than it had been in a year. While Douwe had no desire to go to London, bedding for a night or two in a warm inn on solid ground was welcome. Had he lost his passion for the sea afterall?

They docked in the London port, and the Thames floated with ice. The storm roiled off the coast, purple and gray.

"Three days at most," the captain told Douwe. He and Zubin unloaded Clara and walked her slowly down the icy cobblestones to The Horse and Groom in Lambeth, where a paddock and stable waited.

Icy rain fell, and lightning scratched the sky, illuminating Clara's silhouette as they walked. Her warm feet left clover-like footprints. Her skin was chill to the touch. They settled her with fresh hay and a large bucket of kitchen scraps in the warm stables. She did not eat much. Her sides heaved with effort. Zubin clicked the door shut and followed Douwe into the inn. They settled in with shepherd's pie and rich black bread.

Flyers were printed the following day advertising Clara's brief London stay. Douwe and Zubin sighed and worked despite the chill. A few patrons came, but the cold kept most at bay. The sky was gray as Clara's hide, and Douwe longed for the weather to clear. Two more days, then home to Leiden.

On the morning of the second day, Douwe shot up in his bed. His body was drenched in sweat. A nightmare clung to his mind's eye: Gregor at his bedside, stealing Clara's horn. In the dream, the priest stood above him, horn poised to pierce his heart. A dream. He wiped the sweat from his brow.

It was dark, but he could not sleep any longer. He quietly dressed and checked on Zubin, whose scars were prominent in the firelight. He touched the boy's face with his rough sailor's hands. Zubin did not stir. Douwe descended the steep inn stairs to see Clara.

He opened the stable door and could not see her. Clara slept on her side lately, and her gray feet were visible below the planking. He opened the stall door, but Clara did not stir. Douwe looked for the familiar flicker of her ears as she woke. They did not swivel toward him.

His breath grew short. He lingered, watching, but Clara's sides did not rise with an inhale. He knelt beside her and put his hand before her mouth and nose. There was no breath. He put his hand on her rock-soft skin. She was cold. He rubbed her skin, calling her name.

"Clara?" he said. "Clara, girl, wake up. It's me. It's Douwe."

But Clara stayed unmoving. He sat straight up, praying he was still in his nightmare. He shook her. She did not respond. He did not know how long he had been by Clara's side when Zubin came in and opened the stall gate.

"What has happened?"

Douwe shook his head, unable to speak. Zubin's eyes grew wide with realization. The boy fell to his knees and crawled to her, his scarred hands grasping Clara's face. He drew his hands away, realizing she was cold. He lifted Clara's heavy head onto his lap and rocked back and forth, face collapsing in agony. Douwe trembled, stomach clenching.

Douwe held the boy while tears stained his young face. Douwe felt empty, body shaking with trembling breath. He took Clara's horn from his jacket and placed it where it was once attached, carving the vision in his mind of his gentle, beautiful giant.

Douwe checked her breathing again, but Zubin pulled his hand away from her mouth. She was gone, all essence of the animal and companion she once was alive only in memory. Douwe felt his throat constrict and tried to remember it all: her huffing noises, the way her eyelashes draped when she fell asleep, her earthy horse-like smell, the way she lifted her ears and her lip. Her whistles, her eager trots, the way her body disappeared in a pond. Her rolling gait, her curiosity, her rough warm skin. He flashed back to the first time he saw her, just a baby, not yet his. His mind was filled with memories, but regardless of how strong the visions were, they immediately began to fade. His life without her began.

Clara's keepers stayed by her side, even in death, until night fell again.

The next day, Douwe and Zubin left The Horse and Groom without a basket of fruit, bread, fish oil cask, or Clara. Douwe left her there, where the University of London, contacted in haste by a messenger, was asked to retrieve Clara's 5,000-pound body for their medical school to study.

He wrote on the back of a broadside: "Clara's skeleton will be on permanent display in a museum, so she may be remembered." The college and museum readied a place for her, attending Douwe's wishes with solemn gratitude. He did not watch them haul her away, wanting to shield Zubin from the sight.

The patrons promised a living rhino in London that day left teary-eyed after learning that the Behemoth of Job died in her stall. They offered winter boughs and coins in sympathy. A group of nuns left Douwe with a haunting hymn that echoed around Clara's empty paddock. Word spread quickly in London that Clara was gone.

Douwe and Zubin silently loaded the ship to Rotterdam on the third day. Between them, they had no tears left to shed. Throats raw, the two were silent. Douwe found his idle hands uncomfortable and felt the absence of Clara's care in tandem with Zubin. They did not know any routine but that of keeping Clara alive.

That night in the sleeping quarters, Zubin asked: "What happened to her, Douwe? Was it us?"

Douwe closed his eyes and breathed deeply. "I do not know, Zubin."

"I thought rhinoceros were supposed to live a hundred years," said Zubin. "I thought my children would care for her."

"I am glad mine did," Douwe said.

"I need to know what happened," said Zubin. "Did we harm her?"

Douwe shook his head, thinking back on the last few weeks. It was unusual for Clara to stumble as she did at the ramp in Venice. Her breathing became shallow and fast after Rome. The trauma of losing her horn was the event that marked her change. It was cold here and had been the whole ship ride. He wondered if they should have stayed put until spring. Was it his own selfish decisions that caused this?

"Zubin," said Douwe, sitting up and rubbing his face. Gray circles settled under Zubin's swollen eyes. "We did everything we knew to do with Clara. Her time was exactly as it was supposed to be—with us, loved, for all her days."

"It isn't fair that she died alone there." His voice cracked.

"I must admit that part of me is grateful, Zubin, that I did not watch her die," said Douwe. "I cannot add any more fuel to my nightmares."

Zubin sighed shakily and wrapped his arms around himself. Douwe swung out of his hammock and grabbed his overcoat. He draped it over Zubin and kissed him on the forehead.

Zubin pulled Douwe's coat around his chin and scrunched his eyes, tears coming again.

"This coat smells like her," he said.

Douwe pulled her horn from the coat pocket, sleeping with it near his heart. No dreams came that night.

Rotterdam was white, icy. Douwe's urge to warmly transport Clara bubbled out of him. He would never be rid of earnest plans to keep her safe.

"We would have waited until the sun was highest and warmed her wagon with coals," Zubin said.

Her empty wagon was unloaded unceremoniously. Douwe could not think of what to do with it. Zubin walked the wagon one last time, breathing in the deep, earthy smell of rhino. He wiped his dripping nose and pulled Clara's leather lead from the wall.

Douwe left the carriage by the docks, planning a letter to Verheul, the carriage maker. He'd let him have it for parts. Zubin agreed it was best to not be saddled with the massive thing. Zubin and Douwe took a small coach to Leiden. Snow fell as they passed under the Ziljpoort. The castle ruins where Clara grazed years ago lay under a white glaze.

The carriage dropped them off at the University's church, where Douwe's vision of stepping again on the black slate floor came true. He was brokenhearted, graced with the familiarity of Leiden. Clara was everywhere.

The etching of her from Wandelaar's book was displayed in the shop windows. A model of her stood in the anatomy theater. Johanna's miniature jingle in Douwe's pocket. He still had a soft, folded broadside with notes from Versailles. Douwe counted the things that remained, even after Clara's death: Kaendler's porcelain, paintings, broadsides, medals. Etchings, pamphlets, anatomy sketches. A life-size canvas by Oudry. The scene in Venice with the black-masked onlookers and Clara's droppings. He found a smile. Gregor failed. Clara would live forever. He placed his hand around her horn comfortingly. Zubin and Douwe walked to the Hortus Botanicus.

The greenhouse was shrouded in snow, thick teal glass fogged. Douwe's heart was in his throat—the blurry figure of a woman occluded a pane. He picked up his pace. Zubin followed, white flurries circling them.

Douwe clicked the iron handle of the greenhouse and stepped inside the steam. He wiped snow from his lashes and turned as Lonnie careened into him, knocking his breath away. For the first time in days, Zubin laughed.

Lonnie let Douwe go, cupping his cold, stubbly face in her dirt-smudged hands. He stared into her eyes, but tears spilled over. Zubin sidled up to Lonnie's side, and she wrapped an arm around him, looking at Douwe with concern.

"What is it?" she asked. She wiped a single tear from Douwe's face, leaving a dark smudge of soil behind.

"Clara," said Douwe, unable to continue.

"She's gone," finished Zubin.

Lonnie put a hand to her mouth and shook her head, embracing them.

Douwe and Zubin settled into their apartment that night. Once Zubin was asleep, Douwe silently left, the door clicking gently behind him. He darted through the starry night to Lonnie's small shed, watching his breath fogging the starry sky. She was awake, a single lit candle in her window.

He knocked, and she answered, wearing her gossamer hair loose about her shoulders. She grabbed his hand, but Douwe knelt before she could pull him inside.

"Lonnie," he said. "I have no ring for you." He held, instead, Clara's horn.

On their wedding day in the spring, Lonnie wore a yellow dress with embroidered flowers and a square neckline. Lines of daisies trailed down her waist. On each sleeve, she embroidered a small rhinoceros. She wore pink flowers in her hair, and her freckles blazed. Douwe wore the teal short coat given to him by Maria Theresa. Zubin could no longer get his on.

The willow tree skimmed the pond's surface near the brown brick manor. Though Clara never wallowed there, Zubin smiled, standing by the water's edge. Douwe and Zubin dove into the brown water when summer came and reminisced. Lonnie watched from the window in sailor's pants, hand pressed to her womb, the flutterings of a baby inside her. Elisabeth Clara was born a year to the day after their arrival back in Leiden.

Zubin collected and categorized religious items brought from around the world for the University. Throughout his life, he visited menageries but never saw another rhinoceros. Each time, he brought apples.

When Douwe passed at the age of seventy, his final will and testament, written on the back of Clara's last broadside, left everything to Zubin. His burial instructions placed his remains in the University's graveyard. He was buried in his teal short coat. The last sentence requested that Zubin place the horn of his beloved Clara in his right hand. Douwe's burial plot was marked by a simple white stone veined with black. At the top was a carved rhinoceros. *The Rhino Keeper*, it read.

The river flanking his stone wove toward the sea, away from Europe and onward. The current passed by Douwemout van der Meer's grave and melted into the Atlantic, the Indian, and upward toward the banks of the tea-brown delta of the Ganges, where the waters of the world collided.

The End

Author's Note

The most common reaction to the story of Douwe and Clara is: is this true? Did a rhino really tour Europe? The answer is yes. But unfortunately, Clara's journeys were not documented in detail. Many facts will remain unknown unless primary documents from Douwemout van der Meer or his assistants emerge. If Douwe's journal existed, I firmly believe this little-known history would be common in our societal vernacular.

But there isn't, to anyone's knowledge, a captain's log or journal left behind by Douwe. What primary sources exist from the rhino keeper himself? A handful of signatures, a land deed, a marriage certificate, and a few small portraits of him. We know the path, manifest, and dates the *Knappenhof* sailed thanks to VOC records. We know that Sichterman's wife, Sybilla, really sent her children back to Holland thanks to Jan Sichterman's family papers found in a trunk in an attic.

We can trace the voyage of Douwe and Clara via art—many things were painted and sketched and sculpted with her likeness. It gave me great joy to scour the many portraits of royalty who had some kind of rhino in the background, including the son of Maria Theresa, whose portrait of him holding a rhino book on a small porcelain disk sold at auction in 2022.

As for Douwe himself, even the correctness of his name is debated: some historians see his signature and understand his name to be Douwemout van der Meer, while a newer publication says his name was Douwe Mout and that he later changed his first name to David. While more archives become digitized, the puzzle pieces will shift and mold into a different narrative. All of this is filtered through a lens of fiction in *The Rhino Keeper* to help you, dear reader, keep track of our adventurous captain.

We know that a rhino calf was sold or gifted to Douwe in Calcutta and somehow survived a perilous sea voyage. The dates of the *Knappenhof*'s voyage are not common ones, and when I showed them to my friend, professor and historian Ken Yohn, he was puzzled. Most large ships sail at the same time of the year for favorable conditions. But the *Knappenhof* didn't follow normal VOC schedules—we aren't sure why. But Douwe landed in Rotterdam with a rhino in tow, seemingly unharmed.

There are many questions that emerge—why did Douwe decide to take this animal? Why did he have just one exotic animal when he could have had a traveling menagerie? Who helped him? How did he keep her alive with no vet care, little husbandry knowledge, no idea of what she should or shouldn't eat? For example, citrus in large quantities is danger-ous to rhinos and can cause iron overload. I personally believe diet is one possible reason Clara died. There was no other rhino on the continent during Clara's time, which means we assume no persons knew how to properly care for her. Versailles did end up purchasing a male species who unfortunately was slaughtered by revolutionaries. After Clara's passing, Douwe himself disappeared from the historical record until his own death in 1775.

In the research process of this book, I spoke to real rhino keepers and their responses were much the same when I asked how it was possi-ble that Douwe cared for Clara in the way he did, as a traveling animal. Their answers were the same: a shaking of the head, a wonder-eyed pause, a deep inhale, and similar conclusions: "They must have been bonded." This is truly uncommon for the eighteenth century. Most exotic animals were treated poorly, and died quickly, usually due to lack of knowledge. It needs to be said that Clara's living conditions were unfavorable to her species. I do not believe this was malicious. I believe it was a lack of un-derstanding, and an overwhelming sense of awe surrounding her, that led Douwe to travel with her as he did.

In an analysis of her body condition from her many portraits, which I believe to be accurate to real life as the artists would have no other de-pictions or mind's-eye imagery to skew their art, she was a little thin but healthy. No writings currently discovered mention illness in appearance or behavior, besides the common temper tantrum, that would lead us to believe she was mistreated.

It's important to understand that eighteenth century thinking meant Douwe and his companions had no concept of species survival or conservation. They saw no harm in taking Clara from her natural habitat. Animals in the eighteenth century were treated differently than they are today. Many incorrect and disturbing scientific studies from the seven-teenth century and before took years to disprove—many believed animals making noises in distress were simply squeaking like a machine, and that they did not feel pain. Later in the eighteenth century, people like Vol-taire, who really did meet Clara, argued that animals have souls, feelings, and rights, and that their bonds with people are legitimately emotional.

Rhinos are not unlike dogs or horses with their caretakers, though our society may not acknowledge it as the ancient teachings of Pliny still permeate our view: the image of a violent, charging rhino. Rhinos are wild animals and must be treated as such. Male rhinos are known to charge when threatened, and all five remaining species of rhinos are jumpy and skittish. Due to their large size, this can be dangerous for people. Rhinos in captivity are creatures of habit. They can be trained for blood draws, to open their mouths, to step on a scale, all useful for their survival. They recognize those who care for them and know their own names. They are food-oriented, playful, and responsive. Real life Clara and Douwe likely had a simple understanding of one another.

It is true that Clara was weighed at the Leipzig Easter fair at close to 5,000 pounds. There is one unfortunate report of the death of a young child as the result of Clara's trampling during an event, but the media also reported that she drowned several times and did not. It is unsure what writings about her are true and which are exaggerated. We know she was extremely food oriented, and Douwe could likely get her to do many things with the promise of snacks: bread, beer, oranges (perhaps to her demise), and other produce.

There was a time that Clara did not show up at her advertised appearances. She was in Rome one moment and though scheduled at a few other places in Italy, she did not show up, and when she resurfaced many months later, it was without her horn. We do not know how she lost her horn—according to modern keepers, it's likely she shed it by rubbing it in her wagon due to boredom or stress, or Douwe cut it off himself if it got too long. Cutting a rhino's horn is not painful; the keratin growths are like our fingernails.

Clara lived eighteen years in Europe with Douwe, and while that is around half the life expectancy of a rhino in captivity today, it is significantly longer than any other rhino in the sixteenth to nineteenth centuries. He and his team had to have been devoted to her, or she would have died, perhaps not even surviving the ship voyage. Instead, she died at The Horse and Groom pub in Lambeth, London, in 1758. You can visit the pub today, renamed Horse and Stables.

A few character notes: Zubin is fictional, though there is a dark-haired boy in two paintings of Clara. Douwe could not have cared for her alone, and Zubin was born of those boys tending her in paintings. Lionel/Lonnie is also fictional. Douwe married a woman named Elisabeth, but I absolutely love that a few women in the 1700s would dress in men's clothing to escape their by-the-book lives, usually out of a sense of adventure or for monetary need, and simply had to include her. Lonnie is loosely based on the first woman to circumnavigate the world, Jeanne Baret, a botanist who helped identify many plant species unknown to Europe.

The menagerie keeper, ship's doctor, baytar, crew members of the *Knappenhof*, and stable hands are all fictional. Real characters include Douwe and Clara, all of the royals, the anatomist Jan Wandelaar, and the porcelain maker Johann Kaendler.

For more information on Douwe and Clara, I recommend *Clara's Grand Tour* by Glynis Ridley, who read *The Rhino Keeper* very early on. She and I have continuously corresponded about Douwe, Clara, rhinos, and continue to share new things we learn together. Other readings include *The Rhinoceros: from Durer to Stubbs* by TH Clark, *and Clara the Rhinoceros* by Gijs van der Ham, the newest non-fiction book on the subject which contradicts many things previously reported. I read Van der Ham's book after I wrote *The Rhino Keeper*. My storyline follows Ridley's work more closely. Everyone who has studied Clara agrees on one thing: we don't know everything.

Friend and writer Jenna Blum asked me where Clara's shed horn and remains are today. I firmly believe that Clara's horn is with Douwe. There are no auction records of a rhino horn, no newspaper articles about the horn's placement in museums. We do know that The Grant Museum in London has an old Indian rhino skeleton. The museum cannot confirm nor deny that the skeleton in their collection is Clara. Records are spotty. I hold it in my heart that it is her and would love proof someday.

A few interesting things I left out: Clara was not named right away. She was called Virgin Clara when she made it to Germany, and it stuck. Clara was the first of her species to be scientifically named by Carl Linneaus in Switzerland, Rhinoceros unicornis.

As the years go on and more archival documents are digitized and searchable, we may know more about Clara and Douwe. For now, we can revel in the one unmistakable truth: Douwe and Clara created absolute wonder, and I hope they live long in the collective memory of readers today as they did long ago, when the two-ton queen of Europe walked the cobbled streets.

A note on conservation

Indian or Greater One-Horned rhinos are a vulnerable species in need of our protection. As of this publication, around 4,000 individuals live in the wild. At home in the marshlands of India and Nepal, they're one of five remaining rhino species. In this work, I have chosen to call the species Indian rhinos as during the eighteenth century, the term Greater One-Horned did not exist.

For generations, people have long sought the "magic" of rhino horns and other body parts. Science has proven that rhinos hold no medicinal properties in their flesh or horns. This ancient way of thinking, along with habitat loss, has contributed to the awful truth that less than one hundred years ago, fewer than fifty Indian rhinos remained.

Though numbers are increasing, and new technology allows for animals in captivity to breed more easily than ever before, humans must be aware that large mammals need worldwide support to thrive. Luckily, sanctuaries in Assam mean the Indian rhino can survive in its natural habitat.

I've had the luck of meeting five of the species so far. The first of whom sparked this unpredictable voyage was Joya in Salina, Kansas, at the Rolling Hills Zoo. He has since passed. I've also met Taj in Seattle, and Monica, Stacks, and their baby MJ at Tanganyika Wildlife Park in Goddard, Kansas. I highly encourage you to sign up for a rhino encounter to safely meet these animals. There's nothing quite like getting slimed by a rhino mouth. They are absolutely remarkable and deserve our every effort to protect them through the Species Survival Plan and natural conservation efforts. A portion of the proceeds from this book go directly to rhino conservation funds.

Acknowledgments

This book would not be in your hands without help.

Many thanks to my first readers: Glynis Ridley, Ken Yohn, Kayla Jordan, Janesa Bass, Betty Brewer.

For your guidance, help, and encouragement, thank you fellow writers: Kate Khavari, Jenna Blum, Diana Giovinazzo, my Twitter/X querying group, Maria Tureaud, Paulette Kennedy, Sarah Penner, and Jennifer Howell.

Thank you to the thousands of people who saw my Twitter/X rejection fence, and told me to keep going, no matter how many rejection flowers I had to paint.

For your support and love, my friends and family: Cody Forsberg, Grant Overstake, Claire Overstake, Beth Cates, Annika Wooton, Andrea Bell, Marisa Drummond, Scott Elpers, Kacy Meinecke.

For your belief in this story and its merit: Colin Mustful and everyone at History Through Fiction.

For the opportunity to meet rhinos: Kayla Jordan at Sedgwick County Zoo and Sierra Smith at Tanganyika Wildlife Park.

Thank you to my readers, NaNoWriMo, teachers, professors, and each person who's asked: is this story real? Without you, it would not be.

About the Author

Photo Credit: Kay + Bee

Jillian Forsberg is a historian and author with a master's degree in public history from Wichita State University. Her research on little-known historical events led her to discover the true story behind her first novel, *The Rhino Keeper*. In addition to being the former editor for Wichita State's *The Fairmont Folio*, Jillian is an essayist whose articles have been published in academic journals. With a passion for 18th-century history, Jillian can also be found gardening, exploring antique malls, or reading every label at a museum. Vintage dresses are Jillian's clothing of choice, except when she's at the zoo. She lives in Wichita, Kansas, with her husband, child, and pets. She's currently working on her second novel. To connect with Jillian, please visit her website at jillianforsberg.com.

For exclusive Clara the Rhino artwork, please visit the link below.